SWARMTHIEF'S DANCE

DEBORAH J. MILLER

SWARMTHIEF'S DANCE

BOOK ONE
of
'THE SWARMTHIEF TRILOGY'

TOR

First published 2005 by Tor
an imprint of Pan Macmillan Ltd
Pan Macmillan, 20 New Wharf Road, London N1 9RR
Basingstoke and Oxford
Associated companies throughout the world
www.panmacmillan.com
www.toruk.com

ISBN 1 4050 5074 8

1 3 5 7 9 8 6 4 2

A CIP catalogue record for this book is available from
the British Library.

Typeset by IntypeLibra Ltd
Printed and bound in Great Britain by
Mackays of Chatham plc, Chatham, Kent

To my sisters, Louise and Wendy,
and my brother, Verne.
With love and warmth, always

ACKNOWLEDGEMENTS

My sincere gratitude to my agent, Simon Kavanagh, and my editor, Peter Lavery, for the instinct, wisdom and time they have dedicated to ensuring that *Swarmthief's Dance* lives up to its full, imagined potential. Many thanks also to Gary Taylor for his invaluble advice on swords and weaponry.

❧ SNOOT ❧

ONLY THEIR HANDS could be seen and the stark whiteness of their faces. The chamber was otherwise a medley of blacks and greys. They stared down at the dock, their cobalt eyes devoid of compassion.

'An egg, sir. Ansanzi laid an egg.'

'Do you know what you're saying, boy?'

Snoot nodded solemnly. 'It's true, sir.'

'No, it's heresy.'

❧

IN THE DARKNESS, Snoot could hear them moving: Ansanzi's Swarm. On the very outside edge of his hearing, the clicking and rustling they made whispered like invisible fingers, raising the hairs on the nape of his neck as surely as if they had traversed it with their swift, weightless legs. Snoot steeled himself and walked across the chamber, to stand above the pit, his bare feet soundless in the cold dark. He wasn't supposed to be here at this time of night but Veda, his mother, had left him no choice. His best friend Pik said she knew about Bakkujasi magic, and she was a year younger than he, and a girl.

'Don't tell me you don't know, Snoot. It's easy,' she had mocked. 'I've moved Sarlk's Swarm three times now. I can show you with Ansanzi, if you want.'

'Of course I know,' he lied. 'Ansanzi's special, that's all. She's a queen, so only Veda is allowed to move her.' He ended lamely, 'And me, of course.'

He could tell she didn't believe him, by the way she tossed her dark hair over her shoulder and stalked off, but not before giving him

1

a withering look. It never occurred to Snoot that Pik might be lying, daring him to do something which was dangerous and forbidden – something which she would never attempt herself. She would be far more impressed by his undertaking of it than Snoot realized.

Snoot stared down into the pit where a hundred million tiny dragonflies crawled and flew. Contained within this dimly lit space, their sapphire blue bodies were bright and iridescent, the sound of their wings a hot, constant rhythm. The Swarm was beautiful, Veda had said, a thing of magic, a thing of power. Snoot didn't think so, and his feet itched as though they were crawling over them. He wished he had worn his boots.

He didn't know, of course, how to move the Swarm. Somehow, this sea of blue creatures could be transformed, made to become one entity, an entity that was really Ansanzi – and she was undoubtedly beautiful. Bizarre and majestic as she was, he was sure that possession of Ansanzi was the envy of all other Bakkujasi. Her bright blue abdomen was twelve spans long, her wingspan, easily double that length. Snoot had ridden her behind Veda once – his mother had worn her scary black mask and ceremonial dark blue robes. She had forbidden him to speak of that adventure afterwards, but the flight of the creature still haunted his dreams, the sound of her purring wings filling the dark corners of his bedroom like a warm song. After a week of almost sleepless nights, he thought perhaps Ansanzi was calling to him, but now he was less sure – maybe the Bakkujasi's magic was a female thing? Except that most of the warrior priests were men . . .

Sighing, he was about to turn away to go back to bed, when he noticed the phial. It lay on the lacquered wooden sill which ran right around the glass dome that covered the pit. There was something random about it, as though it had been dropped by accident and then had rolled into this position. Snoot picked it up and held it to the light. It was a long crystalline object containing a thin blue liquid and, as he glanced between the pit, the phial and the Swarm, the possible connections between them seemed intangible, just out of reach. Pulling the rubber stopper from one end, Snoot sniffed and found its smell to be slightly musky and organic. A movement from the pit demanded his attention. In a blue surging wave, as though motivated by one thought, the Swarm had travelled to the side of the pit where Snoot stood. The strange smell had clearly attracted them, pulling them towards it like an irresistible force.

Pushing the stopper back into the phial, Snoot peered more closely at the glass dome which sealed Ansanzi's lair. At the apex of the glass was a slight dimple, long and cylindrical in shape – the same shape as the phial. It suddenly all seemed blindingly clear, and for a moment Snoot felt cheated. 'Bakkujasi magic, eh?' he whispered, realizing his words could be considered blasphemous, even as he spoke them. He glanced briefly heavenwards as though the goddess who watched over all the Swarms might be frowning down on the daring experiment he was about to undertake.

Snoot leaned forward, his arm outstretched, and then groaned aloud as he realized he was too small even to reach the top of the glass. He had always been so small.

'*SmallSnoot, SmallSnoot, SmallSnoot . . .*' Pik's laughter seemed to ring around the chamber and, even in the darkness outside the ring of light which illuminated his goal, Snoot's cheeks burned with impotent anger. Stepping onto the sill, he threw his body forward, wrapping his arms around the curvature of the glass. Another groan escaped from him as he fought to control a sudden vision of the glass breaking and the Swarm covering him with their insect blue. Though his face was pressed against the cold surface, it seemed as though an alien heat was reaching him through the thickness of the dome. This was non-sense, he knew, since insects possessed no soul, and therefore, no heat. Veda had told him so.

Straining every sinew in his legs and arms, he reached upwards for the apex of the dome, questing with the extended phial until, with a high-pitched crystalline 'clink', he located the groove. Pushing forward with his fingertips he slid the phial into position and then sank back gratefully to perch on the edge of the sill. He was warm and sweaty after his exertion and as he wiped his sticky hair back from his brow, he realized that his fingers were moist with the blue liquid. He stared down into the pit.

Just beneath the glass dimple, the liquid drizzled down onto the massed insects beneath. Snoot thought that he would now see their transformation for the first time, but quickly realized that, in fact, no one ever really saw it. Seconds was all the time the transformation needed. Before Snoot's shaky breath had slowed to normal, he saw that Ansanzi was there, in the pit. In a flash of blue fire, the Swarm had merged to produce something more than simply the sum of its parts. In a way, they had ceased to be . . . had relinquished something in order to become Ansanzi.

Slowly, a mechanism triggered by the concentrated weight of the huge insect raised her from the floor of the pit. The glass dome slid back with a hiss which echoed like a sigh around Veda's chamber. Snoot stared at Ansanzi and the huge insect stared back with an iridescent, unblinking gaze. Snoot felt cheated, for Veda and all the Shemari priests claimed that moving a Swarm needed an act of special magic. Well, perhaps they never actually said that – *implied* it was closer to the truth. They had other magics also, but their ability both to move and control the Swarms was the central basis of their power. Snoot was only nine summers old but he sensed that he had stumbled on something . . . dangerous.

'Well, Ansanzi,' his voice was a quiet shaky whisper which sounded to Snoot himself like a shout in the silence of the night, 'it's . . . it's a liquid that does it. The Bakkujasi must carry it around with them.' He sniffed his fingers, which still carried the potent smell. As if from nowhere a thought formed in his mind, and he frowned at the creature in concern. 'Does it hurt you, Ansanzi?'

Ansanzi did not react to his voice, but continued preening her antennae with her fore-limbs; this made a slight rasping noise which was disconcerting. Her abdomen was vibrating slightly, a movement which Snoot had never seen her make before.

Snoot turned to leave the chamber, knowing Ansanzi could not escape. Veda would find her in the morning and there would be some explaining to do. Never mind, perhaps Ansanzi would enjoy her one night of freedom, and could fly around the . . .

Snooot.

Snoot turned around.

'YOU SAY SHE spoke to you?'

'Yes, sir.'

'And this was *before* she laid the egg?' The priest's tone was filled with mockery and contempt. Snoot blinked back the sting of tears and glanced towards Veda, who was also sitting in judgement. She gave him a small, tight smile which did not reach her eyes. If Snoot was judged a heretic, Veda's own position would be under threat.

'Just tell the truth, Simeon,' she said quietly.

'DID YOU . . .? Did you just . . .?' There was a sensation in his brain, as though something was subjecting it to a series of sharp stings.

Snoot? (Sting.) Am Ansanzi. (Sting, Sting.) Not talk. Am thinking.

'I can feel you thinking, Ansanzi, and it hurts.' Snoot swiftly corrected himself. 'Well, not exactly "hurts" . . . but I can *feel* it.'

Help me, Snoot. (Sting. Sting.) Ansanzi began to move slowly towards him, and in the semi-darkness her huge, spindly motion – potentially so fast and deadly – was frightening. Snoot stepped quickly backwards, and then was ashamed of his fear.

Help Ansanzi. (Sting. Sting.) Ansanzi dying am. (Sting. Sting.) She suddenly buzzed her wings, which Snoot guessed to be an expression of grief.

'Dying? I'm sorry, Ansanzi. Veda has told me you are very old.' At least one hundred years he had heard.

Veda! The sting that followed was sharper now, leaving no doubt of the creature's feelings for her mistress.

'Oww!' Snoot yelped.

I am . . . She seemed to be lost for a word.

'Sorry?' Snoot ventured.

Yes. Veda not knowing Ansanzi. Not thinking Ansanzi alive.

Snoot nodded; it was true. Veda had often proclaimed that the Swarms could not be true living souls because they were composed of so many entities. They were like living hives, she had said, and therefore the only 'soul' they could possess would be of the millions of tiny insects which comprised them. 'Does a single beetle have a soul, Snoot?' She had smiled. 'I don't think that's something we need worry about – do you?'

Ansanzi was moving again, that curious jerking of her abdomen which she had exhibited before.

'Ansanzi, what are you . . .?'

'THAT'S WHEN SHE laid the egg, sir – right there in front of me.'

'Oh really, boy, this is too much. What do you propose? How could such a creature lay an egg when she is composed of a Swarm?

5

Even if it were possible, she had no contact ever with a male of her kind.'

Snoot could feel the warm buzz of temper rise in the pit of his stomach. 'I don't know, sir. I didn't stop there to ask her.'

'Simeon.' It was Veda. 'If you persist in this tale, I cannot help you.'

❧

THE EGG WAS not round. There was a slight gelatinous noise as Ansanzi lowered her abdomen to place the object safely on the ground. It was covered in a clear gel, over a pearlescent grey, its surface scored thousands of times in an intricate fantastic design. Snoot stared at the egg, his breath catching in his throat. *This never happens*, his brain insisted, but there it was – as full of life and potential as any egg had ever been.

'It's beautiful, Ansanzi,' he whispered.

Take, Snoot. Run far. Her urgency made the silent stings harder to bear, and her anguish was unmistakable.

'Run?'

Run far, she urged. *Hide Ansanzi's egg – here.*

There was no sting with her final word, rather something that felt like a hard slap. Otherwise unannounced, an image appeared in Snoot's mind of a tiny plateau amid the sharp black rocks of the mountainside, on some west face where the sun seldom reached. A large, gnarled cypress tree and beneath the tree . . .

'When I come back, Ansanzi . . . will you wait?' The question hung unanswered in the darkness, and Snoot could think of nothing more to say to the extraordinary creature. Staring into the huge alien face, he paused and wondered at his feelings of sadness and empathy.

'I will go and hide your egg, Ansanzi . . . but I'm sorry that I will not speak with you again.'

Ansanzi die now, Snoot. Be kind. We are . . . legion. Goodbye, Snoo . . . Sim-ee-on.

❧

'SO, WHERE IS this miracle? Let us see this egg of a Swarm.'

'I destroyed it, sir. I – I put it in the incinerator beneath the temple.'

'Ah, very fitting.' The male judge raised a grey eyebrow.

'Snoot.'

'Yes, mother?'

'Is it not possible that you . . . dreamed all this?'

'*You* saw. You found her in the morning.'

Veda nodded, her face pale, obviously remembering the blue, blue ashes which she swept away; unable to lose the impression that millions of tiny lives had ended at the same split second, the very second Ansanzi – the soulless creature – had passed away.

'She was very old, Simeon.'

Snoot hung his head. 'Yes.'

'Are you sure you did not dream this?'

Snoot looked up, eyes bright with unshed tears, knowing all he had to say was no: no, he wasn't sure, maybe it was a dream. He knew that Veda was giving him a way out.

'Yes,' he said.

IN TRUTH IT felt like a dream now. Disjointed images of pre-dawn colours, which lurched as he ran, were all he could remember. And the smell, that loamy woodland smell which mingled with the tart freshness of low cloud-cover as he descended the mountainside. Then the warm darkness of the tiny cave, which was barely more than a hole, but a shelter from the elements. Had Ansanzi sought help from an adult instead of a boy, they would have been unable to climb inside it and cover the precious trophy with bracken. As the dawn was breaking, he left it there, stopping at the entrance to look back just once at Ansanzi's silver treasure, as the sound of his own heartbeat pounded in his ears.

THE BOY HAD been gone from the city for many years now. In time, talk of his heresy dissipated, trickling from memory as softly as the winter snow from the mountains. In the warm darkness, the waters of the cloud-mist were gradually draining away from the confines of the mountain cave. The larva felt the pull of this new dryness, its skin stretching and drying until finally it split with a faint ripping noise. Otherwise soundlessly, Ansanzi's offspring was born.

Green she was, emerald green. She would be called Ayshena. She spread her wings as wide as she could within the confinement of her hiding place and waited patiently for them to dry off. Raising her eyes to the cave entrance beyond which the warm sunset breeze blew, she stared out into the scurrying clouds.

Snoot, she thought. *Must find he.*

❧ RAAN ❧

S HE NEVER KNEW.
She never knew that I thought she was beautiful, that behind my spite
and malice had lain the weak blind desire of something less than godly;
that in fact, I had loved her.

She was the youngest of the Nulefi – the six spirits whose existence and
movements dictated the cycles of the year for those beyond the veil. And it
is too late to tell her what I felt those many years ago, for I have destroyed
her utterly. Well, I may say utterly – for her spirit and that of her hate-
ful sisters are banished to the void – and yet I know that to we whom men
name gods, eternity is but the blink of an eye. And should she return to
taunt me, I will embrace her anger as though she speaks tender words.
For I have learned that eternity is lessened, diminished without her, and
I would rather have her hatred than nothing at all.

We gods are born of chaos, pure, cold and brilliant. Where a world
begins, we also come into form, and none can truly say which blinks into
existence first. Before belief we are there, guiding, moulding the awakening consciousness of our charges as if they are infants, bringing them to
awareness and worship. Sometimes we are forgotten by those that serve us
and then . . .

. . . so, you see, when I say Aria and her sisters were sisters, I am
speaking figuratively. Only two gods may make gods and demigods anew
– Herrukal and Oshi – and in fact, that is Oshi's main purpose. Perhaps,
I simply mean the 'sisters' were always together. Others thought of them as
identical, created in the same image, but any close observer could have
dispelled this belief. Aria was certainly different from the other five;
dark, graceful and elegant, thus the artists amongst men have painted

9

her image always, believing her a dream. But she was real – is real, if the fates have denied me.

It was in the gardens of Imeris that I finally told her of my passion for her. Created by Imeris for his amusement, it was always warm there. Scented breezes blew in from an ocean so blue as to be almost too intense – that was Imeris for you, subtlety was lost upon him – likewise the trees and flowers were just too, too perfect. True, the place had its charm, but it bored me rather quickly; no insects were suffered there, the lakes and streams – made and remade by magic means – never grew weed or algae. Birds did appear, but of course only the beautiful varieties. Once, as a joke, I left a couple of vultures fishing in the largest lake. Imeris wasn't amused, but the sight of the clumsy brown creatures alighting and defecating on the marble statuary brought a smile to myself and my cohorts. Mischief was never far from my thoughts, but in those days, when the world was still young, I had no grander malice in me . . . However, I digress. On this occasion I was sitting before the lake vaguely appreciative of the tranquillity of the place. I should explain that my thoughts were not like those a mortal might entertain in such a situation; no, I felt no anxiety or nervousness. I had summoned Aria and she would come – we gods were nothing if not bound by courtesy. Also my agenda was very different from that of a mortal – or at least I thought so then. If Aria agreed to my advances, we would couple immediately, and perhaps agree to future liaisons – becoming what mortals might recognize as a 'pair', although we would never live together in the grubby codependent way of our charges. So my thoughts were already somewhat . . . shall we say salacious, anticipating the heady glory of Aria's physical and spiritual form. That is the other difference, our coupling would be more than simply physical . . . But why am I telling you all this when I may show you? I am a god after all. Watch now . . .

IT IS QUIET in the gardens. The peaceful sounds of water and birds break the silence in such a way that their noise seems only part of the stillness. The rich greens of the cypress trees and the creeping flowering vines seem to stretch on forever – which in a way they do, for the garden and its few occupants are perched on the edges of time, and those who visit there assume the guise of mortals because it amuses them to have form.

Beside the lake a youth is sitting, staring into the water at the reflection of his own features; they are square, the eyes too widely spaced, the nostrils flared.

'Wrong', he mutters, 'wrong colour.' He waves his hand almost irritably, and the bright blue eyes transform to a startling vermilion green. Standing up, he paces along the riverbank, his movements deliberately slow so as to feign patience to anyone watching. His stature is short but incredibly broad, deep-chested and stocky. The loose blue robe he is wearing was designed to accentuate his previous eye colour and he absent-mindedly changes this to green in an instant.

'Rann, there you are.' Aria smiles towards him from her vantage point on the sandstone folly at one end of the lake. 'I trust I haven't kept you waiting?'

He stops in mid-stride and stares over towards her, slightly discomforted by the silence of her arrival, wondering if she has been observing his vanity.

'Aria . . .' he still manages to sound almost casual. 'Aria, I've asked you to meet me because I want . . . I want . . .' He gropes for the words mortals use to such effect in these situations.

'Yes?' She looks puzzled.

He smiles, a confident smile which has an edge of arrogance to it. 'I'd like you and I to couple. Together. Now.'

Her eyes widen in surprise. 'What?'

'Well, don't you want to?'

'Well, I . . .'

'Aria . . .' He climbs onto the folly beside her and stands so close she can feel his hot breath on her face. He has perfect even teeth and it seems his smile has gained a feral edge.

'No.' She steps back, and his smile disappears. He frowns, unable to comprehend her refusal.

'Rann, I haven't even seen you for years, perhaps a century . . . so, why?'

'But I have seen you, Aria. I have watched you often.' He reaches forward and touches her soft cheek. It is a greedy, covetous gesture, lacking any tenderness, and she flinches back. 'My passion has grown in the darkness of my realm. With only the dead for company, what hope have I of brightness, of love?' His voice is solicitous as his hand begins to slip down towards her breast.

'Love?' she spits, contempt surfacing on her face. 'Have you

11

borrowed that word, just as you have borrowed the appearance you wear? Get your hands off me, Rann.' Knocking his still outstretched arm away, she turns to leave.

'I – I am sorry, Aria.' She stops although she does not turn around. 'Perhaps I expressed myself badly. I am unused to speaking so.'

But when she turns to face Rann, it is clear the damage has been done; her expression remains cold. 'You cannot help what you are, Rann. Therefore you must content yourself with that, because it will always be this way . . . forever. You come from the darkstuff at the beginnings of creation, so do not aspire to the light.' Then, because she is angry and afraid of his clumsy advances, she seeks to further belittle him. 'Look at yourself. Go and look in the water. You have tried, have you not, to make yourself attractive to me because of our meeting? You cannot do it, Rann. You are dark and ugly to the core.'

She senses she has gone too far, and her face is flushed as she picks up her crimson skirts to flee the scene.

'No!' Rann is almost incoherent with rage. 'Stop!' He reaches out towards her, and sends out *Koshurit* – the binding energy he uses on the restless spirits of the dead. Aria is frozen in motion, her skirts still swirling in the air behind her. Rann fights to control his anger; he could strike her down now, for she is beneath him in caste and wields less power than him. He cannot bring himself to do it though. Walking slowly around to face her, he stares into her eyes. Aria's expression is frozen as an instant in time, and thus she cannot disguise her fear. Although Rann feels secret dismay at her reaction to him, he does not allow her to see his hurt. Concealed and revealed, their emotions hang between them, also frozen, so that it seems even the scented jasmine air is tainted.

'You are wrong, Aria.' Rann says at last. 'I am not truly ugly. Had you existed as I have for aeons, you would know what ugliness is – you would have seen it in the hearts and souls of mortals, as I have. But I will not be denied you.' He clicks his fingers and Aria's robe vanishes, leaving her naked and vulnerable. Although astonished at her beauty, Rann feigns contempt. He leers at her and steps towards her to assault her body – his intention being to despoil her beauty as revenge for his hurt. Although he knows she can remake herself with ease, he needs the satisfaction. After another click of his fingers, he too is naked. The warm breezes in the gardens play against his form, making his skin pleasingly sensitive. Although Aria's body is frozen in motion – her arms still outstretched as when she fled – he takes her by the wrist and moves under her arms as though into an embrace. Their bodies are touching now and Rann is shocked by the warmth of physical contact – a new sensation.

Rann, please . . . She cannot speak in her frozen form but she contacts his mind. *Just release me and I will leave enough animation behind in this body for you to enjoy your sport.* Her voice sounds deceptively calm but there is an edge of panic there.

He steps back. 'But, Aria, you know I deal in souls only. It is you I want, you. This shell' he gestures dismissively towards her, 'we both know it is only a beautiful container for your soul. Nothing I do to it can change that, so I may as well take it now. Listening to your pleas will only heighten my pleasure.' He moves to stand between her legs again, stroking her thigh and delighting in the sensation.

But, Rann, if that is true – if it is me you really want – this is a simple misunderstanding. Release me and I will show you the willing pleasures that mortals enjoy. Look. She sends a sense picture to his mind of herself and Rann lying on her red robe spread out on the grass where they now stand, entwined in each other's embrace, their limbs wrapped tightly around one another.

Rann groans aloud, his desire almost unbearable.

Do you want me, Rann? she whispers.

'Yes.' His guile is as nothing beside her own. He releases her from Koshurit, and does not notice the flicker of her gaze as she casts around for help. She does allow him to kiss her, but does not respond or return the kiss. It hardly matters; it is the first he has ever experienced in his long existence. Smiling, she pushes him gently away. 'My robes, please? Can we not have something on which to lie?'

'Oh yes.' Distractedly he turns around and she seizes her chance to run. She knows she cannot escape alone, and she cannot leave her present body fast enough, so she screams aloud for her sisters to come to her aid. She is still screaming when he catches up with her and flings her to the ground on a pathway at the edges of the lawn. Aria cuts her lip on a sharp stone as she hits the bare earth. They struggle desperately, all godly magics forgotten for the moment. Unnoticed by either of them, the skies above the garden darken and thunder begins to rumble in the distance, for their violence has unbalanced Imeris's playground. Rann is still aroused, and Aria's resistance feeds his desire.

Finally, he has her pinned down, unable to move. Soil is sticking to her sweat-covered skin, moss and twigs are caught in her dark hair, so that she appears almost to have grown out of the garden itself. As it begins to rain, he wipes the dirt and blood from her mouth, then bends over to kiss her roughly. She cries out in pain.

'Let her go, Rann! Now!'

Her sisters have arrived.

SO, YOU SEE, it was her fault – she taunted me. And they should have kept out of it. It's not as though I would have done her any permanent damage. Instead, there began something which would ultimately destroy them, and cause me much pain in the meantime. What's that, you want to see the rest? Very well then, but I must warn you that the Nulefi do not equit themselves with any dignity as far as I am concerned . . .

AT FIRST SIGHT the new arrivals in the gardens look like Aria: five tall, graceful women. They rush towards Rann and their helpless sister, even as Rann gets up and prepares to flee. He knows their strength when together and, by nature a coward, he will not risk this confrontation if he can avoid it – but he cannot. Fajr, the eldest and strongest of them, seeing her sister bleeding and distressed, screams after him. As she approaches him, her anger transforms her into the wind of her season. She howls around Rann, a raging biting torment wrapping his form in cold pain. The others are upon him now, and, before he can recover from Fajr's attack and defend himself, they grab hold of his flailing limbs and move him backwards towards the columns of the folly. Aria is still on the ground. Although she is sitting up now, she is sobbing, with her face buried in her hands. In the midst of his present pain Rann calls out to her but she does not hear, and forgiveness is beyond her. On reaching the central point of the folly, Rann feels icy bonds latch around his wrists and ankles. He knows, in that moment, that instead of calling out to Aria, he should have fought them harder, because the Nulefi are merciless in their rage. He is still standing upright as they bind his limbs to the four pillars at the corners of the open structure, with cords made of icy cold.

They say nothing meanwhile to their victim but, as he comes to his senses and begins to call out his own words of power, they stuff his mouth with leaves and grass. Above this scene, the skies have darkened further, and soon cold drops of heavy rain spatter his body. Once he is bound to their satisfaction, the Nulefi pull short curved knives from their belts and begin to mutilate his flesh. This is purely symbolic, for they know he will remake himself, and perhaps that is their point, because meanwhile he feels the lancing pain of every single cut and incision, being unable to take leave of his physical body whilst at such an extreme of heightened sensation. Refusing, or unable, to scream, he groans and gargles deep in his throat, promising his revenge whilst focussing on the strangely beautiful sight of Aria still weeping, clutching at her red robe and wiping the blood from her face.

WHEN THEY ARE at last finished, the Nulefi sheath their knives and turn to leave. Momentarily, Fajr stands in front of Rann, and stares into his blood-and-sweat-clouded eyes.

'Never touch her again,' she hisses. '*Never.*'

Then they depart, taking Aria with them. At the last moment, Rann manages to spit the gag from his mouth and he calls out to her, 'Aria . . .' His voice emerges as a harsh agonized croak, as if he is unsure of what he wants to say.

Aria turns back towards him, and for a tiny moment there is pity in her gaze as she considers the bloody mess of Rann's body, but then she smiles in a cruel contortion of her beautiful features, and blows an exaggerated kiss. The last he hears of her is her laughter.

And the god Rann is angry. Not because of the pain – he would have dealt out no less – but because they have beaten and humiliated him, who is greater than they. Once they have gone, he gives vent to his anger and shame, screaming curses after them and pulling down the columns of the folly using the bonds they had tied him with. The heavens roar a response. A cataclysmic storm assails Imeris's gardens: the winds whip across the lake, ripping the trees from the earth, lifting the plants into a green-brown frenzy. Torrential rain turns the soil to dark liquid, as though it could melt away the stain of Rann's aggression. All the while, in the ruins of the folly, a maniacal, naked figure capers and screams, as the blood from his wounds is diluted into a lesser shade of red. As his fury dies away, so does the storm until, as the rain becomes softer, almost caressing, he curls up within the lee of a toppled column, tightly hugging his knees as his blood still drains into the earth. His skin is white now, pure white like a marble statue, and his shoulders are heaving. The god is . . .

crying . . .?

STOP IT. Stop now. I say what you can see. Did you see what they did with their stupid little knives? I know . . . I know I handled it badly. Aria was just caught unprepared, that's all. But then it became like a war, a campaign, between us – especially after I discovered the damage they had done me. I thought I could remake myself perfectly, but look at this scar – right down the centre of my face. I petitioned Imeris for healing, but he was so furious at the destruction of his gardens that he denied me. And so my anger became a dark simmering thing, and I quietly watched Aria for another millennium, from the shadows of her life. Often it seemed as though she felt my presence, for she would turn and gaze towards my hiding place, a puzzled look on her face. Occasionally, she would smile, too, and in those moments I truly felt she mocked me. I was waiting for my chance for revenge, although I had not yet decided whether to spare her when the time came, but for her sisters there would be no quarter . . .

When finally the day came, the circumstances of Aria's downfall were something of a surprise even to me. Aria fell in love with a mortal. You should first understand that although Aria was not a goddess herself, she was amongst those beings who you may refer to as godly, in the lower echelons of divinity – and, as such, union with a mortal was denied her. Whilst it was deemed perfectly permissible to elicit the love and passion of our charges, even to use them at our whim, there could be no real relationship of meaning between us. Apart from any 'ethical' concerns involved, the cold reality of being immortal would mean having to watch the object of one's affection decay before one's eyes. If I speak of this with disdain, it is because I have myself tried it for my amusement. It is like keeping a pet: one must accept the inevitable at the outset, and living with the knowledge of the other's demise becomes emotionally tiresome in the extreme. So Aria fell in love, but she was not content to let go of her lover. I knew this because I was there when she told him . . .

THE EVENING IS hot, and Ceer sits waiting listlessly in the field, the drone of the bees matching his mood perfectly, the sound drifting into the distance of the uncaring mountains. She said she would come tonight, and he believes her, although the men of the village have begun to laugh at him, thinking his tales to be the sign of bored intelligence. He smiles to himself; he can tolerate their nudges and their jokes, because only he knows that Aria is real. Below him, propped up against the side of the tree in which he sits, his bag contains the song he has written for her – and when she arrives he will sing it. She loves to hear him sing – his voice is strong and lyrical – and although she sometimes presses him to sing songs which he feels are too romantic, he does not really mind. He would do anything for Aria.

THEN SHE IS there, sitting in the tree branches next to him. It is one of the reasons he knows she is special – like a faerie or changeling, she just appears.

'My dearest Ceer,' she whispers. She leans forwards and kisses him lightly, her dark hair brushing his chest. 'I need to speak with you. Will you walk with me awhile?'

He nods and leaps down from the branch, then holds his arms out to catch her as she follows him. As she comes pliantly into his embrace, he kisses her again, more eagerly this time, the warmth of passion stealing through his frame.

'No, no,' she chides him gently, 'we must talk first, Ceer. Not here, though.' She glances around almost furtively. 'Let's walk into the sunlight.' She takes his hand and leads him into the meadow. Evening moths fly out from the tall grasses as they walk, the tired sunlight catching their wings, flashing silver.

'Is something wrong, Aria? Don't you want me to sing?'

'Maybe later. Ceer, what do you think I am?'

Ceer mistakenly imagines she is 'fishing for a compliment', as his brother has told him women do. However, Ceer is not adept with women and is unsure what he can say to make Aria happy. Looking slightly uncomfortable, he gives her a lopsided grin.

'I think you are beautiful, Aria.'

She does smile at that, but then she shakes her head. 'No, Ceer . . . I mean, do you think I am a spirit, a vision . . . what?'

He shrugs. 'I think you are a changeling, Aria. It's the only way I can understand you.'

'What is a changeling exactly?'

'It's a babe who is born after its mother is favoured by the gods . . . well, one god in particular obviously. Imeris usually.'

'Hmm.' Aria sits down on a log in the middle of the field and idly plucks a cornflower. 'Well, you are close to the mark, my love, but I have no mortal blood at all.'

'Oh.' Ceer looks stunned, then sits down heavily beside her. 'You are . . . immortal then?' He grins again. 'That means you're going to live forever, Aria. I think that's beautiful.'

She groans in mild frustration. It's not that Ceer is stupid exactly, but he isn't a complex man given to sophisticated thought either. That's partly why she loves him.

'But, Ceer, don't you see? That means I'll be always like this, and you . . . you will grow old and die.'

'So? I would have done so anyway, even if I'd never met you. It doesn't bother us mortals much generally. We're born with the knowledge of our death within us,' he plucks a dandelion and pulls off one of its white heads 'like a seed. That is why we are such self-destructive creatures.'

Aria says nothing for a moment, but stares at his broad handsome face. Ceer did this often: just as she was in the throes of deciding she only really wanted him for his beauty, he would say something so astute she would be amazed.

'But it doesn't have to be like this,' she says finally. 'I can change it.'

THERE. THAT'S WHEN *her doom was sealed, when she said it: 'I can change it.' I was watching from the treeline, and I knew her plan the instant she voiced those words. Aria would take the soul of Ceer and ensure it was reborn immortal through mystic means – it had been done before but it was, in your terms, strictly illegal. In fact, the soul of the last being who had attempted the counterfeit of souls did still reside in the*

darkest reaches of my realm. As I thought of this, I realized that Aria's plan could work to my advantage; given charge of her soul for all eternity, I could surely make her love me. So, her plan must be foiled, she must be found out . . . but I am getting ahead of myself again. First, in order for her plan to proceed, Ceer must die and I guessed she would use a poison . . .

'POISON?' CEER LOOKS doubtfully at the vial Aria holds out to him, a tiny amount of green liquid in a glass tube. 'It doesn't look much, does it?'

'Trust me, Ceer, it is enough. Your death will be instant and painless. But, alone amongst mortals, that death will only be temporary. You do want to be with me forever, don't you?'

He shrugs. 'Forever is a long, long time, Aria. You will tire of me, I know it, and then where will I be?'

Again she is amazed by his quiet astuteness but she laughs lightly. 'It will not matter to you, Ceer, for we will be equals, you and I. Immortal, and in love forever.' She reaches out to touch his face and he kisses her palm. 'Are you afraid, my love?'

'Yes. I would be a fool to pretend, would I not? I never imagined my death could be so glorious. Kiss me once more, Aria.'

She does so and immediately their lips are parted, he drinks the poison. She has done her work well; he dies without a sound. Aria glances around once nervously, then touches one hand to his heart and the other to his temple. She is taking his soul for safe keeping. Then she is gone once more.

DUSK IS FALLING when the villagers find Ceer's body. Torches are lit and a small crowd gathers. No one can determine what killed the young man, and they cluster around speaking to each other in hushed tones. They shake their heads and frequently make signs to ward off evil. Only the thin trail of green across his cheek would provide any clue, should they care to notice it. But they will not, because tales of vampir and restless spirits haunt these valleys, and Ceer is soon marked down as one of their victims. Meanwhile, beside the tree, the song he never sang rests unnoticed.

TRAGIC IS IT not? I almost felt for the poor deluded soul. The real tragedy is, of course, that he died for nothing. Actually, I can't recall what became of his soul in the end. I only know that Aria did not complete her plan because, well, frankly I messed things up for her. I told Imeris what I knew and he told Herrukal, who was furious. You see, it was not the first time such a plan had been tried, and that last soul who had been punished for the same reason had been beloved of Herrukal, who had dealt harshly with him to allay any whispers of favouritism. He promptly summoned Aria before him to answer for her crime and, because they came as a kind of set, the Nulefi all came too. I was there, of course, to see my moment of triumph. I hid behind the pillars of Itauc and Iyaur – which support the heavens – and moved as close as I dared. I did not wish the Nulefi to see me or they would recognize my hand in Aria's betrayal. Nor did I wish Herrukal to be influenced in any way by my presence; the Creator scorns me ever, and harries me at every turn, so if he thought the proceedings were to cause some benefit to myself, he may temper his judgement and I would lose my heart's desire.

'WHAT SAY YOU, Aria of the Nulefi? The counterfeit of souls is a crime – an offence against our laws. We have but few of those and I would have them obeyed.'

The huge figure of Herrukal leans forward in his seat, his brows knitted in a furious frown. Of all the gods only Herrukal the Creator manifests himself in the same form constantly, thus allowing his visage to become almost a racial memory to the mortals he watches over. Aria stands before him, slightly forwards from her five sisters, who stand with their arms defiantly folded. They all wear black, as befits their penitence, but their expressions belie this token effort. Only Aria keeps her head bowed, but even she has flouted tradition by wearing her whip and knife before Herrukal. After a moment, when she has said nothing in her defence, Herrukal sighs and sits back. He seems about to speak when Aria decides to defend her position.

'It's not fair,' she begins petulantly, 'mortals are allowed to love – we should be too.'

'And why do we give them this blessing, child?' Herrukal's frown becomes thunderous. '*Why?*' he repeats.

Aria bites her lip, realizing her position is untenable. 'Because they die,' she acknowledges. 'Because without each other they would be in despair.'

'It is only fair that I mete you the same punishment as I did to Tanuk.' Hearing this, Aria staggers back as though struck, and the Nulefi all gasp as one. 'Your soul is forfeit and will be sent to Rann, to be recovered only when the day of our ending comes.'

'No, no . . . Please, Herrukal, don't do this,' the Nulefi begin to plead tearfully. A shadow moves behind the twin pillars of Itauc and Iyaur, as the god Rann can no longer contain his delight and begins to dance for joy. But then, happens something so unexpected that it will forever be remembered in the annals of the gods. It will later be generally acknowledged that the Nulefi – especially Fajr – were only acting true to their nature, but still, it was glorious in its stupidity.

'No.' Fajr's voice rings out, cold and calm. 'We Nulefi will not allow this.' She motions for the startled Aria to get behind her, and then the other sisters close around her in a protective circle. Drawing their weapons – each holds a whip and knife – they begin to back away from the judgement chamber.

Herrukal has underestimated them, and when he speaks his voice is incredulous. 'You dare defy me? What purpose will it serve you to leave this place? I will hunt you down in an instant.' He is almost laughing in his disbelief, but his laughter is cut short as Fajr reaches out – with a motion so fast none anticipate her action – and grabs Luak, Herrukal's favoured minstrel, holding her curved blade to the quaking adolescent's throat.

'Like to hear him singing a bit higher?' she snarls. Herrukal pales slightly at the sight, but then remembers himself and signals to his guards. In the space of seconds, it seems, Fajr realizes the import of what she is doing: there can be no turning back now on her gesture of defiance and all she has done is chosen to make a stand and die for Aria's right to love a mortal.

🌿

STILL, THE STRENGTH of the Nulefi is a sight to behold. The fight is fast and furious, as the guards rush forward with their halberds lowered, only to have their weapons whipped from their grasp by the leather whips of their female foes. Aria herself kills one of them, and his soul blinks out of existence in a flash of purple light. The Nulefi all fight as though possessed, screaming aloud profanities never before uttered in the presence of Herrukal. Their piercing battle calls soar into the vaults above, their black hair and cloaks a whirling mass of darkness from which their knives flash silver as they stab and slash. Below, in the realm of mortals, great storms begin to rage, the seas rising up and swallowing whole cities, while tornados smash through the land, toppling palaces and mud buildings alike in response to the god's anger. It seems, for fleeting moments, that the Nulefi might win an impossible victory, although they are hopelessly outnumbered. Finally they are surrounded by the guards who lock their shields together to form a cage of sorts around them.

'Enough!' Herrukal thunders. 'You dare? You dare defy me?' Never before have the gods seen the white fury at the heart of Herrukal's true nature. Never before has chaos threatened to over-whelm him. For a while there is silence. The guards shift uncomfort-ably, aware of their vulnerable position so close to the captured Nulefi should Herrukal strike out against them. From behind the pillars of Itauc and Iyaur now steps Rann – although Herrukal does not acknowledge him at first. Sensing that he will soon become guardian of the souls of all the Nulefi, he is unable to hide a triumphant sneer. Herrukal steps down from the dais towards the group, before whom lie the casualties of the short skirmish: three guards, and Luak, slain by Fajr. When next he speaks, he fights to control his anger.

'Look what you have done. None may replace Luak's song – *never*.' He pauses as his sandaled feet reach the hem of the fallen min-strel's robe. 'So this will be your punishment,' he says quietly. There is just time for the Nulefi to notice tears in his eyes before he waves his hand, and they are gone.

THERE IS A stunned silence. Then a voice rings out in anguish. 'No . . .'

It is Rann. He knows instinctively that their souls are not his because he senses the traffic to his kingdom as though it is his heartbeat. The other gods are puzzled by his outburst.

'Herrukal, where are they? What have you done?'

'What's this, more defiance?'

'No . . . no, my Lord.' Rann steps back again hastily, but is unable to contain himself. 'But where are they? They have not yet entered my realm . . .'

Herrukal is unmoved by his petition. 'Nor will they. The souls of the Nulefi are forfeit – their spirits scattered to the ether.' He gives Rann a piercing look. 'They are now as gone as they can be, Rann.'

AS GONE AS *they can be. Even Aria, my Aria. What the great Lord Herrukal meant, of course, is that the souls of gods, even demigods, can never truly be obliterated. No, we are part of the fabric of existence and the destruction of one godly soul, never mind six of them, is almost impossible. Thus I was denied my love, my spite and my revenge. All the dark dreams I had conjured of my sweet conquest of Aria's soul, of our eventual omnipotent rule together, as she accepted that my desire was bigger and darker than any idea she may cherish of mortals and their weak pathetic 'love', was now crushed. Crushed by Herrukal's moment of passion. Alone again, but now painfully aware of the ache of my solitude, I plotted my new revenge against Herrukal and the others of our kind, because I was tired of their contempt.*

AEONS HAVE PASSED *in darkness . . .*

BUT NOW, *a soul has entered my kingdom which may change everything. In life his name was Elias . . .*

❧ CHAPTER ONE ❧

He was the power of the lightning.
He was storm. The justice of the gods.
Bakkujasi, Swarm rider . . .

From inside the mask, Nuss saw the world as light and colour. The mask was like skin, warm and enclosing, despite the chill of the clouds and the thin transience of the high air. He could hear them inside the mask, the other Bakkujasi, their spirit voices and deepest thoughts flowed through his mind like a red tide and he was one with them. They knew him also.

He rode Sandeshi, the largest black-and-red dragonfly in the Gremeshkenn Tem flight. Nuss himself wore golden spurs, a dramatic figure in black robes, his Bakkujasi mask the same red as the chitin of Sandeshi's body, in compliment to the Swarm. His cloak and the streamer-ribbons from his headgear flared out behind him, as though the giant creature had grown some glamorous appendage – not that Sandeshi needed any embellishment.

And there was always the sounds of flight, the warm, liquid burr of Sandeshi's wings, loud enough to make Nuss believe he was not, in fact, chilled to the bone, that the sensation of flight was other than a brittle lightness. When grounded, the wings of Sandeshi were a beauteous marvel but only in the skies of Chasia did the leaded veins and silver tautness of them fulfil their true purpose. Even the shriek of the wind was made mute, conquered by her constant thrumming.

Nuss often looked at the ground, exulting as he flew, but he seldom looked at his feet, which were encased in soft stirrups either side of the front of Sandeshi's thorax. For some reason, each time he looked at his own feet, outlined against wisps of rushing cloud, he felt a sick lurching in his stomach, which, being a Bakkujasi, caused him shame.

Below, the southern expanse of the Gurz'taal desert unfolded like shining yellow parchment for a distance of many miles. Occasionally, the flickering light of a shepherd and his small group of animals could be seen. Nuss wasn't sure what the creatures were – strange goats or llamas of some kind, something hardy to survive here since nothing but scrub grew on the salty grit of the plains.

Nuss had been collecting tithes for the Emperor at the temple in Releeza, as this was one of the duties of the Bakkujasi. While he was there, something so exceptional had happened that his head was still spinning from the ramifications of it – mainly in terms of how it could benefit himself, it was true. But although he was an avaricious and ambitious man, Nuss was not without a certain sharp intelligence and he knew that what he had seen – what he now carried in his pack – was worth more than all the tithes he had ever collected, and some-how changed everything for the closeted, timeless world of the temples of the Shemari.

A SUDDEN LURCH of Sandeshi's flight jerked Nuss from his reverie: a heartbeat-quick cessation of the noise of the creature's wings. So brief was the sound, or rather lack of sound, that for a second, Nuss thought he had merely imagined it. Then it happened again; San-deshi's wings stopped moving. For a horrible frozen second, Nuss turned his head to see the sunlight arcing from the stilled silver sur-face, and then they started to fall.

'Sandeshi!' he screamed. 'Fly, damn you!' But there was nothing to be done and, now prey to the winds howling past their plummet-ing forms, Sandeshi began to spin erratically. After the first few moments the creature itself began to dissolve. To Nuss's heart-stopping horror, Sandeshi simply melted away, tiny particles which he knew to be individual insects sloughing away into the sky behind them as the land whizzed towards him in a whirling mass, the dull silver of a river spinning like a dralchi coin in a craze of bright ochre and brown. There was no time or rationality left in which to hope he might land in the water and still survive. Just before he hit the ground,

Nuss was aware of one last thing. A sensation. Like a sharp slap in his mind.

(Sting.) Die.

But there was no time to wonder whose voice it was.

'TIGHTER. GO ON, tie it tighter.'

He flashed a smile at the young woman seated on the other side of the table; reassurance and wickedness in one brief package. She pulled on the ropes binding his wrists with her long white fingers, which probably had little more strength than a child's. The crowd of onlookers breathed a sigh, or sucked air through their teeth in sympathetic reaction as the skin of Vivreki Monvedrian's wrists puckered and pulled beneath the hemp coils. There was certainly no slack there.

'Want to concede before you lose your ale money?'

'No, there's no ropes Viv here c-can't get out of. The wager stands – t-twenty dralchi.' The large man spoke quietly, without a flicker of doubt, but his fingers twitched slightly towards the pile of coins on the table.

'And I'll take a kiss from your lovely lady –' Viv smiled towards the young woman who'd tightened the ropes – 'when I win.' Although he spoke to the man, Vivreki's gaze remained fixed on the face of the girl, who was flushing red from more than simply the heat inside the crowded inn.

'I don't think so.'

Viv glanced towards the challenger. 'Perhaps we should ask her, Ulmo. Maybe she'd like a kiss?' There was a tutting sound from beside Vivreki, as if his brother disapproved of this complication to the wager, but Viv ignored this. He proffered his bound hands towards Ulmo, who clearly relished the unexpected opportunity to pull the ropes tighter still – causing Vivreki's hands to turn so white they appeared almost sculpted – and then moved his hands to beneath the oak table.

'Well, Seesi, what say you?' The young woman shrugged, trying to appear unruffled by Viv's bravado when in fact it was clear from her eyes, and the slight parting of her lips as she gazed at his face, that this was not truly the case. Her expression was not lost on her partner Ulmo either, whose brows were creased into a thunderous scowl. He laid a large, calloused hand on Seesi's shoulder, and the onlookers were silently reminded that Ulmo, a farrier, was almost as strong as the horses he dealt with. Viv seemed unperturbed by this, or chose to ignore it, but his brother Stief shifted uncomfortably in his seat.

'Perhaps not a kiss then . . .' Viv moved his face closer to Seesi's across the narrow surface of the table. He had dropped the tone of his voice slightly, drawing her attention closer, as if to exclude everyone else crowded around to watch this free and unexpected entertainment. The blue-grey of his heavy-lidded eyes regarded Seesi's flushed face with a lazy sensuality. '. . . perhaps something else?' As Viv spoke, he brought his unbound hands back up from beneath the table, holding a long, red rose in his fingers. The movement was so fast, and so smooth, that the crowd was slow to react. There were a few exclamations of surprise and a smattering of applause, which Viv did not acknowledge. Instead, he leaned forward and kissed Seesi hard on the mouth.

With a snarl of rage Ulmo pulled Seesi back, scrunching his hands in her hair and causing her to yelp out in surprise.

'Hey, there's no need for that. I was just fooling around.'

'Oh *yeah*?' Ulmo roared. 'Seesi's my girl.' He lunged across the table, but Vivreki had already pushed himself out of reach. Stief meanwhile was hurriedly sweeping the coins into a leather bag, but was still too slow to stop some of his prize being scattered to the floor. Chaos ensued as the patrons made good on their opportunity and began to scramble after the spinning, rolling coins – Stief ineffectually beating at them with his bag. Ulmo, however, was more intent on serious damage. Vivreki's display of bluster and charm had shown Ulmo up in front of the assembled villagers, and the only thing bigger than Ulmo's fists was his bull-necked pride.

'Vivreki! You goed too far this time!' he stormed. He flung the table out of the way, though it impeded his stocky legs only briefly as he reached for his staff.

'Ulmo.' Seesi thumped him on the back to try and distract his attention. 'Stop it. Vivreki was only messin'.' Ulmo hardly reacted to her blows, which rained down with very little impact. Vivreki raced across the floor of the inn, pushing past the more focussed drinkers who were attempting to ignore this floor-show. At the far end of the bar he signalled frantically to the barmaid to return his sword, all weapons having been checked in on arrival.

The barmaid was distracted by those still scrambling amongst the tables for the coins, so Vivreki vaulted across the low counter causing a chorus of complaints from the drinkers. As Ulmo came closer to him, he rummaged frantically in the pile of leather-sheathed weapons, searching for his own blade. Time was against him and, with few seconds to spare, he settled on one that was roughly the right size, and leapt up onto the bar itself again to meet Ulmo's onslaught.

Vivreki laughed at the absurdity of the rotund smith running full pelt towards him with a wooden staff whilst *he* had gained a blade. Vivreki's laughter was a famously high-pitched, bizarre sound, completely unlike the young man's dark and volatile physical presence, and as such was construed as further mockery by Ulmo who lashed out in fury with the staff.

Around the tavern, Ulmo's friends smirked into their ale. Despite the encounter between Viv and the smith, most had simply snatched up their drinks and moved out of the way. The inhabitants of the small town, mainly shepherds and farmers, could mind their own business to an absurd degree.

Viv's triumphant laughter faded as realization occurred that Ulmo, unwittingly, had the upper hand, because the smith could beat him pretty severely with his staff, while Viv himself had no genuine desire to maim or kill his opponent who was a friend of sorts. However, there was little time to consider this moral dilemma, as Ulmo swung his weapon hard and fast towards his ankles. Viv tried to jump away from the arc of the blow but was impeded by the low shelf above the bar. The staff impacted sharply with his ankle bone leaving Viv crippled by more than simply indecision. Pain lanced up his leg and towards the knee, even as Ulmo was pulling back for another swipe.

Viv lurched clumsily along the bartop, ducking under the shelf of drinking bowls and goblets. Someone lashed out at his legs as he accidentally scattered the tiles of a game of *Mai* which the village elders had been playing assiduously for hours. 'Sorry, sorry,' he muttered. Losing his balance, he did a hasty and graceless leap down, which brought him right back into the path of the frenzied Ulmo.

'Aww, c-come on, you two.' Stief came towards them, slapping coins onto the bar in mute overpayment for his ale. His tone was now conciliatory, and he was tucking his sword belt back around his waist, though his hands lingered near the pommel of the weapon.

'Yeah, come on now, Ulmo,' Viv's tone sounded worried but he still managed a crooked smile. 'No hard feelings.' He laid his sword back on the bar and held his empty hands towards the smith. 'I was just . . . just . . .'

'Sh-showing off,' Stief supplied helpfully.

'Yes,' Viv glanced in meaningful annoyance at his brother. 'And, well, Seesi is just so beautiful, I got carried away.'

Although this statement was intended to placate Ulmo, for some reason it had the opposite effect. He surged forwards with an inchoate growl of rage, grabbed Viv by the neck of his jerkin and hoisted him in the air, pushing his back against the bar. 'Leave Seesi alone. I heard what you said to her before!' He then shook Viv as if to accentuate his point. Stief, who had grabbed at Ulmo's arm to pull him off his brother, hesitated and looked towards Viv in surprise. It wouldn't be the first time Viv's lack of propriety had got him into trouble. The listening crowd were suddenly more salaciously interested, and Seesi – whose virtue was being openly questioned – came to stand meekly behind Ulmo.

'Please put him down, Ulmo,' she said quietly, as if there were any hope that the whole village were not about to overhear a discussion of her fidelity. 'You know it's only you I want.'

Ulmo ignored her.

'Stief. Stief. I . . . can't . . . breathe . . .' Viv was beginning to turn very pale.

'Put him d-down, Ulmo,' Stief urged, somewhat more reasonably than the situation perhaps demanded.

But Ulmo was focussed. He'd known Vivreki and Stief for years, shoed their horses, worked beside them at the farmstead when there had been too much work for just the boys and their mother physically to cope with, but that meant nothing compared to the joy and pride Seesi had brought him by becoming his girl. He intended to marry her and have many children – who would be beautiful like their mother – and then he would become the proudest man in Rinjisti village. Clenching his teeth together with a snarl, he lifted Vivreki Monvedrian higher and higher, oblivious to the insistent patter of Seesi's increasingly urgent fist on his shoulder, or the reasoned tone of Stief's voice. He would keep raising him up until he was near the ceiling, and then . . .

Then he looked up at Vivreki's face.

There had always been something strange about Viv, and Ulmo did not have the capacity to quantify this strangeness; it was just something he felt was there but never considered closely. Now he flinched, startled away from his red fury by the realization that Vivreki was staring at him, quite *calmly,* from those weird, blue-grey eyes of his. Once this thought occurred, Ulmo seemed unable to look away from that pale, calm gaze. It was like a mask – like the Bakkujasi. It could only have lasted seconds but to Ulmo, that short time stretched like molten iron, as he and Vivreki regarded one another.

Just as he was about to say something, relent perhaps, Vivreki's lips opened in a tiny pout, like a carp, and something came out of it. In the slow motion of Ulmo's hypnotized gaze, the object – a yellow and black bead – fell towards him, slick and wet from Vivreki's mouth. But then it ceased to descend, as legs and wings and antennae unfolded from the sheen of spittle – and dived towards his face like vengeance incarnate. The sound of it was the last thing he became aware of before a reaction kicked in, and he dropped the struggling Vivreki suddenly, with a cry of disgust and fear.

It was a hornet.

Ulmo reacted instinctively, swatting the creature away from his face, cursing and ducking back, away from the insect. It persisted though, buzzing loudly close to his eyes. Ulmo began to run, panicked, towards the back of the inn. All the onlookers could yet register was that Vivreki had spat in his face.

Far from being impressed, Seesi now scowled at Viv coldly. 'Did you bewitch him with one o' your stupid tricks?' she demanded. 'I suppose you think that's funny, makin' a fool of a good man?' She then gave him a withering look and stalked off to the aid of her partner.

Stief pulled his brother up from where he sat in a heap on the ale-soaked floor. 'Let's g-go, Viv. I don't think you'll want to see Ulmo again till he's calmed d-down.'

※

AFTER THE HEAT and smoke of the tavern, the crisp autumn air felt good to the two brothers as they stumbled their way along the field track towards the farmstead. For a short distance the light from the village buildings had lit their path but, on reaching the end of the main street, they were suddenly encompassed by the cold darkness of the night, lit only by the pallor of a waxy moon. Stief caught hold of Viv's arm and put it around his own shoulder in order to help support his weight but, given that he was almost a foot taller than his irascible sibling, this was a less than comfortable arrangement. Viv knew what was coming for he had faced Stief's disapproval on many occasions.

'W-why, Viv? Why do you do it?' The question, posed with Stief's habitual stammer, was largely rhetorical. There was no reasonable answer: Viv was just being true to his own rather wild nature. He now winced as he put too much weight onto his foot and was sweating heavily so that the moonlight cast a silver sheen across his face. Despite being in some pain, his grin returned. 'Because I can. And women are just so . . . easy.'

Stief said nothing for a moment, stung by his brother's thoughtlessness. His own dealings with women were few and painful – he never knew what to say to them, worried too much about what they wanted to hear, became easily overawed by their beauty or charm. Their presence made his stammer worse, and the more embarrassed Stief became, the worse his stammer became. He suspected that they often considered him some kind of fool, taking the stammer to signify a damaged mind.

'V-viv, sometimes I worry about your attitude to women.'

Viv laughed at this. 'Maybe you're right. You know I don't think I've yet met a woman I really *like*. Is that strange? I like the business of seducing them but after that . . . they become so needy. I guess if I ever met one I genuinely liked, I might be in trouble.'

'You mean, you might be in l-l-love?' Stief corrected.

'L-l-love!' Viv echoed his stammer. 'Stief, you've been reading books again, haven't you?' Stief was about to respond angrily but, before he had the opportunity, Viv nudged him and pointed up towards the night sky.

'By the goddess,' he breathed, 'what do you think that is, Stief? A new star maybe?'

If it was a new star, it had crept into existence somehow unnoticed. It now glowed and shimmered with a pinkish, slightly sinister light which reminded Stief, somewhat ominously, of an eye. 'P-perhaps the goddess Oshi has put it there, to k-keep watch over you.'

Viv didn't laugh at this feeble joke, but simply stared, transfixed at the unfamiliar star which shone bright enough to steal away even the radiance of the moon. The light washed across his face, bleaching out the laughter lines and making his appearance even younger: a young boy seeing something truly wondrous. As he watched for a few moments, the star seemed to flare, growing brighter and more intense. 'Look,' he whispered.

Stief glanced up but didn't notice anything unusual happening to the star. 'C-come on, Viv,' he moaned. Something about his brother's fascination left him deeply uneasy, though he could not have said exactly why. 'I think your ankle's hurt pretty bad, and Ma'll want to check it over.'

'Uh-huh . . . right.' But still Viv stared for long moments more, before breaking his gaze away from the star with some reluctance to turn towards Stief. Some trick of the darkness caused the starlight to appear caught and held within his eyes, so that he seemed almost to have absorbed it into himself. But before Stief had any further chance to wonder at this, the combination of alcohol and pain overcame Viv and he passed out. Muttering his annoyance under his breath, Stief picked his brother up and carried him home.

BREAKFAST LAUNCHED ITS usual assault on the senses. Everyone rose as usual, before dawn, and already there was a fire in the grate so that the warm smells of woodsmoke and cooking filled the tiny front room of the cottage. Viv sat before the fire looking pale as he always did in the mornings, his tousled hair sticking out in comically sharp angles from his head.

The tiny farmstead dwelling only had one bedroom so Viv and Stief had to sleep here in the front room while Calla occupied the bedroom itself, still sleeping in the big bed which she had shared with their father, Teven, until he passed away three years earlier. In moments of rebellion the brothers teasingly threatened to expel her to the stables, although they all knew full well they'd never dream of such a thing. The warmest, kindest woman one could hope to know, Calla regularly dispensed her wisdom as a side dish to porridge.

'I'm warning you, Vivreki, if a brawl like that ever happens again you'll have to move away from here. You should be married and have settled down by now anyway. Whoever heard of a twenty-three-year-old living with his mother?'

Stief coughed to cover his discomfort over the fact that not only was he too still living at home, but was actually two years older than Viv.

'We've all got to live here you know, not just you, so how do you think I feel when I go to buy eggs from Ferrina and she tells me about the trouble you've been making this time? When will you ever learn to leave well alone what don't concern you?'

Vivreki groaned, looking decidedly pale. 'Ma, I'm still not feeling too great . . .' Calla softened slightly, always ready to give in to Viv.

'You know, you *do* still look a bit pale,' she conceded. 'It seems strange that a sprained ankle should affect you quite like this. Maybe you should go out and get some fresh air. Why don't you go and do some trapping with Stief?' she suggested.

'Cos it's only b-b-birds, Ma,' Stief grinned. Viv chuckled.

'We'll have less of that, young man,' she chided, suppressing a smile. 'I'll make you both some lunch to take but you'd better head off early if you want a decent haul.'

BY DAYBREAK THEY were riding through the Roshann Pass. In the weak autumn sunlight, the reds and golds of the forest looked glorious if somehow frail with the promise of winter. Behind the tree-line the land sloped steeply upwards, eventually rising to the cloudy heights of Vemerrsh Dui, the basalt mountains which bordered on the neighbouring territory of Mecinia. A chill wind was blowing, sharpened by its passage through the jagged black rocks of the pass, whipping the dry grasses into waves so that it seemed an ocean rolled down the lower slopes. It was cold, but not so cold as the freezing climate their potential quarry were flying from in order to escape a winter which made Bywere's look mild by comparison. Quirzel were very colourful birds, some bright blue, others yellow or pink, and the inhabitants of both Bywere and Mecinia prized them as house-pets because of their appearance and song. At the coming winter fair the two brothers could expect to sell them for a few dralchi each.

'Look.' Stief pointed. 'Thousands of them!' A burst of colour flashed between the trees ahead of them, accompanied by the sweet music of the Quirzel's call. Stief spurred his horse forward instinctively, but then reined back. Viv had not moved; he simply sat and stared at the birds as though transfixed.

'Vivreki, c'mon.' Stief frowned. 'The copse there must be directly in their path. Let's get the trees netted quickly.'

'I'm coming,' Viv muttered. He rubbed his sleeve across his eyes as though something had dazzled his vision.

AFTER NETTING THE trees they sat down beneath them for a snack. It was the first time they'd ever used the nets, which had been made by their father several years before. Although both brothers had accompanied him on similar journeys when they were younger, they had never done this on their own before, and climbing the trees to find a secure perch from which to untangle the complex suspended corridors proved remarkably difficult. Even in such a bracing wind they had sweated and cursed. Now as they supped some cool ale beneath the trees, the sound of the tiny birds began to fill their nets. Teven had been a clever craftsman; the nets made to his own design so that no bird was ever injured as it flew through the one-way maze towards the confinement in the end chamber. Stief found it difficult not to feel sorry for the little creatures as they reached what was really a foretaste of their caged existence to come.

Viv seemed strangely silent and deep in thought, staring upwards at the display of vivid colours.

'Are y-you all right, Viv?' Stief asked. It was unlike him to be so quiet. Viv stared back at his brother for a moment and in that time, it seemed as though he hardly recognized him.

'I'm not sure really.' He frowned. 'Stief, if I tell you something, you won't tell anyone else will you? Not even Ma?'

'Of course not, if you d-don't want me to.'

Viv nodded. 'Look at the birds, and tell me what you see.'

Stief looked up at them again dutifully, unsure of how to reply. 'Well . . . they're very fine l-looking,' he shrugged.

'Do you think they're bright?' Viv prompted.

'B-bright? How do you mean?

'Stief, when I look at them they seem like little flames. They shine so bright, I think I can see their souls.' He looked perfectly serious about this statement.

'W-well . . . I don't quite understand, Viv . . .'

'No, I can't really explain it either – but they're just so beautiful.' Viv rarely described things as 'beautiful' and Stief took this as a small sign that he was being deadly serious. Just as he was about to probe further, Viv continued as though keen to unload his secret. In the weeks to come Stief would remember this confidence as something exceptional, but for now he listened incredulously.

'You know when I had the fight with Ulmo? Remember on the way home how I passed out? Well, ever since I woke up the next morning, I've felt . . . different. I can see things like I've never seen them before, Stief. Particularly colours . . . Colours are so alive now: greens and reds and blues, they hurt my eyes. It's as if there's an energy *inside* the colours, and it's so real. Can you understand me?'

'Maybe you hurt yourself when you passed out, Viv. Maybe it's some fever . . . you know, affecting your v-vision.'

When Viv seemed slightly annoyed by this theory, Stief shrugged. 'What do you think it means then?'

'Dunno,' his brother admitted somewhat reluctantly. 'It's interesting but . . .' he rubbed at his eyes, 'kind of tiring.' He glanced back at the birds now crowded in large numbers into the swinging net cages, 'We'd better get them down soon, even if it does give me an almighty headache.'

They worked without pause for two hours, putting each of the birds individually into small muslin bags which restrained them without causing any injury. It was vital that they make good time in getting them back to the farmstead because the worst enemy of the tiny creatures was dehydration. Calla would have provided a large, temporary aviary ready with plentiful water but from the moment the first Quirzel was bagged, the race for their survival was on. Vivreki spoke very little as he worked and Stief watched him closely, his instinct still being that his brother might be suffering from hallucinations or feverishness. Viv occasionally stifled a groan but he didn't slack in his task.

'V-Viv, why don't you take a break?' Stief yelled over the din of the birds. Viv glanced up briefly, but simply smiled and shook his head.

'C'mon, Stief, we've got to get them all down.'

THEY MADE GOOD time on their return journey, pacing their mounts at an easy canter rather than a breakneck gallop which in the hilly terrain of the foothills could easily result in a broken leg for one of the horses. The ground was riddled with the holes and homes of ground squirrels and rabbits, and in places, the scree weathered out from the mountainsides made the going particularly treacherous. Behind them, a storm was approaching from the north, and as they cantered silently through the overcast landscape an unnatural sense of foreboding descended on Stief. The hairs on the back of his neck stood up suddenly and he felt fidgety and uncomfortable in the saddle. Viv showed no sign of reacting similarly, but merely stared ahead, totally focussed on reaching home.

Quite abruptly it began to rain, in a chilling downpour which limited visibility to only a few paces ahead, drenching both riders' clothes within moments and cloaking the surrounding landscape in a sodden silver shroud. There seemed little point to spurring on the horses, so they slowed them down to a hesitant walk. Saying nothing to each other, the brothers simply carried on, knowing that they could not afford to stop and still hold onto their prize.

For Viv, their day's work was deeply significant; he was hoping Calla would allow him to buy a new horse – a stallion – with the proceeds of their forthcoming trip to the fair. His current mount, an aged piebald named Jest, was a small, sturdy mare; unglamorous yet practical, while Stief had borrowed Calla's brown gelding, a mount that was equally calm.

As they approached the Fideawere river, Stief's thoughts reached a worrying conclusion which the first sight of the river confirmed; it had become a rushing torrent, its passage down the mountainside swollen to deluge proportions by the heavy rain. Both men stopped and stared aghast at the same instant knowing that re-crossing the Fideawere would be impossible and so their hard day's work would be in vain.

'What should we do, Stief?' Viv said gloomily.

'Look, there's a cave of sorts over there. Maybe we should at least take shelter f-for a while.'

'We'll have to let them loose, won't we?' It was a rhetorical question, since they both already knew the answer.

'Otherwise they could d-die,' Stief sighed.

For a moment, Stief presumed he had his brother's agreement, but then Viv clicked his tongue in annoyance. 'No, there's got to be something else we can . . . come on.' He turned, spurring Jest, and began to canter upstream.

'Where are you g-going?' Stief yelled after him, for Viv was heading full-tilt into the direction of the storm. As he raced ahead, the silver light of the deepening dusk shone all around him like a halo, and as it caught the rainwater breaking around his dark figure, it glanced off like bright sparks.

'The weir.' His voice drifted back, as though from a great distance. 'We can cross at the weir.'

❧CHAPTER TWO❧

I T WAS THE silence which always chilled him most.

Achios knew that above him the feet of the faithful were treading the mandala of the Abax, that they prayed and chanted as they walked, their voices and their constant pacing like the whispers of the sea. The Abax collected those prayers, entreaties, whispered celebrations or echoes of despair, transmuting them all into a physical moving river which wove in secret channels through the bedrock of Gremeshkenn Tem in an endless, shining representation of Herrukal's eternity. And from the Abax came *kyermah,* the most precious elixir used to move the Swarms of Myr . . .

But down here, in the chambers beneath, no breath of sound reached him. Down here in the secret depths of the temple city, few were permitted to enter and those who did were seldom cheered by the prospect.

Most would suggest that Herrukal's adherents were characterized primarily by their love of space and sky, that the blue of the Shemari monks' robes signified the freedoms of their faith, that the Swarms of Myr carried the spirits of thousands on their backs but, as Achios knew only too well, there were other skies, signifying a darker, deeper twilight which was equally the domain of their hierarchy of gods. Here, entombed in the bedrock of the mountain beneath the jewel of Gremeshkenn Tem, was the main power base of the Shemari and it was not a thing of bright transience but rather the brooding, beating heart of the world.

The cold walls of the passageway were for the most part unadorned, except that occasionally, with a randomness which could only suggest deliberation, there hung the ruined masks of dead Shemari Swarm riders – the Bakkujasi – placed upside-down to symbolize their wearers' descent into oblivion. Faint breezes stirred the faded ribbons and laces attached to their sides, as if the spirits of the dead would not relinquish them. Achios found himself surprised by this fanciful thought but then, spending any time in the depths of the citadel could lead one to such morbidity.

It might surprise many to know that the Hani – Exalted Voice of the Divine – maintained audience rooms in such a place where he conducted matters considered, in his indisputable opinion, too sensitive or important to the operations of his church to be held under the open scrutiny of the faithful. In fact to Achios, who knew the machinations of the church better than most, this polarity seemed entirely appropriate, for the Shemari, after all, were keepers of balance above all else.

He stopped before the unguarded doorway, glancing furtively up and down the length of the corridor. This was purely a reflex action, for no one knew of his summons here, any more than he might be privy to any other meeting the Hani might call. Achios had in fact been here only once before, although he encountered his leader often in the Sky Temple. If any thought had comforted him on receiving this summons it was that at least he might find the atmosphere easier this second time – even if the meeting itself would do little to salve his tattered nerves. He knocked on the door with more assertiveness than he was actually feeling, but when no one answered he shifted from foot to foot and waited long moments before deciding whether to knock again. Then, just as he drew his hand back to knock, the door swung silently open. Achios straightened his robes and paused to summon his poise before entering the Hani's chamber.

Just as he remembered, the chamber was much, much larger than the insignificance of its entrance would lead one to expect. It was gloomy to the point of darkness, and although numerous lanterns were mounted along the walls, their light barely penetrated to the central floor space, creating instead a lazy orange nimbus around the room's outside edge. Up above, a rough ceiling was pitted by dripping extrusions of lime. Achios knew he was now far beneath the plateau of the temple complex, for it had taken him an hour to make his way down by various hidden routes and stairs, passing the level of the Abax which the pilgrims walked. He found himself wondering what lay beneath his feet, what further levels of darkness the Hani might know.

'ACHIOS, HOW GOOD of you to come.' The voice was dry, almost rasping. Achios said nothing in response to this meaningless welcome, but he bowed low and slowly.

Ahead of him, the Hani was seated behind a table strewn with papers and books. To either side of that exalted presence sat two elderly men dressed in hooded purple robes. Although it would seem that they gazed towards the position where Achios was standing, he knew this was not the case, for they were Neruk'eel, special advisors to the Hani, and therefore would have been ceremonially blinded at their ordination. It was often speculated that the Neruk'eel provided the vital link between the gods and the Hani, but Achios felt fairly sure that they exerted a more earthly, and overtly political pressure on their leader. Certainly the most powerful families in Chasia patronized this obscure sect with gifts and donations for what appeared to be little material return.

They spoke only to the Hani, but even this exclusive communication was preceded by a curious practice of writing symbols in a small handful of sand which each placed before himself. The man sitting nearest to the Hani was even now scratching out some message before him, his index finger hooked like a gnarled white claw.

The Hani bent forward, somewhat stiffly, to read the text. 'Ah. Yes. We are reminded, Achios, that the scholars of the last age believed the world was created anew each night as they slept – that each man's reality was as a separate thing, overlapping like the ripples on a pool . . .'

Achios smiled thinly but did not yet respond. How the Hani could divine so much from just one scribbled symbol was beyond him! The old man often liked to prevaricate before settling to his point.

'But that is not my own belief, Achios. No, I feel that reality is rather more of a shared dreaming . . .' The sightless eyes of the Neruk'eel continued to stare towards Achios, making him shift uncomfortably. He noticed the man who had created the apparently redolent symbol had no visible pupils, only white eyeballs like glowing opals.

'Indeed, illustrious one,' Achios muttered absently. When the Hani gave him a momentary look of annoyance, Achios realized belatedly that his leader had been hoping for him to embark on some kind of philosophical discourse. He could only imagine how stifling it must be to live constantly surrounded by people who never questioned a word one said. 'In fact,' he floundered, 'only the gods can direct our dreaming.' He congratulated himself silently on the neutrality of this statement.

'An interesting point. Very pertinent.'

Achios frowned. 'Pertinent, sir? How so?' He noted that one of the Neruk'eel had scribbled something else, but the Hani waved a hand dismissively as if to quiet the man – surely a wasted gesture. When the old man next spoke, an unexpected chill passed down Achios's spine.

'We are in peril. I feel it.'

THE LOW LIGHT of the lanterns flickered, making the image of the Hani indistinct and somehow unreal. If this same audience were being held in the Sky Temple, the Hani would be seated on a gold and ebony throne, his face obscured by an ornate ceremonial mask, but here, where such ostentation was deemed unnecessary, he appeared in his natural state, that of an extremely old man. His bare arms were wizened, white as a corpse, his face slack and drooping, almost as if the flesh was melting from his aged skull. However, he then leaned forward and fixed Achios with a steely-grey, flint-like gaze which belied any physical frailty.

'Can it be that you do not know? Oh, this is good . . .'

Achios failed to see how he – as the most senior Shemari – being ill-informed could be in any wise construed as 'good'.

'Do you mean the loss of power in the Abax, sir?' he ventured.

The Hani nodded. 'That is the end result of it, yes. That and the fact that four Bakkujasi have suffered dissolution in the last ten days.'

'Four!' Such a number of deaths was unprecedented. Over the past decade very few had suffered such a fate – falling from the skies as their Swarm inexplicably reverted to its countless individual members. The Bakkujasi would glorify such deaths, claiming that Herrukal had taken the unfortunate rider for some special reason.

'I have ordered that the Swarms be used only sparingly, Achios . . .'

'You think there is a connection between their deaths and the loss of power in the Abax?'

'Yes. Yes, I do. Tell me, have you ever heard mention of the egg of a Swarm?'

'I . . .' Achios glanced at the Neruk'eel, his mind racing – this could be some kind of trick. Perhaps the Neruk'eel had suggested some lack of piety on his part, or perhaps one of their powerful patrons had . . .

'You may speak freely, Achios.' The Hani appeared to sense his panic – for such things should never be spoken of. 'You will not be judged.'

'I – I have heard of such a thing,' he admitted. 'There was a case some years ago, regarding a heretic. I was on the panel of inquiry.'

'Yes, a young boy. What happened to him?'

Achios shifted uncomfortably. The fact that the Hani already knew about the boy suggested that he also knew very well what the outcome of the case had been. This question could only be rhetorical therefore, leading Achios into some kind of admission – but what?

'He was sent away, north to Jerrguti, for correction. We judged his mind to be frail.'

ONE OF THE Neruk'eel began his infernal scrivening once more, his hooked finger making a faint scratching on the surface of the table. The Hani nodded wordlessly, as if agreeing. 'Bring her in,' he motioned to someone at the side of the chamber whom Achios had failed to notice earlier in the gloom. There were other entrances, at least four that he could now discern.

'Would you like a seat, Achios?' the Hani asked, unexpectedly solicitous.

'No, sir – thank you. I am a bit unclear, however, as to what this is about. I . . .' He fell silent as a Shemari acolyte entered the chamber. He was supporting a woman who seemed on the verge of fainting. Achios felt that he knew her somehow. She wore loose nightclothes which were richly embroidered, and it was clear she had been abducted from her bed, possibly during the previous night, and was also one of the more affluent of the temple city's inhabitants. As they drew nearer, her head rolled backwards, shifting the hair which had obscured her face.

Achios let out a gasp of surprise. 'Lady Veda! What madness is this? Does she stand accused of something?'

'Only of being a rather too diligent mother,' the Hani replied. It was difficult to detect any irony in his tone. 'It was her son we were speaking of. His name was Simeon.'

'Yes, I remember now, she was on the inquisition panel also – something of a conflict of interests but an opportunity to prove herself impartial. It was mainly due to her presence that the child was not executed . . .' Achios was aware of a rising anxiety and checked himself before he began to sound defensive or panic-stricken.

'Do we often execute mere children?' This time the Hani's tone was unmistakably one of disgust.

'N-no, your Highness. That was an exceptional case. The boy was given every chance to recant his heretical tale, but he adamantly refused.'

Another scribble from the Neruk'eel beside him and the Hani nodded. 'Did it never occur to any of you that the boy might be telling the truth?'

'No, of course not,' Achios said flatly. 'Why would the gods reveal their will through a mere child? What he claimed was unthinkable.'

'Truth often is. It stretches us, reveals us . . . Let that woman sit,' the Hani snapped. From the indistinct shadows of the room, someone brought forward a chair and Lady Veda was helped onto it. There she slumped sideways over one arm, her long, glossy hair swinging in heedless motion. Where one side of her face was revealed, Achios noted the shape of a jewelled insect glistening on her cheek, its silvered wings moving slowly as it pumped a soporific into her head. There was something avaricious about this movement, something coldly smug, as if it were feeding on a defenceless victim. Despite years of training and his knowledge of the Swarms, Achios had to fight down the urge to slap the thing away.

'The boy swears he saw the egg of a Swarm being laid. As far as we can tell, he took it and hid it somewhere.' The Hani shuffled through some papers which lay on the desk before him, and Achios realized they were transcripts of the trial. 'He was sent to Jerrguti, as you say. However, according to the manifest of the institution, he never arrived there.'

'Oh?'

'Now, it doesn't take much thought to realize that, whilst not the most powerful woman in the city, as a Bakkujasi Lady Veda commanded a certain amount of influence at that time. I would probably have done the same in her position – spirited the boy away, perhaps even substituted him for some starving peasant.'

'Then she is guilty of treason!' Achios frowned.

'Well, yes, but I am inclined to be lenient. She has now told us where the boy was sent, and her motivations were understandable.' Achios raised his brows in surprise but he said nothing. If *he* were Hani, Veda would be executed without trial and he wondered if the current incumbent was losing his grip on affairs of the realm. 'The point is, the egg – assuming it was real – was laid in precisely the year and the season when our first Bakkujasi riders suffered dissolution. It is my theory that the existence of this egg somehow affects the energy of the Abax, thus lessening the potency of the *kyermah* used to move the Swarms,' he waved his hand in a small cyclical gesture, 'thus causing them to dissolve.'

Despite the circumstances, Achios was almost unable to check a derisive laugh. The Hani's idea seemed preposterous – a leap of thinking which seemed tenuous at best. 'But, sir, you say there have been four dissolutions in just the last ten days. Why would the existence of this supposed egg cause that after so much time?'

'We have no way of knowing what happened to that egg. No, my theory is not extrapolated from so few known facts. There is a *new* egg now. In Releeza.'

'Where?'

'It is a small town far to the south-east, beyond Cantroji. The egg was discovered by fishermen only a week after the annual tithes had been collected there. We have requested it be sent to us but there is a slight problem. The people of Releeza have decided it is the egg of a dragon, and that it will bring prosperity to their town. Miraculous healings have already been attributed to it, and they don't want to give it in.'

'But they have no choice. They *must* obey.' Another unthinkable scenario within the space of moments, for no one dared defy the church – at least, no one ever had before.

'We are in negotiations with them for now, but I fear an example must be made.'

'Indeed, how can I be of service in this affair, my Hani?' Achios was instantly keen to make amends, since the obvious implication of this special meeting was that both he and Lady Veda had made a serious error years before.

'Veda's boy must be found. I entrust this to you, Achios.'

Achios bowed in relieved thanks. 'What is to be done with Lady Veda?'

The Hani narrowed his eyes slightly suspiciously. 'What would *you* do with her?'

Achios recognized this as a small test of his character for he knew the Hani was inclined to pardon the woman and was probably checking whether Achios would dare challenge this opinion.

'As you say, her crime was being a diligent mother. Perhaps it would be appropriate to strip her of her rank. Perhaps she might learn due humility as a maid to the Emperor?'

'Yes, yes, a good choice, Achios. I will leave you to . . .' The Hani stopped, as if listening. One of the Neruk'eel was scribbling another symbol. 'Oh yes, I almost forgot to mention, your niece – I believe she is called Asoori – once had some connection with Veda's boy, didn't she?'

This caught Achios completely off guard. Asoori was his only family, and he had ambitious plans for her advancement. Insofar as he was able to acknowledge such an emotion, Achios was fond of her. 'No,' he glanced at the insect still quivering on Veda's face – if it remained there long enough the woman would have no memories left, her brain becoming like blank parchment. A small frisson of fear clutched at his stomach. 'No. No I don't believe so. They were friends as children, but Asoori was never implicated in his heresy. She is a very devout young woman, sir.' *Devout to the point of zealousness*, he thought silently.

The Neruk'eel wrote something else and the Hani gave a short nod of assent, but did not give any hint to Achios of what had been written. Achios's mouth went dry and he found himself clenching and unclenching his fists. He was sure the silent message must have been in reference to bringing in Asoori for questioning.

'You may leave us, Achios.' The Hani gave him the briefest of smiles. 'Let me know about the heretic boy when you have found him. If indeed he still lives, he may be of use to us. We can only assume the gods had a purpose for the lad,' he paused. 'And take the Lady Veda with you.'

Achios bowed again, trying to remain calm. He well knew that the

Hani's mind was like the jaws of a boar: once he settled onto something, nothing could wrest it from him. So if he was considering bringing Asoori in for questioning and appraisal, the best thing Achios could do was to get himself out of sight as quickly as possible. He gave brief instruction to the acolyte regarding Veda and walked briskly back to the door. Only after he was in the corridor again did he pause, his mind racing. It was clear there were two things he must attend at once: get Asoori safely out of reach and find the heretic boy.

THE SWARM LUNGED effortlessly into the breathless blue of a clear sky. Achios gripped the rope tightly and stared down into the dark crevasse of the mountain with some trepidation. He was one of the very few people who, while not himself Bakkujasi, was allowed to fly as a passenger behind one of the Swarm riders. The white-clad figure of the Bakkujasi seated before him had said nothing the whole time. Awaiting him in the courtyard of the Sky Temple upon instruction from the Hani, he had already been wearing his mask when Achios arrived there. The expressive white-and-gold mask displayed a visage of calm contemplation, gold and black ribbons streaming from the temples in echo of the rider's own hair which was tightly concealed beneath a white cowl. Many of these masks were less serene, some leering and frightening, but Achios knew the Bakkujasi were not given a choice in this, for their individual masks were preordained and allocated to them when they took their orders. The hood had slipped loose as they flew, so that from where Achios sat he could see the man's brown hair poking like stubborn straw through tiny gaps in the cloth bindings. This remained the only indication of the Bakkujasi's humanity, the only proof that a living, breathing being was behind the totally immutable mask. Its wearer moved with the smooth detachedness which was the habit of the Bakkujasi; they were allowed to speak but were often by choice silent. At this moment that suited Achios very well, for it was difficult to put aside thoughts of the Hani's warnings – and the fear of a sudden dissolution would not leave him. It was impossible to tell what the Bakkujasi thought of their new-found vulnerability, but he knew the Swarm riders would never refuse to fly – it was their passion.

❧

Despite his current misgivings Achios could not fail to be dazzled by the panoramic view which opened up before his gaze the instant the Swarm took off from the side of the mountain. He was reminded of Hani's comment about the world being made anew when men slept, and this was how he felt each time he flew. The land seemed remade beneath him each time he rode one of the Gremeshkenn Tem flight, so intrinsic to the existence of Myr had they become in the decades since their discovery.

Below him he could see both of the twin cities: Gremeshkenn Tem still closer to his right, and Gremeshkenn Sor, the martial city, in the distance over to his left. The temple city he had just left appeared as some bright, golden phoenix, its roofs crusted with gold and the carved likenesses of mythical creatures such as djinns and dragons. Few birds ever dared land on the tiles of the temple except for the white eagles which lived there, making their eyries amongst its spindle minarets with the arrogant impunity of creatures considered sacred. Red and gold flags snapped and flickered constantly, as if to lend some kind of levity to the constant drone of the prayer wheels and the monotonous solemnity of the monks and Shemari elite who made that place their home.

And if Gremeshkenn Tem was a phoenix, his destination was the ashes from which it was born. Gremeshkenn Sor was a stark matron in comparison to her shining sister; the grey solidity of its buildings – the ancient core of which had been hewn from the mountaintop itself – formed a crumbling citadel which Achios held in quiet affection. Most of its residents would not profess to the same fondness, merely because Gremeshkenn Sor was always, *always* so cold. A large plateau girded the citadel's western extremity before suddenly giving way to the jagged gorge which made the journey between the twin cities far from simple. Because of the plateau, Gremeshkenn Sor was less sheltered; the winds howled up from the depths of the crevasse and across the open expanse, unchecked until they slammed into the grey walls of the city, whistling through the tiniest of breeches, over time eroding the ancient structure like the crazed weatherbeating of an elderly face.

Wordlessly, the Bakkujasi directed the Swarm south, as it was impossible to fly straight across the intervening gap, the winds of the gorge being so capricious that three Swarms had been lost there in the past. He would skirt down the perimeter of the Gremeshkenn Tem side, and then describe a long loop back north-west to bring him over to the calmer side of the martial city. At the southern limit of the mountains, the landscape of Chasia stretched out before him, falling away steeply towards the elegant darkness of the great forest. Once the true mountain terrain ended, the land still undulated for many miles, its rocky surface blanketed by trees becoming gentler and less sharp in the blue haze of distance. The great forest – named Wakku Fend by the mapmakers of Myr, but simply Sorib Tu (The Greenness) by most of the inhabitants of the towns and cities on its distant fringes – covered a massive area, that gave way in turn to further mountains ranges in the east, and a smaller, single one immediately on its southern boundary, behind whose shelter the relatively balmy climate of the Cantroji region began. Achios could just see the conical tip of this southern guardian, Taqua'heen, in the far distance, with its pinnacle, permanently covered by snow, basking in the low autumnal sunlight so that a pinkish blush was now painted across its summit.

Wakku Fend was so dense in places that it was largely unexplored. In the summer months, even this far north, it would occasionally steam as if some sleeping behemoth underlay its soil who one day would rise to shake the irritations of both trees and sparse human settlement from its back as if they were lice or ticks.

As they reached the southernmost point of their flight the Swarm banked right. If Achios had timed his journey correctly, he should arrive at the martial city around midday, time enough then to settle into his own rooms – he was one of the very few, even amongst the elite of the Shemari, who maintained rooms in both cities. He planned to stay there for a few days this time, sending a message to his niece and attending to some other business for the Emperor. He had conceived a proposition for Asoori which he rather hoped she had the wit to appreciate.

ASOORI PIKRESH GLARED coldly at her opponent for a moment, then attacked so swiftly it seemed as though she had scarcely moved at all before her body was back in its starting position, her wooden *shenai* again held upright against her face, touching her lips in salute. The only thing to belie any motion was that her opponent – a younger woman exuding far too much confidence – was now clutching at her shoulder and staring at Asoori in disbelief. Although the light wood of Asoori's weapon could not have cut into the girl's arm the blow had been hard and stinging so that she dropped her own blade as her hand had involuntarily spasmed.

Asoori stepped forward and touched the tip of her sword to her opponent's breast. 'There now, Cloe, I have killed you. Or rather you have killed yourself by dropping your blade when all I would have had inflicted was a flesh wound.' She smiled thinly. 'Go and get some more practice. Think particularly about how your reactionary senses may betray you in combat.'

'Yes, Tavidar.' The pupil turned to go, her cheeks burning with shame. Her humiliation was not complete, however.

'Cloe,' Asoori snapped, 'get back here!' The defeated girl stiffened and then turned, her expression a mixture of fear and indignation. Asoori noticed the flicker of rebellion in her eyes and she was quietly pleased. She walked up to the pupil and grabbed her by the lapels of her white training shirt.

'Never, never leave my square without bowing to me first,' she hissed, pushing her face right in front of the girl's line of vision so that she could not avert her gaze. 'Do you understand me?'

Asoori shook the girl slightly and then pushed her away, Cloe bowed stiffly and then turned to walk back to the residential halls. As Asoori watched her go, she felt faint admiration that her pupil did not break into a run as most would, but moved calmly as though she had not a care in the world. In fact, Cloe was easily the most promising swordswoman amongst her contemporaries, but the girl was spoilt and used to having her own way. Asoori had heard how she had been bullying one of the other girls mercilessly, until the girl broke down in tears. Her victim had refused to name her aggressor through fear of reprisal but Asoori knew it could only be Cloe.

Turning to the other young women who had been watching, she bowed.

'Dismissed.'

The girls left hastily; it was not unknown for Asoori to change her mind and call them back again. The courtyard emptied quickly and Asoori was left alone. After putting on an extra layer of woollens against the chill, she began some stretches to aid her aching muscles as they cooled.

❧

'ASOORI PIKRESH, when are you going to learn that you are not allowed to do physical injury to your charges?' The question was asked with only the slightest hint of amusement. Kilmer leaned against the stone wall of the refectory, watching her perform her exercises with interest. Asoori continued with her stretch: lunging forwards and pushing down her heels, until she felt the tension in her calves. 'That girl deserved it. She's a bitch and a bully. Learning some humility won't kill her.'

Kilmer assumed a pained expression. 'Need I remind you Tavidar, that your student's parents do not pay for her to come here and learn humility. Your pupils are training in the hopes of joining an elite section of the Emperor's guard – that same ladder you are still climbing, somewhat precariously I might add.'

She gave him a tense smile which did not reach her eyes. 'I thank you for your concern on my behalf, Earl Torroshi, but my career path is really of little consequence to you.' Asoori knew she should act more politely towards him: she would never have dreamed of addressing him so bluntly if anyone had been listening to their conversation. Kilmer Torroshi was her superior both socially and by rank, for despite his apparent youth, he was a philosophy professor on the teaching staff at Gremeshkenn Sor. He did not seem offended, however, and merely smirked at her rebuke as she grabbed a towel and, sketching the minimum bow possible towards him, began to walk away towards the monolithic building which housed the teaching-staff quarters.

'Asoori, your uncle wishes to see you at eight bells,' he called after her.

She spun around, an expression akin to fright on her face, 'What – about Cloe?'

He shrugged, 'I doubt it. Even here, news doesn't travel that fast. Perhaps he has found a patron for your commission, at last . . .'

'My commission?' she echoed, and her face lit up with a remarkable smile which her students rarely saw. '*Yes!*'

BEFORE KNOCKING ON her uncle's door, Asoori stopped to fidget with the skirts of her garments; the underskirt had become caught and twisted around somehow. These same blue robes had lain unpacked in her luggage chest since the day, almost six years before, when she had first settled her belongings into her tiny room in Gremeshkenn Sor. Her mother had insisted she take a couple of formal *hannar*, gods knew why. Asoori realized now that she, a mere sixteen-year-old at the time, had a more realistic view of the possible depredations of life here than her mother. That first winter, the ancient citadel had been gripped by ice and storms and, as she huddled in her bed writing home with cold cramped fingers, she had wryly remarked, 'The lovely blue and red *hannar* you made for me, mother, are just a little too light a fabric for the climate here, but I am hoping to have the chance to wear them during the summer.' In fact she never had worn them, the version of the summer season up here seeming to be only a brief respite from the biting winds of the mountain top, despite the occasional break in the clouds to reveal a sky as vibrant as Asoori's neglected blue robes. Still, she had become acclimatized now and could allow herself a small smile whenever she saw a new intake of her pupils shivering in the cold grey light of dawn. She finally gave up on her skirts and knocked on the door.

'Come in.'

It came as no surprise when the door creaked open under her touch; she was sure her formidable uncle deliberately kept it so. There were no lights in his room; only the flickering movements of a blazing fire illuminated the cold stone walls. His chamber, which doubled as her uncle's study, was cluttered and untidy, with books and papers strewn around every surface. Only heavy green drapes and a large tapestry above the fireplace allowed the room any feeling of warmth. The tapestry depicted a hunting scene centring on a strange bear-like beast watched impassively by a woman in a tower over to one side. Asoori disliked such adornments, on the principle that they were almost always stitched by long-suffering women waiting for a husband to return home, or some such nonsense.

She had not seen her great-uncle Achios for months now; he rarely bothered with the mundane day-to-day business of the citadel, being one of those Shemari elite who moved back and forth between the ancient cites of Gremeshkenn Sor and Tem like shadows whose existence and activities remained unquestioned, yet somehow inherently essential to the fabric of both places. It came as a shock to her therefore to see how thin he had become. He exuded old age and frailty in his movements as he walked towards the chamber door to welcome her. She frowned at this, almost forgetting to bow.

'Are you well, Uncle?'

He sighed heavily but then smiled, his dark heavy-lidded eyes still retaining the spark of great intellect. 'Direct as ever, Asoori. Come, sit over by the fire. My old bones chill easily these days.'

Asoori sat down obediently and watched as Achios poured her a drink into a tiny filigree-decorated silver bowl without first asking if she wanted it. When he had poured the liquid, he turned the bowl ceremoniously three times, before proffering it to her.

'Thank you, but I am afraid I do not allow myself any alcohol.' She smiled uncertainly, aware that Achios might somehow be testing her. 'It clouds my mind and fuddles my thinking the next day. I cannot afford to let my students get the better of me.'

'Indeed not, Asoori, but I can assure you this is no ordinary alcohol. In fact it sharpens the mind wonderfully, even the next day. It is called Dremsi. You may have heard of it.'

'But Uncle, I'm not permitted . . . Only Shemari are entitled . . .'

'Consider it a foretaste of things to come . . . Anyway, who will tell on us? I am the leader of the Gremeshkenn Sor chapter. There is no authority in this gods-forsaken citadel higher than I. Now, drink it.' His last words were more command than invitation and Asoori hastily took a large swallow of the drink which smelt of heady spices. Immediately she felt something react in her brain, a sharp but not altogether unpleasant shock as though her mind was recoiling from the forbidden spirit.

'Oh, it's . . . nice,' she ended lamely. Her uncle appeared to be watching her closely as he sat down opposite her by the fire. He arched his brows questioningly, as if inviting her further opinion of the strange liquid. For some reason his demeanour irritated Asoori, and she scowled in response. 'Is this about my commission, sir?'

'Indeed.' He paused to take a sip from his own bowl. 'You may consider this something of an interview.'

Suddenly Asoori sprang to her feet, snatching the long silver dagger from the sheath fastened at her side. 'Sit very still, Uncle. There's a large . . .' she squinted closely at the fast-moving shadow hovering on the back of Achios's seat, '. . . rat on your chair.'

Achios threw back his head and laughed, a surprisingly warm sound in the dark stillness of the chamber. 'Put your weapon away, girl. It's only Niyya. She's a pet of sorts.' He reached out one arm and clicked his fingers; with an unerringly fast spring the rat shifted from its perch on the back of the chair, and darted down Achios's arm to rest on his lap. The animal remained quite still, poised upright on its back legs, its silver whiskers twitching, sensing the air, as though Asoori's threat was somehow still tangible. Asoori sheathed her dagger slowly, hardly daring to breathe in case she frightened the creature. Its sleek brown fur was tipped with black, and its coat shone in the firelight. There was something precise and purposeful about its bearing to which she could instantly relate.

'It's quite . . . it's quite attractive really, in a way,' she whispered.

Achios arched his brows, his expression radiating amusement. 'Why are you whispering? She will be fine as long as you make no sudden moves towards her. Sit down and finish your drink.' Asoori did as she was bid, taking another swig from her drinking bowl. She couldn't take her eyes of the rodent and it seemed equally fascinated by her, its bright black eyes reflecting the firelight as it returned her stare. She was fleetingly aware that something strange had happened to her thought processes, and this must be entirely due to the Dremsi. It seemed as though she could see every tiny detail of the creature, every clean pink patch of skin on its feet, every tensing of its relatively powerful muscles, and this was all, for some reason, important to her.

'Is she old?' She wasn't sure why she asked this, except vaguely that the rat emanated a similar air of venerability to her uncle. 'Yes. Niyya is very old for a rat – almost twenty years. I fear our association will end soon.'

'You mean, she's dying?' Asoori felt inordinately sad about this.

'No, not yet. But she has . . . disobeyed me.' Achios's statement appeared perfectly serious. His smile had vanished and he now looked down at Niyya with an expression of grave disappointment.

'Disobeyed?' Asoori echoed.

'Yes, she has produced offspring.'

'But Uncle, she's only a rat. How could she know that you had forbidden her?'

'Never underestimate such creatures, Asoori. They are highly intelligent. Would you like to see her brood.'

'Yes . . . if she doesn't mind.' Asoori took another sip, getting used to the strange flavour now, though aware that it was affecting her strongly. Things were happening around her in the room; the light seemed to be shifting, her uncle's figure becoming indistinct although his voice was strong and focussed. She smiled brightly, enjoying the sensation but hoping that she looked sober.

'Come here, then,' Achios stood up in one swift movement, and for a split second Asoori expected Niyya to drop to the floor. However, sensing its master's intention, the rat leapt back onto his shoulder.

Asoori had no sensation of herself getting up, no idea how she arrived by the window, but the next moment she was peering behind its heavy drapes. Within the skeletal hollow of an empty sconce, left discarded on the wide stone sill, a ragged nest of sorts was moving with new life. Five young rats were sleeping there in a chaotic heap, their bodies wrapped closely around each other. Niyya leapt down onto the sill, surveying her brood with an air of dispassionate interest. To Asoori's present heightened perceptions, it became clear that the adult creature saw her own babies as a threat. The mother rat moved with agitated little jerks, her outline – like Achios's – becoming indistinct, a fluid shadow. She remained watchful, on guard, a small halo of flashing colour surrounding her tiny form like a warning.

As though in answer to her unspoken question, Achios spoke. 'You see, they are almost old enough to leave her and she knows that,' he remarked. 'It will be soon, within the next two days, but to Niyya they are already gone. They have no further need of her, or she of them. Such is the nature of beasts. Even a common rat has much to teach us, Asoori. While their need was strong, she would have given her life to protect them.'

'Surely, such is the nature of all mothers?' Asoori started as she realized it was she who had voiced the question. It was true what she had heard about the effects of Dremsi; although her vision had become warped, her thoughts still ran like a sweet clear ribbon through her quickened mind.

Achios smiled wanly, 'Alas, I know nothing of mothers, Asoori. When your grandfather and I were children our own mother died very suddenly. And now,' he spread his hands expansively, his fingers casting long, filtering shadows, 'I live here, entombed in rock and surrounded by male acolytes.'

But Asoori was not listening; she was peering transfixed at the baby rats. 'Look, Uncle,' she breathed.

There, beneath several larger brown bodies, lay a hooded black-and-white rat. For some reason, Asoori was instinctively sure that this one was female. Achios nodded at her, as though agreeing with the same unspoken thought.

'Come, niece, let's have another drink and discuss your commission.'

She blinked, and she was back by the fire, but how had she got there?

'. . . and so you see, what I am proposing would mean more than just a commission to the ranks of the Brengarmah. For you, Asoori, will be a Shemari. It is rare for women to be accepted, but not unheard of. I see it in you clearly: you are a mystic not a soldier.' Achios paused. 'Asoori? Can you hear me?'

IT HAD GROWN darker in the chamber, and warmer. But not to Asoori; to her the room had suddenly become ablaze with white light, which bleached out all surrounding detail except for her uncle and the firelight. The fire now blazed with a green flame, casting shallow shadows onto the figure of Achios in his chair. She knew it was due to the Dremsi and understood now why its use was widely banned. Fighting to keep an expression of panic from her face, Asoori focussed hard on her uncle's features, which seemed even longer and thinner than before. He was watching her patiently, but there was something questioning in his gaze.

'Just relax. Relax.' Though it was Achios's voice, it seemed to come from very far away.

She frowned. 'I think . . . I *have* to be . . . Brengarmah. I've been saving my . . .' Her voice seemed to ring loudly within the white room, sounding young and high-pitched. 'Uncle, is this Dremsi stuff drugged?'

He shook his head, the movement seeming slow and sustained, leaving a visual trace of the second before. 'No, Asoori, it allows a certain freedom to the mind, that is all. I simply wondered if you have the gift to become Shemari, should you wish. What can you-you-you see-see-see?'

His words echoed in the whiteness, for long moments seeming so much meaningless sound. Asoori licked her lips and tasted salt, realizing she was perspiring suddenly, as though her uncle's question had provoked an intense physical response. She watched the slow unnatural curl of the green flames in the hearth for a while, controlling her breathing as she would on beginning a duel.

'What – can – I – see?' She repeated the words as if feeling for their meaning. Slowly, as though with massive effort, she managed to turn her gaze back towards Achios. She blinked. There seemed to be two people sitting in his chair now, their images overlapping one another and drifting in and out of focus. 'What – can – I . . .?' She narrowed her eyes, trying to pull the double vision together, and to make sense of it.

'It is not your eyes which can perceive more, but your mind.' Achios's disembodied voice came again. He raised his arm as though he was speaking normally, but the other Achios did not move. Asoori's gaze fixed onto the arm which still rested on the chair, following the line up from it to the shoulder and then to his face. It did not look like Achios at all.

Dark hair clung in tiny tight curls to the head of this Other. Its features were broad, there was something almost bull-like about them; the wide-set green eyes were gazing at Asoori dispassionately.

'I . . . I can see . . .'

'Yes?'

'Another being.'

Achios's reaction to this was one of alarm, and he sat forward abruptly, gripping the arms of his chair. The Other remained exactly where he was, a small, slightly unpleasant smile playing on his lips.

'What are you saying, girl? Can you not simply see my aura?' It was difficult to tell if Achios was enraged or frightened.

'Please do not raise your voice, Uncle.' She frowned. 'It hurts my head.'

He sat back. 'I am sorry, Asoori, but usually, people can see an aura – a shadow which reveals the colour of a man's soul.'

She nodded, 'Yes, I can see it. Yours is a kind of dull purple colour, which I believe signifies you are ill and driven by something like . . . bitterness. I am sorry, Uncle.' Instead of appearing hurt or offended by her words, Achios seemed relieved. He nodded agreement and was about to say something else, when Asoori continued. 'The Other's is red – violent red.'

Achios appeared to consider her statement for a moment, which felt like a long time to Asoori; she twitched and fidgeted, something she would never normally do, the sign of a disordered mind. 'I don't think this Dremsi really clarifies one's thoughts,' she remarked a-propos of nothing. 'No, not really . . .' The Other smirked at this, and she smirked also in return.

'Listen to me, Asoori,' Achios leaned towards her and she sensed immediately that he was now going to attempt to hypnotize her, at least plant some counter-suggestion in her mind. She almost laughed, remembering how her cousin Meb had tried to do the same once but had given up, declaring Asoori completely immune to suggestion. The brightness was fading now, faint details of the room becoming visible again.

'Yes, Uncle,' she said meekly.

'Listen.' His quiet controlled tone did seem to effect some change in her, and her outraged senses of a moment ago began to still, slow down. She stared at the dual image of Achios, no longer frightened or puzzled by it; and as she met his dark eyes, the Other began to fade, flickering in and out of existence.

'What you have seen here is . . . a shadow, a ghost from a previous existence of my soul. You do believe, don't you, in the eternal life of the spirit?'

'Yes.'

'Shemari are the guardians of that life. Perhaps what you saw was a lost soul that I am meant to help.'

No. In her thoughts she rebelled against this, because lack of control was unthinkable.

'Or perhaps what you saw was indeed my own soul – myself when I was younger and stronger.'

He had green eyes, the Other.

'Who can say what the untrained vision of a young acolyte may conjure up?' Achios smiled warmly.

Green eyes.

'You should forget it . . .'

Light now – or rather darkness, a natural absence of light. Golden orange flaring from the fire.

'Forget it. You must be very tired, very, very . . .'
Green . . .
'Yes, I'm tired.'
'Why don't you sleep now?'
He was evil, wasn't he?
'I'm very . . .'

ACHIOS HAD BEEN right about one thing; Dremsi didn't actually cause a hangover. However, Asoori was unused to missing her regular sleep. Usually she sprang from her bed at first light and made her ablutions in the cold mountain spring water which was left in a pitcher by her door, not bothering to heat it first as most would. This morning she groaned as she sat up rubbing her eyes. She knew the moment she opened them that she was already late for her first class; the sharp morning sunlight flooding through the casement window filled the room with unaccustomed brightness. Her students would already be waiting down by the cairn for her to set them off on their morning run, and in her absence she knew they would soon fall into mischief – such being the nature of girls of their age. Cursing, she stood up to strip off her *hannar*, still worn from the night before. She assumed she must have been carried here by one of her uncle's menservants, and vaguely remembered falling into unconsciousness. There was something else though; something else had happened.

Just as she was about to fling the robe aside she noticed a movement from within the pocket that was sewn into the deep fabric of the sleeve. As she carried on removing her underwear, she frowned at the blue garment as though this could somehow make the tiny movement stop. When it continued, she tiptoed towards the bedside table and grabbed a heavy paddle hairbrush. For some reason she held her breath as she raised this weapon, but then curiosity overcame her. Crouching naked on the cold stone floor, she peered inside the pocket of her discarded robe.

She gasped at what she saw, then murmured, 'C'mon little creature. I won't hurt you.'

Just then, Kilmer's voice sounded from beneath her window. 'Asoori? Asoori Pikresh, are you there?'

She frowned, then folding the cloth back carefully to conceal the pocket and flinging another robe around her shoulders, she peered out of the window blinking in the sunlight.

'Ah, good morning.' Kilmer smiled up.

She smiled back. 'Good morning, Tavidar Kilmer.' She considered Kilmer a good friend. And one she was about to ask a favour of. He gave an exaggerated bow in return to her reference to his rank.

'Kilmer, I don't suppose . . .' she began.

'Already done. I took the liberty of instructing your girls to run twice around the perimeter wall. That should keep them busy until noon.'

'But you do realize there isn't actually a track right around, don't you? It peters out beyond the north tower.'

'They'll be fine.' He shrugged. 'They have brains in their heads after all, so they're not going to run over the edge of the cliff just because the path runs out.'

'Oh, I don't know about that.' She grinned.

'So, now that you have the rest of the morning free, Tavidar, would you like to come riding with me? Stable block in twenty minutes?'

'I'll be there,' she said. Turning sharply from the window, she almost stepped onto the garment which had held her attention so closely only moments before.

'Ah, yes.' She pulled back the folds of the skirt to find the creature had already climbed free of the pocket and now sat cleaning itself in the crisp morning light. It was the young black-and-white hooded rat. Asoori chuckled in delight and picked up the stowaway, holding it right before her face on the flat of her palm, where it nonchalantly continued its assiduous grooming. It seemed clear to her that this was a present from her uncle as a result of her fascination with Niyya the night before. Unperturbed by her close attentions the rat skipped up the length of her arm onto her shoulder, tangling itself in her dark hair.

'Oh, well, if you're so comfortable there.'

She proceeded to dress in her jerkin and leggings, enjoying the warm tickle of tiny feet on her shoulder as the rat occasionally shifted its position. 'Come, you can't just sit there while I'm out riding.' She gazed around her sparse little room, but there didn't seem to be anywhere obvious to house her new charge. 'Well, I guess you'll have to come with me after all,' she frowned. 'I know.' Flinging open the lid of her clothes chest she rummaged frantically before finally unearthing an old brown leather purse which she could wear around her neck. The rat quite willingly hopped into its snug interior, and Asoori smiled at the little pink nose which could just be seen sensing the air.

❧

THE MORNING WAS glorious; the clear air held the sweet promise of winter sunshine, and now that some snow had fallen it was actually warmer than it had been for the past week. Asoori and Kilmer rode across the Gremeshkenn plateau at a gallop, their horses ploughing up the snow so that they appeared to ride on a pure white cloud. The beasts were eager for their exercise, their flanks heaving, great gouts of steam flaring from their nostrils. After a while Kilmer reigned back, and Asoori slowed to join him.

'Ah, there can be no beast quite so fine as this one,' Kilmer said, clapping his mount on its neck, 'not even those which can fly.'

Knowing he was referring to the Swarms, Asoori pulled a reproachful face. 'Kilmer Torroshi, you know the Swarms are beloved of the goddess. Why do you dislike them so? How can you hope to find favour in the beyond if you despise the goddess's favourite creations?'

'I do not know, Asoori Pikresh, but I've never liked them. Maybe it's fear.'

'Fear?'

'Yes, I pulled the legs off so many of the little ones when I was a boy, I'm damned already.' He laughed at his own joke as he often did, flinging back his long tawny hair. His green eyes reflected the light of the surrounding snow for an instant, but then his expression changed and he sighed heavily.

'Is something wrong?' Asoori frowned.

'It's nothing, really.' Kilmer assumed a more animated expression and Asoori knew instinctively to hold her peace, as something in his voice still belied his apparent cheerfulness. She knew he was a private person and if he wanted to tell her his problems he would do so in his own time.

'So, tell me how your meeting with Achios went,' he prompted. 'Did you get your commission?'

'I'm not really sure. It's difficult to remember. We were drinking Dremsi and –'

Kilmer's brows shot up. 'Dremsi?'

'Yes. That's it, I remember now. My uncle doesn't want me to become just Brengarmah, so I don't think he's even tried to find me a patron. He wants me to be Shemari, maybe even Bakkujasi.'

Kilmer whistled in surprise. 'He has ambitious plans for you at least. It is good to have friends in high places.'

They had reached the small woodland at the eastern edge of the plateau where Asoori reined in her horse and dismounted.

She looked up at Kilmer, still astride his own mount, and her face appeared serious and worried. 'I think he is mistaken,' she said quietly. 'I am a warrior, Kilmer, and I have spent the last six years preparing myself for a commission in the Brengarmah. I know more about the art of killing than is healthy for a woman my age. I am the best swordswoman in the realm. None can best me.'

Kilmer dismounted also and his expression was thoughtful. As they walked to the rock where they often sat whilst having a break from their ride, Kilmer stopped and took her hand.

'Think very carefully about your uncle's suggestion, Tavidar. Being Shemari brings great power, and status, much greater than accorded an officer even in the Brengarmah. But then, at least if you are Brengarmah . . .'

'What?' She pulled her hand away, looking irritated. In fact, she was embarrassed by Kilmer's closeness and by the frank intensity of his gaze.

'Well . . .'

'What?' she demanded.

'As Brengarmah, you can still marry.'

'Marry?' she stormed. 'What do you mean? I'm never going to marry. I don't even much like men.' She stalked towards their rock and sat down, glaring at Kilmer. 'I can't believe you even said such a thing.'

Kilmer's expression was now one of bemusement, 'Asoori, you did not think that I was about to propose to you then, did you?'

'Well, I . . .'

Kilmer laughed so hard and so loud that his horse skitted uncomfortably. Calming his mount he tethered it next to Asoori's and went to sit down next to her.

'I'm sorry, I just . . . you should have seen your face.' Eventually his grin subsided and he looked at Asoori seriously. 'I'm sorry,' he repeated. 'We're still friends, aren't we?'

She stared at him for a moment in surprise: she hadn't thought their friendship so important to him, even though she herself knew the loneliness of Gremeshkenn Sor intimately. 'Of course,' she muttered.

'My parents would be delighted if I got married myself though,' he said as something of an afterthought. 'It would certainly take the pressure off me.'

'What pressure? Surely it's up to you when and who you marry?'

'Not really. I am an Earl, remember. When my father dies I will become Duke and inherit our family estates in Cantroji. Falloden Sen, our ancestral home, is one of the most powerful houses in the south, and my family would like me to ensure they had a grandchild by the time I inherited.'

'Oh, that is indeed pressure.' Asoori could not imagine suffering the dictates of such a social position – her own family consisted of just her mother and Achios. Her father was now rotting in Rann's territory of hell, or so she hoped.

'If I don't marry soon, they'll choose someone for me.' He shrugged, 'I'm just not ready for the whole business.'

'Gods, I didn't realize people still arranged marriages like that.'

He gave a short, humourless laugh. 'Happens all the time in the nobility . . .' Kilmer suddenly frowned. 'What's that?' He was staring at the purse looped around Asoori's neck. She had forgotten it and her passenger, and now a pink nose and whiskers were sticking out of it in quest of air.

'It's my new familiar,' she joked. 'Uncle Achios gave it to me.' She then took the warm, furry bundle out of its pouch and sat it on her arm. The rat seemed quite calm and sniffed the woodland air appreciatively. 'At least I think Achios gave it to me. Ye gods. Kilmer, listen. I must tell you about last night. Something else strange happened . . .'

'. . . So, what do you think?'

Kilmer frowned at her. 'I think your uncle could be right. The other presence you saw could have been what he called a "continuing soul". It's no wonder he wants you to be Shemari if you've shown such latent mind-talents.'

'No, he was wrong. That being was . . . well, I think it was *evil*.' It had begun to snow again, and as she thought of the strange, otherworldly shape she had seen so clearly the previous night, a new chill seemed to seep into her bones and she shuddered.

'C'mon, I think we should get back before we get snowed out of the citadel,' Kilmer suggested.

'If you don't mind, Kilmer, I'd like to visit the shrine first.'

They walked in the woodland, its quiet calm enveloping them, their feet making crunching noises in the blanket of untouched snow. The shrine was not far, within a small clearing, just a simple stone shelf under a larch tree whose drooping branches almost obscured its sides. A statue fashioned from a kind of dull green rock stood on the plinth: an ancient stylized image of the goddess Oshi, smiling beneficently with one hand outstretched in her traditionally depicted pose. Asoori quietly walked forwards and bowed before the shrine, her lips moving soundlessly. Kilmer stood politely at the edge of the clearing, watching her devotions. Once she had finished, he turned back immediately, to head back towards the citadel, forcing Asoori to hurry to catch up with him.

At one point he turned back towards her, a slightly pensive expression on his face. 'It never ceases to amaze me, Asoori Pikresh, that you can retain such faith in selfish gods, especially after the childhood you experienced.'

She pursed her lips in annoyance but she said nothing as they walked out of the treeline and back onto the expanse of the plateau. As they re-mounted their horses, she gave Kilmer a tremulous smile as though he had somehow unnerved her.

'My faith is all I have. It has allowed me to endure.' After a brief pause, she asked him, 'Have you no faith then?'

'None at all,' he replied.

LATER, AS SHE washed and prepared for her afternoon lessons, she thought about Kilmer while she dried with a rough towel, forcing the blood to tingle warmth back into her limbs. She always enjoyed Kilmer's company and found herself increasingly looking forward to the occasional afternoons they spent together. It was as if an affection for him had somehow sneaked in beneath her guard – because the truth was that Asoori did not generally like or trust men. That was something everyone seemed to know about her, and maybe the reason that Kilmer had found the joke about him making a proposal earlier so funny. But very few people knew how Asoori's loathing originated, and they never spoke about it.

As with most young women, her attitude had been formed by her own experiences with her father. Gellan was a swordsmith. He had been an angry man his whole life, dominating and bullying those around him with an unquenchable rage, fuelled by some sourceless flame that blazed within him. Asoori's birth had been the ultimate disappointment to him – the gods had cursed him, he claimed from the day she was born, simply because she was not a boy. While the preference for boy children was considered normal, Gellan's reaction to this bitter disappointment was less so. He treated Asoori as a boy, making her mother, Helis, dress her only in boy's clothes and beating Asoori herself if she made any female friends. By the time she was five, it seemed almost as if Gellan had convinced himself it was true.

Asoori grew up with the painful awareness that Helis did not scream or cry out when her husband abused her and, as she reached her mid-teens, the realization came that her mother deliberately kept silent in the hope that Asoori would not hear. And so shame, secrets and anger hung over their tiny household like a constant thunderhead. Sometimes Asoori wondered why her mother had not simply taken her and left Gellan. But she never would, for Helis would consider such an action as a failure.

Unwittingly, the flame of Gellan's anger passed on to the next generation – it was all Asoori could ever say she inherited from her father. For years she was angry all the time, and frequently this rage was directed at her mother. *Why did she not stab her bullying husband as he slept? It was all he deserved.* Asoori knew that Helis was not a weak woman; far from it, strength of character ran through her like steel wire. Perhaps it was a kind of sheer courage or bloody-mindedness that made her stay. She never looked brow-beaten, did not walk like a victim – hunched over and staring at the floor – no, even when she had bruises which no observer could ignore, she would still walk tall, forestalling any questions, and glaring at any about to make comment. Only once though did she hit back at her husband

and then it was strongly enough to break Gellan's jaw. Asoori did not realize she lived in an exceptional climate of fear and violence, because that was all she knew.

On the day Asoori turned sixteen she resolved to join the Brengarmah but she knew she would somehow have to find money for a commission if she ever wanted to make the rank of officer – her family being of a lower caste than those normally seeking entrance. She walked to her father's forge that morning to tell him her intentions. It was raining, she remembered, but the air was warm and Asoori felt curiously dizzy at the mere idea of leaving home. She was shocked to find Gellan near to the fire, a branding iron poised to burn into the flesh of her mother's thigh. Helis was pinned down against the massive anvil and she was struggling and kicking. In the second before she herself screamed, Asoori could see that her mother had already been severely beaten, her nose was bleeding heavily and her blouse was ripped away from the neck.

On reflex, Asoori grabbed a weapon from a pile of discarded and broken blades on the floor and charged towards Gellan, heedless of the danger to herself from the branding iron he held. He turned towards his daughter with a curse, and Helis wrenched free from his grasp, sliding to the ground as she fought to recover her wits.

Gellan was yelling and cursing at Asoori as she ran towards him. His face turned purple with heat and rage, spittle foaming at the edges of his mouth. As he ordered her to put the blade down, Asoori stabbed him through the gut without hesitation. The brand fell from his fingers and he staggered back, reeling in shock, eyes bulging and round with fear. She knew nothing then of the art of killing swiftly, but Asoori had enough sense to realize there was now no turning back. Nor did she want to – the hatred and repression of the last sixteen years resonating through her body in a wave of red heat. She could hear Helis sobbing – *now* at last, her mother let her hear the pain – and in those very few heartbeats everything seemed right. Asoori stepped forward and, with icy calm, plunged the blade in again, twisting it from the hilt.

She had stared down at his corpse, her face an ugly rictus of raw emotion, then she turned and vomited onto the sawdust floor.

Soon after, Helis had led her out of the forge into the rain. Even now, years later, Asoori could remember the feel of her mother's arms around her, how wet and warm they both felt from the rain, tears and sweat. People had come running to the forge at the sounds of trouble but no one stopped them from leaving and no one – even the magistrate who visited them the following day – accused them or asked any detail. Gellan, it seemed, had fallen on the blade he was making; the women of the community had exerted their quiet influence.

ASOORI FOUND HERSELF chilled all over again, thinking back to that day. She was under no illusion, despite the solidarity of their home community, that she had in fact murdered her father, and so she did not deserve their silence. She left the village – which was perched amongst the foothills beneath Gremeshkenn Tem – as soon as she was able. It wasn't far to travel to the martial city and she had joined the Brengarmah as a rating. That had been almost six years earlier and she was still waiting for her commission – still saving. Because it was unlikely that any patron would take her if they enquired closely about her past.

LATER THAT EVENING she saw Kilmer again. This was most unusual because, in the huge landscape of Gremeshkenn Sor, normally they hardly saw one another for a week at a time. But this time he deliberately sought her out as she was reading in the college library. A vast network of archives extended under the main citadel buildings as though tunnelled by some intellectual worm. Because its passages were hewn from the solid rock of the mountain they were always cold. Asoori liked the libraries, whose treasure trove of scrolls and books seemed to her full of potential and unfulfilled dreams. She always felt safe down here, embraced by the silence of the corridors. Tonight was bitterly cold so she had come well prepared, wrapped in a thick coat and wearing fingerless gloves, and had quickly wedged herself into one of the old padded chairs which seemed to retain some of her body heat. Even so, her fingers were growing increasingly stiff as she turned the pages, and she was about to give up and go back to her room when she saw Kilmer striding towards her through the gloom.

'Tavidar Kilmer,' she stood up stiffly and gave a small, polite bow. It was an unspoken understanding between them that here, within the confines of the citadel, they behaved with more formality than on their external jaunts together. 'We don't often see you down here,' she smiled.

He glanced around at the darkened spines on the bookshelves, curving away in all directions, reminding him of some huge sleeping animal. 'We?' he said. 'Who's "we?" I can't imagine you see anyone else down here ever.'

She ignored his remark. 'Were you looking for me, sir?'

'Yes, I've had an – um – an idea.'

'Really?'

'Yes, really.' He crouched down beside her chair, then glanced around slightly nervously. 'Remember what we talked about this morning? When we joked about getting married?'

'Sort of,' she frowned. 'But it was your joke, I recall.'

He paused. 'Asoori, I mean it, let's get married. It's a great solution. I'll buy your commission for you – finance your equipment and your squire. You then won't be allowed to be Shemari because for that you'd have to stay celibate . . .' She stared at him aghast, a kind of sullen dismay creeping across her features. '. . . then I'll inherit. Well, we'd both inherit. You'd love it in Cantroji and you'd be mistress of everything. And, it will keep my parents happy.'

'Kilmer, you're talking about a marriage of convenience. A loveless match?'

'That's a bit unfair.' He frowned. 'Since I'm very fond of you. We're friends, are we not?'

She coloured, unused to receiving even such casually dismissive affection. 'Yes, but there would be no real marriage, would there?'

'What do you mean?'

'I mean . . .' She could feel the colour in her cheeks and was frustrated at her own naivety, 'I mean, *physically*.'

'Well, maybe not at first but . . .'

Asoori frowned again. 'I know I'm not the most worldly of people, Kilmer Torroshi, but it was always my understanding that people were supposed to be in love when they got married.'

'That's nonsense. Arranged marriages happen all the time.'

'Yes,' she snapped, 'but this wouldn't be an arranged marriage in the normal sense of being chosen by our families, would it? It would be for *our* convenience.'

He laughed at this. 'The world is not so black and white, Asoori,

and there are many kinds of marriage.' His tone had changed, somewhat, a defensiveness creeping in. Asoori realized that she was in the
process of rejecting her friend and he would take such rejection to
heart. However, she wasn't about to agree to his wild idea simply to
save his feelings – or please his family.

'It may have passed you by, sir, but I do have some principles. You
are talking about *buying* me for the price of my commission. My soul
would be forever damned for being part of such an arrangement.'

'You're serious, aren't you? Do you think the gods give a damn
about the motivations of mortals' relationships? Don't tell me you
really believe in all that damnation stuff?'

Asoori's eyes darkened, and for just a moment Kilmer could sense
the dangerous edge to her zeal. 'You know I do,' she hissed.

Her glare didn't flicker and Kilmer sighed. 'Asoori, you said yourself that we are friends – good friends – and that's more than many
people have going into such a union. I'd take good care of you,' he
ended lamely. He realized he had made a big mistake the moment the
words escaped him and Asoori bristled visibly. 'Not that you need
looking after. Oh damn, I've made a complete mess of this.'

At last she smiled. 'You're right,' she said. 'It has to be the worst
marriage proposal ever made.'

Finally Kilmer gave up. He patted her arm distractedly. 'Just give
it some thought, Asoori.' He stood up and began to walk away, his
bearing visibly dejected, the purple swathe of his cloak, catching the
gloomy light of the sconces, matching his mood.

❧CHAPTER THREE❧

A S HE FELL, Viv cried out in horror. Jest was pulled after him, her legs and hooves flailing hopelessly in the darkness. Lightning flashed once more and was caught and reflected for a second in her desperate eyes. Stief was screaming Viv's name in panic as he turned and ran downstream, following the white bulk that was Jest as she was swallowed by the river.

'Swim, Viv! Icanti's teeth, swim!' he bellowed, vaguely aware he was stating the obvious. Below the weir extended what looked like half a mile of white water, with jagged shards of black rock that protruded from the banks or cropped out in the middle of the river. For long moments Stief lost sight of the pair and even above the sound of the rain and retreating storm, he could hear his own ragged gasping. 'Viv?'

Suddenly, they broke the surface; Jest ploughing gallantly onwards through the icy torrent with Viv now clinging to her side. They were swept rapidly along with the current, helpless to make any change in direction or to slow their progress. Stief could just make out Viv as he raised his arm, although it was unclear whether this was an involuntary movement or whether he was waving back towards Stief on the bank. Not for the first time, Stief cursed his brother inwardly.

'Hang on, you idiot!' Stief yelled. He saw the rocks ahead before Viv and felt his guts twist in panic. 'Look out!'

But there was nowhere to go. At the last moment Viv managed to twist himself around to face Stief and poor Jest took most of the impact. There was a terrified scream and, in an instant, it was all over. The unconscious forms of Viv and Jest were caught behind the rocks for mere moments before the surging water took them away once more; this time unable to help themselves in any way.

❧

IT WAS DARK by the time Stief finally found them. The slope of the riverbank was too steep and slippery for his own mount and so he'd left it tied up near the weir and had been walking through the wet mud in search of them for a long time. The storm had abated, leaving only the subdued sound of the river beneath a low freezing mist which clung to the contours of the land like a shroud. He could not imagine they had been carried this far by the current, and was just on the verge of giving up and doubling back to the weir. He would still face the problem of crossing over should they have been washed up on the other side. For the moment, his mind was working quite calmly, stubbornly refusing to accept the idea that Viv might have drowned. Much as his thoughts reeled away from such a suggestion, he kept hearing in his mind that scream of terror as Viv and Jest hit the rocks and disappeared. Despite the freezing air, Stief was sweating profusely and sniffing loudly.

When he first heard a noise he almost thought he'd imagined it, so low and quiet it was. He stopped walking and listened, fighting the urge to sniff, then the noise came again. Slightly louder this time, it was followed by a muffled curse. Running unsteadily down the bank towards it, he began to slip and slide helplessly in the mud. Losing his footing completely, he went careering down towards the water's edge and landed in a crumpled heap beside his brother and Jest. Viv raised his head, which seemed to be bleeding all over, and grinned wryly.

'Ah, the rescue party.'

Stief sat up, rubbing his knee which had taken the brunt of his tumble.

'V-V-Viv?'

'Yes, I'm still alive, Stief – but look.' It took a couple of seconds before Stief realized that his brother was fighting back tears. 'Look what I did.' He gulped, nodding towards Jest. She was clearly dead, her neck lying at an impossible angle and her flanks not moving at all. The panniers holding the sacks of Quirzel were completely water-logged; one was still attached to her while the other lay a few feet away near the water's edge. There was no movement coming from within the sacks and it was clear that the tiny birds had drowned. Jest had been Viv's mount since he was only thirteen; an unremarkable beast in most respects except for the manner of her death. Stief guessed the last image of her gallant flight through the rapids would remain with him for a long time. Viv had been planning to put her to pasture for the rest of her days once he acquired the coveted stallion. As Stief gazed at the sad white outline of Jest with her dead cargo, he felt the first flicker of anger.

'B-bloody imp-p-etuous fool, Viv. You've killed her with your s-stupid heroics – and all the birds. Now we'll have nothing to show for this trip except b-b-bloody c-cuts and bruises.' He crawled towards her body and stroked her cold face and neck. 'S-s-stupid,' he fumed.

For a moment Viv said nothing, but hung his head because he could not deny the truth, and it was not the first time he had led them both into trouble. 'I'm sorry.' He mumbled, 'I'm really sorry, Stief.' He crawled towards the dead horse also and stroked her nose. 'She's . . .' he sniffed loudly, 'she's so cold.'

'She's dead,' Stief replied sullenly, 'that's what happens.'

He looked up at his brother to read his expression. Viv's face was covered in his own blood, which looked black in the moonlight, his hair plastered defeatedly to his head, but it was his eyes which caused Stief the most concern. They were glinting with a cold silver light too bright to be merely a reflection from the river. Instinctively, Stief drew back from his brother, sitting back on his heels, and sinking his hands into the freezing mud of the bank.

Viv seemed unaffected by the strange change in his appearance; just sat turning his hand under his own gaze, examining it closely as, slowly, his fingers began to glow with the same cold light. Suddenly he was reaching forwards to touch Jest lightly on her forelock.

'W-what are you d-doing?' Stief whispered. 'L-leave her . . .' He didn't know why he said that, except a tight band of fear was gripping his chest, making his breathing seem harder.

Slowly, Jest began to stir, first with a long shuddering exhalation, and then a series of shorter bursts until she must surely have emptied all the air from her lungs – before sucking back in a huge breath which drew with it some of the silver-blue light from Viv's fingertips. Her eyes – until now pathetically rolled back into her head – flickered, gained animation, some dawning intelligence once more. Despite this transformation, she was still too stunned to rise.

'Jest,' Viv crooned. 'Jest, you're back.' Then he threw back his head and emitted his high crazy laugh, his delight echoing down the low river valley. Stief just stared dumbly at his mud-spattered brother, unable to share his unnatural joy.

'The birds,' Viv gestured over towards the loose pannier.

'What?'

'Give me the birds.'

'V-viv, you can't. It's . . . not right.'

Viv cocked his head, eyeing his brother as if he was some strange curiosity. 'What would *you* do, Stief? It's all my fault, remember.' Viv frowned, the nimbus of light around his hands flickering like ethereal marsh-fire. For a tiny instant Stief felt an entirely new emotion in regard to his younger brother: *fear.* But he knew, with certainty that his instinct was right – bringing back creatures from the dead could only be morally, intrinsically wrong. The goddess Oshi would punish them for this. He sighed, picked up the pannier lying at the waterside, removed the sack and threw it to Viv, aware of the weight of tiny wet corpses within. Viv caught the sack by the bottom and sat for a moment cradling it in his arms.

'Do you know what you're doing?' Stief tried to reason with him again.

'Shh,' Vivreki cautioned. 'Listen.' There followed a further few seconds of silence and then, a sweet high sound from within the sack, unmistakably the song of a solitary Quirzel. Then, the whole bag began to move within Viv's grasp, as more and more of the birds awoke from their deathly sleep. He laughed again, reaching for the other pannier still attached to Jest's saddle, and began warming it too with the strange fire.

'Here,' Viv reached over to pass the sack it contained to Stief. As he did so, their fingers touched briefly, and purely instinctively, Stief recoiled.

There was a frozen moment between them as both men assimilated what had just happened. For Stief, it offered further confirmation that he was frightened of this thing which had somehow possessed his brother. And this fear became transmuted into something entirely visceral and instinctive. For the very first time, Stief was actually *afraid* of Vivreki. The shock of this realization was written plainly across his exhausted features.

For Vivreki, however, the same awareness brought different

emotions: dismay that Stief could ever think he might be a threat to him, but also a shameful tinge of self-satisfaction. This was all about *himself* after all – perhaps this current 'gift' might never happen to him again but, for this moment it was *his*, and how he used it was entirely up to him . . .

He coughed, breaking the tension of the moment. 'Well, I think they've suffered enough, don't you?' So saying, he ripped open his sack and they streamed out joyfully into the darkness. Some of the birds had caught tiny echoes of blue fire on their wings and tails so that they carried the strange light away like a thousand fireflies. Stief ripped his sack of birds open too, ignoring any sensible thoughts of salvaging anything profitable from this bizarre day's endeavour.

Viv reached out to the escaping flight, and as he did so somehow discharged the last of his luminous gift to them. The brothers watched as the flock of Quirzel flew back towards the mountains trailing a shining mystery in their wake.

IT HAD BEEN a great day. Asoori stared at the shimmering array of her newly acquired weapons. She had spread them out across her bed and they glinted with a satisfyingly cold flare, catching the light of the new star which shone through her window like some baleful accusation. *So what*, she reassured herself, she wasn't the first woman in history to sell herself into wedlock for money.

It had taken her three days to change her mind. She had returned to her room after Kilmer's less than romantic proposition, counted up her savings, prayed for a long while, and then done some cold hard thinking. At the rate she was managing, it would take yet another five years of saving to finance her own commission. A new officer had to prove they had the means to equip themselves and also finance the pay of a squire for at least the first year. Most of the young men and women buying themselves into the Brengarmah were financed by rich parents and, in truth, it probably meant little to them. If they didn't enjoy the military life they would just quit to do something else – to Asoori, it meant so much more. She didn't really know why she was so set on this course, and she didn't like to examine the reasons too closely, but when she did, occasionally, an image would come back to her from her past. It involved her father, and his expression of disbelief as . . .

Enough.

The lighter side of the bargain was that during those three days she'd come to examine her feelings towards Kilmer more closely. Eventually she reached the conclusion that being married to him was quite appealing – she was obviously more fond of him than she had previously realized. When she told him of her decision, and he had picked her up in his arms and whirled her round in rather boyish enthusiasm, she had found herself sharing his excitement. This new arrangement would take some adjustment she knew, but it no longer seemed as arduous as she had imagined it might.

SHE PICKED UP her new shortsword and examined the blade closely, admiring the craftsmanship of the folded steel which, in the dull light of the early evening, had a subtle, almost reptilian sheen. It was half of a stunning pair Asoori had requested, and she was looking forward to wearing them both when in dress uniform. It did vaguely annoy her that all her new equipment had Kilmer's family emblem on it but then, what did she expect? In reality, he owned these weapons as surely as he would own her once they were married. She swished the blade experimentally, lunging forward onto her left foot. It was good, perfectly balanced, the grip could have been moulded to her hand. She began to move in a slow practice pattern, stilling her breathing, stopping her thoughts, focussing only on the pink-silver light reflecting off the new blade.

There was a knock at the door, and Kilmer entered. He wore a long informal robe and was carrying two goblets of red wine. Asoori could smell the warmed spices as soon as he came through the door. 'Ah, your new weapons.' He smiled. 'Do they meet with your approval?'

She nodded and took one of the goblets from him. 'Thank you,' she said, in response to both offerings.

'No, thank *you*.' Kilmer looked so earnest as he said this that, for some reason, Asoori felt slightly patronized although she could not have said why. It was exactly the way he might have thanked his groom for something. Since returning to Cantroji, Kilmer had changed somewhat, coming into his own and exuding the easy self-confidence of a highborn earl.

'What for?' She frowned, sipping her wine.

'You chose a local boy for your squire – Merric, I believe. The villagers will talk of it for years. It is a dream, an ambition, for all the local lads.'

'The peasants you mean.' She scowled.

He arched his brows and looked at her questioningly. 'Is there something wrong – something making you uncomfortable, Asoori?'

'No . . . well, maybe. It's just this – all this.' She gestured towards her new weapons. 'It feels as if you're buying me somehow.'

'It was our agreement,' Kilmer replied flatly. Putting down his drink he wandered over to survey the weaponry. He picked up the long dagger and balanced the blade on his forefinger idly, testing for its point of balance.

'I know,' Asoori sighed. 'I just didn't expect to feel like this about it. I no longer feel your equal here, the way I did in Gremeshkenn Sor.' She stared out of the window across the lush woodlands of the Cantroji estate. 'We were both just teachers there, colleagues. Now . . .'

'I'm sorry.' He shrugged. 'I hope once we are married, you will feel my equal once more. You will become a titled lady, Asoori.'

She nodded. 'I hadn't thought about that much – the title, I mean.' There was silence between them for a while as, outside, it began to rain – hissing and beating down on the darkened tops of the trees, tainting the sky and diffusing the bright light of the new star. 'Do you think that the star is some sort of omen, Kilmer?'

'The Shemari are certainly very worried by it.' He moved nearer and the warmth of his closeness sent an unexpected shiver through her. 'I'm told they're holding special councils and their most learned men have been discussing it.' She did not ask how he knew this, only assuming that someone of Kilmer's high-born caste might have access to such information. 'Some are suggesting it is the dawn of a new age, others that it might signal the end of the world.'

'What do *you* think?'

He shrugged. 'I think it's beautiful – a new star in the heavens to light our union. What could be better?'

She laughed quietly, but she was cold from standing by the

window and the sound caught in her throat. 'You're such a romantic!' She meant it as a joke, perhaps a slight admonishment.

'What? Oh, yes, I suppose it's always been a shortcoming of mine.' She could tell he was smiling from the sound of his voice. As she sipped her wine, feeling his breath warm against her scalp, she found herself vaguely wishing he would kiss the top of her head. She leaned herself back against him, and he wrapped his arms around her as they watched the rain in comfortable silence.

TWO WEEKS LATER and the unseasonal rains had vanished, while the sounds of laughter and music drifted across the lake; Asoori's wedding party was in full swing. The evening was warm, even this late in the year, and most of the revellers – who she had never met – had spilled out into the parkland. Asoori sat by the small boathouse, staring out at the water, her unaccustomed red gown billowing out around her like a moonlit flower. She felt a strange grudging contentment – deception was so easy, it seemed. Even when Kilmer insisted on ostentatiously kissing her every five minutes, it didn't seem too onerous a task. She found herself smiling at the sense memory of his warm lips on hers, but then checked herself for being easily influenced. It would be easy to give in to the idea of being the Mistress of the Cantroji estates, to sit at home and do . . . she frowned . . . what was it that Kilmer's mother actually did all day? Needlework or something . . .?

Falloden Sen – the big house and estate were so beautiful, nestling here in the river-valley. The people, the wildlife, even the plants were different here – strange and somehow intoxicating. She closed her eyes, inhaling the scent of jasmine and the cool freshness of the lake.

'Ah, there you are, milady.' The tone was slightly ironic, the voice unsettlingly familiar.

'Uncle?' She turned to see the frail darkened outline of Achios picking his way through the low shrubbery towards the boathouse. 'I wasn't sure you would be able to get here in time.'

'You are my only living relative, Asoori, and since Kilmer's father invited me, it would have been both a social and political error not to accept, hmm?'

'I suppose so.'

She didn't like Kilmer's father; the man showed no trace of

humour, only a kind of low cunning was evident in his eyes, which raked up and down her body at every opportunity. How such a man had ever fathered someone possessing the grace, charm and intelligence of her new husband she couldn't understand.

'He didn't.' Her uncle sank down beside her, obviously glad to find a seat.

'Pardon?'

'Forgive me, Asoori, sometimes I forget to . . . well, switch off my mind-talent as it were. Duke Detri is not his father. Your new husband is a bastard.'

'Oh,' Asoori floundered, trying to find an appropriate response to such information.

He shrugged, secretly amused by her shocked reaction. 'It's of no consequence since Detri will never know, and he dotes on his son. Don't worry about your new inheritance Asoori – it's quite safe. Unless, of course, he discovers the truth about your happy union.'

'The truth?'

'That it is to be a mere convenience, both for you and for Kilmer. You get your commission, and he gets to carry on seeing whatever serving-girl he may imagine himself to be in love with. Of course, it's up to you, but if you seriously expect this arrangement to work, I'd give the Duke what he wants straight away.'

'What?'

'A grandchild.' Achios stared out impassively across the waters of the lake.

'But Uncle – Kilmer and I . . .'

'Oh, so he hasn't told you – about wedding night traditions in these parts?'

'No.'

'Well, in about an hour and a half, the members of the wedding party will come to escort you both to the bedchamber.'

'So?'

'They don't leave . . . for a while.' He said it mildly, but Asoori immediately knew. 'No, you're not serious?'

'But I am, niece.'

'I'll kill him first.'

Achios snorted in derision. 'No, you won't. He may have his disadvantages as a husband, but you like him, don't you? He has a certain charm.' Peering at her glowering face in the dim light of the sconce, Achios tried to temper his obvious glee. 'You're angry with him because he didn't warn you about tonight's little ritual humiliation but, ask yourself, would you have gone through with this charade if he had?'

'That's hardly the point,' she fumed. 'He lied to me.'

'No he didn't. He just didn't mention it – which is not the same thing. Anyway, that's not what I came all the way here to talk to you about, despite the superb hospitality. I've brought you details of your first mission at last.' He smiled, but then his hooded eyes narrowed slightly. 'The significance of your marriage is evident, Asoori – as I am sure you are aware – the Shemari is closed to married women. Your recent choice is a great disappointment to me personally, since I had hoped to train you myself.'

Asoori flushed with pleasure at her uncle's small admission of defeat.

'However,' he could hardly hide his self-satisfaction, 'we do not easily lose sight of those people who may be important to us. It has been agreed that during your probationary mission as a Brengarmah officer you will report to me. I have been authorized by General Rewyn to brief you with your first assignment. We – that is, the Shemari – have had disturbing reports from a town in the far southeast of this region, named Releeza. Have you heard of it?

She shook her head.

'I am not surprised,' he continued. 'I understand it is an uncultured backwater – literally as it is on the shores of a freshwater lake. Releeza itself is in a small region previously known as Thian, but has subsequently become engulfed by Cantroji region for understandably practical reasons. They have silver mines there, which I believe Falloden Sen estates have an interest in, but mainly it is a poor farming area. Anyway, the people are fiercely independent – which is why this current problem arose.'

Asoori wanted to interrupt the old man and get him to the point – she did have her wedding guests to attend to after all. However, she held her patience, knowing her uncle was merely being thorough.

Achios paused as if wondering how best to continue. 'It seems the people of Releeza have found an egg – a large egg which they imagine to have been laid by a dragon. We of the Shemari suspect that it is, in fact, the egg of a Swarm.'

'But that's impossible. We know Swarms can't . . .'

'Yes, impossible, Asoori. It would be a miracle. As you know, people have been tried as heretics for even suggesting such things aloud. The problem is, the people of Releeza will not relinquish this egg. It may be that we must take it back by force, so a regiment of Brengarmah is making its way to Releeza now. But it will still be some time before it arrives so I want *you* to travel there separately Asoori. We need you to find out the truth and then recover the egg. The Brengarmah are under instruction to assist you – and your companion. Remember, we of the Shemari are not blind to the idea of miracles, but we need to know for sure in order to inform the faithful . . .'

'My companion?'

'I'm sending a representative of the Shemari with you – Cion Gezezi.'

'Cion Gezezi?' she echoed, unable to keep the dismay from her voice. She had heard of the Shemari's star warrior-priest, and nothing that she had heard could be construed as good. The man was said to be a fanatic, a powerful and dangerous one. 'But isn't he Bakkujasi? Can't he just fly to Releeza and I'll meet him there?' She found it hard to hide her dismay, but Achios chose to ignore it.

'The Swarms are currently grounded. Their power is being . . . diminished, affected by something.' He shrugged. 'We're not sure by what yet.'

'You know of Cion then?' he continued mildly. 'He is something of a specialist when it comes to miracles. He has studied such phenomena for many years and has validated – or invalidated – such claims before. Because the Swarms are limited to greatly reduced flights for the moment, he could not travel the whole distance on one.'

Achios did not elaborate further and Asoori was too preoccupied to wonder at the grounding of the Swarms.

'But surely I can manage without him, Uncle? How am I supposed to prove myself if I'm being wet-nursed by a Bakkujasi?'

'For goodness sake, girl,' Achios snapped, 'this matter is something bigger than your commission. If you and he retrieve . . .' he could hardly bring himself to say it again and looked around furtively. 'If you can retrieve this egg, you must bring it back to Gremeshkenn Tem without delay.'

He stood up, straightening his ceremonial robes. Their gold and silver braiding caught the moonlight, giving them a garish, almost ridiculous aspect, as though swamping the old man. 'I will send Cion here to collect you in three days' time. Meanwhile, you have some time to accustom yourself to married life.' Making his way back through the ornamental bushes he hacked out at them with his cane. 'My blessings on your union, Asoori. Don't worry too much about this evening's festivities. The guests will all be drunk anyway.' He shrugged. 'Fake it. Women have been doing so for centuries, so I am told.'

Just before he disappeared from view, Asoori recalled the vision she had seen in his chamber. 'Uncle,' she called, 'be careful.' But there was no sign that the old man had heard her. Her thoughts turned to Kilmer; her new husband was in deep trouble.

※

'KILMER, CAN I speak with you a moment?'

'Ah, there you are, my darling.' He kissed her lightly on the cheek.

She frowned in response. 'I need to speak to you *now*.' Something of her expression convinced Kilmer that his first marital tiff was imminent.

'Do excuse us, Lady Harrim.' He bowed smoothly. Then, taking Asoori's arm, he gently directed her into a nearby copse of silver birch trees, that were gaily decked with tiny lanterns.

'What's wrong, my darling?' Asoori lifted her skirts and kicked him hard in the shins. 'How dare you not tell me? How dare you assume . . .'

'What are you talking about?'

'So tonight – me – I'm meant to be some kind of sacrificial virgin! It's – it's so barbaric . . .'

'Oh, you mean . . . but look we can . . .'

'Pretend, you mean? No, no we won't. Sleeping with you was never part of this bargain. Not so . . .'

Suddenly she felt betrayed and stupid and tearful . . . and then shocked to see the expression on Kilmer's face, he looked so hurt. 'I'm sorry, Kilmer. I'm sorry.'

He took her hand. 'Look at me, Asoori. Do you really think I would force myself on you? Believe me, there are ways around this. And we will not be the first to have used them.'

'Are there?' She looked up into his face, and was embarrassed and surprised to find tears streaming down her cheeks.

'Of course.' He wiped her cheek with his thumb. 'A little subtly added sedation goes a long way, and those guests scheduled to attend our bedchamber have been imbibing it for the last two hours.'

She grinned through her tears. 'So, we're going to spend our wedding night in a room full of snoring people?'

'Hmm, you said I was a romantic, didn't you?'

AFTERWARDS, HOURS AND days afterwards, he would remember how the world changed, moment by moment by moment, crashing like a land-slide, gaining momentum, until nothing could ever be as it was . . .

The visceral brightness of that night would forever be etched on Stief's mind . . .

IT'S GETTING LATE as they return from their unsuccessful trip, no birds to show for their endeavours, clothes torn, scratches and bruises coming to purple-black prominence. Dusk is falling, pushing the pink resistance of the light across the sky. In the east, clear, sharp stars are already visible, but at the other extremities of his vision there is still a stubborn ridge of low cloud and enough light to cast shadows.

They crest the low hill before the farmhouse in intractable silence. They've hardly spoken on the day's journey back home, a swathe of time spent in dull, low-level pain, their minds too blasted to talk about the happenings of the night before. Stief mutters, 'I'll be g-glad to get back.' It's the type of pointless comment that people make to one another, the type which still gives the last normality to the day.

Viv does not respond. He's stopped Jest at the top of the dirt track, ahead of Stief so, when he calls back to him, his brother initially misses the trepidation in his tone.

'Stief, there's something happening at the farm.'

THERE'S A BAKKUJASI Swarm in the yard before the house; surreal in the half-light, casting a long black shadow. It is gold, and the last vestiges of sunlight seem to be trapped, made red, in the sheen of its body. Its legs and face are black, the vast wings still, and it stands there like a strange statue awaiting instruction from its rider, who is currently nowhere to be seen.

Before either brother can pass further comment, however, something happens – actually *two* things happen, but as mere seconds separate them, the brothers assume they are connected. Something passes overhead, flying so close that the air is disturbed and pushed towards them in a chilled gust. There is only a brief sensation but their hair and clothes are ruffled, the horses fidgeting nervously, Jest clashing her teeth, when the second thing happens. Down-slope to their left, a green flare is fired into the sky and casts its sickly, anxious light over the silent farmstead.

'What's going on?' Viv whispers.

'Don't know. They've s-spotted us though.' The flare could only have been a signal – Stief has a vague idea who 'they' might be, and his gut is churning already. The flare has landed on the roof, its green light dispersing to warmer orange flames as the tarred willow thatch begins to smoulder immediately.

'Icanti's tits,' Viv hisses, spurring Jest quickly down the path. Stief follows close behind, knowing that Viv himself can have no inclination of any Shemari interest in him, but as the flames begin to spread and his anxiety spirals with the sparking roof, a horrible inevitability grips like a fist in Stief's chest. He knew this day would come. Ma knew it . . .

As they reach the yard Viv reins in, and leaps from Jest's back – she is whinnying in fright, unused to the sight and scent of a Swarm.

'Ma!' he yells. 'Ma, where are you?' The roof has fully caught fire now, but for the moment the blaze is confined to the thatch itself. Stief dismounts just as Viv begins to run towards the house. At that moment the front door is flung open and, in the corner of his vision, Stief notices the movement of two men running up behind them, closing the trap. But there is no choice but to go forward. His mother is inside there. His mother is in danger.

They both stop suddenly, as if someone has worked some bizarre magic and turned them into stone. In the doorway stands a Bakkujasi, a Swarm rider. He's tall – at least a foot taller than the struggling form of Calla, whom he is grasping by the hair – and his gold mask glints and flickers in the lurid light of the flames, its fixed expression one of savage fury.

There's a moment when fear confines them, when superstitious belief holds sway: the belief that they cannot approach or speak to a Bakkujasi whilst he wears the mask. But this moment is broken when Calla cries out, her voice surprisingly strong. 'Get him away, Stief! Get him away!'

'What?' Viv's confusion reaches Stief through the crackle of the flames.

The Bakkujasi addresses Stief. 'Give me the heretic. I will exchange him for your mother.' The voice is not muffled by the mask, as one might expect.

'No. No!' Calla twists in his grip and he effortlessly transfers the black fist to her neck. Stief's mind is reeling – moments seem to stretch. *Why can't she just run? Why doesn't she just kick . . .?*

As if she knows his thoughts, Calla lashes back with her foot, her heel impacting hard on the Bakkujasi's shin. But the Swarm rider fails to react – as if she is of no more consequence than the burning building. And perhaps, if things had been different, Stief might have had time to consider the idea of trading Viv for Calla. He knows why they want his brother, even though Viv is completely mystified. But he also knows that Calla would never give him up. *Never.*

But there's no time for thought now, despite the dripping, stretching of each second. For Calla takes her destiny into her own hands. As the Bakkujasi looks from one to the other of the still immobile pair, she reaches behind her and pulls out the rider's sword.

Everyone reacts at once, so unthinkable is her action. The Bakkujasi rarely draw their blades because when they do, a life must be taken. Everyone knows this, even Calla, therefore her action is suicide. 'Run!' she screams again. Firelight flares off the arc of polished steel, but once she has it in her grip it seems her hands are too weak to cope. She waves it uselessly, unable to focus on how best to wield such an arcane, deathly instrument.

Viv breaks free of his indecision and starts forward a couple of steps. But he has no weapon, and no clear idea of how to save his mother. Stief, just behind him, grabs hold of his arm, sick certainty coursing through him that Calla is buying them precious seconds. Vivreki glares at Stief's hand gripping onto the cloth of his jerkin, a look of complete horror and incomprehension on his face. 'No,' he protests. 'No.'

There is no time to explain something so vast, how such a lie became woven into the fabric of Vivreki's life: how the woman selling her own life to buy them time – because she loves him so dearly – is not even his mother. How he is not even named Vivreki. No time now for any of it. And there is no question of them defeating a Bakkujasi, or however many Shemari are sliding silently through the shadows at the periphery of the scene. But they still have to try . . .

Viv stumbles back towards Jest, and his sword latched to her saddle; it is a poor weapon to pit against the Bakkujasi but he will do it. At the same time Stief grabs a hay rake which is lying near the back legs of the Swarm. At any other time, he might have been afraid of the strange creature, but now he ignores it as if it were the statue it appears.

Too late. As he turns, grasping the rake, he hears a sound which chills his blood. So alien and unrecognizable is it that he thinks it must be from some animal. But then he sees Vivreki sink to his knees, and realizes it has been torn from his brother's soul by something unimaginable. Stief glances back and sees the Bakkujasi and Calla, outlined by the now blazing frame of the doorway. The Bakkujasi's right arm is pulling down, just finishing a savage downward stroke with the long dagger. Calla is now falling, dropping like a doll, her face still caught in a moment of sheer determination, but the sword clattering from her grasp as the shock abruptly steals the life from her limbs. A red gash crosses her throat, and the moment of her death is frozen in time as she falls, sparks from her home blazing like cruel diamonds in her unbound hair.

The Bakkujasi does not even stop to look down at his handiwork, and who could know what expression he wears behind the mask. Is it triumph? Contempt? Stief is standing staring at the tableau even as the rider drops Calla's corpse and retrieves his blade. Just then the roof of their house collapses, expelling the fire out towards them in a billow of heat and flame.

Ignoring the heat as if it is an irrelevance the Bakkujasi strides towards them – *his eyes are blue*, Stief realizes – just as Viv surges up from the ground, screaming and brandishing his sword as if he is vengeance incarnate. And still Stief is watching, transfixed, unable to assimilate what he is seeing, denying that the crumpled heap of faded fabric in the doorway is . . . was . . .

Viv covers the distance between himself and the murderous Bakkujasi fast. The rider strides on towards him, apparently emotionless, definitely fearless. Stief hears Calla's last words to him echoing in his brain. *Get him away, Stief! Get him away!*

Yes! He's not sure if he says it aloud, but he is galvanized into action as surely as if Calla still spoke to him. He runs towards Viv and the Bakkujasi and shoves one arm out hard, to send Viv sprawling out of reach of his opponent's blade, then thrusts out to the other side with the hay rake.

It is sheer folly, of course. But Stief cannot allow himself to stop and consider his action, or it will be his undoing. The cursed blade gets caught between the trident prongs of the rake, and Stief twists and pulls it aside, grabbing the sword from the Bakkujasi's grasp and then propelling it through the air for some distance. Fortunately, he does not make the mistake of mentally congratulating himself and lowering his guard. His opponent pauses for what can only be an instant but feels much longer, as those blue eyes – so *wrong* in the context of the gold lacquer face – stare at him in apparent disbelief.

Viv has recovered his balance and races towards the horses, but his way is now blocked by the two Shemari Stief noticed earlier. He lets out another ragged scream of anger and engages both of them at once, his blade moving like ghostly silver lightning in the encroaching dark. Stief backs towards the three combatants, still jabbing towards the Bakkujasi in mute threat with the rake. As the blue eyes regard him calmly, Stief realizes that he and Viv, frantic with despair, are now most likely to make fatal mistakes. If they cannot retain clarity of mind the foe will pick them off within minutes. The blue gaze tells him this – despite the fact that he has just managed the unthinkable and dis-armed a Swarm rider.

There's a strangled noise behind him and then a nasty, humour-less chuckle which he recognizes as Vivreki's. He wants to turn around and look but he knows it would be his undoing. For the moment the Bakkujasi is side-stepping to recover his blade, so Stief turns with him, as if they are the ends of a pendulum. He jabs forward with the rake again, determined to keep his aggressor as distant as pos-sible. The Bakkujasi does not even flinch, merely side-steps again, closer to his weapon. It is a ridiculous situation; Stief cannot let the rider regain his sword but neither can he bring himself to attack – he has the upper hand but seems incapable of following through. He cannot *kill* a Bakkujasi – can he?

Only seconds have passed, but Stief feels like he is drowning.

'Viv!' He cannot look away. 'Viv, get the horses.' There's a grunt from right behind him, and Stief realizes he and Vivreki are now standing back-to-back. He's pretty sure his brother has managed to incapacitate one of the Shemari, but he cannot even glance back to check. The taste of sheer panic becomes like copper and ashes in his mouth.

Suddenly he is yanked from behind, pulled out of this never-ending dance by Viv shoving him towards his horse. Viv covers his retreat by recklessly stepping towards the Bakkujasi, flailing with his sword and screaming obscenities. Stief has only a fleeting impression of this encounter as his horse's welcome brown flanks come into view. He throws himself gracelessly across its back, clutching at the beast's mane as he struggles to right himself.

'Viv! Viv!' he yells desperately, and manages to wheel around just in time to see Viv racing after him. The strange stalemate is broken, the Bakkujasi finally making a bid to retrieve his sword. This gives Vivreki precious moments to reach Jest and, as if in payment for Viv's gift of the night before, she does not fail him. Viv makes a desperate lunge for the saddle, before spurring her back up the hill road towards the forest. The two horses need little encouragement, they gallop as if a predator is snapping at their heels. Their eyes bulging, snorting through flared nostrils, they leave the farmyard behind them and the world becomes a racing frenzy of darkness. A streak of silver flashes past Stief at waist height, Vivreki lets out a long cry of anguish, but Stief simply clings to his horse, insensate, like a drowning man.

BEHIND THEM, the Bakkujasi removes his mask and hood, and bright white hair flutters in the smoky breeze. He watches their escape with some measure of annoyance. He could follow them on the Swarm, but then, where will they go? The forest stretches on for many leagues and they are on horseback, easily overtaken by anyone on a Swarm when they finally break cover. The Bakkujasi only needs to know their whereabouts, and they are inevitably his.

He walks over to the Swarm, which has remained immobile despite the heat from the raging fire. As he crosses that distance, his lips begin to move as if he is singing to himself; it is an incantation to the god Herrukal and he is very precise with his formulation of the words. Standing by the Swarm's massive head, dwarfed by its iridescent compound eyes which sparkle in the light of the flames, the Bakkujasi might seem to be singing to the giant beast. He reaches up as though to touch its face but then, rather than make static contact, his hand continues further and plunges through the creature's hard exterior as if it is merely illusory. There is no visible reaction from the Swarm and when the man withdraws his hand again there is something pulsing and glowing in the expanse of his gloved fingers. The many lights are green, blue and yellow, and at each core something is writhing in silent anticipation.

The Bakkujasi smiles mirthlessly at the mute defencelessness of his prize. Then he opens his hand and, directing it up the hillside where Vivreki and Stief have vanished from view, he blows the strange seed towards them.

❧CHAPTER FOUR❧

T HEY HAD RIDDEN these paths for years, but seldom in the
darkness and never in fear of their lives. The world became a con-
fusing, jagged whirl of harsh red breaths, crashing branches and snorts
of steam from the horses' increasingly laboured efforts. For the first
hour neither of them spoke, as if to communicate would break their
focus and a moment's lapse in concentration would bring their pur-
suer upon them.

Stief didn't know how long it was before he became aware of his
own sniffing and breathing, as the world settled back into stark focus
– it was moments later he realized he was weeping uncontrollably, raw
emotion exploding forth unchecked into the night air. He leaned his
face forward into the warm sweetness of his horse's mane and closed
his eyes, drawing in the scent, the bobbing motion of the beast's neck
a tactile comfort. His horse, Tally, had been stabled with Jest for years
and the two followed one another without hesitation. After a while,
he raised his face again and looked ahead at Vivreki; as far as he could
tell his brother had not given way to hysteria and grief as he had, for
Viv sat on his horse rigidly, every fibre of his body attuned for sounds
of pursuit.

'Viv? I . . . I don't think the Bakkujasi is c-coming. Can we s-
stop?'

Viv turned round in his saddle, having already slowed Jest to a
walking pace. In the darkness, Stief could only just see Vivreki's face,
but the tightness of his jaw and the look of blank shock in his eyes was
sufficient for him to recognize that Vivreki was as traumatized as he
was. 'Let's just walk the horses some more,' Viv said.

There was room on the path for them to ride side by side, and it was not until Stief drew abreast of Jest that he noticed that Viv's leg was bleeding at the top of the thigh. 'You're injured,' he remarked.

'Yes.' Viv held up his hand and he had the Bakkujasi's silver dagger in his grip. Stief realized this was probably the same weapon that had killed their mother so he passed no comment, as there seemed nothing appropriate to say. They lapsed back into silence for a few minutes as neither dared bring themselves to talk about what had happened. The horses seemed to take comfort from this proximity as well, jostling up against one another every few steps, their loud breathing beginning to calm once more.

Eventually Stief spoke. 'We should be looking up.' As he said this he gazed at the night sky, to where the new star was directly overhead, an uneasy, argent glow.

'Huh?'

Stief shuddered, the residual tightness of sobbing still gripping at his chest. 'He'll come on the S-swarm, won't he?' Viv did not respond but rather glanced behind him. 'What's wrong?'

'Don't know . . . Think I . . . Did you hear something?'

Before Stief could say anything Viv's question was made irrelevant. Eight separate orbs of light came into view behind them on the trail, their glow made intermittent by the waving of night-dark branches. They moved with prescient determination, swerving and diving fast, the sound they made a quiet but high-pitched screaming.

'Move!' Viv spurred Jest again but she needed little prompting as the sound made her instinctively want to flee.

Stief urged Tally forward. 'What are they?' he yelled.

'*Darhg*. Bakkujasi trackers. That's why he's not following us.'

THE NIGHT DISSOLVED into chaos once more, and Stief was aware of the cutting wind which dried the salt of his tears into tightness against his flesh. As the path narrowed, he allowed Jest to go ahead, and again the ragged breathing of the horses and the sounds of their hoofbeats filled the forest. He could hear the screaming wail of the *Darhg*, coming closer and closer, then falling back for a moment as the horses managed to widen the gap.

But the *Darhg* were inexhaustible whereas the horses were not.

The terrain was growing rougher which slowed them further. Stief had heard of the Bakkujasi's trackers, but was vague about what happened when they actually caught up with their prey. There was a squealing, buzzing sensation by his head, and he glanced aside and let out an involuntary yelp of terror. The *Darhg* were alive, not magical inanimate lights but insects just like the Swarms. Within each orb of light was an impression of jagged, almost metallic, sharpness. The sound they made was generated by their wings which were composed of black chitin, and behind them they each carried a wicked-looking sting, half as long as their body.

Stief lashed outwards with one arm. 'Don't touch them!' Viv shouted back to him. 'They'll kill you!'

The *Darhg* were gaining, there was no mistaking it. The sound of their wings seemed to envelop the whole world. Stief gritted his teeth against a wail of dismay, but suddenly the breath was knocked out of him as he was wrenched sideways from Tally's saddle.

The smell of loam hit him sharply in the face, and then he was rolling down a steep hill, brambles and twigs catching and cutting at his flailing body. At the bottom of the slope he landed in a cold pool of mud, which at least softened the impact. Stief's exhausted senses struggled to discern what was happening to him, and he thought he heard Viv's voice. He sat up and was immediately pulled back down into the mud.

'Get down, you fool!' Viv hissed. 'Here, plaster some more mud on you.' This comment was accompanied by a freezing wet handful of mire being rubbed into his hair.

'What are you doing?' Stief's face was now dripping with muddy water and he blinked to try and clear his eyes. The only spots of warmth he could feel on his body were those areas where he was bleeding. As he managed to focus on Viv, he realized that his brother's eyes were glowing in *that* way . . . *Was it only a night earlier he had saved Jest and the birds?*

'Shhh. Like most insects,' Viv explained quietly, 'they can *see* our heat. The mud will help disguise it.' His voice sounded strained, the words seeming a trial to him as he held out his hands which radiated that inexplicable light once more.

Viv had always had a strange affinity for and knowledge of insects, so Stief did not question what he said, merely stared dumbly. 'How can that help now?' he whispered.

91

Viv did not answer, intent on his own hands where the silver-blue light was growing stronger, gaining a nebulous shape – or rather shapes. These new orbs were the same size as the *Darhg*, and Viv cast them into the air as one might release a bird. They flew down the path in the same direction as their prey.

'W-what about the horses?'

'Will you shut up?' Viv snapped, then he sighed. 'Sorry, Stief. This magic – or whatever it is – pains my eyes. I'm hoping my lights will act as a decoy. But there's no way of knowing if it will work unless they come back this way so I think we should stay put for a while.'

'In the m-mud?' Stief considered this prospect as the chill crept deeper into his bones. 'Viv, people die of exposure, you know.'

'And you have a better idea?'

There was silence for long minutes as the physical shock of events caught up with their bodies. Stief didn't want to fall asleep there in the muddy pool, didn't think it was even possible to sleep in so much discomfort, yet his anxiety about the cold fought with the tug of physical and emotional exhaustion. His mind turned to Calla, and he knew that in calmer moments his sadness and anger would return, but for now he could weep no more; it seemed his grief had been ripped out of him. As if sensing his thoughts, Viv suddenly spoke, his question catching Stief unprepared.

'Stief, what did she mean? When she said, "Get him away." Why say that? It doesn't make sense.'

Stief tried to deflect Viv's curiosity. 'I am your elder brother, Viv. She was putting me in charge.'

'No,' Viv insisted, 'it wasn't like that. It was like she knew the Bakkujasi had come especially for me.' He looked back at his hands as he spoke, but the light had gone, and only his eyes retained a vague, unnatural brightness. 'Is that true?'

'I . . . I can't explain. Truly, I don't know all the details, b-but . . .'

'Tell me.'

Stief sighed. Only yesterday he could never have imagined any circumstance which might wring the truth from him – but now the world had changed. 'Vivreki . . . I'm s-sorry. Ma – Calla – she wasn't your real mother.' He expected some reaction to this from Viv but none came. In fact, from the dark detail he could see of his brother's face, Vivreki's expression hardly changed. 'You were sent to us when you were young, from Gremeshkenn Tem. I'm n-not really sure why, but it was something to do with heresy. You won't remember 'cos they did something to your mind . . .'

'Not my mother?' It was as if Viv were experimenting with this idea, as if speaking it aloud might make it more real. 'Teven . . .'

'No, he wasn't your f-father either.'

'Then why did they take me in? Why did my own parents send me away? Why . . .?'

Stief sighed. 'Look, you were in some serious trouble, and your own mother had to give you up. I remember the night you came and you were . . . I think you were unconscious or something. The first day or so, you didn't say anything, just stared around the room like you were in a dream.' He shifted, trying to keep his legs from going numb beneath him in the cold. It was such an age ago but, as he spoke, he could still remember the blankness of Vivreki's young face, how pale and defenceless he had seemed. 'D-da said that he rescued a dog once, when he was younger, f-from a neighbouring farm,' he muttered. 'The owners had abused it, been beating it, and it took weeks before that dog found its bark, he said. J-just like you. You had some funny wounds on your cheek and t-temple, like something had been dug into you, and it seemed as though you came right again only as the wounds faded.' He shrugged, 'Could've been just coincidence, of course. I'm s-sorry, Viv. If it helps, I've considered you to be my brother s-since that first day.'

Viv seemed to be reeling with bewilderment. 'Calla, she wasn't my mother but, Stief, she was killed tonight, trying to help me. Why would she do that?'

Stief gave a short, pained laugh, unbidden tears starting to his eyes. ''Cos she was a stubborn so-and-so.' The tears spilled over, tracking through the drying mire on his cheeks. He smiled over to Viv but his smile had a broken, unconvincing quality. 'Because she loved you – like a son.'

IT WAS THE third morning since the wedding and, as usual, Asoori awoke alone. She sat up in bed listening to the high, bright tone of the rain glancing off the roof tiles. The rooms were beautiful, a world away from her chamber in Gremeshkenn Sor. They were located in the oldest, stone-built part of Falloden Sen, and the walls were plastered and painted with some kind of sepia tint. There were plants everywhere, even a small tree in a pot by the screen doors which led out to the terrace. The reflections of the raindrops on the screens threw soft drizzling patterns onto the walls.

There was little in the way of furnishing in the room, just one hugely oversized dressing table with what must have been a valuable mirror above it. The bed was raised on wooden legs, in the southern style – rather than on a platform – and it was covered in opulent silk and soft cotton blankets.

Despite the lushness of her surroundings Asoori felt listless and depressed; she was beginning to feel she had made a bad decision. Kilmer, as kind and polite as he was, did not want her physically. Last night she had made the error of asking him to stay, and that was not something she had done lightly. Asoori had decided she would commit herself to the marriage in all senses; possibly that way her bad conscience concerning the buying of her commission would be assuaged. Not only that, she had feelings for her new husband that she sensed might be worth exploring. She had no true idea of what love or even attraction felt like, only that her stomach tightened and her cheeks flushed each time he spoke to her. This was a recent development, and one which made her feel childish and slightly annoyed with herself. For all she knew, it was just as likely to be the result of food poisoning except, if that was the case, why was she now watching the doorway in the hope he would come in to wish her good morning?

Anyway, she had asked him to stay with her last night and he had refused. 'You are under no obligation, Asoori,' he had commented, somewhat coolly.

'Kilmer, this is not easy for me,' she said. 'Please understand I'm not asking you from a sense of obligation. I . . . I like you, and . . .'

'I like you too, Asoori – you know that.'

'No, listen, I mean, just stay. It doesn't have to be anything . . .' she glanced away, losing her nerve and wishing she could match the frankness of her request with her gaze.

Kilmer said nothing for a long moment and the silence stretched between them, becoming increasingly awkward. Finally, he replied to her quietly, his tone measured as if he had thought through his words before speaking.

'I realize what you are saying, Asoori. You want to know me more closely. I'm not talking about sex, and neither I think are you – it is intimacy you want. I would like to sleep beside you, to hold you, talk to you as you fall asleep, but that would not be fair. It is not possible.'

She looked straight back at him then. He had retreated a couple of paces towards a pool of darkness at the edge of the room. Taking his leave of her for the night had suddenly acquired a strange, almost bitter significance. 'What do you mean?' she frowned. 'Surely in time . . .?'

There was another pause before he spoke, and it seemed to Asoori that he wanted to say something else, something that would require a long explanation, but he did not. Instead he just shrugged and said, 'Perhaps. Goodnight, Asoori.' Then he turned and left.

SHE HAD STARED at the doorway for a long time, almost as if she could will him to come back through it. Something like fright had seized hold of her and, although she knew this was irrational, she could not shake it. She must have fallen asleep while still looking at the door.

As soon as she woke, her thoughts raged unabated. All he had said – all he had *really* said – was that he wasn't ready. It was just as they had previously discussed, before they entered into their agreement; they were simply friends who had married. Perhaps she was the one being unreasonable, since they had only been married three days and already she was changing her demands.

Or, he already had a mistress? This thought came completely unbidden to her mind and it was not as though Asoori had any experience of such situations, so she examined the idea as though it were some exotic stranger. It would all make sense – the sudden proposal, the quick wedding – but then he had spent so much time with her since they had come here, there were simply not enough hours in the day for any dalliance with a rival. Still, in planning for the long term, it would be worth his while to spend some time apart from his lover in order to secure Asoori's full cooperation. As she considered all this, Asoori got up and wandered over to the ornate lacquered dressing table. She began to brush her hair with a silver paddle-brush, her strokes measured, in concert with her musings.

Perhaps it was some serving girl, a kitchen wench or a stable maid. She stopped her brushing; perhaps there was a child . . .

'Good morning, Asoori.'

She jumped, startled by his voice, guilt at her recent thoughts causing her to flush. 'Oh, good morning.'

'Asoori, I'm sorry about last night. We need to talk things through, and we will, in a few days.'

She frowned. *Why would they have to wait a few days? What could change in that time?* Then she smiled, allowing the subject to drop. 'There's no need to apologize, Kilmer. Let's forget it just now.' She pinned back a stray hair with some ferocity. 'I've got to put on my new uniform today. Cion Gezezi is arriving from Gremeshkenn Tem.'

'Yes, I know. I've met him before actually.'

'What's he really like? I've heard some reports about him – that he's dangerous and arrogant.'

As Kilmer laughed, air whistled through his teeth with a sound that seemed strangely insincere. 'I suppose you could say those things about him, but I found him to be a charming and erudite man. Of course, having only met him at social functions, I'm not familiar with how his Bakkujasi persona might be. Is he to become your superior?'

'No, well, not really, because I'm Brengarmah – although I suppose in the absence of any superior officer . . . But I haven't actually been instructed to take orders from him.'

Kilmer patted her shoulder reassuringly. 'I'm sure you two will get along finc,' he said.

As Asoori stood up to go and get changed in her dressing room she noticed her husband's appearance for the first time. He wore a richly embroidered dark green *yurik*, with a wide sash belt and soft leather riding boots. She noted the silk threads plaited into his long hair and also that he was wearing a ceremonial longsword.

'You look good this morning,' she smiled at him.

'You think so? Thank you. I'm expected to represent Falloden Sen when Gezezi arrives.'

'But your father will be here, too?'

'Yes,' he shrugged, dismissively, 'but it never hurts to make a good impression on the Shemari.'

'Indeed.' As she watched him walk out, to await her in the main hall for breakfast, she sensed a tenseness about him she could not fathom. Perhaps *she* was coming today – his mistress – perhaps she was even in Gezezi's entourage. Asoori resolved to watch all the Bakkujasi servants closely.

CION GEZEZI HIMSELF arrived on a Swarm, but his entourage would not catch up with him until the evening, as they were riding more commonplace mounts. Asoori was unsure of his precise position within the Bakkujasi hierarchy, but he was obviously considered fairly important. The Swarm he rode was golden, a prestigious colour that was highly significant to the Shemari. It touched down close outside Falloden Sen, its wings causing enough noise and backdraft to bring running those estate workers who had not been expecting the arrival. Although the Swarm's main body was gold, its black legs and face gave it a frighteningly aggressive appearance.

Cion dismounted but no one dared approach him, due to a long-standing mixture of etiquette, superstition and fear, for none touched a Bakkujasi until he removed his mask. And Cion's mask was one most likely to enforce such fear: it was gold lacquer, the mouth turned down into a fierce snarl, the eyes ornamented by brows bunching into whorls and creases above the bridge of the nose. His robes were black – no skin showing anywhere – and black gauntlets covered his arms to the elbow. Asoori had the unsettling impression that there was really no one in there at all. She had seen Bakkujasi often before, and she always felt uneasy in their presence.

No one spoke as Gezezi removed his mask and cowl. Once freed of this constraint, a shock of thin white hair fluttered in the breeze as he bowed formally to the Lord and Lady of Falloden Sen. Then he strode across the courtyard and up the steps of the great hall, two at a time. He was, as Asoori expected, a tall skinny man; his white hair was not due to age, and she was sure he was an albino. His movements were quick and self-assured, and both bearing and manner gave the impression of an almost obsessive tidiness about his person. He kept smiling broadly, and only as his intense blue glance alighted on her did he show any uncertainty, which confused her, if only for a moment.

Asoori stepped forward to salute him formally as all Brengarmah must salute the Shemari and Bakkujasi. She was wearing her new officer's uniform: a light silver-mail vest under the long navy *yurik* sporting the symbol of Imeris on her left shoulder. Her new pair of swords were belted to her hips, but because she was greeting a guest informally she had dispensed with the accompanying silver headgear, and had scraped her hair back into its customary tight plait. Cion smiled thinly towards her.

'Kilmer, you old dog, I had no idea . . .' He mouthed the words in a distracted fashion, as he turned towards her husband, as if knowing that pleasantries were expected of him but for some reason hardly able to deliver them with any sincerity. It was in that moment when the two men's glances met, as they clasped hands and bowed to each other, moving a tiny fraction closer to one another than mere politeness demanded, it seemed to Asoori that the very essence of intimacy, of extreme comfort in one another's presence, was laid bare. Her gaze became fixed on the sight of their fingers entangled together, and Asoori simply *knew* – and the reason for all Kilmer's anxiety fell into place. She stifled a gasp, clapping a hand over her mouth; there was no mistress, no serving wench with a baby, or any such ridiculous idea. It was Cion Gezezi who was Kilmer's lover.

As both men turned to look at her, it was plain from her wide-eyed expression that she knew. Kilmer widened his own eyes in mute appeal that she say nothing untoward. Cion's gaze held a slight tinge of fear if only for a second, but of course she said nothing and would say nothing. She fought to maintain her calm.

Kilmer's parents stepped forward, eager to meet such an influential Bakkujasi. Asoori fought hard not to show any displeasure but thought – *perhaps they wouldn't be so keen to greet him if they knew* – and too late, she remembered the mind talents of the Bakkujasi.

Cion turned and fixed her with a hard, disdainful gaze. Her thoughts in turmoil she turned her attention back to the huge black shape of the Swarm, now sitting virtually motionless, only its great wings trembling slightly in the breeze. As she studied the creature, a movement to the left, just behind it, caught her eye. Three people, all men, were moving forward, an unnatural tightness to their otherwise nonchalant movements. They were dressed as grooms, in Falloden Sen colours, but they looked smart and tidy – *too* tidy. Asoori's hand dropped instinctively to her sword at the same moment as the men broke into a run. Side-stepping, without stopping to think, Asoori shoved Cion forcibly out of the way.

'Kilmer!' she yelled.

But he was already beside her, any non-combatants pushed behind him into the doorway – custom demanded that Cion would be weaponless as he entered their home. From the trees over to her left, two further men emerged. Moving with one thought – unwilling to be cornered on the steps – Asoori and Kilmer ran down to meet their aggressors. Unable to stop a thrill of pleasure at their first use, Asoori drew both of her swords. One in each hand, she ran to take the first thrust of both men's blades more through luck than judgement. She then kicked out hard with her left foot, catching the first man in the midriff and knocking the breath out of him. Knowing this would only detain any determined fighter for a few precious moments, she turned her attention to the other man, just to her right. She was in luck, he was young and inexperienced, and she could see the look of mild fright in his face and the shock of realizing he was fighting a woman. She attacked efficiently, her movements controlled and precise. As the young man moved back quickly on the defensive, for a moment Asoori felt a small tug of sorrow that she had to kill him. Perhaps if she could just disarm him . . .

'Asoori, look out!'

Realizing the other man had recovered, she lashed out blindly to the side with her short sword and was satisfied to hear an anguished howl of pain as her blade bit into his shoulder. Distracted by this, the younger man's gaze was becoming ever more panicked.

'Focus!' she snapped at him. She said it without thinking – he was about the same age as her students. Then he rallied and she cursed herself roundly for her outburst. Finally his retreat forced him back hard against a tree; Asoori whirled her longsword in a figure of eight, flipping his weapon from his inadequate grasp. Again, his desperate eyes betrayed him, and she turned on her heel, to run her shortsword straight into the ribs of the older man, who collapsed forward onto the blade. Kicking his dying body away to clear her weapon, she turned back to the young man, who had now sunk to his knees.

'Don't kill me,' he sobbed, his terrified gaze fixed on the fallen man. 'That was my father you've k-killed.' It seemed as if, bizarrely, the youth had never even confronted the idea of how this encounter might end.

'He died with honour,' Asoori snarled at him, annoyed at his cowardice. She began to lower her blades. 'Who sent you?'

He looked up at her, and opened his mouth to voice a reply, but none came. A silver throwing-knife thudded home into his throat, pinning him firmly to the trunk of the tree. With a last expression of surprise, he convulsed once, and then died.

Asoori turned and saw Cion still standing at the top of the steps, a look of cold satisfaction on his face. His action was an inconceivable breach of etiquette, but the Bakkujasi knew that none would challenge him over it.

'There was no need . . .' she began to protest.

'Asoori, when you're ready?' Kilmer shouted. Staring at him for a moment with hesitation, a shocked realization gripped her; that he was a stranger to her. As she watched this graceful man who fought with agility and speed as if the fight were merely some deadly dance, the thought raced across her mind that, at this precise moment she did not know how she might feel if her husband were killed. Then she checked her thoughts and ran to Kilmer's aid although he had seemingly little need of it, having already killed one man and injured another who was stoically ignoring the blood oozing from an injury to his neck or ear. Both opponents looked much more competent than those she had killed, but they stood little chance of survival against Kilmer. Still, Asoori quickly engaged the injured man, as she knew Kilmer must be tiring.

Her assailant did not wait for Asoori to gather her wits, but went into the attack immediately, lunging forward, bringing his blade down in a strong two-handed strike. He didn't waste his breath on curses or stupid battle cries either, so Asoori felt a faint respect for her opponent as she just managed to dodge aside. However, the speed of her evasion unbalanced her and, twisting her ankle, she fell hard onto the stony path. All her instincts told her to lie there, gasping and cursing (her leg had been cut on a stone, the warmth of the blood was coursing down her calf) but she ignored them. Twisting onto her back she pushed herself up, just as the swordsman raised his blade once more to take advantage of her vulnerable position. This left his belly exposed and, without hesitation, Asoori lunged forward with her longsword, stabbing him through the gut, and twisting the blade as she withdrew it. He toppled onto his knees, his strength dispersing as shock claimed him. Knowing this was a horrible way to die, as a mercy, Asoori cut his throat with her shortsword.

She turned back towards Kilmer, but his opponent was already down, stabbed through the chest, his muscles twitching in their dying spasms.

'Well done . . . darling.' Kilmer grinned at her. She scowled back at him, trembling with an acid reaction in her stomach. It had been years since she had actually killed anyone, and the drills, the theory, the art of battle all ultimately came down to this deed. Asoori was more than capable with a sword but she could never deal with death lightly. Kneeling on one knee, she rested her head against the still-warm grip of her blade and uttered a silent prayer to the goddess Oshi to take the defeated men's souls into her care and to forgive Asoori for their slaying.

Kilmer stayed silent through this, then turned back towards the horrified watchers in the doorway where his parents were staring at Asoori open-mouthed.

'What, did they really think they let me join the Brengarmah as a cleric?' she snapped on seeing their reaction. She and Kilmer then headed back up the steps to receive the frightened congratulations of the little gathering before making their way into the hall where a small, and now somehow irrelevant, welcome party was laid out for Cion's arrival. Asoori lagged behind, walking behind the guest himself, and as though he felt her gaze on his back, Cion turned and gave her a small nod.

'Many thanks, Asoori. It would seem Kilmer has met his match – in more senses than one.'

'You didn't have to kill the boy,' she replied evenly, though she could feel herself colouring as she spoke. Even as she knew she was being insubordinate, she wanted this man to know her opinion. 'He had no weapon,' she said aloud. Then, she added the thought, *And you should not have had one either*.

His cold quiet eyes studied her face carefully before he spoke. 'And yet he was a danger, for not all weapons are steel,' he replied. 'These heretics threaten not just our lives but our very souls.'

As he turned away again she thought, *And where is his soul now, Gezezi?* She meant him to pick up on her thoughts as he had done before, and he did. He turned back sharply. Asoori herself had no previous experience of heretics, having lived for so long in the unquestioning grandeur of Gremeshkenn Sor. So, despite her anger, her curiosity was aroused, for Cion Gezezi seemed perfectly serious about the perceived danger.

'How?' she frowned, her tone defiant. 'How can they threaten our souls if we are strong in our faith to Herrukal?'

Cion sighed. 'Now is not the time for such discourse, but sufficient that you know the danger. They worship one – and *only one* – goddess. They claim she is in somewise older than the true gods, but I will not speak her name lest this house be blighted. Bad enough that the Duke has had to suffer such an embarrassment today.' He gave an unattractive, humourless sneer which was perhaps intended to be a witty smile. 'So, the state of that boy's soul is no longer our concern. He forfeited the god's patronage once he aligned himself with the followers of the goddess.'

'One?' Asoori muttered to herself in momentary confusion. 'Only one goddess?' The idea seemed preposterous, for how could just one deity be responsible for everything occurring on Myr, she wondered. Cion had turned away from her, as if dismissing her enquiries in a manner that irritated her immensely. Her instinctive dislike of the man and the memory of his dagger thudding into the boy's neck conspired to rouse her anger once more.

A throwing knife is a coward's weapon, she thought, but she kept her expression deliberately innocent as though she had intended the thought to remain private. Though Cion said nothing further, his icy expression could have cut glass, as a small muscle in his jaw ticked slightly.

Kilmer came towards them carrying a drink for her. 'I see you two are getting acquainted,' he smiled. Within five minutes of the skirmish outside, Kilmer was already reverting to Lord of Cantroji behaviour, only his eyes betraying any concern as he looked meaningfully towards Asoori. She accepted a drink and sipped at it, meeting his gaze over the rim. Cion moved towards Kilmer's parents without comment.

'I'm sorry, Asoori,' Kilmer continued. 'I had hoped I would have a chance to explain.'

She cut him off with a dismissive wave of her hand. 'Forget it,' she snapped. 'There's nothing to talk about.' She gulped a large mouthful of the drink, feeling the warmth of the alcohol burning its path to her stomach.

Kilmer looked annoyed by her abrupt tone, but she was past caring. He glanced over to where Cion was now conversing with his father. 'You're getting under his skin already,' he remarked dryly.

'I should care?' Asoori frowned. 'He's not *my* lover . . .'

'Keep your voice down!' he hissed.

She snorted. 'I don't *have* to like him Kilmer. And I don't trust him either.'

SEEKING CRYSTAL INNOCENCE
THE SEED OF BRIGHTEST HOPE
REMEMBERS THE FUTURE

❦CHAPTER FIVE❧

ANY YEARS AGO, when he had first arrived in the temple city, the sound of the prayer bells, constantly turned by the invisible fingers of the wind, had seemed quite frightening to Achios; their melancholy tones like wailing spirits of the dead. Now, though, the sound seemed restful, part of the fabric of the city. Achios knew that pilgrims who visited – perhaps only once in their lifetime – venerated the deep sound as if it were representative of a different character for each bell. This idea was heresy, of course, so not spoken about openly, but Achios heard many things, knew each of the secret names the bells had been given.

He walked slowly past the largest, highest prayer bell marking the point at which the ground-rock gave way to the suspended pathway leading towards the Sky Temple. It would be folly to rush, for the path twisted and turned in a seemingly random fashion, the swaying, creaking walkway sometimes doubling back on itself, sometimes dipping precariously away so that it vanished into the white oblivion of the clouds. Only those few permitted entrance to the Sky Temple knew that if seen from above (something only possible whilst riding a Swarm) the pathway formed the shape of a symbol which described the dark chaos of creation. And for those people, like Achios, this symbol was something writ upon their very soul.

Achios knew he was weakening, and one day soon he might find himself unable to complete this fraught journey. As the wind shook the walkway, whipping through the complex knotwork of the rope handrail, he found his heart beating faster and his mouth becoming dry. Men had fallen to their deaths from here: priests, acolytes, the occasional careless servant. Their bones were left unrecovered in the crevasse below, for the sun to bleach and the great white eagles of Gremeshkenn Tem to pick over. They would be known to have died in the glorification of Herrukal the Creator – even those lowly enough to have been charged with the mundane cleaning of the Sky Temple – and so their souls would be blessed in the afterlife; spared the dark attentions of Rann and his minions. A red flag would be raised for each of these deaths – something of an irony as these flags at the end of the path were such a welcome sight to those who completed the walk in safety.

Achios had done the walk many times, possibly hundreds, and he knew none would criticize him even if he arrived for this important meeting on the back of a Swarm. Indeed, none would dare – despite the present curtailing of their flights – but he felt it was important to show little sign of weakness. He would be gone soon enough.

And so he walked the torturous route with all the meditative solemnity it deserved. The cloud mist had wet the wooden boards, making the tenacious green algae dangerously slick; his bare feet grew numb with the cold, his hands increasingly shaky as he gripped the guide ropes. Behind him the sound of the prayer bells faded into the mist, and the emptiness of the mountains and the sky encompassed him in purifying silence, broken only by the keening of the eagles.

It took him an hour. In times past he could have done the route more quickly but he chided his own weakness and vanity for thinking about this. The Sky Temple was vast – a golden mirage which wound around a thin core of rock; the very pinnacle of the highest mountain – apparently defying gravity on those days when its spire core was obscured by white cloud as it was today. The eagles which perched on the golden roofs of the complex proudly surveyed the lower reaches of the mountains as if this special, somewhat sumptuous, eyrie had been built purely for their benefit.

Swarms had already landed, bringing both Bakkujasi and those few other Shemari priests deemed important enough to be invited to this discussion. Achios glanced up at the sky before entering the outer courtyard of the temple complex, but the object of this extraordinary consultation was obscured from view by clouds heavy with snow.

It was as he entered the outer courtyard and passed the massive stone statues of Herrukal that he heard the voice again. He had heard it drift through his consciousness quite a few times over the last few weeks – since that night he had tried to persuade Asoori to become a

Shemari – and he remembered now how she had called out to him as he walked away on the night of her wedding: *Be careful* . . .

But Achios was unable to decipher any message in the voice he now heard – it was as if a sound carried on the wind, haunting, disquieting but meaningless. He had decided that his mind must be reacting to the physical changes his body was suffering as he began his new path to enlightenment, and that the voice could only be of his own making, whether conscious or not. But this time it seemed more like a scream of rage and, mystified, he gazed wordlessly at the magnificence of the nearby statues. He had no quarrel with the Creator . . .

'Achios, my friend, it is good to see you.'

One of the white eagles had alighted on the carved hand of Herrukal, and was eyeing the aged priest with the arrogant disdain of a natural predator. So confused was Achios at the sound of the scream that, for a moment, he imagined it was the eagle who had spoken to him. He peered at the creature myopically but then heard a quiet chuckle behind him.

'Oh,' he turned, trying to conceal his consternation. 'Pava, it is you. How good to see you.' He gave a small, formal bow, touching his middle finger to his heart as he did so.

Before him stood an aged Shemari priest clothed in the simple pale blue shift of the Sky Temple. Pava was as bald as Achios, for the most part, but a thin black plait ran from the back of his head down to his belt, where it was neatly tucked away. His weather-beaten face, although obviously elderly, was marked by years of kindness and smiles and he was smiling at Achios now with unfaded geniality. It would be a foolish man indeed who mistook Pava's demeanour for weakness though; he was one of the most powerful of all the Shemari, and the only one to have a permanent set of rooms here in the Sky Temple – apart from the Oracle herself, of course.

Pava made a quiet 'tut-tut' sound and the eagle hopped onto his outstretched arm – Achios noted he wore no leather glove like a falconer and wondered why the massive talons did not scratch his flesh. 'Come, Achios, the Oracle will make her pronouncement before dusk, and you are the last to arrive.'

They walked through the cold mist from the clouds, and across the marbled courtyard. Before Achios, the light figure of Pava with the eagle seemed to fade and then appear again as the mist swirled

and parted around them. There were a few worshippers about who
– caught unawares by the presence of Shemari dignitaries – hastily
prostrated themselves upon seeing Achios's golden cloak. Achios
smiled and nodded absently to them. He could never lose the feeling
of being suspended, up in mid-air, when he was in the Sky Temple.
He tried not to dwell upon the sensation, but he was always aware of
the absence of ground beneath him. It gave him acid in the pit of his
stomach, and he was at a loss to know how Pava could spend so much
time up here. He quickened his pace and followed Pava closely into
the inner temple.

THE FLOOR OF the sanctum was studded with jewels to represent the
wheeling movements of the heavens. The Shemari had gathered in
grave silence, and each man sat rather uncomfortably on a 'star' which
signified their varying importance. At this time of early evening,
Achios always fancied the place looked at its most magnificent; its
lapis blue walls and golden filigree caught the lazy warmth of the
setting sun and reflected a rich intensity of the light in such a way it
reminded Achios of the chitin bodies of the Swarms. The smell of
incense and sandalwood drifted through the chamber like an echo,
faint wisps of ever-present smoke contending with the stray ghost-
fragments of cloud which floated in through open panels in the vaulted
ceiling. As the darkness of nightfall descended, the character of the
Sky Temple would gradually change until the place truly seemed at
one with the sky – a glittering, gilded island upon which all must now
remain until daybreak because of the perilous return journey.

ONCE ACHIOS AND Pava arrived, taking up their positions near the
centre dais where the Oracle would appear, the praying and chanting
began. Though Achios's lips were moving, he was not concentrating
on the wandering melody of the prayer; for the voice was back, and
this time he thought he could discern words amongst the sound of it.
It seemed the voice must be mocking him, mocking all the gathered
assembly, because wherever the sonorous chanting fell away, the voice
became clearer, its profanities so loud that Achios feared others could

surely hear them, that the sound could not fail but be involuntarily voiced by his throat. He clamped his mouth shut and, without turning his head, ran his panicked gaze across the rest of the priests who seemed blissfully unaware that one of their own number was suffering from some obscene delusion. Only when he glanced at Pava did Achios notice the other man frowning in his direction. He grimaced a smile and rubbed vaguely at his chest, hoping that Pava would interpret this as an attack of heartburn.

Time passed slowly and torturously for Achios. He knew the Oracle would appear in her own time – their prayers did not summon her, but were simply a show of devotion. As the voice within his head grew more agitated, profane and frightening, he found his vision began to blur: the room became a streaked canvas of blues and golds, the seated priests soft pillars of wax-like colours. But nothing else significant happened until the Oracle finally appeared.

SHE APPEARED, as always, clothed in a white wraith of cloud. And for some reason, despite the confusion of colour in the room, Achios could still see her very clearly. She was as white as the enveloping cloud, her skin and her hair *white* – not pale pink or silver blonde – for the Oracle had been distinguished thus at birth. Only her eyes had any colour and they were intense, almost shocking in contrast to the pallid background of her features: one was blue, the other green. She was clearly ageing now, no longer nymph-like but a full-figured woman whose demeanour seemed at one with the power and significance of her office. When she 'spoke' the sound carried around the dark confines of the temple in much the same manner as the voice which was still echoing through Achios's brain. Though she did not move, her eyes raked across the assembly, their intelligent scrutiny like needles in the soul.

'You have come about the star.' Her voice echoed slightly around the wide space. 'It is a sign from Herrukal the Creator . . .'

She doesn't know . . . The voice in Achios's head became frantic. *She knows nothing . . . It's a lie . . .*

'He is displeased, and you will all be punished.'

Pava stood up and bowed solemnly. 'We, Lady? Do you mean the Shemari?'

Her gaze remained cold, detached. '*All* of you, priest. The whole world of Myr.'

There was a shocked silence after this pronouncement, and it was Pava who recovered his wits first. 'How have we erred, Lady? Tell us in what manner we might make amends.'

'You cannot. It is late – too late. Prayers from the Abax are lessening and heresy is increasing in the world. People are now worshipping a false god. I will not speak her name.'

Trust Herrukal to use this to his advantage . . .

'The world will end, and the star is the signal. It is falling from the heavens. The Sky is falling.'

'No, please, Lady, petition the gods for us. We must atone.' Pava's words of stark fear echoed around the chamber, as many of the Shemari priests began rocking back and forth in babbling prayer.

'I do not know if it will atone, but perhaps there is *something* the Shemari can do. The eggs . . .' Some of the priests looked confused by this, as news of the Swarm eggs had been a well-protected secret. 'The eggs of the Swarms . . .'

He wants them back! There was no mistaking the sudden panic in the voice in Achios's mind.

He felt as if something had landed a physical blow to his gut, but even that would be preferable to what occurred next.

The door of the sanctum flew open and a young man burst in. He wore a bright red cloak which, against the solemn backdrop of the room, appeared as violent as his intent. Beneath the cloak he wore a tunic emblazoned with the swirling sigil of the One goddess. And he was drawing a curved dagger from his side . . .

Achios had long moments to consider the boy's appearance because, at the moment he entered, something else happened. Everything, and everybody but Achios, immediately froze.

Without conscious thought, Achios stood up and took two steps forward. Around him the room had suddenly come back into sharp clarity – the priests' expressions ranging from those still showing rapt attention to the Oracle, to shock and alarm amongst those who had noticed the intruder. They were all now frozen in their positions, as if time itself had been stilled – by what force it was impossible to tell. When Achios turned back around, he saw *himself* still seated above his designated star, an equally shocked expression on his normally inscrutable face. Achios instantly understood that magic was at work here, but he had no time to consider this further. Still without much conscious thought, he walked over to the boy – the sound in his head not the voice any longer, just a low hissing – and peered at the face beneath the shadow of the hood. The intruder was young, perhaps only eighteen or so, and there was no mistaking the raw energy of the idealistic zeal in his brown eyes. Achios realized this was a suicide mission: the boy was about to kill the Oracle of the Sky Temple, and there could be no escape for him thereafter.

Achios stared around at those priests who had been frozen whilst turning to look, after hearing the sound of the door. There were at least three who had shown very quick reactions, already reaching for the gold ceremonial daggers at their belts. As these priests were positioned between the boy and the Oracle, it was clear to Achios that the assassin's mission would fail.

Again, there was no thought, no conscious decision as Achios leaned towards the boy's ear. 'Throw it,' he whispered. 'Throw your dagger.' This said, he touched his finger to the weapon, a kind of distant horror growing in his confused mind. A dark green nimbus of light flickered lazily between his outstretched finger and the dagger itself and then, as Achios began backing away towards the Oracle, the light extended like a malevolent thread to reach her – who seemed as transfixed as all the others in the chamber. Then Achios turned and touched his finger to the middle of her breastbone, exactly above her heart. He had no idea why he had done this thing, but just as he finished his strange mission he glanced into the Oracle's face; she blinked, as if she were aware of him.

He wanted to say something to her, but appeared unable; he opened his mouth, gawping uselessly – watching the dark sorrow blossom in her gaze like a silent flower. When the sound of his own voice came back to him once more the words were equally as foreign as his instruction to the young assassin. 'They're *mine*.'

Whatever it was that had taken control of his spirit tried to turn away, but Achios was caught, drowning, in the intensity of the Oracle's gaze – the sensation of his spirit body being wrenched in two directions at once caused the most encompassing pain Achios had ever experienced. He groaned, sudden nausea lancing through his belly. And when he opened his eyes again, he was back in his seated body, his head just turning towards the disturbance caused by the arrival of the red-clad boy.

Someone yelled out, but to no avail; the assassin's purpose was set. Screaming the name of his heretical god, he pulled free his dagger – as Achios, sickened in every sense, already knew he would – and threw it with deadly force. Distantly, among the screams and the panic, Achios knew that the weapon was travelling the same course he himself had marked for it. Without his guidance this attempt would have failed – he, Achios, was killing the Oracle before she had the chance to deliver Herrukal's divine message.

The force of the dagger throw lifting her off her feet, she fell back, dead even before she hit the floor. It was, for her part, a strangely undramatic demise given the pomp and fanfare of her life. She did not cry out and did not move once the killing blow was struck. Only Achios noted that, as her life drained away, her increasingly deathly gaze was fixed on him.

THERE FOLLOWED PANDEMONIUM in the chamber. A group of priests rushed the assassin and bore him to the ground, their golden knives flailing in a horrible frenzy of retribution. Unlike his silent victim, the boy was voluble in his fury and pain; the sounds of his death, which seemed to take an inexplicable length of time, would haunt Achios for months. The unleashed aggression of the Shemari, so contrary to their piety only moments before, was sickening to see and hear. Even after the sounds of the boy's pathetic protests died away, some continued to slash and stab at his dead flesh as if they could hurt him yet further. Not until Pava intervened to stop them, did they pull away, leaving the youth's warm, bloodied remains on the floor.

Others had rushed to the aid of the Oracle, and hushed sobs were coming from the dais where they were tending her body. In a daze of confusion, Achios stared at this sad tableau, warm tears slipping silently from his eyes, and dripping unchecked onto his hands which he still held folded in his lap. He could not see her, surrounded now by her faithful mourners, except for one white arm that had fallen limply away from her body, her hand brushing against the floor, nerveless fingers open, questing for something. A reason perhaps?

'Are you all right, Achios?' He looked up to see Pava staring down at him, sadness and concern in his gaze.

'I will be.' He nodded absently looking back towards the bloody remains of the assassin. A gasp escaped his lips unbidden as his mind grasped what he was seeing.

'It doesn't signify anything,' Pava said calmly, and Achios stared doubtfully into his friend's eyes to see if he believed himself what he had just said. For on the star-map floor of the Sky Temple where the heretic's blood had been spilt, the boy had died in the precise position of the new star.

Cion Gezezi was 'inducting' Asoori's new squire into the secret of their mission. Asoori watched from beside the tiny woodburner, feigning disinterest. Merric seemed a bright lad, a tall gangly youth with a shock of unruly blond hair and a tendency to blush scarlet at very little provocation. He had been cleaning Asoori's swords, and the faint aroma of the clove oil mixture he had used on the blades gave the cramped galley the scent of winter spices. On Merric's first day Asoori had given him the rat which Achios had gifted to her, and the creature was now sitting on Merric's knee, cleaning its whiskers with apparently no care in the world. Since she'd entrusted her squire with the rat it seemed his habitually edgy excitement had calmed down, and Asoori was pretty sure he spoke to the creature when no one was listening. It was difficult to guess Merric's age – anywhere between fifteen and twenty – but she was sure he was already missing home, despite the excitement of the journey. He looked nervous, but was holding up to Cion's scrutiny well.

'You understand, of course, that we are chasing the impossible.' Cion was watching the boy's reactions closely. 'There can be no egg – that's only a story put about by the heretics of the One goddess, Mauru.'

'But why would they say such a thing?' Merric frowned, genuine incomprehension twisting his features. 'In what way would it advance their own beliefs . . . I mean, heretical claims?'

Cion's gaze flickered slightly as he tried to fathom whether Merric was being deliberately obtuse or surprisingly clever. 'Do you know what their beliefs are?' he asked.

'No . . . no. I mean . . .' Floundering, Merric spread his fingers wide in a vague gesture. 'I just heard that they don't believe in *our* Gods . . . Our *true* Gods,' he added hastily.

'Indeed.'

Asoori sighed wearily. They had been travelling for three days now, heading south-east out of Cantroji town, after having established the route of the missing Swarm and the Bakkujasi, Nuss.

Yesterday they had commandeered a ship – one of the feluccas which plied their trade on the inlets of the eastern sea. It moved fast, much faster than Asoori might have expected, clipping down the relative shallows towards the south of the region. Overland transport was difficult across the central area; to the south of Cantroji the forest was underlain by unstable rocky scree and vast areas of volcanic ash. Further to the south-west began the barren saltpans of the inhospitable desert – the Gurz'taal. They would be making landfall at an outpost town, which Cion had visited before and where he knew he could purchase horses to travel onwards.

Travelling by ship as far as they could would shorten their journey by several days, but for Asoori, the moment she stepped back onto firm land could not come quickly enough. The sensation of the boat combined with the salt smell of fish left her feeling light-headed and sick, although she did her best to hide her discomfort from the others.

She was sure it would have been easy for Cion to travel ahead on the Swarm – despite what Achios had told her at her wedding party, she knew that Cion was transporting his Swarm with him in the special sealed casket the Bakkujasi used for the purpose – but when she had done her best to try and persuade him of this he had declined without giving his reasons; in fact, she felt he was being deliberately obtuse. The trouble was, Kilmer had found reason to travel with them on business for the Cantroji Estates and his presence made the atmosphere in the party rather strained. To Asoori's dismay, her first mission for the Brengarmah felt like neither a mission nor a honeymoon, just an intolerable jaunt with a supercilious Bakkujasi priest – self-styled 'miracle hunter' and intellectual minefield. For the life of her, she could not understand why Kilmer admired, possibly even loved, this pompous swine. But when Cion and Kilmer were together her charming, affable husband turned into something else entirely – and all the gauche posturing of the Lord of Cantroji came to the fore. That *other* Kilmer, who she could not believe was anything more than a lifetime's training fronted by a smooth smile.

Asoori's heart was sore, and she could not understand it. She had known the terms of their agreement. But last night she had woken alone in their cabin, the lazy slap-slapping of the waves against the hull the only sound to break the night silence, and as she tried to get back to sleep she heard low quiet laughter from some other room on the barge, suggesting an intimacy which she did not want to think about. She still felt angry, and had spoken little to Kilmer since discovering the truth of his relationship. They had now become distant and civil to one another. She told herself that she might feel better about the whole thing if she liked Cion in the slightest or even thought he was good enough for Kilmer.

'Asoori?'

'I'm sorry?' She glanced over to find both Cion and Merric were looking at her expectantly.

Cion smiled, perhaps noting her discomfort. 'Merric here has just posed an interesting conundrum. He asked us what will happen when we get to Releeza and find the egg. For how will we know if it is the egg of a Swarm? What if the people of Releeza are right and it is in fact the egg of another mythical creature – like a dragon.'

Asoori blinked, then frowned towards Cion. She could hardly believe he had said such a thing. Talk of dragons was completely outlawed, considered as heretical as any mention of Swarm eggs. He could only be testing the boy, trying to trip him up.

'I d-didn't actually say that word,' Merric said hastily.

Asoori tried to make her answer noncommittal, sure that Cion was simply amusing himself. 'It would be a miracle, Cion,'

'Ah yes, miracles.' Cion nodded, his fingers tapping an irritable little tune on the table. Merric, obviously relieved to be absented from further conversation, bent his head and paid close attention to the sword he was cleaning.

'You must believe miracles are possible, otherwise you would not devote yourself to the important work that takes up your time. Surely we must allow that if what we find is indeed a real egg of some sort – then no one can know what is inside it until it hatches. Apart from the Oracle perhaps.'

'Indeed,' he shrugged, 'it is not given to us to speculate.'

Asoori had the distinct impression he meant it was not given to *them* to speculate, but he considered himself as something quite separate. 'And what would you do with it if perhaps it hatches before we even get there, and it's not what we assume?'

117

'We of the Bakkujasi assume nothing. I would simply do as we have been instructed, and take it back to the Temple City, to your uncle.'

Asoori had a brief and satisfying image of Cion being shredded by a dragon. It was childish, she knew, but it made her feel slightly better about things and in her confusion she took her comfort where she found it. Before she could discuss the probabilities of a dragon further, however, their discussion was interrupted by a sudden juddering of the vessel and a jarring sound, as something scraped against the timbers of the ship.

'My swords, Merric,' Asoori snapped as she stood up. Merric stared at her in brief confusion but reached for the newly cleaned weapon. 'It could be brigands,' she explained. 'They might know we have a Bakkujasi on board – not to mention the heir to Cantroji.'

Cion raced ahead of her, having drawn his silver dagger. 'Not to mention his wife,' he remarked casually over his shoulder as she hurried behind him up the narrow stairs to the front deck.

THEY FOUND KILMER already on deck, talking to the captain. The boat was at a dead stop in the water, but seemed to be rocking slightly more than usual. Asoori glanced over the side into the darkness to see if there was another ship alongside, but she could not see much as the water was a boiling mass of steam.

'What's going on?' she asked.

'You tell me. It's the strangest rainfall I've ever seen.' Kilmer gestured out over the side, and Asoori peered down into the water. All around their boat, large chunks of flaming debris floated on the surface; until the water extinguished their flames into hissing steam.

There was also a quieter sound, a cracking, splitting noise as the floating material cooled. As one of the objects surfaced right next to the boat, Asoori leaned over the rail in order to get a better look.

'It's *rock*,' she breathed in awe. 'How could rock just fall from the sky? And how can it float?'

Behind her she heard Merric whisper a curse and then, remembering the company he was in, hastily offer up an invocation to Oshi. One of the sailors began ringing a bell on the prow, its unmelodic clashing intended to warn other ships in the vicinity, but also adding a jarring sense of panic to the scene. The hail of unnatural missiles could only be considered an ill omen, and as the other sailors moved silently about their tasks they carefully averted their gaze from the smouldering rocks.

Another ship came alongside, drifting silently through the steamy mist – it had also been caught up in the strange storm but, less fortunately, had been struck by one of the flaming rocks. A fire was burning just behind the main sail and the crew was fighting desperately to contain the blaze. The captains of the two vessels called out to one another, exchanging reports and consolations.

ALL WAS CHAOS for a few minutes, although there was nothing to be done except stand and marvel at the lurid scene on the water. Plumes of smoke and steam rose, backlit by the orange glare of the short-lived flames, while here and there gouts of blue and green gaseous flames flared out from the floating rocks. A sulphurous smell clung to the back of Asoori's throat and her eyes began to water, even though the starfall had finished before she'd arrived up on deck.

'We should pray.' Cion's voice cut through the haze which lingered even though a breeze was now wafting the smoke and gas away from the deck.

Gazing up into the night sky, half-expecting further missiles, Asoori turned towards Cion, frowning at his suggestion. For a moment it seemed almost nonsensical, and certainly impractical. The captain and some of the sailors were busy, using long poles to push the rocks away from the hull lest they still be hot enough to set the ship aflame. The captain of the other felucca had approached the rail of his own vessel and was talking to Kilmer with low urgency. From his serious expression Asoori guessed there must be casualties aboard.

'We must pray,' Cion repeated. 'The gods are angry. We must plead with Oshi to intervene on our behalf.'

'But we . . .' Kilmer had just taken up one of the poles to help push away the hissing debris. He glanced at Asoori, who raised her eyebrows at his imminent objection. It hadn't occurred to her before that Cion might not know that Kilmer had no faith in the gods at all.

'Yes, of course,' he muttered. He quickly dropped the pole and joined the little cluster of people now gathering around Cion Gezezi.

FORTUNATELY, THE BAKKUJASI had enough practical sense to keep his prayer short, and everyone soon dispersed to go about their tasks. Once the fire was brought under control the captain of the other ship came up and asked Cion if he would go over and visit the injured crew members and bless his vessel; Cion assented, nodding beneficently.

'I suppose it might bring some comfort.' Kilmer had come to stand beside Asoori and was also watching Cion.

Asoori sighed; she felt too emotionally wrung out to keep up her frigid anger. 'His faith demands that he behave in a compassionate manner. Otherwise . . .' she shrugged wearily.

'You don't like him, do you?'

'You know I don't.' There was a short silence between them as both reached for something to say which might alleviate the situation or, at least, distract them from it. 'So what do you think is happening, Asoori? Is the sky falling down?' Kilmer pushed his long fingers through hair which would smell of smoke for days.

Asoori looked up at the night sky which was now mercifully clear. Her attention fixed on the new star; it seemed different, slightly larger, and behind it, a long stream of light extended like a tail. 'I don't know if the gods have sent it or not,' she said, 'but my instincts tell me the new star means a whole lot of trouble.'

❧CHAPTER SIX❧

'ARE YOU SURE about this, V-viv?'

The rain had turned to sleet and snow, barely stopping all night. Both Stief and Viv were in sour moods, having spent sleepless damp hours in the shelter of a larch tree. Cantroji was still quiet. Only the low wooden roofs of its houses had held onto the snow, and looked bright white in the morning sunshine – below, the dirt streets were a mire of red mud. There was to be some kind of fair held by the docks, and people were setting up stalls there or unloading produce from feluccas and long wooden barges. There was a subdued air about the city, further exacerbated when the prayer bells of the temple began to toll, sounding a dolorous wail from the cliffside. Smoke drifted lazily across the scene.

'We've got to get some food soon and we're safer in among the crowds than out on our own anyway. Once we've eaten –' Viv shivered – 'maybe warmed up a bit, we should try and get passage on one of the ships. We could work our way from here to anywhere in Myr.'

'We could be seen by someone we know, the f-fair is on. We're not *that* far from Rinjisti.'

Viv stopped and glared at Stief. Four days and nights in the forest had not been kind to either of them. Much as they were capable of survival, at this time of the year it was a cold and bleak prospect. Both were unkempt and muddy, their hair damply plastered to their heads – even Stief's usually irrepressible curls having given up the fight.

'We could split up, of course, if that's what you want,' he snapped.

Stief recoiled slightly, taken aback by the idea. 'N-no, it's not what I want. Why would you say that?'

'No reason.' Viv sniffed dismissively, and did not meet Stief's gaze. 'Shall we try and find some food now?'

'I'm still your brother.'

'Yeah, I know. Let's forget it can we?' Viv smiled at an old woman who was hurrying towards the marketplace. 'Good morning,' he said, but she merely scowled in response. 'Friendly bunch, aren't they?' he muttered.

'There's a b-bad atmosphere here.' Stief frowned. 'Why's every-one so quiet? And where's that smoke c-coming from?' he sniffed.

'I've got an idea to get us something to eat,' Viv mused. 'Where's the one place people give out food for free?'

'The temple? But, Viv, that's just s-stupid. I'm guessing we're wanted heretics now. Well, *you* are . . . Anyway, that food is meant for pilgrims.'

Viv shrugged. 'Well, we can be pilgrims for an hour. Do you think they actually look at the worshippers as they slop that stuff out?'

'It's still a bit, well, blasphemous.'

'I don't care. They burned our house down and killed our mother – breakfast is the least they can do.' There was not a trace of humour in this statement.

Viv seemed to assume Stief's agreement, because he turned and began heading up the hill towards the Kamyaaz Tem temple without further discussion.

THERE WERE FOUR pyres raised in the temple courtyard, though not for the dead. Their unfortunate victims must have still been alive when secured to the torturous iron-clad stake which ran through the middle of each one. Three of these pyres had been used the day before, and were the source of the acrid smoke, but one remained pristine and untouched. A tiny mass of green leaves still grew from one of the branches used to construct it, and they danced merrily to a rhythm of their own, buffeted by the slight breeze.

On the used pyres, the twisted corpses of the victims were still bound, their flesh now reduced to charcoal and soot. As they stopped at the edge of the courtyard by the nearest one, Stief found himself unable to tear his gaze away. The victim appeared to have curled up as he or she died, the legs were drawn towards the chest and twisted across to one side, as though desperately attempting to protect the torso. Towards the back of the head a few patchy remnants of hair survived, and smoke curling up from the charred flesh below caressed the sooty blonde wisps with deceptive gentleness.

'What the hell happened . . .?' Stief began.

Viv did not reply but nodded over to the pyre positioned nearest to the temple. Monks were now emerging from between the pillars, and for a moment Stief assumed they had come to clean away the remains of the executions. But instead, they moved in slow procession towards the furthest, unused pyre, their gazes not even drawn by the horror they had already committed in the name of their god. There were about twenty of them, led by a Shemari priest who wore pale blue robes rather than the red of the lesser monks. About two-thirds of the way along the column, held firmly between two guards, was a girl they were presumably about to kill in the same manner. She was not composed about her imminent demise, since no one had seen fit to mercifully drug her. Under short-cropped red hair, which was sticking to her sweaty, tear-stained face, her green eyes were huge and round with terror and the girl emitted a low visceral wail, like an animal in pain, as she struggled with complete futility. Stief felt his stomach heave. More people had begun to trickle back into the square, returning from the fair perhaps, but the small crowd remained silent.

'Look.' Stief pointed over to the left side of the square. A darkly clad man was walking into the open, leaning heavily on a staff which was topped by the bleached dome of a skull. His shapeless, heavy robes were a motley of black and grey which trailed through the wet mud in tatters. His face was hidden by lank and stringy black hair, but where the pallor of his skin could be seen, it was as deathly white as a corpse. As he walked he rang a small bell that sounded through the muffling sleet in sweet denial of its owner's squalid appearance. The crowd jostled silently forward to see him closer, their eyes full of frightened curiosity – and some even spat into the mud before him.

Viv and Stief stood motionless, for what felt like a long time, as everyone's gaze was locked on this strange apparition.

'A Sin Eater,' Stief breathed. There could be no doubt that was what this being was, and yet neither Viv nor Stief had ever seen one before. Sin Eaters were the stuff of bedtime stories for little children – existing on the periphery of 'normal' life. In many regions they had fallen out of use, no longer countenanced by local patrons. They were never spoken of in company, only whispered about in the darkness of temples, and never referred to as 'he' only 'it'. 'Do you think it's t-true?' Stief was morbidly fascinated by the strange being. 'D'you think a s-spirit really comes?'

'Dunno – just a lot of hocus-pocus probably.' He tried to appear unaffected by what was happening, but Stief could recognize the tension in his tone. 'Doesn't look like they're feeding the faithful today.'

'No.' The sleet was beginning to fall harder, making the scene sodden and miserable. 'Don't think it's going to be easy lighting the bloody fire.'

THE SIN EATER glanced at the crowd and then back to his client, his grey gaze flickering from side to side. Their fear of him was laughable – or it would be if he didn't know, from experience, that it brought out the very worst in such ignorant, insular people. If they could hear him, *really* hear him – the constant, unremitting diatribe which surged through his burned-out brain, would their fear turn to pity? He doubted that very much.

I'm frightened, Sevim. Frightened.
Be still. They have called us . . .
Why they hate? Why they spit? Whhhyyy . . .
Be still, child.
They have not called us for long time.
Yes.
But why her?

THIS JERKED THE Sin Eater's attention towards the unfortunate victim, whom this delay would only serve to torture further. He knew why, knew all about it, for Kalia had refused the advances of a powerful local man, who had taken his spiteful revenge by naming her heretic. But Kalia came from a good family, unlike the other wretches whose sins would even now be weighing them down, drowning their souls in the caverns of Rann. Kill her they would, but still the proprieties had to be observed. His heart was sore – she had been kind to him once, and he had watched her often from the fringes of the forest, only a deep patch of shadow against the colours of Kalia's life. But Sevim had no name for the ache which now assailed him.

She is special, that's all. Don't make me think of it.

He glanced over at the lead Shemari, fearing the priest might be picking the thoughts from his brain – but it was more than obvious that the priest would not sully himself by entering the splintered mind of such an odious creature as the Sin Eater. His expression was one of distaste.

'Sin Eater,' the priest began, giving the smallest possible bow, 'this woman is accused of both heresy and witchcraft. We therefore fear she might be possessed by a djinn of some nature. Can you see anything in her? Any disturbance?'

This was completely unexpected. Sevim opened and shut his mouth a couple of times, groping for words. Finally, he said, 'I will investigate, priest.' He had a queer, high voice, as if he were constantly being strangled, and the priest blanched slightly at this strange, garbled sound. Sevim did not care though, as this gave him an opportunity to move nearer to Kalia. He walked closer and peered into her face, but her head was lolled to one side, her red hair obscuring her eyes.

'What do you see? Do you see anything?' The priest stood beside him, regarding him closely.

Sevim shook his head. 'No, there is nothing.' He then turned his attention back to Kalia. In her terror she was as corpse-white as he himself was, only her full lips and a red blush across her chest showed that her heart must still be beating, labouring to fight her descent into total fear.

In the hands of the weather-beaten guards she seemed as delicate as a moonflower.

She looks funny. (Laughter.)

Stop it. She is afraid. Like you.

'Is the witch dead already?' he asked, trying to keep his tone as level as possible.

'Just fainted,' the priest replied without emotion, then he nodded at the guards, who shook Kalia awake roughly.

'Pay attention, heretic,' one urged. 'The Sin Eater has come for you.' Her green eyes snapped open and she stared directly into Sevim's face. However, there was no sign of recognition from her; instead she emitted a low, thin wail of abject misery.

She doesn't know you.

It's . . . it's just her fear.

In truth, Sevim was fighting back his disappointment. He realized how unlikely it was that Kalia would know him, but he had allowed himself some hope – a foolish hope. If only she had, perhaps a faint glimmer of hope might have entered her faltering gaze.

'You must step back,' he said to the monks. They glanced at the priest for guidance, and he frowned at Sevim.

'Why?'

Sevim fought for calm. 'Would you have me eat everyone's sins, priest?' he snarled.

'My men are monks, their lives are dedicated to Herrukal's service. What sins could they possibly have?'

There followed a loaded silence, during which only Kalia fidgeted slightly. Her gaze grew more focussed as she continued to stare at Sevim. Her lips were moving, stumbling to form words.

Make them move! She's going to speak. Sevim! Make them . . .

Be still!

Sevim nodded towards the other three pyres. 'If your men assisted yesterday, they have taken life – so they have sin.'

'Only the lives of heretics and witches,' the priest replied sourly. Then he sighed, 'Very well.' He signalled to his men, and the whole entourage moved back to the perimeter of the square. As Kalia's arms were released, Sevim was sure that she would fall in a crumpled heap into the mud. Surprisingly, she did not; she merely wavered like a willow twig in the breeze.

'Bring a seat,' Sevim rasped and, when the monks hesitated, he added, 'You may bind her to it, if you require.' As they went to fetch a chair, he began chanting in a low voice and sprinkled ashes and herbs from the pouch at his waist. For the most part, this was unnecessary – all he needed to do now was to release Spall – but he had learned through the years that the townsfolk expected a certain amount of preamble. Normally, the Sin Eater's services were only required when the recipient was recently dead – more than a couple of hours and it became too late – but on rare occasions such as this he would use his herbs and scented smoke to calm the dying.

Glancing back to make sure the priest was out of earshot, he moved in closer to Kalia. Despite her state of anxiety, she recoiled at his proximity. Sevim felt dismayed; perhaps he should change his plans . . .?

Sevim, tell her! Or you will be angry with yourself after. Tell her!

'K–Kalia,' he whispered, then he continued with his chanting.

She blinked, unsure that anyone had spoken her name. The moment of recognition was so precious to him that he could barely bring himself to look at her – although he must. Through the damp veil of his hair, he watched her closely, the sound of the chant fading gradually from his mouth. Her lips moved soundlessly, seeking to form meaning and sound. When it came, it was barely more than a breath, slipping out like a sigh. 'Sevim?'

He nodded, only a tiny spasm of his head, but Sevim's empty heart rejoiced: she knew him!

He whirled and danced dramatically before Kalia, motioning with his staff, chanting, wailing, drawing forth black crows from his cloak. When the opportunity presented itself – as the priests, the monks and the crowd looked increasingly bored – he hissed into her ear. 'Be ready.'

'IS HE ACTUALLY going to kill her, then?' Viv frowned.

'N-no, he'll just absorb her sins – then they'll burn her,' Stief explained. Viv stared at his brother, surprised at his apparent nonchalance. Stief wore the same blank gaze as most of the watching crowd, seemingly unable to look away from the young woman's abject distress. Viv realized that it was not ghoulish enjoyment but something more subtle – Stief simply could not bring himself to *believe* they were going to take that girl, tie her to a stake and murder her. *Here, in front of his eyes.* Viv believed it though. Fingering the Bakkujasi silver dagger he had kept from a few nights earlier, his eyes skimmed over the grey monotone of the scene. For the moment there was no conscious intention in his mind, only a rising, unformed denial of what he was witnessing.

'I'M SORRY.' Sevim leaned in close to the chair. 'He won't come without sensing the blood . . .' Then he turned his back on Kalia and made a few final gestures in the air. He had played the crowd as long as he could and, while the townspeople seemed grudgingly impressed, the

Shemari remained impassive. He turned back, 'I won't let him touch you . . .' he hissed to her. Kalia, still terrified, was not yet reacting to his confused attempts at reassurance but merely watching his theatrical movements with a glazed expression which suggested a complete failure of mental capacity. Without hesitation, Sevim pulled forth a dagger and drew it across her arm – before her mind managed to latch onto the significance of the weapon.

What do you mean, you won't let me touch her? She's mine. Her sins are mine.

Yes, but she's not going to die, if we can help it.

Not caring. Don't care. Her sins are . . .

No, but you cannot. I warn you, Spall.

Too late. (Laughter.)

THE BLOOD FLOWED freely from Kalia's unresisting arm, staining the side of her wet, white dress a mottled red, Sevim lifted the arm and touched his lips to the wound.

A sudden flare of blue light coruscated out across the square, pushing the sleet and foul weather before it. Sevim and Kalia stood at the eye of the brief magical storm. The onlookers gasped and blinked to try to rid their eyes of the aftershock. Once clarity returned, the black-crow figure of the Sin Eater was no longer standing next to Kalia. It was someone else.

He was a child physically, perhaps twelve to fifteen years old, but Kalia still had to look up at him from her chair, her eyes focussing once more as the crackle of the sin-spell faded into the distance. The boy wore a robe which had once been pure white, except that from the bottom where the hem trailed in the dirt, in mute echo of Sevim's, streaks of black and brown had begun to leach their way up the fabric. Above this height he was still pristine. He had brown hair, swept back from a face which was a marvel of innocence, the blue eyes shining with a strange laughter. He looked as though he had been dipped into something foul and yet borne the outrage simply by denying his ruin. Only the quirk at the corner of his mouth betrayed the fact that he was slowly suffering the corruption that he had taken into himself. One day he would be lost, and so would be Sevim, his host.

'Kalia,' he smiled, 'are you ready?' The boy's voice was young and melodious. He lifted her arm again towards his mouth, and his lips drew back to reveal impossibly white, impossibly sharp teeth. Kalia, as if awakening from sleep, grew afraid with fresh, new reserves of terror she would never have dreamed of in her deepest nightmares.

Spall! Spall! I'm warning you! Remember what we said – I will never eat another sin, you'll live longer, Spall – as long as me! Remember? That was our bargain, our bond . . . please.

Spall stopped with Kalia's arm a hair's breadth from his mouth, his gaze boring into hers, and she could feel the strange sensation of something gathering inside her, ready to explode.

'Are you ready?' he repeated.

There was a pause and, at the edges of the square where the sleet was still drifting, the townspeople held their breath as one. They would tell their children and their grandchildren of this day when they saw the emergence of a Sin Eater's innocent avatar. He was *beautiful*, they would say, but only the Shemari priest had the presence of mind to realize the avatar was almost spent, consumed.

Finally, Kalia found her voice and whispered, 'Ready?'

'Let's do it!' Spall reacted instantly, as if her frightened whisper were a shouted command. Grabbing her from the chair, he tore the bonds from around her wrists. Just as the Shemari began to react, sensing something strange in Spall's actions, he flung his hand out-wards in a sudden gesture. In the air between Spall, Kalia and the many onlookers something sinuous and black burst into being.

'What the hell is . . .?' Kalia gasped.

'Sin,' said Spall. 'What else would it be? Come on!' They began to run towards an unguarded exit leading from the square, Spall drag-ging the weakened Kalia by her wrist as she tried to find her footing on legs which only moments earlier had been paralysed by fear. She glanced back to where the black thing writhed and shimmered in the air. Most of the townspeople were on their knees praying, but the monks were standing their ground, the Shemari priest shouting some order, although his face had turned white with shock. Spall tugged her arm. 'Don't stop to look, Kalia,' he said. 'It's just an image, and we won't have long till they realize.'

As they reached the centre of the square, near to the remains of the used pyres, a temple guard tried to block their way. Spall stopped running abruptly, Kalia careering into the back of him, while the lone guard brandished his spear towards them, obviously thinking to delay them until others arrived. But then he fell to the ground, inexplicably it seemed at first. As he landed face-down in the mud a tall, dark-haired man came over and pulled a dagger from the fallen man's back. Although only injured, the guard sensibly made no move to get up, just lay there gasping in fright.

'This way!' the stranger urged, and there was no time to ask questions. As they raced across the square another man joined them, taking Kalia's other arm and helping Spall to pull her forwards. Without argument they all rushed towards the south-east corner leading out onto the main street. Spall noticed how Kalia immediately pulled away from his grip and allowed the stranger to guide her. He had agreed with Sevim in advance to get Kalia into the forest where she could be more easily hidden, but he realized now that the place was bigger than Sevim's bizarre optimism allowed, with many streets, and the river, still between them and the forest.

'They're gaining on us.' Kalia was panicking. 'Can you do it again – the sin stuff?'

Spall snorted to himself – did she know how long it took to amass that much 'stuff'? – but he paused in order to try and oblige her suggestion. Their pursuers stopped dead before the malevolent mass he flung towards them, three of the monks turning to run and the others dropping to their knees.

When he turned back he found Kalia and the two strangers were now some distance ahead. 'Where are you going?' he yelled after them. 'The forest is this way.' He started running to catch up – he could only imagine Sevim's fury if Kalia was able to credit her rescue to anyone else.

'I can't b-believe you, Viv,' the second man stormed as they ran. 'You c-could have warned me!'

Viv was running ahead. His lightness of build made him fleet-footed, and the other three had some difficulty keeping up. He glanced back at them, his blue-grey eyes flashing annoyance. 'They were escaping already. Would you rather have watched her burn?'

Spall had no idea who these strange people were, but he knew one thing, he was tiring already. Cramps were seizing up the muscles of his arms and legs, his vision was blurring . . . so, whatever plan these men had for escape, it had to be soon. Because Sevim's soul was fighting to take back possession of his body.

VIV WAS ABLAZE with directionless anger as he ran; he didn't even know why he had become so rashly involved. He wasn't sure of any of his reasoning anymore. Maybe he just wanted to defy the Shemari, hurt them in some small way, to answer their thoughtless murder of Calla, and give them a bit of trouble of their own. He could do more maybe – perhaps return and burn their bloody temple around their ears . . . But first of all, he had to get the girl and the Sin Eater away safely.

He glanced back at his brother, who was visibly tiring. Stief had skidded in the mud, almost pulling Kalia down with him, but the Sin Eater in particular seemed to be struggling.

'Come on,' Viv urged, 'up here!' and he turned a corner just as the three pursuing guards came into view behind them. There was a strange, high-pitched sound close by, and it took him a few seconds to realize that there were archers aiming at them from the rooftops. With a curse, he turned to run the other way, only registering that the alley was a dead-end even as his feet propelled him forward. 'No,' he groaned. Instinctively he hugged into the wall where the arrows could not reach him. As the others came closer he heard their exhausted exclamations as well.

THE GUARDSMEN HAD reached the bottom of the alley now. Its upward slope would impair their progress slightly, but they could see that the four were trapped so they slowed their own pace, puffing and panting for breath.

'Throw down your weapons,' one of them shrilled. 'You, Sin Eater, keep your hands where I can see them.' As Spall moved to comply, there was a sudden flurry above them as a strong wind began to crash around the alleyway, picking up grit and bits of debris, spattering splashes of mud in chaotic patterns against the walls. The guards drew back, instinctively putting their arms up to protect their faces. But the four escapees had nowhere to run.

It was a Swarm, and it landed right before them. Its bright green bulk came to rest with a slight vibrating motion on the suspension of its huge wiry legs. Kalia screamed in surprise and hid herself behind Stief, who began backing away from the creature although he could retreat no further than the wall. If the Swarm was carrying a Bakkujasi, it meant they were finished – but as the massive wings stilled, it became clear that this Swarm was riderless.

Contrary to all logic, Viv walked over towards the massive dragonfly.

'Viv, get b-back!' his brother yelped. As Viv glanced back towards them, Stief noticed that, once again, his eyes were glowing with that strange eldritch fire.

It was all too much for Kalia, who gripped Stief's jerkin and tugged at it feebly. 'What's wrong with him? Has he gone crazy?' Her voice became a breathless sob, and Stief could see the shock of the past hour etched deeply into the lines of her face. Spall was silent, as he watched Viv closely.

'It's all right,' Stief heard himself replying. It was laughable; he *didn't* know that it would be all right. Viv was now beside the beast's head, which the Swarm tipped to one side as if regarding him curiously. Through the arch formed by the creature's legs, Stief could see that more guards had caught up with the first ones, but they all stood paralysed by indecision. The archers had stopped firing, for no one would dare fire on a Swarm.

Something strange was happening to Viv – but it was so fast that no one watching would have been able to identify the precise instant. Except perhaps Stief, who had witnessed the changes in his brother for the past several days. But now it seemed those changes were coming to a strange fruition. All he could say for sure was that Viv's back stiffened, as if something had hauled him upright by his collar.

Viv heard her speaking to him. The Swarm was filling his mind. Yet he felt no sense of threat from the creature, only a strange, almost wilful joy.

Ayshena, she said. Her name was Ayshena. *Helping Viv-reki. Helping.* That voice was unmistakably female, and her words sounded as a low buzz inside his head.

Viv felt his gaze drawn upwards to the blank iridescence of the Swarm's eyes, but he saw nothing there to be discerned as an expression. Before he had time to assimilate his thoughts further, she urged. *Fly.*

THERE WAS THE sound of shouted orders from the guards massed at the far end of the alley – there were perhaps twenty of them now. Viv reached out and touched the face of the Swarm – it felt hard and cold, almost shell-like.

Fly, she repeated.

'Yes,' he replied. He turned to Stief and the others. 'Come on, she wants us to fly out of here.' They stood motionless with expressions of mute disbelief. Just then two of the temple guards started to edge forward nervously, their spears thrust out in front of them. It seemed likely they had been instructed to walk under the legs of the Swarm.

'Come on,' Viv snapped impatiently.

There was a knotted rope hanging down from the Swarm. He had no idea how it got there, but neither did he have time to wonder. Leading by example, he began to haul himself up. Although his heart was still hammering in his chest, Vivreki felt only the thrill, not the fear, of the fact he was about to fly.

❧CHAPTER SEVEN❧

F LYING A SWARM was easier than Viv had imagined – easier but infinitely more terrifying. And if *he* was terrified, Stief, clinging on behind him for dear life, was now a gibbering, near-hysterical wreck. As such behaviour was so unlike his elder brother, it somehow added to the surreal nature of this, their first journey on the back of a Swarm. Viv himself yelled and screamed in exaltation even though he could feel his legs tremble and the muscles in his belly tighten with visceral fear.

Beneath them the forest whizzed by, the landscape altered by their speed into a blurring frenzy of deep green interspersed by silver flecks of rocks and rivers. Only Bakkujasi had ever seen such a transformed view of the world before, and Viv had heard that they had to train for months before they were allowed to fly these precious creatures. It seemed little wonder, then, that their priestly caste was so different, so set apart from what Viv might consider 'normal'. Such an astonishing experience as this could only change a person's view of the world and Herrukal's creation of it.

AYSHENA LANDED THEM some twenty-five leagues north of Cantroji – effectively a day's distance from any likely Shemari pursuit, unless they had another Swarm in the city. The forest stretched densely for seventy leagues, so Ayshena's first problem was finding a clear enough space to set down in – the second problem being that she was in imminent danger of losing her passengers.

As soon as Kalia had been hauled onto Ayshena's back by Viv and

Stief, Spall had come running up behind her. This strange young man had saved their lives by the use of the sin-spell, so Stief had let down the knotted rope in order to pull him up also.

'Leave him!' Kalia shrieked, grabbing the rope away. 'Leave him, he's . . . he's unnatural.' Stief couldn't believe what he was hearing – surely the girl was still confused by the ordeal of her trial.

Spall himself looked as if he was about to pass out. 'Help me,' he called up, his expression pained and confused.

Stief moved to clamber down towards him but Kalia gripped his arm. 'Don't you know what he is?' she hissed.

Stief glanced over to Viv, who also seemed surprised at her violent reaction. But Viv was in no mood for such dispute, and he frowned at the girl. 'He rides or you get off,' he snapped. Viv's threat seemed to carry enough force, and Kalia fell silent – her lips pressed into a thin line of annoyance. Spall had only just managed to climb up the makeshift ladder as Ayshena's wings began to thrum – even as the guards raced forward, brandishing their temple longspears. As they realized their quarries were about to make their escape on the back of the Swarm, their bullish expressions transformed into stupefied amazement.

'Come back here,' one yelled, somewhat ridiculously. 'I command you in the name of Herrukal.'

As Ayshena began to lift off from the ground, the powerful air current she created forced the guards back, fighting to stay upright while shielding their eyes. 'Yeah, yeah, we'll come back,' Viv scoffed, 'so you can burn us all, you sanctimonious bastards! Herrukal be damned!'

Stief tutted quietly, wondering if Viv finally adding blasphemy to his burgeoning list of crimes would make any difference in the long run. He had to concede to himself that it would not. After the last few hours work, they were as good as condemned men, and the Shemari could only kill them once.

As THEY GAINED height, Stief became aware of the girl behind him struggling and shifting. She was shouting, yelling too, and although her words of complaint were whisked away by the force of the wind, her tone of bitter complaint was still clear. Stief twisted around from the waist to warn her to sit still lest she unbalance them all.

'Tell him to take his hands off me,' she spat, as soon as she realized she had Stief's attention. 'Get him away from me!' She lashed out ineffectually behind her. For a moment, Stief was puzzled until he looked past her shoulder and realized the Sin Eater had reverted to his original, unclean form. The wind was blowing aside the lank screen of his black hair, and his face was now fully exposed; although surprisingly young, his features were so deathly pale as to seem blue tinged, his twisted mouth a liverish purple. The young man's appearance was truly frightening, and he had reached forward to grip his gnarled hands around Kalia's slim waist in order to steady himself.

'Sit still, both of you.' Stief frowned, but a few moments later sensed a further disturbance behind him. There was nothing he could do to solve the situation, short of flinging Kalia off the Swarm's back, an idea which, as the journey wore on, gained a certain amount in appeal.

As soon as they landed, Kalia leaped recklessly down from Ayshena's back without waiting for Stief to pass her the rope. There was little doubt she planned to continue her diatribe of complaints, but she underestimated the distance and landed badly, squealing in pain and indignation as her ankle twisted beneath her. The three men remaining on the back of the Swarm stared down at her with a mixture of disbelief and faint amusement.

They dismounted in turn – Sevim slowly and stiffly, his movements reminding Stief of someone really ancient, despite his earlier impression that Sevim was in fact far younger than he would have expected. As soon as he touched the ground, near to Kalia, she recoiled. 'Just get away from me,' she muttered and limped away from him.

Viv ignored the rest of them and stood in front of the Swarm as if listening to something, his gaze sliding over the others in a distant, detached manner.

'I'm sure he d-didn't mean to upset you, miss.' Stief had put himself between Kalia and Sevim in case she decided to lash out as she had during their flight.

'Upset me?' She arched her brows. 'That would be to presume I even cared.'

'Am I m-missing something here, because it s-seems to m-me' –

Stief's stammer worsened under Kalia's scornful scrutiny – 'that he s-saved your life. Isn't some gratitude therefore in order?'

Kalia looked only vaguely chastened at this. She brushed distractedly at her blood-smeared robe as if that could somehow remove the marks. 'You must ask yourself, then, for what purpose this foul creature saved me.'

Stief bridled at her easy dismissal of Sevim's courage but, then, he had not stopped to question the Sin Eater's motives. 'He's n-not a foul creature . . .' he began to argue.

'It's all right.' The strained, sibilant voice came from behind him as Sevim hobbled forward. 'I am used to people's reactions to me.' He nodded meaningfully towards Kalia who had wrinkled her nose in dainty disgust as he stepped closer. 'You know me then, Kalia?'

'Yes,' she replied, hesitantly. 'I remember when they . . .'

'They cast me out,' he supplied. 'It was not so very long ago. Five years or so. Kalia, you were then the only one to show me any compassion. I can see now it is gone from you – perhaps I should have let you burn.' He turned away from her, mumbling about finding somewhere to sit down. Kalia stared after him, her gaze fixed on his bowed back.

SHE REMEMBERED HER act of 'compassion' and, in truth, it had been no such thing. The villagers of Hevino had reached a fever pitch of speculation about Sevim. The child lived alone after his parents had died, no relatives coming forward to take the lad in. As a result, Sevim had become increasingly remote from normal village life, speaking to no one. Few people saw him about, and when they did, Sevim appeared to have neglected himself. His clothes and hair hung in tattered rags and his bare feet were covered in filth. When a young girl went missing, this strange, withdrawn creature in their community seemed a likely suspect.

It was Kalia's own father, Tarrauk, who had been the main instigator of Sevim's persecution. He was an influential man in the village and his cronies would do much to retain his favour. 'We must cast the boy out,' he roared, 'for he has become unnatural – an abomination in the sight of Herrukal.' It was raining very heavily that night, a wilder storm than the villagers had seen for years. This added further fuel to their superstitious ire. Deep in their cups as they were, they went and dragged the boy from his hovel to the yard of Tarrauk's house, literally tethered by the waist and hauled along behind the horses. Afterwards, they would remark, 'He said nothing to defend himself.' His uncanny silence under this treatment had made the participants even more uneasy, as though he somehow denied them their ignorant satisfaction.

Kalia's father had stumbled out drunkenly into the yard, as they taunted Sevim. Stripped of his clothes, he stood there in the cold deluge, water sliding off his deathly white skin, his black hair plastered over his face, making no effort to brush it aside in order to see the faces of his tormentors.

Watching unseen from the side doorway, Kalia was curious at first, having never seen a naked man before. But her curiosity quickly turned to dismay, as she watched her father behaving like an imbecile. That was far more upsetting than anything else. She hung back in the gloom of the doorway, her hand over her mouth, and she watched as they sought to dehumanize the boy. They spat on him, pissed on him, ridiculed him and finally Tarrauk branded him with a poker, making a crude emblem of Herrukal between his shoulder blades. At that point, Sevim collapsed in the mud, still making no sound – and with his collapse the desire for violence among the small mob seemed abruptly satiated.

Her father tossed the poker aside. 'Let's go in,' he said. But before he turned away, he kicked Sevim hard in the ribs – and Kalia somehow *knew* that this kick was because Tarrauk was angry with himself, unsatisfied but unable to articulate his anger. In all the times in the years since that night, that Kalia had unwillingly replayed the scene in her mind, she could perhaps have forgiven her father everything but that final kick; it showed the narrow, petty limitations of a man she had idolized until that moment.

As she had watched, unnoticed, Kalia slid down against the doorpost until she was slumped on the floor, her hand still clutched in horror around her mouth now wet with tears and snot. After they abandoned Sevim there in the mud, the scene was even more desolate: the lashing rain pooling around the prostrate figure who made no move to stand up again. Her father had gone back to his beer and his warm while she sobbed quietly in the dark, listening to the hissing sigh of the storm.

'Kalia?' It was her mother who eventually found her there. She never knew how much her mother had witnessed of what had happened in the yard. Although she glanced out at the boy, it was as though she failed to see him. She seemed far more concerned with her daughter's comparatively trivial tears.

'It was Father,' she wailed. 'Father . . .'

'I know, dear.' Her mother shushed her with meaningless words of comfort. She had brought a blanket with her and she reached down to put it round Kalia's shoulders. 'Come away, child. Come on . . .'

Kalia stood up slowly, her legs stiff with the cold. She had started to follow . . . but then she glanced back to Sevim. He had not moved. He could be dead of shock or cold – and her father had done this!

'No, wait,' she muttered and ran out into the rain.

'Kalia, your father will be angry,' her mother called after her, but Kalia could not turn back.

When she reached him, she was overcome with relief to find that Sevim was still alive. Her first intention had been simply to throw the blanket down to cover over that startlingly white form, but as she stared curiously at the bloodied curve of his back, he suddenly groaned and shifted feebly in the mud.

'Here.' She crouched down to cover him with the blanket as he sat up. She tried her best to avert her gaze but Sevim was too confused to worry about modesty. He gathered the blanket around his neck, and there followed long moments of silence between them as Kalia caught the flash of his grey gaze fixed upon her from behind the lank curtain of black hair.

'You must go now,' she stammered. 'You – you are branded . . .' She had realized that the only thing for him now was to leave the village and be content to have escaped with his life. Kalia certainly did not want him here as a constant reminder of her family's shame. She cast her gaze around the yard and saw her mule sheltering under the inadequate lean-to her father had constructed. She went over and pulled the reluctant creature towards him, only to realize with some embarrassment that Sevim was too weak to climb onto its back unaided. She certainly had little intention of helping a naked boy sit astride, so once she had managed to slump him across it side-saddle, she hastily thrust the rope bridle into his numb fingers and stepped back.

'Thank you, Kalia,' he whispered, so low that she hardly even heard him. They were the only words he uttered all night but none would ever know of it except Kalia . . .

NOW, SHE WATCHED him shamble slowly across the woodland clearing towards the good-looking youth who seemed somehow able to communicate with the Swarm. Sevim had turned his back on her, dismissed her almost, and perhaps it was all that she deserved. For what he had once perceived as an act of compassion had been motivated by the desire to remove him from her sight. A desperate attempt to expunge her father's guilt – ultimately, nothing other than complicity.

They scrabbled together a meagre encampment; it was a cold night but fortunately the snowstorm had not reached this far. The ground remained dry and hard, enabling Stief to get a fire going from windblown dead wood. Sevim, despite his slow, pained movements, even managed to help by bringing haphazard bundles of twigs clutched in his white fingers.

Fortunately, both Viv and Stief still had their sparkstones in their pouches, but that was about the only survival equipment they possessed. They were even hungrier now than when they had entered Cantroji earlier that day. Kalia, meanwhile, had lapsed into stony silence, sitting defiantly with her back to them some distance from the fire.

SEATED ON A rotted log facing the Swarm, Viv ignored the snow and the chill. His head was tipped back and his muddy hair scraped away from his face, while his eyes were shining with that eerie glow. Occasionally, his lips moved as if he were speaking to himself, or he nodded in agreement to some information the Swarm seemed to be imparting. Ayshena herself sat inanimately at the edge of the clearing, looking for all the world like one of those brightly painted temple statues.

Stief was uneasy about his brother's behaviour, but there was nothing to be done about it, Viv did not appear to be threatened by the Swarm in any way; in fact, he seemed a willing participant in their strange communion. There seemed nothing he could do but wait for Viv to come over to the fire.

'So, what happens to that other person?' Stief turned to Sevim in an effort to alleviate the burgeoning silence of the forest.

'You mean Spall? Nothing happens to him. He's part of me. He only comes to receive the sins.' Sevim replied. Although he answered willingly enough, Sevim did not show any sign of expanding on this subject, and Stief had the impression that the relationship between Sevim and his avatar was intensely personal to him. He cast around for something else to talk about. 'So, you already know Kalia, then? That was why you tried to save her?'

Sevim nodded sharply, with a glance over to where Kalia was sitting. Stief sighed, she must be freezing by now – wearing nothing but the white shift they had planned to burn her in, which was clinging damply to her body. The pink stain of blood gave it a perversely soft appearance and lent the wretched girl a further air of vulnerability. She was shivering from either cold or delayed shock. Perhaps her ingratitude towards Sevim was atypical of her, Stief thought. After all, the circumstances of her rescue were incredible.

Stief stood up, took off his riding cloak and walked over to drape it around Kalia's shoulders. 'Why don't you come over to the fire now, Kalia?' he said gently.

She did not reply, did not move, merely sat silently in the snow like some ice carving. Stief fastened the clasp around her neck and then, just as he moved his hand away, she reached out and grabbed it suddenly, her grip like a freezing vice. 'Kalia, you m-must come and get warm,' he insisted. He put an arm around her and drew her to her feet, and gradually across the clearing. She walked as if in a dreamstate, not even looking once at Sevim. Stief settled her by the fire, hoping that she might thaw out both physically and emotionally.

It was over an hour later when Viv finally moved away from Ayshena. He looked different to Stief, although at first Stief could not place the reason for this. A small smile flitted across Viv's face every few moments as he spoke as if something had lit him from within.

Viv crouched beside Kalia, extending his hands to the fire 'Well, Ayshena has a lot to say.' He chuckled dryly. 'She's told me why the Bakkujasi want me so badly. You were right, Stief. I was judged a heretic when I was just a boy – seems they don't even make allowances for children.' He tilted his chin and regarded Stief warmly. 'And you may not be my real brother, but you always will be, in here.' He tapped his chest, above where his heart was. Stief frowned: it felt as though Viv was patronizing him, bestowing on him some obscure blessing – as if his love was divine. Sevim sensed this too and he glanced over uneasily.

'Are you all right, Viv?'

'Never better.' Again, that unsettling smile. 'I have to leave you in the morning though.'

'L-leave, why? Where are you going?'

'To Releeza. I've promised Ayshena I will help her recover the eggs of other Swarms. Just like I did for her mother, Ansanzi, when I was a boy. That's why I was judged a heretic, Stief, because I took Ayshena's egg and hid it away. The Shemari would have destroyed it. Now there are other eggs and they will seek to destroy those too.'

'What will you do with them, Vivreki?' Sevim asked, suddenly.

Viv glanced over at Ayshena. 'Same as before: hide them until they all hatch. The Swarms that come forth will be the same as Ayshena – special.'

Sevim was now leaning forward, keenly interested by this strange conversation. He too glanced over to Ayshena. 'It has a soul?'

'*She*,' Viv corrected. 'Yes, she does.'

'It must be sin free,' Sevim observed. Something salacious in his tone made Stief feel slightly uneasy.

Viv did not seem to notice the Sin Eater's close interest. 'I suppose so. I hadn't thought about it.' He stood and returned to take up his position by Ayshena, his manner dismissive.

'W-wait, Viv,' Stief called. 'If you're going anywhere, I'm coming with you. You c-can't just go around stealing the eggs. The Bakkujasi won't allow it – it's not that simple.'

As Viv turned to answer him, Stief suddenly recognized what seemed different in his brother. In the gathering dark, Viv's form had acquired a solidity, and an aura of musky warmth – something intangible – crossed the distance between them. Viv was made stronger, made *more*, by whatever power it was that had gripped him. It was clearly the presence of Ayshena that made it so.

'I'll ask Ayshena if she will carry you too,' Viv replied simply, sounding neither pleased or displeased.

'And us? Please ask her,' Sevim said.

Viv did register some surprise at this; his brother's request was predictable, but Sevim and Kalia had no reason for wanting to remain with them. Sevim was presumably well able to look after himself, having been an outcast for such a long time. Kalia was quite the opposite of that . . . but then, Sevim would look after her, whether it was what she wanted or not. Having saved the girl's life, Viv felt that his own responsibility to her was ended; after all, she was a stranger, whose conduct was hardly endearing.

'Why would you want to come?' Stief frowned at Sevim. 'Viv and I will probably end up in the same situation as Kalia was. We're wanted men now, and the Bakkujasi will be looking for us.' It was only as he spoke these words that Stief acknowledged to himself that his allegiance to Viv had become something inherently unquestioning.

They both looked over at Kalia as Stief spoke. She was staring fixedly into the fire, her arms crossed over her chest as if protecting herself. The blankness of her gaze was still impenetrable, as if she was thinking of the flames she had been destined to die amongst.

Sevim shrugged. 'Kalia and I, we came from the same community – the same people have abused and abandoned us. No one ever protected us or interceded and took our part, except for you two. We owe you our lives . . .'

'But you were already escaping,' Viv pointed out. 'You did that without our help.'

Sevim nodded. 'I was doing it for her. You must think that pathetic since she cannot stand to look at me, but remember I have known her for most of her life, and it took every grain of my courage. I would not have done it for a stranger, as you did.'

Vivreki appeared unmoved by Sevim's words of praise and Sevim sensed that he had not convinced him. 'I can be of use to you,' he protested. 'You have seen what powers I can summon to protect us.'

Viv merely nodded but did not respond directly; he turned to walk back towards the Swarm. Sevim watched closely, wondering why he felt such a need to remain close to Ayshena and the miracle of her soul.

SLEEPING, WAITING FOR
IRREFUTABLE, UNTAMED BEING.
WAKING IS TO KNOW.

❧CHAPTER EIGHT❧

THERE WAS NO doubt in Uriel's mind that he was a heretic – he had been since he lost his wife and children to sickness a year before. The gods of Myr had forsaken him then, he reasoned, and so it seemed right that, in return, he have nothing further to do with them.

A chill breeze was blowing from the north, its stiff fingers tousling his greying hair so that even his scalp felt the cold. He pulled his jacket more tightly around himself, sighing as he gazed across the river at the lights of the Brengarmah encampment. It was hardly a massive force, but it would be sufficient to kill most of the population of Releeza should the town finally make a stand against them.

And then Uriel himself would be responsible for those deaths, because the people of this previously soulless backwater had listened to him and believed in him, rallied around a man who was devoid of belief. Well, perhaps it wasn't *all* his fault, perhaps he had only given voice to the existing feelings of those farmers, miners, builders, brewers – because Releeza was composed of such people   who were unable to articulate their wonder. Uriel himself was a cooper by trade, as his father had been, and he was also a rarity amongst his fellows in that he could read and write. This ability had garnered him much respect in the community, and it was this respect which had gained firstly the townspeople's indulgence, and then, their trust.

He was sitting on a raised platform in the middle of Releeza's town square, his back resting against the wooden framework they had constructed to contain the precious egg. The egg itself glinted with a heavy pewter hue under the stark moonlight, and Uriel found himself wishing it was warm to the touch, that somehow the thing might give him a sign that he was right in his defence of it. Rationally there was nothing there to support his belief since the egg was effectively inanimate. Korri Peryju, one of the town's many publicans, had even suggested cracking the thing open to discover its contents; a suggestion that certain other people had tentatively agreed with. That was over a week ago, and since then Uriel had taken to keeping watch here at night, lest someone come staggering from the tavern and think it an interesting suggestion to follow up on. To most of Releeza, although they listened respectfully to Uriel's imprecations, the egg remained totally an enigma.

Not to Uriel, he *knew*, in his heart and in his bones. Inside this egg was a dragon. From the moment he had seen it, he simply knew. The egg had been discovered on the same night that the new star had first been sighted from Releeza. It had become clear to him then that this was the reason he had survived that first long winter after the death of Mia and his boys, when all he had wanted was to walk out into the freezing calm of the snow and die a numbing, unthinking death. No, he had been destined to survive in order to defend it, to watch over it, to make Mia proud of him. He was its guardian. Sometimes he had sat here in the silence before dawn in the sleet or the rain, and visualized the hatching of the creature inside, imagining the look of joy and wonderment on the faces of his two boys if they had lived to see it. Perhaps brightness would return to the world in that moment, he really did not know.

When such secret doubt assailed him he held onto this precious imagining. His certainty was strengthened by it and Uriel's certainty had motivated the townsfolk of Releeza: the dragon's egg was *theirs* alone, they said. They had built and painted the rough-hewn dais it rested on, and people came to visit it each day – some even claiming it healed their illnesses.

Eventually, hearing rumours of this marvel, Shemari priests had come all the way from Yotu Tem, seventy leagues away, to examine the treasure, and it was they who had reported its existence to the Hani in Gremeshkenn Tem. They declared it a miracle of Oshi, but the inhabitants of Releeza were not happy with such requisitioning of their local wonder. Word spread throughout the region that the official gods had no claim on it; that perhaps, the *Other* had sent it – *She*, the goddess Mauru. Of course, that was heresy, but in the past no one from the temple city had cared about the workings of the unimportant minds in this barren and blasted corner of the world.

❧

THEY OBVIOUSLY CARED now, though; something had moved the Hani to action. A delegation from Gremeshkenn Tem had already been sent packing from the town – much to the glee of Korri and his cronies who were still treating the whole business as something of a joke.

'Yeah, that'll show Gremeshkenn Tem that we're not to be messed with,' he had exulted. Uriel had just smiled distantly, at Korri's naivety. When the second delegation had arrived three months later, it was with a whole battalion of Brengarmah at their backs to protect them. Negotiations had begun badly, with Uriel and the town council maintaining an entrenched position from the start. The young Brengarmah commander, named Fodukiz, had seemed reasonable to begin with, promising a financial reward for the town in exchange for the precious egg. To be fair, it would have been a winning ploy if Uriel had not been present.

After the Commander had gone, leaving them to discuss his proposal, Uriel rounded on the other members of the council. 'This is not about money,' he argued. 'Why do you think they really want it? Because it is *ours* – that's all. Because it signifies that we are special, chosen.'

'Chosen by whom, Uriel?' the mayor asked quietly. His grey-faced expression showed that he foresaw Uriel's answer, and was already nervous of it.

Uriel did not pause. 'Chosen by Mauru. The One. She sent it.' There was an instant of shocked silence, then everyone began to talk at once. 'You know that it's true,' Uriel did not release the mayor's gaze. 'The old gods have long forsaken us here in Releeza, but she is our new protector.' In the silence that followed, he turned to walk away, leaving them to a debate which he knew would rage for hours. He did not like to be away from the egg for too long.

The mayor came after him and caught hold of his sleeve as he reached the door. 'Uriel,' he said gravely, 'my heart tells me that you may be right. Talk of the goddess is on everyone's lips. But to make a stand, to deny Gremeshkenn Tem, that could lead to death for many of us. People go about their everyday lives here with little thought to the gods. They labour and feed their families, and hope to survive through the hard winters. This new cause you are creating is dangerous. Let it go, I beg you. Is the anger which rages in your soul worth the cost?'

THAT HAD BEEN two days ago, and nothing had happened since. The town had not made any declaration of their stance with regard to the gods, nor had the Brengarmah come back across the river to press them for their answer. They all seemed to be waiting for something.

It began to snow. In the silence of the night Uriel could almost hear the breathless softness of the flakes; it seemed as if the heavens were weeping. He pulled the leather blanket over him which kept out the most biting of the weather – it formed a bell-like shelter around him and within a few minutes, as the familiar scene gave way to whiteness, Uriel was surrounded by a shallow layer of snow. Without much thought he took a stick and began to draw shapes in it around himself, only realizing as he finished that perhaps he had some notion of protection, of warding off . . . what? As ever, the snow brought out the worst of his morose nature.

'Uriel.'

He started, then peered around. It was Ruji, a boy who used to play with his youngest son, Dan. The lad stood uncertainly in the snow, a steaming mug of *kashis* in his hand. The scent of the spices wrapped themselves around Uriel's heart. 'My mother thought you might be cold out here,' he explained.

Uriel took the drink gratefully and readjusted his cover. Ruji suddenly asked, 'Is that the dragon?'

'Huh?' As he looked at where the boy was pointing, he realized he had in fact made a poor representation of a dragon amongst his snow pictures. 'Yes, but it's not a very good likeness though, in the snow.' Ruji smiled somewhat uncertainly, revealing a gap between his front teeth. He had just reached that age when they began to fall out, just as Dan's had. Uriel felt a familiar tightness in his chest.

'When will it come, Uriel? Mama says it will heal all the sick people . . .' He paused briefly, remembering how Uriel's family had all died of the blight sickness, his discomfort flitting across his open features, but then he continued, 'and it will make our fields all lush and green again, so we can grow better crops and even . . . even orchards.'

'That would be good, Ruji. But we don't know yet when it will come. We've never hatched a dragon before, have we?'

Ruji shook his head, and looked like he was going home to ponder this notion. Just before he turned away, he frowned. 'But what if that takes hundreds of years?'

It was a worrying thought Uriel had also toyed with, though his instincts told him it would happen soon. 'Well then, a new guardian will have to be found after I die. Goodnight, Ruji. Thank your mother for me.'

The snow became heavier and Uriel was left alone again, brooding on the realization that this might be true. The hatching could take years yet, so he would have to set about building a shelter of sorts. No one else could take his responsibility from him, for he was the First Guardian.

CION'S PARTY HAD landed at last, at a tiny hamlet named Daikamya, where the low, salt-blasted wooden houses nestled like eyries amongst the sharp clefts and inlets of the jagged cliffs. At the quayside were moored boats of such extreme dilapidation as to make their modest vessel look like the Emperor's barge. They hired a guide, six horses and two mules, and started off immediately into the desert-like scrub of the plains, without so much as a break for food. This area lay in the south-westerly extremities of the Cantroji region, a harsh and empty environ where the barren plains extended as far as one could see.

And yet the nomadic Gurzz horse tribes managed to eke out some kind of living here. The Gurzz, although subjects of the Emperor, were afforded a certain sovereign autonomy and this included the Shemari turning a blind eye to their worship of a whole panoply of spirits. These, if Asoori understood correctly, were the spirits of their ancestors, which supposedly manifested themselves in natural elements and features such as the rain and the rocks. Herrukal knew, there was little else to revere out here . . .

They had now arrived at the approximate location where Nuss had disappeared – as determined by some divination done back at Gremeshkenn Tem – and spent three whole days just riding around scouring the area for any sign of the accident. After the first day they knew they were being watched by the Gurzz, because the tribesmen made no secret of their observations. Leaning back casually in their tall-pommelled saddles to chat and smoke their pipes, while letting their horses crop at the meagre scrub, they watched with a strangely unengaged expression as though the travellers were creatures from a distant world.

On the third day, a sandstorm blew in from the west and caught the small group completely unawares. Their tents proved unsuitable for the terrain as Cion had elected to bring only lightweight supplies – Merric's was little more than a lean-to which he shared with the guide. Asoori and Kilmer's tent collapsed first under the weight of the sand; Merric's was also blasted away although he had managed to grab the escaping canvas.

Except for the guide, who had chosen to stay with the horses in the lea of a nearby dune, they were all now crammed into Cion's tent for the night, while the wind shrieked and howled outside. It was a prospect guaranteed to put both Asoori and Cion into a black mood, as the undercurrent of their sharing of Kilmer's attention became unavoidable. Settling down with her husband on the other side of the tent, Asoori had flashed Cion a tiny smile as she wrapped her arms around Kilmer's chest.

The loose edges of the tent buffeted and snapped, gripped by the unremitting blast of the storm. The wooden frame swayed slightly, its movement causing the lantern to swing almost as though they were still at sea. Its yellow light cast lurid shadows on the sleeping occupants, who had lain awake for hours listening to every creak of the tent, until eventually, their weariness won out. As Asoori drifted into sleep her last realization was that Cion, over on the far side of the tent, was sitting cross-legged with his back to them. He was probably meditating.

THOUGH DRAINED BY the journey, Cion was trained not to require sleep, rather to remain awake if necessary and spend those wakeful hours in prayer. Tonight, however, he could delay no longer – he had to reconnect with the Abax. If he failed to do so, he doubted he would find enough strength to move his Swarm again after they arrived at

Releeza. He quietly opened the battered cedar box which he had kept tied to his back since his arrival at Falloden Sen. Inside, despite its tattered surroundings, the golden mask shone in luxuriant splendour. He touched its cold unmoving brow as if it were a breathless lover.

Sometimes the demands of being Bakkujasi were such that Cion had to wonder if he could survive in service, and he prayed constantly for strength. By nature a secretive, private individual, the sharing of consciousness involved in his vocation harrowed his mind. None could match his mental alacrity, however; he had learned how to pull back, to channel his secret thoughts away from the Abax, no matter how it sought to unravel him. This time would be harder, the reason he had delayed – he planned to lie to Achios. He knew the fate of the heretic boy in Rinjisti had been important to his superior, although he had little idea why that might be so. It seemed pointless to tell Achios of Vivreki's escape from him; it could only damage his own reputation for no practical end . . .

He glanced back across the tent to ensure everyone was asleep, before putting on the mask. Normally he would only attempt such contact in a temple or secret place, but time was pressing and the storm outside too severe. Everyone appeared to be sleeping and so he slipped the mask on, the familiar cold rush of physical contact making him suppress a shudder.

Cion did not even need to close his eyes. The yellow billow of the tent walls vanished from his sight and before him appeared a lush garden arbour: a miniature temple replete with wrought-iron curlicues and guardian dragons. Seated on a stone bench at the top of the steps, Achios was waiting for him, as Cion had known he would be. Cion also knew this illusion was a mere fancy – perhaps Achios's way of showing his effortless power to manipulate the magics of the Abax. As he walked forward, Cion could hear the disembodied voices of other Bakkujasi – those also currently wearing their masks – drifting through the air like discordant birdsong.

Achios wasted no time on ceremonial niceties. 'Where have you been, Cion?' he snapped. Perhaps fortunately, he did not give Cion any time to respond. 'Where is the heretic boy? Why is he not on his way back to Gremeshkenn Tem?'

Cion's projected avatar bowed low before Achios, fighting to keep his features blank and his mind calm. 'Sadly he is dead, Master Achios. He put up a fight when being taken into custody and killed two

Shemari.' Even as he spoke, his sense of conviction began to fade. Although Achios's expression did not change, it seemed to Cion that, somehow, the old man could detect his duplicity with ease.

'*Really*, Cion, I have to admire your gall. I take it he evaded capture?'

There seemed nothing to be gained by protesting. 'Yes. I sent *Darhg* to track him but they were lost – I have never known anyone evade them before.'

Even Achios looked impressed. 'I will seek him by other means for the moment. When do you arrive in Releeza?'

'In two days, sir.'

'Very well, Cion. It is of the utmost importance the egg be removed from that town. My sources tell me that it has taken on wider implications there. The local townsfolk are turning away from the gods and embracing heresy.'

A whole town. Cion was genuinely dismayed. The very idea gave him an acid feeling in his gut.

'Yes,' Achios continued, 'you must deal with it as you see fit. Commander Fodukiz is already there with three battalions of Brengarmah, so liaise with him on your arrival.' Cion felt some small satisfaction about this; he knew Fodukiz of old, and that he was a nasty little man easily manipulated through his vanity.

'How is my niece?' Achios asked, unexpectedly.

'Very well, sir.' Cion fought desperately to disguise any emotion. As far as he knew Achios was unaware of his affair with Kilmer, and for the moment he wanted to keep it that way.

If he had sensed anything, Achios did not react to it. 'Keep her safely with you when you arrive. She is not to join any fighting.'

Cion frowned, 'But why, sir? She is keen to join her battalion.' He had been looking forward to ridding himself of Asoori.

'My decision is no business of yours, Cion Gezezi. You may go now.' Achios looked irritated and Cion belatedly wondered if he had been unable to conceal his true feelings about Asoori. He backed away with a bow, allowing his senses to retract smoothly from the vision of Achios and the arbour.

'Cion.' Achios had spoken again, keeping him suspended in the Abax dreamstate.

'Yes, sir?' Cion looked up, just as Achios opened his hand as if to release *Darhg*. But it was not *Darhg*. Instead, something mottled brown and sinuous snaked through the air towards him, covering the distance in a heartbeat. Its face filled his vision, a reptilian nightmare, its eyes lurid yellow and black, its gaping maw displaying rows of tiny lethal fangs dripping ichor. It hissed and spat into Cion's face, throwing open a fan of neck-spines. The sound it made was a wailing, gaseous hiss.

'Never lie to me again!' Achios's cold voice filled his mind.

The thing reared up in a hellish imitation of a cobra, and he backed away, frantically seeking to break the link between the planes of reality, screaming, 'No, no, no,' as he scrabbled to remove his mask with numb fingers.

As his consciousness came back to the warm confines of the tent, hearing again the now reassuring shrill of the sandstorm, Cion was fighting for control as he stared down at the golden mask. After a few moments he became aware of someone's gaze and turned to see Merric sitting up amongst the nest of his blankets staring across the tent with an expression of alarm echoing Cion's own.

How much had he seen?

Cion's embarrassment manifested itself as anger: 'What are you staring at, boy?'

'Nothing, sir.'

'Get me something to drink. Now!' Cion snarled. In an irrational surge of emotion he picked up the nearest thing to hand and hurled it at Merric. It was a ceramic drinking bowl, which glanced off the boy's cheek. Perhaps it was simply because Merric had only just woken, and his brain had no time to catch up with the situation, that he yelled back in outrage, his voice a plaintive chord against the keening backdrop of the storm.

'Why the *hell* did you do that?'

Asoori woke up and immediately shook Kilmer into wakefulness, sensing trouble.

Cion was reaching over to put the mask back into its box, but he froze in mid-step. So *alien* was the idea that a servant might talk back to him – never mind raise his voice – that he was almost unable to believe his ears. 'What did you say?' he gasped, turning to look at Merric over his shoulder.

Merric flinched, realization of his misdemeanour seizing him though his ire was roused. His features now drained of all colour, his hand held to the stinging graze on his cheek. 'But why . . .?' he began.

There was had no chance to finish his accusation, however, because Cion was already upon him.

The Bakkujasi grabbed the youth by the neck and shook him hard enough to rattle his teeth, screaming blasphemous obscenities that no priest should rightly know. Just as Merric seemed about to black out, Cion flung him to the floor, and then began to kick him in the stomach.

Asoori screamed at the Bakkujasi to stop, then made an ill-advised lunge towards him. Cion jabbed her away with an elbow to the ribs, which sent her reeling backwards across the tent. During this tiny second of distraction, Merric hauled himself onto his back, and found he could not breathe as Cion pinned him down with a knee on his chest. Despite the silver point of a dagger now held in front of the boy's nose, far more frightening was the animalistic fury in Gezezi's blue eyes.

'I should kill you, you little . . .'

Merric tried to say he was sorry, but could not inhale so his lips moved soundlessly. Black flecks began to swim across his vision.

'That's *enough*, Cion.'

The Bakkujasi was pulled away from the boy with some force and Merric folded his legs up in a spasm of coughing. He opened his eyes again, to witness Gezezi holding a threatening dagger out towards the Earl of Cantroji. This unthinkable scene appeared to be frozen in time, as a howling wind buffeted the tent with renewed energy, as if in elemental outrage.

Kilmer regarded the Bakkujasi calmly, and when he spoke, his voice was flat and emotionless.

'Cion?' he murmured.

It was Gezezi's turn to have been duped by circumstance – his actions had been dictated by instinct. As a Bakkujasi he should have remained master of his emotions. In the blink of an eye he had shamed himself; his honour was now hanging by the most gossamer of threads. And now it seemed, all reason had deserted him. He twitched the tip of his dagger at Kilmer, grinning dangerously.

'Come on, Cion,' Kilmer began.

There was no way of knowing how this stand-off might have ended, for in that moment, with a loud crash, the main tent support finally succumbed to the sandstorm. As the lantern shattered just behind them, their world became a stinging fury of flame and confusion.

❧CHAPTER NINE❧

I KNOW WHAT *you're thinking. You think it was me, don't you? That I sent the cursed star? Well, it wasn't me – it was Herrukal. The star was intended to teach the mortal world a lesson in humility because the Abax – that magical organism which feeds his precious vanity with belief – was failing. Something was wrong with it, and less and less belief was sustaining Herrukal. Ultimately if this degeneration persisted, it would affect us all, but Herrukal sensed its unease first, initially blaming the problems on growing heresy on the world of Myr.*

Personally, I think he overreacted, but then his ire has always been swift and deadly. Elias was one of the first victims of his fury and came to be standing in front of me, his trembling contrition unmanning him. Look, I'll show you as I did before, but do not blame me if the sights of my realm burn themselves into your feeble mind . . .

IT'S DARK IN here, as seems right. High, high above, at the level where the sky should be – thousands of creatures are flying, with leathern wings snapping as they swoop and dive. The details of those creatures are mercifully indistinct, but they are too large to be mere birds and their scabrous flight is an obscene parody of their brighter avian rivals.

Black cliffs rise upwards in a rough-hewn natural amphitheatre, with innumerable hollows and passageways cut into its tiered sides like the burrows of some vast worm. From within these recesses emerge disembodied sounds; sudden sharp screams or – somehow more frightening – visceral moans. Other inexplicable noises too: a slow, inexorable drumbeat, an insect, either a cricket or a cockchafer . . . This is were the damned go when Rann has judged them worthless, damned for all eternity perhaps, or until their souls just fade into shattered nothingness . . .

The man standing in the centre of the amphitheatre does not know what eventually happens to the souls, but fears he is about to find out. In his abject terror his bladder has failed him, and the smell of his own urine is sharp in his nostrils. He finds the strength to remain standing even though his legs are shaking uncontrollably and he cannot know that many in his position do not maintain even this small dignity but grovel on their bellies or lie hugging their knees as their minds desert them. Exploiting such weakness comes easily to the god Rann, but this man is different and his kind seldom end here; he is a Shemari priest and his name is Elias.

THE GOD APPEARS with no fanfare. Many will pass this way and never see him, but Rann is attuned to his realm and, whatever else he may be, he takes his responsibilities seriously – perhaps more so than any other god. Elias stares at the deity's shifting features; it may be a trick of the dark – Rann's eyes appear first blue then green, and provide the only splash of vibrancy in this place. It gives an irrational comfort to Elias to realize that Rann, although a god who holds the allocation of his mortal soul in the balance, does not have either the wit or the power to make himself appear more than he is.

'Is this some kind of joke?' Rann demands.

The rough question takes Elias by surprise; he had expected some degree of formality and Rann's voice sounds sharp and irritated – unexpectedly human. 'My Lord?'

'You are Shemari, are you not? Has Herrukal sent you to test me?'

Elias frowns as he tries to fathom Rann's thinking. 'No, Lord. I have sinned against Herrukal, and I must be p–punished.'

'Affecting humility will avail you nothing here, priest. It is far too late to make any amends. You say you sinned against the Creator – how so?' Rann seems vaguely interested, and this ignites a spark of hope in Elias. Perhaps he can convince the god there has been a mistake!

But Rann has heard so many explanations over the millennia. The only reason he is asking is because he is bored, not boredom on a human scale but rather an ennui which has gripped him for a hundred years – since Aria. If this priest before him has succeeded in irritating Herrukal, his impassioned plea for his soul might prove rather more diverting than average grovelling.

'I-I am very old, Lord, by mortal measure. I am also the c-creator . . .' he stumbles over that word, aware of the inherent blasphemy in it but equally aware that he is damned anyway. 'The creator of the Swarms.'

Rann looks impressed. 'What, those giant creatures that the Shemari use to bolster their petty empire? But surely that cannot be sinful. You were clever enough to dedicate their service to Oshi . . .'

'Yes, Lord. But I continued to work with them over the last fifty years. My work was kept secret so that the population would believe that the Swarms are the creation of Oshi.'

'As if *she* cares,' Rann mutters.

'A few years ago I was working on the flight of Gremeshkenn Tem when . . . when s-something happened.'

Rann arches his brows impatiently. Without comment he snaps his fingers. Elias flinches but nothing harmful happens to him. A large object appears behind the god; it is gnarled and twisted, and Elias initially thinks it is a tree until Rann steps back a pace and sits down on it. It is in fact a throne, magnificently carved into the likeness of an ebony and silver tree. Rann drums his fingers idly on a branch which forms the armrest.

'The creation of the Swarms was – is – an act of combined alchemy, magic and prayer. One day I was working on changing the *kyermah,* in order to extend the creatures' lifespan. I was praying and chanting when—'

'Is there a point to this?' Rann demands.

Elias has the distinct impression that the receptiveness of his audience is running out. 'L-l-lord,' he stammers, 'I trapped accidentally some s-spirits that Herrukal had vanished into the ether.'

Rann's expression changes instantly. He sits forward on his throne. 'You did *what?*'

'I . . .'

'How can you know that?'

Elias senses that his importance has suddenly grown – that he has bought himself precious time and all might not be lost. 'I saw them,

Lord Rann, the spirits. They were beautiful: only shapes, shimmering and changing, but those of beautiful women.'

'How many?'

'It was difficult to guess.'

'Guess!'

Elias blanches at Rann's sudden passion. 'Five – perhaps six.'

'And where did they go?'

'It all happened so quickly . . . into, into the Swarms, I think. I was surrounded by them at the time. And . . . and the spirits were so indistinct, like lights that f-flowed.'

Rann gives a smile which chills Elias to the bone. It is a contemptuous, triumphant expression. When next he speaks, his tone is almost conspiratorial. 'Why did it take Herrukal so long to react? Why punish you now?'

'I do not really know, Lord, except that strange things have begun to happen with the Swarms recently which may have brought these spirits to his attention. There have been rumours that some of the Swarms have laid eggs, even though they are, by definition, sexless beings. A bright new star was sighted only recently, and we of the Shemari have come to believe that it is a sign of Herrukal's displeasure – although for the most part we do not know why he is angry.'

Rann nods. 'You are almost correct, priest. Herrukal has sent the star. But what makes you think the Creator is displeased with you in particular?'

Elias twists at the wet folds of his blue robe. 'Because Herrukal struck me down by lightning . . .'

Rann starts to laugh, and the sound of it fills the massive space, even drowning out the screams and the moans and the drums. Never before has Rann's kingdom been filled by unadulterated laughter. Not understanding the significance of what he has just told Lord Rann, Elias imagines this laughter to be at his own stupid misfortune. And yet he recognizes a joy in the sound which surely does not belong in such a place as this. And as the god laughs, his tree-throne begins to move in sinuous sympathy, its roots and branches twisting, the silver veining on the trunk writhing and flashing through the strange dead wood until, at the tips of the branches, silver buds explode into leaves and blossom. But, brought into being as they are by Lord Rann, these cannot long survive and wilt away, before sloughing down like fragile silver rain.

Elias, at his wits' end, laughs nervously too, although his predominating fear makes the sound rusty and broken. Silently, he wishes there was nothing beyond death, just oblivion. So when Rann finally stops laughing and observes him closely, the god can see Elias's tears of despair. It does not move him. It never does.

'Do you realize what you have done, priest?'

'No, Lord.'

Rann nods beneficently. 'I should really give you what you crave. It is so little to ask.' Elias knows he has not yet asked for eternal rest, so the god must have read his thoughts. And while it might have seemed a strange thing to wish for while still alive, now it seems a treasure indeed. Dark hope flares within him as he watches the last of the silver leaves flutter to the ground. 'Sadly, however, I cannot afford to provoke Herrukal any further – nor bring your precious eggs to his attention.'

The last thing Elias sees of Rann is the god idly pointing a finger towards him. After that, there is only the blood-bright flare of eternal pain . . .

ALL RIGHT, I know I should have spared him, but then I'm not Imeris. I am Rann. Even in the midst of unaccustomed joy I had to look to my position and, as I told the doomed Elias, take care not to bring myself to Herrukal's attention (nor Imeris's as he is ever Herrukal's toady). And Elias was just one more soul in the greater scheme of things. Compassion is something rare to me and the mere fact he caused me to consider it – even though I did not then act upon it – was a remarkable thing. Perhaps it was tempered by the excitement I felt to think that the soul of Aria was still out there somewhere – either in one of the Swarm creatures or those 'miraculous' eggs they had begun to lay. Such a sublime act of creation, where none should naturally exist, was an elemental act of defiance which could only indicate the workings of the spirits of the Nulefi.

In the space of mere minutes I felt emotions again which had been lost to me for many years: excitement, yearning and fear. Fear because I knew it was possible that I could be wrong in my assumptions, and if I were, what then? How could I hope to return to the empty echo of my

kingdom and still find succour in its hollow, limitless spaces, if this frag-
ile hope was then denied me?

IT WAS SHORTLY after the meeting with Elias that I made contact with
the mind of the Shemari priest Achios for the first time – he was in a pos-
ition to know what was happening with the Swarms of Myr.

VOICES. SHE COULD hear voices, muted and low as if from a great distance, and there was some pain. While her thoughts drifted, she concentrated on the pain as if to examine it better, in the way she might have probed an aching tooth with her tongue. A dull ache gripped her skull in a vice-like hold; it centred on one side of her head where she guessed something had hit against it, hard. Down the side of her leg throbbed the sharper pulse of a different kind of injury; a burn, quite a small one, but intense enough to cause her body to brace itself against the pain. A tear escaped the corner of her eye and slid down across her cheek, stinging sharply as its salt traversed a smaller burn on her face.

'She is wakening, sir.'

There is a pause, and soft shuffling of footsteps. 'Asoori? Asoori my love . . .' Kilmer's voice. Kilmer's gentle touch, as he stroked away a stray lock of hair. '*My love*' he had called her. She wanted to weep but she couldn't remember why.

She opened her eyes. 'Kilmer?'

He took her hand and kissed it, then pressed it to the warmth of his face. His expression radiated concern, but there was something else there: anger or perhaps guilt?

'What happened?'

'The sandstorm destroyed our tent and then the lamp set fire to everything,' he paused, trying not to look at her leg, which lay above the blankets so that the air might cool the burns on it. 'The Gurzz found us in the morning and . . .'

'Miss, would you like some water?' Merric had returned from somewhere and stood by the end of her narrow sleeping platform. He looked happy to see her also, but Asoori was shocked by his appearance; his lips were cracked from dehydration and exposure, but more noticeable was the black eye whose bruising extended over most of the right side of his face. Asoori frowned as her recollection of the storm – or, more exactly, what had happened just before the destruction of their tent – came flooding back to her. She turned to Kilmer, who was still watching her reactions closely.

'Where is he?'

'Please don't upset yourself, Asoori,' Kilmer said quietly.

'Where is Gezezi?'

Merric poured water into a bowl beside her bed, studiously ignoring the awkward silence that ensued between her and Kilmer.

Kilmer sighed. 'He has apologized for his behaviour.'

She sat up sharply. 'Oh. And I'm guessing you just accepted that straight away. "Yes, Cion. No, Cion. Whatever you say, Cion . . ."' She sank back with a groan as her head throbbed in reaction to the sudden movement. She knew she had overstepped her boundaries even as the words left her mouth but, of course, it was far too late. Kilmer flushed angrily, all his solicitous concern gone.

'I think you will find that the chastising of a servant is not deemed shameful amongst the nobility. I understand, of course, that not being born into the nobility yourself might exclude you from such knowledge.'

Asoori glanced at Merric, who was still making a great show of ignoring the altercation and had begun to tidy up some blankets that had dropped off her bed. 'The man is a vicious bully and you know it,' she snapped. 'Why else would you have intervened? You saw how violent he became – he could have killed Merric. It does nothing for your honour to be his . . . friend. He lessens you, Kilmer.'

He stood up, his expression still angry, but clearly affected by her words. 'You don't know what you're talking about.' He scowled.

'Yes, I do. I know you care about people. You must know Merric's family – I bet you knew every family who put a boy forward to be my squire. I heard you gave them horses to ride during the selection parade. Do you think for one moment that Gezezi is capable of such thoughtfulness towards others?' She glanced over to Merric, now over the other side of the room, putting the blankets away, and lowered her voice. 'He doesn't deserve you, husband.'

'I will be the judge of that,' he said, stiffly.

Asoori felt suddenly weak and tearful. 'Whatever you say.'

Kilmer looked as though he wanted to say more, and fidgeted from foot to foot, pushing his fingers through his hair distractedly. 'Are you . . . are you sure you're all right, Asoori?'

She didn't reply – in truth she didn't know what to say. She only knew that she'd give anything if only he would hold her for a while – the way he had that evening in Cantroji before their wedding. And that made her despise her own weakness.

She heard him sigh and turn away, felt her heart sink, heavy with impotent anger as she thought he was probably on his way to reassure Cion that he had smoothed things over with her. 'Kilmer,' she called after him, her voice straining, 'tell Gezezi, if he touches my squire again, I will deem it a point of honour to kill him.'

As she drifted back to sleep, Asoori remembered how, just before she had antagonized him, her husband had addressed her as 'my love'. Merric had been out of earshot and there had been no one there to pretend in front of – it had been just between them.

WHEN SHE WOKE again hours later, it was to find Cion Gezezi himself standing at the end of her bed. It was after nightfall and the light of the oil lamps flickered over his unnaturally white skin, so that for the first few moments, until he actually spoke, Asoori thought perhaps she was still dreaming.

He stared at her, his expression suddenly candid and unguarded. 'I know you dislike me, Asoori, and I don't blame you. Your position seems tenuous, but even if I were not here, Kilmer would have another lover. You cannot change what he is, nor should you want to. He is a good man, is he not? At least we can agree on that much.'

She nodded curtly. 'I would rather not discuss my husband with you.'

'I understand. I simply wish to apologize for my behaviour the other evening. It was inexcusable. I hope that when you return to Gremeshkenn Tem, you will not—'

'What?' she frowned. 'We're going to Releeza. We have a mission.'

'Asoori, you have a serious burn to your leg. It is taking me much time and mental energy to block your pain.'

'You?'

'For the moment – and I am doing it for Kilmer,' he said. 'Burns can cause excruciating pain. However, I plan to move my Swarm and leave in the morning for Releeza. We are only two days' distant, and the Brengarmah are already there, outside the town. It seems likely that the local people are about to put up a fight to retain the egg . . . Such stupidity.'

'Oh yes, the egg,' she muttered. 'Their supposed miracle.' As she spoke, something jolted at the back of Asoori's consciousness.

'Perhaps.' Cion was still reluctant to decide on the status of the egg until he saw the thing with his own eyes. 'Whatever it is, it belongs in Gremeshkenn Tem.'

'When I was a child I had a friend who claimed he had seen the egg of a Swarm. He said he witnessed one of the Gremeshkenn Tem flight lay the egg.'

'Really?' Cion's curiosity was piqued. 'What happened to him?'

'I'm not sure, but he was named a heretic . . . I *think* he was sent away for correction.'

'We were too easy on such heretics then,' Cion remarked darkly. 'That is why we have come to this crisis. That's why belief in the one goddess still grows, and their power grows. For now they are simply a disorganized rabble, but if their heresy is allowed to continue, who knows what may become of us? The gods are justly angry.'

'I didn't know,' Asoori frowned.

Cion's expression grew guarded once more. 'So your friend never came back to the temple city?' he asked, in a rather obvious effort to change the course of the conversation.

'No. I was told that he died of pneumonia about six months later.' Asoori frowned. 'The correction seminaries in the far north are hard places, are they not? But he was just a boy, a skinny little thing. It doesn't seem to me that he got off so lightly.'

'He could have recanted his tale,' Gezezi shrugged.

'But he never would, and now it seems he could have been right. He died for nothing. No, he died for the truth.'

Cion looked extremely uncomfortable at this assertion. 'We do not know that yet, and you should be careful what you say.'

'I'm sorry, but he was my friend, and he had no one to speak for him.' She grew thoughtful for a moment and then suddenly smiled, remembering Snoot's devotion to her. 'I was only in the temple city for two summers, while my father was making swords there, special ones' – she nodded towards Cion's weapons – 'like those. They were commissioned for the Shemari and the Bakkujasi. I met Snoot soon after we arrived . . . I remember he had these amazing, huge, blue-grey eyes and he'd follow me everywhere. I should make sure I see this miracle, for his sake if nothing else. It is my mission to go there.' she insisted.

'But you do not owe *anything* to his memory. He is still a named heretic – and he died as such.'

'I do – I *do* owe him something.' Asoori looked suddenly listless, as her memories caught up with her with unexpected savagery. 'It was my fault, he told me his secret – only me,' she swallowed, 'and I did not keep it.'

❧CHAPTER TEN❧

A CHIOS HAD NEVER been afraid of death, had always known that
Herrukal would be waiting to reward him when he passed over.
Granted there had been a few power struggles in his youth, soon after
the Swarms first came to Myr, when he had perhaps acted less than
honourably, but then, no Shemari cleric of his generation would be
any different in that respect. And he had been planning to die anyway,
in a glorious and revered fashion – already his body had become thin
and wiry, his arms and legs as insubstantial as driftwood. For he had
been in the process of committing himself to *Imicia*, the gradual
process of living mummification, so that when his end came he would
be displayed to the faithful, even prayed to as a minor deity.

The only food he had eaten for the last two months had been pine
nuts and he had been drinking dilute lacquer which he had planned to
concentrate more strongly within the next few months, thus coating
and preserving his internal organs. It was a delicate process, aided by
many hours of meditation and prayer, and he was in constant, sometimes overwhelming pain, but he had remained resolute, focussed on
his goal, believing in his ultimate destination. Now, since his visit to
the Sky Temple, all that had changed – because he had murdered the
Oracle.

He sat alone on a freezing outcrop of rock, facing the silent lurid
immensity of the northern night sky, where the lights pulsed and
danced in weird concert. Even here in such solitude it seemed to
Achios that the whole world had changed because of his action: a
disharmony had crept into the universe. The sky lights now seemed
agitated, their pulsing movements suggestive of elemental worry. A
chilling wind blew from the north and, although it was not particularly

strong, Achios rocked back and forth slightly, as if buffeted by it, so delicate had he become. He kept reminding himself that Herrukal had shown signs of displeasure even *before* the Oracle had been killed – the star, that accursed star, having been already set in motion, on a path – or rather descent – which, all the sages of the world now agreed, put it in line for a collision with Myr. So Herrukal had already sent it for reasons of his own which Achios could not fathom, not that the intentions of a god should ever be transparent to mere, sinful mortals. It was true about the spreading heresy in the world – but then, had it not ever been a risk to contend with? He rocked some more, realizing he had lost all feeling in his limbs, and welcoming the numbness which overwrit his pain.

Now, for the first time in many years, he *was* afraid to die because he realized his one act of murder must have doomed his mortal soul. Ironic, then, that he sat here with his shortsword set before him, ready to kill himself. His thoughts had been ablaze with confusion since the incident in the Sky Temple. He had settled on only one explanation for his actions – that he had been possessed by a demon, used to further the aims of some evil entity – and he was exhausted now, with a lassitude which encompassed him so completely he could see no way forward from this point. On his return from the Sky Temple he had moved through his own life as insubstantially as a ghost, his emotions and his sanity stretched as thin as rice paper. He could wait for the end of the world that was clearly impending, but why now suffer the agonies of *Imicia* any longer?

He had become convinced of the existence of the Swarm eggs, and he had no clear idea why they might be so important. But the Hani was right, there was something significant about them. He had been dreaming of them constantly and had even set in motion their discovery and collection by Cion Gezezi, a man he knew was used to operating in the grey areas of faith – the dichotomy of truth and myth. He would not live to see the outcome of this task, but he had left a letter of instruction in his rooms addressed to Pava – the only man in the Shemari he would deem as incorruptible as he had previously believed himself to be.

As Achios picked up the sword, freezing moonlight lanced along its length of folded steel almost as if providing a pale pathway from *Jannu*, the moon, along which to lead Achios gently into the dark.

Except it would not be gentle, not for him – not now. It would

be hell, but then, that was all he deserved. Achios realized he was pre-
varicating – how long had he been sitting here anyway? Minutes or
hours? He turned the point of the blade towards his own body, his
cold, stiff arm only just able to perform the ritual movement, the first
of twelve. Somewhat belatedly it occurred to him that he would be
unable to complete the full rites as required – his frail body had
become too stiffened and debilitated by extreme cold and lack of
energy. He laughed bitterly but no sound came, unless his laughter
was echoed in the cruel biting tone of the wind.

Just as he decided to dispense with the elaborate formalities and
simply aim for his heart, Achios felt a strange change within him, and
recognized the presence of the same demon that had used him before
in the Sky Temple. Renewed warmth flooded through him and, as he
watched through eyes crusted with frozen tears, the flesh of his arms
and hands regained colour, blood surging again through the shriv-
elled, damaged veins. The damage of wasted muscle magically regen-
erated so that, even in the neutral silver of the moonlight, the flesh
attained a pinkness that Achios associated with his youthful vigour. He
could soon feel his entire body resonate with this unnatural fire.

Achios felt no joy in this transformation, however. Whatever it
was, it would not claim him again. Even as such thoughts were
formed, he stood up on strong, warm legs and stared down the mountainside to where, far in the deep distance, a tiny clutch of lights
glimmered from the building used by the monks who guarded
the pilgrims' access. All he needed to do was take one step off the
edge. Trembling, because his sudden renewal brought back with it
the natural desire of youth to survive, he stretched out his left foot –
noting how it blotted out the distant lights.

No!

The voice was the same one – that of the blasphemer, the murderer.

You cannot have me, Achios thought, sternly calm.

If you jump, I will bear you up again.

Achios stepped off the ledge and fell, plummeting like a stone. He
did not believe the demon could save him; now he would be free, he
would be judged, he would be . . . yet a sharp stab of regret seized
him, as he was carried on a screaming current of the wind. He closed
his eyes as his breath was ripped from his chest.

I told you.

Achios opened his eyes, and he was strangely unsurprised to find himself back on the outcrop where he had started. He knew he had fallen, for the skin on his body was stinging as if he were flayed and his breath was coming hard; he looked back down at the lights seeking the reassurance of mundane reality. Dying, it seemed, was not going to be easy but his sensibilities were too distracted for regret or anger.

Who are you? he thought.

As the pearlescent colours of the dawn thrilled his newly young eyes with wonder, the answer came.

Rann. I am your god.

WHEN ASOORI AWOKE once more it was still night-time. She had only a vague impression of the passage of time. It was warm in the tent and she found herself gazing aimlessly at the thick felt of its walls which the Gurzz tribesmen could dismantle and shift within the space of an hour. An insect flitted around the yellow orb of the lantern, its wings making a brittle whirring sound. Asoori rubbed at her eyes and found them still gritty from the sand; it reassured her to know that no one had tried to wash her while she was unconscious. The pain in her leg was still evident, but it was faded now. The Gurzz women had placed a compress made from the fibres of some desert plant against the wound. It felt cool and soothing, drawing out the heat from the area. Her head and neck still ached, but not as much as she remembered.

At the end of her bed platform Merric sat dozing upright amongst a pile of cushions. His chin had slumped forwards onto his chest giving a comically saggy look to his young face. She nudged him lightly with her toe. 'Merric?'

He jolted into wakefulness. 'Lady Asoori, you're awake! His lordship will be so relieved – we've been worried about you.' His delighted expression seemed to falter for a moment, as if a shadow had moved across his face.

'Merric, is there something you want to tell me?'

'No, Miss. It's just that . . . as I understand it, Lord Gezezi was talking about leaving here without you on the Swarm.'

'Yes, yes,' she muttered, 'I am aware of his wishes.' She studied the purplish bruising around Merric's eye, which served as a reminder that the Bakkujasi was an arrogant bully. 'Merric, has Cion threatened you again today or treated you badly?'

'No, Miss Asoori.'

'Good.'

'I'll go and tell his lordship you're awake now?'

'Yes, and tell him I should like us to have supper together.' Merric smiled in response and left the tent. 'Oh, and bring me some water for a wash,' she called after him.

Once she was left alone with her thoughts Asoori wondered what exactly Kilmer and Cion had argued about. She imagined Cion wanted to leave her behind, and go on to Releeza alone. He could reach the town within a day on the back of his Swarm, so why should he wait for her to recover?

It must have been Kilmer who had prevailed upon the Bakkujasi to wait, but surely Kilmer would have been glad to get her out of the way, to be taken back to Gremeshkenn Tem or even to Cantroji to be looked after by his parents. Then he could continue to Releeza with his lover, unimpeded by his duty to Asoori. She had the distinct feeling that, if she allowed herself to be sent away thus, displaying any such frailty so early on in their marriage, she could end up closeted in Falloden Sen, sitting embroidering with Kilmer's mother.

When a smiling Kilmer rushed into the tent soon after this thought, she eyed him suspiciously in response to his greeting.

'Did *you* tell Cion to wait for me?'

'Yes,' he seemed confused by her coolness. 'But we are only delayed by one night so far. Do you want to go home instead? Did I do the wrong thing?'

'Well . . . no, I just don't understand why.'

'Does it matter, Asoori? Why do you have to make everything so complicated?' His tone settled into reassuring smoothness, 'I know how important your commission is to you – this first mission is really important, isn't it?' She nodded, almost mollified. 'Well then, we don't want the Bakkujasi taking all the Brengarmah's credit, do we?' he smiled.

She studied him carefully, unable to believe her husband was effectively protecting her interests over Cion's. Then the simple truth seemed blindingly clear to her. Cion would have gone ahead on the Swarm, leaving Kilmer to travel alone with the horses and the staff. It would have only taken two or three days at the most to follow Cion but Kilmer was selfishly scheming to remain in the Bakkujasi's company for as long as possible. 'You just didn't want him out of your sight, did you? You're loving this gentleman's expedition – it's just a bloody game to you. All the secretive sneaking around is just bloody *fun*. You can try and wrap this up any way you like, but don't try and convince me of your selfless, honourable reasons. I'm not some stupid, half-wit village wench.'

'*No*.' He looked angry but seemed at a loss for something to say in his own defence. At least he had better sense than to fall back on his rank and tell her again that she had overreached her position. If he had, Asoori felt she would finally lose all respect for him.

'Just go away, please. I want to be on my own for a while.'

'What about supper?'

'I'm not hungry any more.'

When he had departed, she curled up into a ball and began to cry. She didn't know what she was crying for, possibly the knowledge that her union with the Earl of Cantroji was doomed to failure, or possibly because, as Kilmer had stalked from the room she knew she'd hurt his pride badly and he might never forgive her. It was as if they were caught in this inevitable dance, since she could not make him love her. And only now her anger allowed her to voice it, silently, to herself; she was in love with him.

RELEEZA WAS WAITING. It was a town with no defences because no one had ever coveted anything they possessed before. In fact, it only merited being called a town because of its size, for Releeza had originally been merely a loose cluster of buildings thrown up when the local silver mine had been at its most productive. It was because of this that the place had no discernible layout, no grand structures, just long, low wooden houses which looked attractive enough in their unassuming way but were no indicator of any importance bestowed on their residents.

What the inhabitants of Releeza prized most in the flat, empty reaches of their valley were trees. It was difficult to get them to grow in the thin, acid soil, and those that did – juniper and larch mainly – grew twisted and gnarled by the salt blast of the winds which blew constantly from the tidal lake to the east. So, trees had to be grown in pots of soil which was brought downstream by somewhat bemused traders. Each family nurtured its trees, for the soft sweep of the colourful branches softened the stark dilapidation of the buildings.

The town's only square – where the 'dragon's egg' was now displayed – was simply an empty space where nothing had been built by virtue of the fact that a thick layer of rock lay just below the soil. After the arrival of its celebrated occupant, it had become a place to congregate but, now that the Brengarmah were camped just across the river, the townsfolk hurried about their daily tasks, averting their gaze as if this tiny act of denial could have any effect on the might of Gremeshkenn Tem. The recent snows were still crisp and white, while smoke drifted from peat fires in a sleepy smouldering underlain by whispered fear.

Preparations had been made; primitive spiked palisades had been placed along the north side of the square where the gradual slope down to the river began. To the east, where the fishing fleet landed, the banks of the lake were too steep to allow the Brengarmah easy access, but the quays had been rendered unusable – much to the dismay of the fishermen. To the west, more solid barricades had been built between the river and the southern crags, and checkpoints had been set up allowing only minimal traffic in and out of Releeza. To some extent this was irrelevant; the nearest town was thirty leagues to the west and it was almost as insignificant as Releeza. The larger city of Nesha with its temple, Yotu Tem, was another forty leagues still further to the south-west. Some Shemari priests had arrived from there only a few days ago, and their bright blue robes could be discerned moving amongst the darker throng of the Brengarmah even from the Releeza side of the river.

The river Rel itself provided little real barrier; it was wide but shallow, so in places it could easily be forded by horses, when not in flood. The current snow melt would help swell the waters – each day the Brengarmah delayed their assault was advantageous – although no one in their encampment appeared to have reached that conclusion. Still, even if the Rel began flowing faster than normal, it might still be fordable on horseback or raft. The people of Releeza were under no illusions that the Brengarmah would come and steal away their precious egg, but for the first time in their history, they had found something worth defending. Through all the time of Releeza's existence, the precious silver from the mine had been traded too cheaply, flowing like the river out and away into the world of Myr, taken for granted by the pragmatic citizens. This though, their egg, was their very own miracle, signifying that Releeza had been touched by the divine. Whether this divine patronage was a benison of the goddess Oshi or the goddess Mauru was still being debated in each of the four taverns and in every marriage bed in town.

URIEL FELT RESTLESS and nervy although he could not readily identify the reason for this. His eyes were tired from straining to peer across the river into the gloom of the Brengarmah encampment. As far as he could tell they were not readying for an attack; in fact there was little in the way of activity. The local people had begun to speculate that the army might simply remain dug in over the winter. Perhaps that was the cause of Uriel's nervousness, the fact that his fellow townsfolk were beginning to relax somewhat. A delegation from the camp had forded the Rel a couple of days earlier, headed by some young lieutenant that Uriel had not seen before. He seemed a reasonable sort; his open expression and dirty-blonde hair gave him an unthreatening persona. Uriel had watched him closely though, noting the way his green eyes flickered back and forth across the town square as if checking for concealed defences. There were none, of course, there being no military experts in the town. All hopes had been pinned on the palisades, their archers, and the river; no one had thought that step further or could countenance the idea of their simple defences being breached. No agreement had been reached and the stalemate remained, although Uriel sensed the decision was closer this time – the Brengarmah deliberately gave the impression they could wait as long as it took for Releeza to come to its senses. A few of the other council members were now beginning to waver, at least in private. The mayor was doing what he could to unite them but he was hopelessly out of his depth; Uriel could see the man's hair turning greyer with each day that passed.

Uriel still had not built himself any shelter. He felt that such small comfort might somehow lull him into a deep sleep or at least a warm lethargy. Sometimes he himself felt as if he were being turned to stone; he would then glance at the egg and see the stubborn dullness of the pewter shell as something which found echo in himself: a dormancy, a waiting . . .

He looked over at the Brengarmah encampment, blinking the dryness from his eyes, and noticed something which made sense of their delay. Flying from the north, colours muted by the frozen moonlight, was a Bakkujasi Swarm. Even from this distance the faint thrumming of wings could be heard, and Uriel could only just discern the shape of the human rider on the fantastic creature's back. Someone else called out from where the young men stood watching by the palisades, and the sound of feet crunching through the crust of the snow filled the night-time quiet of the square.

'Look, a Bakkujasi!'

'A Swarm! A Swarm from the Temple City!'

The amazing creature appeared to land just behind the encampment, and was soon lost from view. Uriel could not tear his gaze away, and a thrill of fear coursed through him. Without thinking he reached over and touched the chilled contours of the egg as if to reassure it somehow. As he did so, something pulsed and tapped from within the shell.

❧CHAPTER ELEVEN❧

ACHIOS IS DREAMING.

He knows it's a dream, sent to torment him by Rann. Each night the war for his soul rages on and each night he refutes the god's promised comfort. But simply knowing he is dreaming is not enough to alleviate his fear . . .

He is now sitting on a hilltop looking out over a valley. He has the sense that this is a real place: it is night and in the distance the silver fragment of a river moves beneath the moonlight, its reflection clean as the blade of his sword. It is very cold here too, but Achios is not worried by the temperature because he knows that this is not true suffering, merely discomfort, and this god is a master of pain and terror.

The star is clear in the sky, brighter, more poignant than any of its paler sisters. He knows the Shemari mystics have named it Orlannoni – Shining Ghost – and tonight she appears to be falling towards Myr – who must be mother of all lost souls, even ghostly ones.

As Achios watches, though, it seems that Orlannoni is no longer alone. Other new lights appear in the heavens beside her, first one, then another and another, blinking into existence until the night is glorious with their illumination, until the lone star becomes something else, made stronger and more dazzling by their companionship. Just as this light renders his vision to uselessness, they begin to fall, crashing to the floor of the valley, sending shockwaves billowing towards Achios . . .

. . . who is walking amongst them. The bright fragments are fading, tongues of flame caress their jagged edges as if in consolation, eddies of wind whip at Achios's hair and robes. He does not understand why he is being shown this vision and, although it does not hurt him, he realizes he is afraid – but cannot articulate his fear. He stops

176

and stares into the midst of the nearest heap of rubble, feeling a strangely *crawling* radiance on his skin. There is something there in the midst of the broken fragments, something large and solid – an egg. As he watches, it begins to hatch. He can hear the cracking, splitting, not just of this egg but hundreds, possibly thousands, amongst the rest of the debris. The sound becomes all-encompassing, repeating over and over again. It stirs his blood, gets into his skin, so that he wants to shriek out for it to stop.

But before he can speak, the one nearest to him is spewing forth its content. Even as it does so, its luminescence dies, its life spent or stolen by its hideous progeny. Achios finally cries out in raw fear, because he now knows that the creature is something hailing from darkest legend.

It stands impossibly tall, illogically so to have emerged from the egg. It resembles a man in many respects – *the dreamplace is growing darker now as the stars are dying, long shadows form* – its legs wide apart, it stands as if claiming the world for its own. Behind the naked torso, huge black wings stretch out in an expansive, expressive threat. The creature's face is dark, with a covering of short, spiny feathers, and dominated by a strong hooked beak. It (*they* – Achios looks around in panic) are the epitome of pure malevolence: *tengu.*

All of a sudden he is so afraid of them he can hardly breathe; they are tainted, foul light-eaters, and there are hundreds of them. The *tengu* hold spear-like weapons or swords in their clawed grip, and the night air is filled with their fecund stench. The creature right before him opens his cruel maw and Achios sees the sinister blood-purple of his tongue – panic surges through him.

He turns to flee but fear makes his legs weak and useless. He is gasping in harsh, ragged sobs, and each breath comes hard as if through a cloying strain of feathers. He stumbles and falls.

Help me?

Laughter. It is Rann's voice. He knows it now.

No. His denial is born of panic. *These creatures are not real things. Indeed they are, Achios. They are mine to command. As are you.*

HE AWOKE, GASPING for air, and sat bolt upright in his bed. His mind was desperately trying to shake off the dream – images of those cruel, alien faces of the legions of *tengu* assailed him. He swung his feet over the side of the bed, rejoicing in the cool sensation of the flagstones, and padded across the floor, fighting to control his shaking. There was a knock at the door of his rooms.

'Master Achios . . .'

Achios realized he had been holding his breath in the same instant he released it in a sigh of relief. It was Rimmin, his acolyte.

'I am just coming, Rimmin.' Achios fought to make his voice sound authoritative. As he made his way across the room, wrapping a blanket around himself, he called out. 'What is it that can be so important at this time of night, Rimmin?'

'Sir, you asked me to tell you immediately of anything unusual occurring . . .'

Achios grimaced in the darkness as he threw open the door. He was unprepared for the sight that greeted him: Rimmin was carrying a large, apparently heavy sack over his shoulder.

'Icanti's teeth,' Achios breathed. 'What is it?' He ushered his acolyte into the chamber.

'I do not know, sir,' Rimmin replied. 'But it was handed in at the temple in Kamurka by a farmer who found it lying in his stream.' He set the object down and reverentially pulled the sacking aside. 'I cannot imagine what it might be.'

It was large, reaching to waist height on Achios, its surface was a heavy pewter colour, and Achios knew straight away that it was nothing like the *tengu* eggs in his dream. There could be no thinking this came from starstuff – it was completely dense and covered all over with scoured markings which were harsh and strangely unornamental. Achios had an impulse to crouch down and listen for sounds coming from within, but his recent dream was still with him and he dared not get too close. The beginnings of dawn light trickled through the narrow slitted window and touched on the object, bringing it to a somewhat reluctant shine.

Achios glanced at Rimmin who was staring with a horrified fascination. 'Leave it with me, Rimmin,' he said. 'I will speak with the council about it. Meanwhile you must keep silent about it.'

'What do you think is inside, sir?' Rimmin's unguarded excitement was disconcerting.

Achios sighed and contrived to look calm. 'Probably nothing – I imagine it is made from rock . . .'

Rimmin's expression became guarded. He was astute enough to know how the Shemari operated through a morass of secrets and half-truths in matters of power and advancement. 'I will tell no one, Lord Achios, sir,' he confirmed.

RIMMIN LEFT THE chamber, promising to return with breakfast. Achios was eating once more although he still found it difficult; it would take time for the lacquer to dissipate from his gut and eating would never again be pleasurable as it used to be. Once left alone, he waited, for he knew that Rann was watching. In fact he was certain the mere presence of the mysterious egg would attract him – and, sure enough, he soon felt the slight scratching sensation which denoted Rann's arrival in his mind.

Can he be trusted?

I would trust him with my life.

Your life is nothing – but your soul is mine, Achios.

My soul, then. Leave him alone.

The god said nothing in response to this, but turned their thoughts to the egg. He instructed Achios to hide it safely while he, Rann, advanced his plans further. Achios was relieved that the god appeared to have forgotten about Rimmin, so he was saddened – if not totally surprised – to learn two days later that his acolyte had been killed in an accident on his way to the Sky Temple. It was notable that he had been going there to meet with Pava.

IN THE END, Cion did set off ahead on the Swarm. It would take only one more night and day until they reached the Brengarmah encampment, so it would be a comparatively easy ride – they were leaving the fringes of the desert now, and needed to cross only the foothills of the mountain range in whose valley Releeza sheltered.

They had taken leave of their Gurzz guides early that same morning and before dusk were pitching camp early for the night. Asoori was relieved about this, as she wanted to be fresh when she reported for duty the next day. The burn on her leg was healing rapidly, thanks to the skills of the Gurzz womenfolk with their herbal poultices. It was still a constant gnawing pain, despite her best efforts, but at least no one was treating her as if she were a liability.

Tonight she was in a positive mood, mainly due to the fact that Cion had gone. For once, she and her husband were to have supper alone together, and she was looking forward to it. Kilmer had been politely distant with her since their last argument – she knew she had offended him deeply – but there had been no mistaking his pleasure when he saw her riding her horse astride that afternoon, rather than side-saddle as on the day before so as to alleviate any undue pressure on the burn. They rode for a couple of hours across the sparseness of the browning grassland until she eventually gave in to her growing discomfort and changed her position.

'Well done, wife,' he had said, smiling.

She berated herself inwardly for the swell of pride this comment brought her. Something about Kilmer's undeniable charm could always make her feel like a child in need of approval. She had resolved at that moment to try and make amends for her stupid tantrum; surely he would realize that her bitter comments had been exacerbated by the pain?

'How is the supper doing, Merric?' she asked. Merric had been left instruction on how to cook the massive game bird the Gurzz had presented to Kilmer before they left. Asoori assumed it was a turkey or something similar but, being already plucked, it was difficult to tell. 'Just fine, my Lady,' he replied cheerily. He too seemed in a lighter mood at the prospect of an evening without the Bakkujasi.

'Lady Asoori, have you seen Iro?' he asked her unexpectedly.

'Iro?'

Merric coloured slightly. 'Your rat, I mean . . .'

'Ah. No,' she frowned. Merric usually kept the rat somewhere in his vicinity, and everyone was quite accustomed to its presence by now – though Cion still seemed to view it with an inordinate contempt. Remembering the affection with which her uncle seemed to regard these creatures, she hoped Merric had not lost it. 'He was in his cage when we set out this morning.'

'Well, yes, but not this afternoon when I went to fetch him,' Merric frowned slightly pensively. 'You don't suppose Lord Cion took Iro with him, do you?'

She almost laughed, 'Don't worry, Merric. I can't imagine Cion would want to take Iro anywhere. He seemed hard pressed to even pick him up, as I remember.'

Merric nodded, pursing his lips tightly in an effort to hide his feelings on the subject of Cion.

ASOORI HEADED BACK into the tent which the Gurzz had gifted to them for the remainder of their journey. It was a much smaller, less solid affair than those they normally used themselves, but she could understand why they would not want to part with one. She wanted to dress smartly for supper, but all she really possessed was her uniform *yurik* and her travel clothes, which were already beginning to look worn despite Merric's best efforts with steam from the water kettle. She did, however, have a couple of silk scarves, which Kilmer had given her. So she tied one across her brow as a bright bandana; the other she plaited in amongst the black lustre of her hair. After that she put on her *yurik* along with her full-length navy riding skirt. On their marriage Kilmer had given her a gold necklace decorated with the phoenix crest of Cantroji. This evening she hoped Kilmer would note she was wearing his family crest.

There was no mirror in which to check the final result, but Asoori was not given to preening at the best of times. Just as she finished gently prising her injured leg into her low-heeled boots she heard Kilmer's voice somewhere outside, in an exclamation of surprise. She snatched up her longsword as she ducked out of the tent-flap, but she needn't have bothered – Kilmer's surprise was not caused by any adversary.

It was snowing heavily. She blinked, for a moment not trusting her eyes. The snowstorm had arisen as if from nowhere. It was still autumn and even in winter, snow was a rarity in the salt of the desert. Besides, it had not even been cold. The flakes were beautiful, large like feathers, drifting whiteness. Kilmer laughed, the unexpectedness of it catching him off-guard, he stood with his arms outstretched, his fingers spread wide as if to catch the gentle deluge. Flakes settled in his brown hair, rested on his cloak and jerkin, without dissolving. 'You must be joking,' he called up into the heavy blankness of the sky. 'Snow *here?*' He laughed again.

Asoori laughed too and then, mindful of their fencing practice, she swished the blade she was still holding in a pattern she had only just learned, slicing through the tumbling snow, the clean cold silver of the sword reflecting the white purity, becoming like a brand of white fire. She moved her body slowly, with what elegance she could still muster, her other hand feigning stylized blocks and pushes, her feet describing the ordained steps with precision.

'Oh, very good, Asoori.' Kilmer chuckled in delight. 'But how about against a real opponent instead.' He pulled his own blade from his saddlepack, and swished it in mocking threat.

'Come on, husband, I could take you any time,' she replied gleefully. They both knew that was true but it was not something that bothered Kilmer much; Asoori was a professional, that was all. He dived into the attack – clumsily as it happened, but Asoori let that one pass, while mentally noting she could have disarmed him within a few seconds.

They sparred for a while, throwing mock insults back and forth. Merric watched them from beside the fire with a look of bemusement. The snow continued unabated, but the fencers' swift movements kept their blood flowing fast. Asoori found herself swept up in the moment, pressing her attack until a vaguely worried expression flitted across Kilmer's face – she was just about to pull back slightly, when she skidded backwards in the snow, her injured leg failing to take her weight and buckling under her.

'Asoori!' Kilmer dropped his blade. 'Oh gods, are you all right? What was I thinking?' His face was a picture of consternation as he rushed forward to help her to her feet, only realizing as he took her hand that she was laughing at her own indignity. He smiled in relief as he pulled her towards him and held her close, rubbing the tops of her arms in an abstracted effort to warm or comfort her. She smiled, holding his gaze and returning the warmth of it. For a brief moment there was something between them that was only theirs. Asoori knew then that her apology was no longer necessary.

HE SLEPT BESIDE her that night, and held her while she drifted into sleep. In the last hour before dawn she was awakened by his kiss, warm against her neck. Ironically, there were so many reasons why making love to her husband was a bad idea. He did not speak at all but made love to her with a gentle but intense passion, careful of her injury, kissing her mouth instinctively when she drew so much as a breath to speak. To allow rationality to bear on their lovemaking would be to ruin its magic.

Afterwards, they said nothing to one another either but it was an easy, satiated silence. He fell back to sleep before her and she lay watching him, as if he were completely new to her, as the dawn came up and the first skylarks began to sing amongst the remnants of the snow.

THEY HAD NO horses so all they could do now was walk. That meant it took a long time to reach Releeza. Although Ayshena consented to carry them where she could, she could not fly openly above inhabited areas, lest she be seen. This was how she had survived by herself in the wilds for so long, as a rogue Swarm skimming only above the empty spaces of the world, shunning those bright red and yellow lights which was how she perceived the body heat and the souls of human beings.

Stief had lost count of the days, and found himself unwilling to measure the passing of time from the death of Calla, that bizarre night when the world had suddenly betrayed them. He thought often of his mother but did not speak of his sorrow, merely kept it close to his heart. As they travelled across the rocky terrain of the forest, he felt this as a physical hurt which slowed him and kept him withdrawn from the others . . .

For the first four days, Kalia had also proceeded in silence, scrambling across rocky scree, ducking beneath the canopy of pine and larch as though she had died after all, and now merely moved through some ghostly representation of the world. Her feet bled but she ignored them, her green eyes staring ahead like empty, tortured pools. Stief remembered the brittle vivacity with which she had berated poor Sevim when they first landed in the forest, before her fright claimed her overwrought mind. It seemed almost preferable now, to her silent distress. Despite her earlier rejection, Sevim stayed close to her, lending a steadying hand or helping guide her across a stream. He was clearly fretting about her condition, but there seemed to be little hope of his breaking into Kalia's defensive silence until she was ready.

Viv seemed curiously annoyed at Kalia's withdrawal, as if it were some personal rejection. But then, he could hardly complain when he himself spent every evening communing with Ayshena, who came back nightly to find them. Stief knew that Viv must also be mourning the loss of their mother, but neither of them seemed able to discuss it with each other. And so, the days went on – each of the travellers locked in their own self-indulgent misery – until the morning of the fourth day.

A rumble of distant thunder boomed from far to the west, sending a squalling flock of birds scattering above the forest canopy, their erratic flight catching the first rays of the dawn. The travellers had started early and were now climbing up a gradual slope which proved deceptively hard work – there was still a light dusting of snow here which lay in the cracks of the underlying rock. Ayshena had already gone when they woke up, but Viv had not commented on it. After the first two hours he suggested they stop for a while, and it seemed like a good idea. There had been no sign of any pursuit from Cantroji to impel them, so only Viv's zeal was pulling them forward.

They reached the crest of the ridge, and below them at last found a break in the unremitting green expanse of the trees. Here and there amongst the carpet of grass and snow, yellow flowers gladdened the eye, their wavering blooms glinting like displaced sunshine. As Sevim and Stief began to lay a fire, Kalia sat herself down on the damp grass, heedless of the cold. She had simply stopped, as if needing further commands to animate her again.

'Kalia, here, sit on this.' Viv had found a small section of tree trunk for her to sit on, and he motioned to her to stand up so he might position it comfortably for her. Viv was not given to small acts of kindness, but Kalia's vacant stumbling could not fail to move anyone to pity. She stood up and then sat down again as suggested, as biddable as a child. Viv remained crouching in front of her, his eyes searching her face keenly for any hint of expression. He took hold of her hand and squeezed it. 'Kalia,' he said gently, 'you must come back to us.' She did not react and he sighed helplessly.

'Look.' Lightly he moved his hands before her face, displaying his empty palms. Then he reached up as though to touch her ear – she did not shrink away, as he feared she might – and when he put his hand in front of her face again, he opened it to show one of the yellow blossoms. 'Magic, eh?' he smiled. Still she did not make any movement but Vivreki thought he detected something, some tiny flicker in her gaze. He wasn't sure, so he tried again, tucking the first flower behind her ear where it nestled beautifully against her flame red hair. 'Look, see, nothing. Empty hands . . .'

Sevim and Stief had now stopped what they were doing to watch. Stief was smiling widely; this was the first sign of the 'old' Viv he had seen since Ayshena appeared. For in seeking to reach through to Kalia, Viv unwittingly allowed himself to relax.

Sevim frowned. 'Is your brother magical? A mystic?'

'No,' Stief laughed. 'It's only sleight of hand. He used to d-do this in the tavern to impress the g-girls.'

'Does it work?' Sevim seemed reluctant to take his gaze away from Kalia.

'Sometimes.'

'Ta-da!' Viv produced a second flower, and put it behind Kalia's other ear. Then another one. 'Ah.' He scratched his head in mock confusion, as if at a loss where to put this new flower. As if he'd had a sudden revelation, he smiled and tucked the blossom behind his own ear – and the next he tucked behind his other ear. The sight, although meant in jest, was actually rather attractive, if not very masculine. Vivreki's blue-grey eyes danced with laughter that concealed his growing concern that Kalia might never recover. After he made the next flower appear, he went through the same exaggerated mime and then stuck the stem between his teeth. He held out his empty hands again, as if about to repeat the trick, but did his patter as though he could not speak properly because of the flower in his mouth. 'Nnnngh – nng – nnng . . .'

In the very moment he was about to give in, and just as the laughter began to fade from his expression, Viv was rewarded by a reaction. Kalia's mouth twisted slightly as if in an unnatural contortion, and she emitted a tiny, choking laugh, then reached forward to touch his face. Her pallid fingers were icy cold against his skin, but Vivreki did not flinch.

'Funny,' she murmured. As if the uttering of that single word brought her back to herself, her vision suddenly cleared and she stared at Viv as if seeing him for the first time.

'Kalia?' he said hesitantly.

She glanced about uncertainly, pulling the dark fabric of Stief's cloak tighter around her. 'It's so cold,' she said, her voice now distinct and clear. The fact that her first conscious words were also a complaint struck Viv as ironically amusing.

'Yeah,' he grinned. He turned to where Stief and Sevim were standing, transfixed by the encounter. 'We had better get that fire going.'

She came back to the world, little by little, during the remainder of the day. By the following morning Kalia seemed restored to herself – as if her withdrawal from reality had never happened. She even seemed easier with Sevim, although she did not allow him to touch her or support her as he had when she was insensate. If ever a good result became something of a double-edged blade, Kalia was it. She moaned and complained constantly: it was too cold . . . it was raining . . .

Sevim managed to trap a pheasant so they had a delicious supper of it, with mushrooms and dandelions and wild garlic, but even then she complained the meat was tough and stringy. The strange thing was, no one minded.

And, after the first couple of days, the acerbic sting seemed to go out of Kalia's comments. Perhaps her perception of her companions gradually shifted and it seemed as though she no longer railed against them but simply passed comment on things that they all must endure together. Perhaps she merely felt the constant need to bring these trials to their attention.

Much later, Viv would grow to realize that Kalia was actually the force that bound them together; she drew them all from their introspection and opened the way to their communication. One evening she even spent time talking at length to the previously despised Sevim. It was the night before Ayshena flew them across the Gurz'taal desert and they camped by the quiet shore of the lake at Honashu.

LOOKING OUT OVER the water, Sevim could see why the people of the region revered the lake. It was a full moon tonight, and it hung above them as though it was some great paper lantern, silver and bloated like a child's drawing of a moon. Its unreal reflection shone across the lake, shimmering from darkness to light with the ripples of the water. Of course, now the moon had constant competition from the troublesome star, whose light was becoming ever more yellow as if it strove to out-glamour its larger cousin, by flashing and flickering the filigree light of its tail. It could never succeed – the moon would ever be more sedately beautiful.

'Sevim, do you mind if I join you?' He turned to see Kalia standing nearby. The brightness of the moon accentuated the red of her hair, and the sharp green of her eyes. She was gnawing her bottom lip as she seemed to do when she was unsure.

Sevim felt his palms start to sweat. 'Of course, Kalia.' He moved along the shore a little way, hardly able to believe that she might follow him and, when she did, he sat himself down on a fallen tree trunk. She sat beside him, close enough for him to feel the faint heat of her body.

'I'm sorry,' she said.

'Why? What for?'

'Stief told me what I said to you just before I . . . well, I should never have said those things. I owe you an apology – and my thanks. You saved my life.'

He shrugged, faintly embarrassed. Although her words pleased him, he realized she was merely setting things right. 'I – I couldn't have done it without Spall,' he announced as if to deflect her good opinion.

'Spall? I only vaguely remember him. That day is all a bit hazy to me. I understand he is like . . .' she cast around for the words, 'like a part of you. Another part of your personality?'

'In a way,' Sevim replied guardedly, 'but it's not that simple. I have to bring him forth when my services are commanded. It is my duty – and his.'

'What would happen if you refused?' Her gaze remained fixed on his face, watching him closely, her curiosity piqued.

Sevim shifted uncomfortably. He did not like talking about Spall and the mysteries of their duality; it seemed disloyal somehow. 'I . . . I don't really know. I think Spall would then leave and I would be alone.'

'But that would be good . . . wouldn't it?'

'No, I do not think so,' he said stiffly.

'I'm sorry, Sevim. I didn't mean to offend you.' She gazed out over the lake and a slightly uncomfortable silence bloomed between them, which Kalia felt she had to fill. 'He's not your only friend any more, Sevim Salasho.' She tried to pat his hand reassuringly but he noted the way she pulled back at the last moment, merely brushing it with her fingertips instead.

It seemed a spark of energy surged through him. 'What did you call me?' The sound of the water seemed suddenly loud, disturbing the precious softness of her voice. She looked concerned. 'That's your name, is it not? Sevim Salasho?'

He nodded again. 'No one has ever spoken my name since . . . since the night I was cast out. I had . . . forgotten it.'

'How could you forget your own name?' she asked incredulously.

'You would be surprised how easy it is, when there is no one else to speak it.' He smiled slightly at the shock which had registered on her moonlit face. 'Also, when I take other people's sin, it makes my own self somewhat . . .' he struggled to express himself, 'fuzzy,' he ended lamely.

Another silence – but this time, subtly, more easy. Both of them stared at the water, listening to the high mourning call of the loons. 'Did you know,' Kalia said, 'that this is a haunted place? The local people sometimes just walk into the lake to drown themselves.' She gestured towards the water.

'Yes, they call it *karresatu*: the end of spirit.'

'My father would have nothing but scorn for such an action.' She stiffened slightly as she remembered Sevim's personal experience of her father. Actually, he didn't mind what she said; the fact that she was having this conversation with him, apparently at ease in his company, was a joy.

'Indeed,' he smiled darkly, 'but he will never know their courage, Kalia. It is their own choice to take their leave and we should respect it.'

'Yes.' She was looking at him intensely, but Sevim found he did not mind that. He turned towards her, brushing his hair absently away from his face. 'I *do* understand Sevim. Perhaps in time you might real-ize that I am rather like the lake, there.'

'Pardon?'

She smiled – a thing of rare beauty on a face still ravaged by recent horror. 'Not quite as shallow as I appear.'

BEFORE DAWN THE next day, Ayshena flew them swiftly most of the way across the Gurz'taal desert, veering to the south-west in order to avoid the opening of the river valley in which Releeza was situated. They camped the last night of the journey by the Rel itself – thirty leagues upstream from where the Brengarmah were now preparing for battle – and had a bland but sustaining supper of eel and yam stew. Although their mood was light to begin with, they had no idea what awaited them at Releeza until Ayshena returned.

She had been loath to fly too close to the town, and so could only make out the shapes and colours of masses of people – but she had gleaned enough to know that some kind of conflict was imminent. Viv recounted these rough details to the others, while Ayshena sat silently in the background. 'You don't have to come with me,' he pointed out. 'I'm grateful for your companionship on the journey but I cannot ask you to risk everything.'

'Why not, Vivreki? That's what you risked for us. Everything,' It was Kalia who spoke and Sevim nodded his agreement.

'Thank you.' Viv made a weak smile which did not reach his eyes. It was clear he was really worried about the dangers of Releeza.

'Do you have any plan, Viv?' Sevim asked.

'No, well, not exactly. Ayshena is going to wait for me behind the town, but we'll have to go there tonight while it's dark. Then we'll have to enter the town and assess it from there. We don't know how well the egg is being guarded but I'm hoping we can take it while the town is under attack. It's a pretty big diversion.' He shrugged. 'Sevim, I wondered if you might be able to go in as Spall?' Although they had all now become used to Sevim's presence, it was obvious that he would still be very notable in a crowd. Whilst Spall was just as remarkable in his way, he would be more easily disguised.

Sevim did not seem to take offence, but nodded slowly, considering the practicalities of Viv's request. 'I will try,' was all he said. Kalia looked concerned, but she said nothing.

'When are you planning to s-set off?' Stief asked.

'As soon as we're ready.' Vivreki's expression was tight with anxiety. 'It seems the Brengarmah are now readying their attack, and there is at least one Bakkujasi Swarm in their camp.'

'Well,' Kalia remarked, 'I just hope we can steal some extra clothing in all the confusion. I'm sick and tired of feeling cold.'

❧CHAPTER TWELVE❧

'HOLD OUT YOUR *hand. Go on, I want to give you something. What, don't you trust me? Look, this is all it is.' Rann opens his hand and something bright, a tiny bright ball, floats gently to just above the level of his palm, spinning gently like a tiny world.*

'What do you think this is? Very good, it is a representation of a soul, a being which once enjoyed the gift of life on the world of Myr. If you observe it closely, you will see that within the nebulous outer layer is a hard opaque core. That is the fundamental essence of a being's soul – what makes them good or evil, if you will. Most beings do strive for good-ness, within the constraints of their understanding of such a term – thus an executioner may still believe himself to be a good man, while a priest may secretly consider himself deeply flawed, even wicked and perverse. Many do not even bother to strive – few embrace what they are knowingly.

'Why am I showing you this?' Rann crushes the soul between thumb and forefinger, and the light goes out with a tiny breaking sound. 'It's because I'm trying to explain about Achios. I started all wrongly with the Shemari, believing him to be of only average aspirations. I tried to impress him with my power, I tried to frighten him into submission, to browbeat him as I could those of lesser intelligence. And, much as it pains me to admit it to myself, I was wrong. For Achios was astute enough to realize that despite my wilful blustering, I needed something from him. And so he simply waited, with the tenacity of a fox, even though in deep fear over the fate of his own soul. He kept the egg, as I instructed him, but I could sense he was not committed to following my plans. I also read in his overwrought mind that he was considering confiding in his friend Pava.

'So I had a closer look at the structure of his soul, and can you guess

190

what I found in there? To my delight I learned that my new lackey possessed a deep propensity for evil – but only in selfish pursuit of his own ego. That ego was a fragile thing, shored up by decades of prayer and meditation, but still weak. This gave our friend a certain cunning, which I sensed I might exploit. And once I realized this, I knew I could win him over completely with the one thing which he did not even know he craved: power.

'After that, I could just sit back and relax.'

ACHIOS WAS IN his garden. He had found that sometimes, observing the flowers and the myriad insects, his mind achieved a welcome state of calm. He clipped and pruned away meticulously at specimen yews and cedars which already looked near perfect. In the past this taming of nature, removing every audacious bud and leaf which did not fit with his grand plan, had pleased him – but now he was less sure. It seemed a hollow, arrogant activity, and he wondered how he had ever fooled himself into thinking that it was a salutary exercise in discipline. Lately he had developed instead the urge to wander through the wild meadows on the lower mountain slopes. Having removed his sandals first, he wanted to revel in the glory of untainted nature, though his pragmatic mind insisted on reminding him of the discomforts of thistles, insects and sharp stones. He knew such notions were part of what the god had done to him, part of being younger and stronger; his sap was rising in just the same way as for any tree so he would be surrounded by life – by living energy – whenever he could.

He stared in dismay at one of his previously beloved miniature trees. Twenty five years earlier he had been given it as a sapling, by Pava. Now it was no taller, only wizened and twisted as he too had been.

On a sudden impulse he pulled the plant from its pot and tore away the soil from around its roots. There in the centre of the clump, like a white, defiant worm, was the new growth of the tap root. Up till now, each year he would repeat the process of trimming the root, which would keep his tree small and delicate, a masterwork of craft. This year, however, he would not, could not do it. This year he would . . . The thought trailed away from him as the first soft splish of rain whispered across the terraced garden. What could he do? The tree was bound – it did not know how to grow any longer. It would simply die, as was only right and natural; a thought which gave him a sharp pang of envy.

He continued to stand there in the rain as it grew heavier, aerial waves of raindrops surging out across the mountainside in a mocking, elemental freedom. As the soaking robe began to cling to his rejuvenated flesh, he dropped the tree onto the nearby grass where the rain whittled away the remaining soil from its roots. Staring at it with emotional blankness he thought that he might watch the death of the tree over the next few days, or weeks, to remind himself what he had lost.

The sound of the door to his room opening played at the periphery of his awareness. He ignored it for a moment, as the strong feeling of moving through a wakened dream state kept him from rousing any interest, but then followed the sound of footsteps running out onto the terrace. Undue haste was not something either the Shemari or the monks of Gremeshkenn Tem were given to or would encourage in others.

He turned in the direction of the sound and was surprised to see Pava standing there, looking agitated and vaguely frightened. Pava had brought with him one of his white eagles from the Sky Temple and he had just perched the creature on the railing, where it sat hunched moodily, ruffling its feathers against the rain.

Pava was staring at Achios in puzzlement – his desire to remark on the dishevelled state of his friend obviously vying with whatever news he was bursting to tell. Years of training won out and he expressed his concern first.

'My friend, what are you doing out in the rain? You will surely catch a fever.' Pava himself still stood beneath the bowed eves of the terrace. Achios glanced down at his own appearance with some degree of humour; his sodden robes clung to his skin and soil from the uprooted tree had left a muddy stain down his front. He looked like a little boy again, who had been playing in the mud, and he understood that Pava might think his behaviour strange.

'What is it, Pava? Is something wrong?'

Pava hesitated for a moment. 'Come in out of the storm and I will tell you.'

Achios smiled. 'When did you last embrace the elements, my friend? The rain is soft and cleansing, and yet its strength shapes the landscapes of our world. No, come on out.'

Pava did not look too amused at this suggestion but as Achios seemed intent on remaining out in the downpour he stepped into the garden, his thin blue robe darkening as it absorbed the rain. 'Achios, I bring grave news, the Hani is dead.'

Achios was not expecting such devastating news, and at the same instant Pava finished speaking every bell in the twenty temples which formed Gremeshkenn Tem started to peal, plunging the whole city complex into official mourning. The Hani, 'Worshipful Leader', Herrukal's emissary on Myr, was still a relatively young man at sixty-four. Achios had seen him conducting prayers only a few days earlier and he looked to be the only Shemari in Gremeshkenn Tem whose state of rude health might rival his own. He frowned, 'Do we suspect foul play?'

Pava looked decidedly uncomfortable at Achios's frank suggestion, but he shook his head. 'No, it was his heart that failed, most unexpected – the healers suspect it was the strain of the whole Orlannoni situation. He glanced skywards as he spoke.

Achios sighed, 'That has been a strain to us all, my friend. If the church does not declare its position to Herrukal's displeasure, all the people of Myr will despair. They look to us for guidance.'

'Indeed. But we must now attend the Sky Temple promptly. I believe the Hani left instructions with regard to his successor.'

'Really?' Achios paused. He was loath to revisit the Sky Temple since the death of the Oracle, but he realized his presence would be expected and absence more likely to raise questions. 'That is most unusual,' he murmured. Normally the Council chose the new Hani, in a process which took days, sometimes weeks of debate. Achios and Pava were both members of the Council and had been so when the newly deceased Hani was inaugurated only four years earlier.

Pava nodded. 'But necessary and practical. In the current climate of uncertainty we cannot be left without leadership.' He turned to walk back under the shelter of the eves, so wet now that Achios could see through the fabric of his robe. As he reached out to lift his eagle from the post, the bird ruffled its massive wings to shake off the rain, and cawed as if in annoyance at his keeper. Achios shuddered at the unexpected sight of the creature's tumescent purple tongue, his dreams of *tengu* surging into his consciousness once more, anxiety gripping him.

As he headed slowly back through the sodden garden, Rann's

voice came to him, an unwelcome intruder as always. *Well, Achios, call it my gift to you in anticipation of your loyalty.*

'*What?*' He stopped, as the implication of Rann's gloating words hit home. Achios was unable to keep the thought to himself, and spoke his incredulity out loud. 'You killed him? The Hani?'

Possibly. Maybe I just helped his ailing heart to find rest . . .

This was so typical of the capricious, irresponsible god that Achios whispered, 'Does it not worry you that Herrukal will avenge his emissary?'

Rann chuckled nastily. *He will not stir himself – not yet.*

ASOORI WALKED BRISKLY along the bank of the river, appraising the fortifications across the other side of the Rel. Considering their lack of experience in such matters the townspeople had done pretty well, she thought. She could make out the plinth where the egg was displayed, although the precious object itself was difficult to discern in the gloom of the early evening. There was something like a sail from one of the fishing boats covering the top of the structure so it was in rather more shadow now. Apparently this was only a recent development since they had spotted Cion arriving on his Swarm the day before.

Her mood soured at the thought of the Bakkujasi. She had only seen Cion briefly since arriving at the Brengarmah encampment. He had glared at her as if ice-water ran through his veins and she wondered if he somehow knew about her tryst with Kilmer in the desert.

She had an ache between her ribs: a dull, sickening ache which she could not find a name for. But deep inside her mind, somewhere where she was truly honest with herself, she knew what this was: a physical manifestation of her hurt. Denial was still sweet enough to hold onto, so long as the memory of their night together remained strong, the sense-memory of his arms around her, his breath warm against her skin. She knew that when she turned to embrace her anger, as was inevitable, all this feeling would be lost, and she would grieve for it.

He had not spoken to her this morning, but was already gone from their tent when she awoke. She emerged to find him sitting at the fire with Merric, tightly wrapped in a swathe of blankets although the morning was not that cold. It seemed as if he wanted to hide his body from anyone's gaze, as if he were ashamed by the weakness of the flesh which had overcome him the previous night.

'Good morning,' she said.

His smile was merely a tight contraction of his features and he did not meet her gaze. 'Good morning, Asoori,' he said. That was it. In the cold silence of their ensuing journey, she had tortured herself by imagining him enveloping her in the blankets and leading her over to the fire. He did no such thing, of course, and while Asoori returned Cion's glare when she reported to him she could not understand how he managed to conceal any look of triumph.

'CION TELLS ME the Brengarmah will attack before dawn, thus catching them with their guard down.' Recognizing her husband's voice straight away, Asoori did not need to turn around. She heard his footsteps crunching through the brittle snow towards her. 'Can you not even bear to look at me, wife?' There was no accusation in his tone, only a slight sadness or puzzlement.

'What do you care?'

He sighed. 'I thought it was what – what you wanted.'

'Really.'

'I behaved rather badly this morning, Asoori. I am sorry. I was just . . . I've ruined everything, haven't I?'

'What was there to ruin?' she replied bitterly. He had moved to stand beside her now, but still she did not look at him and continued gazing out over the river. She realized that if she turned there was a danger she might be overcome, although she wasn't sure if it would be by fury or tears – of course she would rather it was the former, she was not given to easy tears – but it could go either way.

'I had rather hoped our friendship would continue throughout our marriage. It is all rather too soon to be unable to stand the sight of one another.' Another sigh. 'We would be like my parents.'

She did turn towards him then, and was unable to deny to herself that she was still gladdened by the sight of him. There was not much light yet, just the soft blue reflection off the snow and the distant orange glow of a hundred torches. Kilmer held her gaze with candour, his green eyes searching her face for some sign of hope that bitterness would not divide them so soon. He did not look likely to grovel for any crumb of forgiveness and she was mutely glad of that. They stared at one another for a long moment, both unsure where to go from here, and if they could salvage their pride. Fortunately, neither of them had to make the next move, for Cion was striding across the snows towards them with an almost unseemly speed – even before they turned to face him it was clear he was unusually excited.

'There is news from Gremeshkenn Tem. The Hani is dead!'

'How do you know?' She frowned.

'We must conduct a ceremony here in the temple, after we have routed the heretics,' he said.

Asoori was surprised that Cion appeared so ready to assume a victory – the people of Releeza seemed easily dismissible to the Bakkujasi. Although she would pray to Oshi for victory before she slept for a couple of hours tonight, she would offer no disrespect to her foes. It seemed almost an irrelevance to her at this juncture who might be the new Hani. It came as something of a shock to her when Cion added, 'The new Hani is to be your uncle.'

'What?' she stammered.

'Your uncle Achios has been selected as the new Hani.'

'You're joking.' She knew he wasn't; it was a reflex response. Beside her, Kilmer let out a gasp of surprise. It was likely that he realized immediately the social impact of this news. As the only living relative of the new Hani, Asoori would henceforth enjoy a new status that would propel her into the highest echelons of society. 'That changes nothing as far as I'm concerned,' she said.

'Oh, but it does, Asoori,' Cion replied without a flicker of humour. 'It secures your marriage and makes it probable that the Cantroji estates will end up belonging to the church – if you do not have any heirs of course. It also means there is no chance now that we can afford to risk your life in battle.' He knew what a disappointment this was to her, and finally, a tiny spasm of expression crossed his face which may have been pleasure in her misfortune.

IT WAS MADNESS. Sheer madness.

Asoori stood silently in the shadow of the buildings, the taste of bile spiking in her throat. Finding a way across the river to the Releeza side had proved relatively simple for one person; she had crossed further upstream using a small punt she had found amongst the reeds. Then, she had sneaked back towards the square – the old buildings which edged the eastern side were packed tightly together, but she had found a narrow passageway between two of them. It was a tight squeeze, and she had snagged her cloths on various nails and splinters of wood as she passed. At the end of the vennel, the gap onto the square had been closed off in a perfunctory fashion with large beams and driftwood. It was still possible that one person might break through – but such a tiny gap would be easily defended and was the least of the Releezan's problems. But Asoori intended only to watch, at least until such time as the Brengarmah stormed the town, then she would participate whether her superiors wanted her to or not.

She had never witnessed a battle before and, although she had known in every rational sense that it would be a horrible experience, nothing had prepared her for the furore, the hellish chaos, sounds and colours which would haunt her for many months. The scene before her was so unlike the grace and discipline which she taught her students that she realized, with a stab of remorse, that she had done little to prepare them for the reality should they too come to this.

The Brengarmah had finally made their first move two hours before daybreak. The front areas of their encampment, easily seen from the other side of the river, had been kept deliberately still and quiet to avoid alerting the townsfolk. When the battalion was ready to ford the river, they moved silently, the metal of their bridles and weapons muffled lest their sound alert the sleeping population too soon. Fodukiz's plan was to get as many of his men over the ford area as quickly as possible, and then fan out along the entire length of the palisades. It was a risky manoeuvre as there would undoubtedly be a bottleneck; the ford was so narrow that only four or five horses could cross abreast at one time. There had been sentries on watch from the other shore, of course, but Brengarmah concealed earlier in the night, exactly where Asoori now hid, had dispensed with them swiftly at a given signal. If Releeza was alerted too soon, those still fording the river would be vulnerable, easily picked off by archers.

For the first twenty minutes it had gone well; almost a hundred men had crossed the ford with no losses either to the freezing water or their opponents. Their silent progress might have continued undetected for some time, but for the strange man who remained seated beside the plinth at all hours. The man was named Uriel and was almost certainly insane. Fortunately, even the insane slept – unfortunately, they slept fitfully. Asoori, who had concealed herself in her present hiding place at nightfall, was close enough to see him clearly.

As Uriel reacted to what he saw happening at the ford, there was no sound at first, only the ceaseless murmur of the river, but his alarm was plain to see. He whirled back towards the treasured egg as if about to fling his arms around it in mute protection. Turning back to the river he tugged at his hair, panic evident in the gesture, looking left and right in puzzlement towards where the sentries had been stationed. For a long, breathless moment the man seemed torn by silent indecision, but then he began to shout out a warning which could not fail to bring people running. The mixture of a scream and a shout he uttered seemed an entirely appropriate presage to the death and carnage that would follow it. If the strange sound could have had a colour, it would have been bloody red. Thereafter, as the first moments of battle unfolded, as alarm bells were struck and shouts rang out from both sides, Asoori could not have said if, or when, the sound ended.

But the people of Releeza were not so unprepared as they might first have appeared. Those responding to the alarm were already fully dressed for action; furthermore she could count at least thirty archers amongst them. Once his warning was acted upon, Uriel hastily uncovered a large barrel off to the side of the plinth, and soon Asoori could smell the sweet aroma of tar. The archers dipped their arrows into it and set them aflame before firing them into the midst of the enemy. Within minutes the night sky was ablaze with missiles, their light-tails flaring behind them, arcing across the space with deadly purpose, causing chaos in the ranks of the Brengarmah. Although carrying shields, many of the riders were too slow to raise them amongst the crush of the horses – and those who so did only ricocheted the blazing arrows onto their fellows. Small fires broke out everywhere despite the slushy ground. Meanwhile, Asoori could see Fodukiz berating his men from the shoreline, as many grimly continued in their purpose of tying ropes to the wooden palisades in order to pull them down.

Should have dug them in, she thought. It was in the details that war was fought, she knew that. She had been telling her students something right at least . . . The spiked barrier posts were mounted on flat bases which were in turn secured to the ground with long wooden pegs. Fodukiz had rightly guessed that these supports did not go deep enough into the wet earth. Soon after the ropes were attached to it, one of the barriers was heaved aside. Releeza defenders swarmed into the breach, armed with swords or whatever other weapons they had been able to find. This point was where most of the carnage was now happening. The townsfolk were a mob not an army, but their indignant fury served them well. Horses screamed and reared in terror as their Brengarmah riders were torn from their saddles, to be hacked and trampled into wet, bloody tatters.

Once the defences had been breached, though, it was only a matter of time. Sheer weight of numbers and the Brengarmah's highly trained discipline would prevail. Asoori's gaze drifted back towards the platform where Uriel stood – the archers were still firing to the left and right of him. But something else was now happening there, something Uriel had not yet noticed. A black-clad figure was standing behind the egg itself and had begun to rock the object out from its base.

Had Cion sent him? she wondered.

Whoever it might be would have only seconds before he was noticed. The egg was too large to be simply spirited away unremarked.

Even as she thought this, Uriel turned round and caught sight of the thief.

ALL HE CAN think about now is the egg. Ever since Ayshena came into his life he has shared her desire to protect the unborn Swarms: a desire so strong that he often feels consumed by it. Occasionally he worries that Ayshena may have done something to him, something physical – planted a splinter of chitin inside his heart whilst he slept, making him merely a human extension of her Swarm.

As he runs through the back streets of Releeza, his senses are alive with the heightened awareness Ayshena confers on him; the scent of the earth beneath the snow and the ancient wood of the buildings sing a bright song. The city is aflame with the shimmering of souls, against which the normal dark of the sky becomes a muffled black. The souls mass at the river like moths to a lantern, and in their midst is the beating, pulsing gold of the other Swarm. He senses Ayshena's excitement; indeed it courses through his body in fervid red flame. He senses the location of the egg – even though he has never set foot in the town before he knows where it is, he feels it. His eyes are glowing once more, but this time he embraces the strange sensation as if it is a bright benison received from his protector and friend . . .

'VIV, SLOW DOWN. I want to look in here. I think it's a washhouse.' He had thought Kalia was joking about getting warmer clothes; after all, he currently had far greater worries on his mind. But as soon as Ayshena landed and they ran off into the alleys of Releeza, Kalia began peering into the darkened back yards and outside spaces of the houses.

'We haven't got time for this,' he hissed desperately, as she pushed past him.

'Viv, it might be worthwhile,' Sevim said. 'We do need to disguise ourselves somewhat.'

'It's a waste of time,' Viv insisted. He glanced at Stief, expecting his brother's support, but Stief merely gave him a shrug in wordless apology. 'It could help, V-viv. Wait here if you d-don't want to come.'

'But I have to . . .'

'We'll be quick.' With that, Stief sidled through a gap in the wooden fence, which Sevim was holding open for him. Viv paced up and down the alley impatiently awaiting the results of their foray. He could hear the sweet, pure sound of Quirzel song coming from the yard opposite, and it stilled his agitation for a few moments. That sound reminded him so much of the day he and Stief had gone trapping, before his whole world had been turned upside-down, that it was almost unbearably poignant.

He stepped across the alleyway and parted the thin screen of bushes to peer into the yard from which the sound originated. A long aviary took up most of the available space and, although fairly basic in its construction, it had an air of permanence about it. A lantern burned inside which, at first, he assumed would be to deter weasels and rats, but then he noted the small figure curled up in a quilt on the floor. There wasn't much to be seen of the young boy, just a shock of black hair emerging from the top of his cocoon-like cover. Probably his family were in the town shelter, but he had sneaked back to watch over his Quirzel.

Just then, the sleeping figure moved, and a small hand squirmed its way out of the quilt to pull the layers away from his face. Coal-black eyes snapped open, and the boy was looking straight over at Viv.

Fearing the boy might think he was a spirit or demon of some kind, Vivreki smiled at him encouragingly and touched a finger to his lips in a shushing gesture. The boy stared unblinkingly at the strange apparition. Finally he asked, in a querulous voice, 'Are you Brengarmah?'

'No,' Viv replied quietly. 'You can go back to sleep.'

The boy continued to fix Viv with his persistent gaze. 'Don't touch my birds.'

'No, of course not,' Viv agreed hastily. 'Did you breed them yourself?' The boy nodded in response, pushing his nose into a warm edge of the quilt. 'So you can sell them?' Another nod.

'Viv?' Kalia's urgent whisper distracted him. 'Viv, come over here.' He smiled again at the boy, who this time gave him a hesitant smile in return.

'What is your name?'

'Masu.'

'Goodnight then, Masu.' Vivreki let go of the branches and turned back towards the others who were waiting for him beside the gates of the washhouse. Kalia held out an armful of clothing. 'This should be your size,' she said. She herself was now wearing cotton trousers and about five layers of clothing over that – as if overcompensating for her week of cold.

'Thank you.' He snatched the black robes from her and dressed without further comment, his frustration returning.

'Listen,' Sevim frowned.

The distinctive sound of battle had begun to carry from the riverside – the Brengarmah had made their attack. Without further pause, Viv began to run for the river and they could do little else but follow.

AS HE DRAWS nearer to the square the lights in his head become too much. The precious egg is within sight now, its vibrancy, its molten gold light almost obliterating any normal vision. Nearer the river, bright flares of colour jostle and move as the Brengarmah and the townsfolk do battle to possess the egg – as if such a lustrous object could truly ever be the possession of mere mortals. The cries and the crashing of weapons scream

in audible concert with the lights Vivreki is actually seeing, and his over-loaded brain cannot cope. He skids to a halt in the night-time gloom beneath the deeper shadow of the town hall. 'Ayshena, you will have to stop. Let me do this,' he whispers. 'I just can't see properly.'

Even as he speaks, the lights afflicting his gaze dim almost to normal, and he knows she has heard him. He glances round at the others, still limned with a pale nimbus of light but one that is no longer overpowering. Kalia's eyes are massive with fear, the way they had been when they first found her. Stief and Sevim wear grim expressions as they survey the crush of fighters at the barricades. Even at this distance, the close-quarter fighting resembles a sweaty, crushing hell. Leather armour has been set ablaze by the arrows of the Releeza archers, so that some of the enemy are burning where they stand. It seems clear that their com-mander should order them to retreat – but no order has yet come. It will be over soon enough, so Viv knows his opportunity is limited.

'Right, I'm going in now – there's never going to be a better dis-traction.' Viv has trouble tearing his gaze away which amply proves his own point. 'Wait here. I'll need help to carry it. Have your swords ready.' Without further comment he darts forward to place himself directly behind the egg, whose bulk shields him from view. Peering cautiously around the plinth, he notes that a group of archers are gathered around a barrel of pitch some few feet away, but all eyes are still fixed on the river. Viv is well aware that the egg will be missed almost immediately due to its size – he glances back to where the others are standing, trying to esti-mate how fast he can run and reach the cover of the shadows before pursuit begins.

He reaches out a hand to touch the surface of the egg itself, his fingers trembling as if Ayshena's excitement is still discharging from them. This close to it he notes the strange patterns which scour its surface, and it is only then that he truly remembers that night in his childhood, and his frantic, gasping race across the slopes of the mountain, to hide his secret treasure. A small smile plays on his lips, even amidst the chaos, and as his fingertips make contact with the cool surface, a ripple of light pulses out-wards from them, illuminating miniature gullies and grooves. He can feel a quickening of the Swarm inside, a dull squirming sensation which carries through the flat of his palm. But fortunately, nothing else hap-pens, as hatching now could only bring disaster. Reaching up with his other hand, he experimentally rocks the egg prior to taking its weight.

Before he can act further, however, there is a shouted curse from the other side and he knows he has been seen.

Viv recoils backwards as if in mute denial of his intentions. A man comes running around the side, brandishing a makeshift weapon of some kind. There is something very odd-looking about him, which Viv cannot immediately identify. He holds his hands up apologetically, to show his surrender, but the man is not easily placated.

'What are you doing?' he demands. 'Did Fodukiz send you?' He moves closer, jabbing with his weapon, which Viv can now see is one of the flat shovels used for loading pitch into the cauldron where the archers are standing.

'Who?' Viv continues to back away, keeping a guileless expression on his face. Once his retreat takes him out of the circle of firelight and into shadow, he lowers his hands slowly, his fingers twitching towards the hilt of his sword. 'I – I just wanted to see it . . .'

The man is fully around the back of the plinth now, obscuring their confrontation from the preoccupied archers and warriors – this is a blessing at least, Viv thinks.

Uriel frowns. 'How can you not know who Fodukiz is? Everyone in Releeza knows that name.' As he watches the man carefully, Vivreki realizes what is so unusual about him; he has no aura of light about him as all the others do. Rather, one golden rope-like strand of light drifts through the air between him and the Swarm egg. Vivreki recognizes that the egg has enslaved this man to it somehow.

Without further warning Uriel strikes him hard with the shovel. As the iron blow crashes into his ribs, knocking the breath from him, Vivreki blacks into unconsciousness. His last sight is a glimpse of his assailant raising his weapon for another blow . . .

❧CHAPTER THIRTEEN❧

KALIA FOUND SEVIM sitting on the steps of the inn, staring out at the corpses of the Releeza fighters. There were fifty-seven in all, a much lesser death toll than among the Brengarmah, although that would bring scant comfort even if the townsfolk had known. Kalia had gone out in the clothes they had stolen from the washhouse, in search of something suitable with which to bind Vivreki's chest. She had to cover her red hair, which could attract unwanted attention. It was rare in this region where most of the inhabitants had dark, coarse hair and were much shorter in stature.

It was easy to find abandoned houses towards the rear of the town and her mission had been accomplished quickly. As she cut back towards the boatsheds lining the quay where they had dragged the unconscious Viv the night before, Kalia became distracted. It was a beautiful day; marvelling at the purity of the colour, she stared up into the high blue of a cloudless sky. The autumn sun was low, casting long, chilled shadows, and looking out towards the tidal flats, she could see wading birds raking through the rich brown mud, their chattering calls and haunting music carrying clearly across the distance. Wrapping her arms across her chest, Kalia drew in a deep breath; if one looked only in that direction, away from the besieged town, it was possible to believe that nothing could ever threaten the very nature of the world of Myr, and that life would continue on, regardless of man's stupidity.

Just then, from somewhere behind her rose another sound; that of profound grief. It was the dull, tuneless wail of a newly widowed woman. Kalia sighed, and turned to follow the sound, intending to pay her respects.

Sevim was sitting on the top step, gazing down mutely at the tidy rows of bodies which covered the grey ornamental pebbles. He did not acknowledge Kalia at first, so she sat beside him.

'Sevim? We need to go back – get these bindings back for Viv.'

He looked at her blankly, and she was shocked to see he had been weeping. For most people this might seem a normal and explicable reaction, but for the Sin Eater, death was intrinsically part of his existence.

'What's wrong, Sevim?'

'They had all converted to Mauru before they died,' he said quietly. 'They converted to the One.' Kalia did not understand why this might upset him so much, but she held her peace, waiting for his explanation. 'I cannot absorb their sins, Kalia. Spall tells me the gods will not take them to their rest because they have denied Herrukal. But she – Mauru – has not come for them either.' He turned his gaze towards her, the pain of his knowledge evident on his face. 'They have no release, Kalia. Do you understand?'

'No. I –'

'I can *see* them – as ghosts.' He nodded towards the bodies. 'They are all ghosts now, with nowhere to go.'

'Oh.' She gazed out helplessly at the desolate scene before her, unable to think of anything meaningful to say in response to such an awful situation. 'Are they . . . frightened?' she whispered.

Sevim regarded her with some surprise. 'Yes, they are.'

She took his hand and they sat together in silence for a long time.

'DID YOU SEND someone over already to seize the egg?' Asoori was taking advantage of her new found importance by sitting in the damp chill of Fodukiz's tent while he was engaged in subdued conference with Cion and his other senior officers. Kilmer was also in attendance, but was astute enough to know his input would not be valued amongst the military gathering, so he kept a low profile for the moment.

The Brengarmah officers were in a state of shock, as they had badly underestimated the resolve of their opponents. What had begun, for them, as something of a minor skirmish had resulted in the death of a hundred and twelve of their soldiers. This reflected badly on Fodukiz's leadership and the presence of Cion must have served as an uncomfortable reminder to the man that the gaze of the Temple City was now fixed upon this previously insignificant backwater. Possibly more lamentable was the growing dissatisfaction of Fodukiz's own men at his leadership. Asoori had overheard some of them grumbling openly outside her tent half an hour earlier.

Fodukiz looked up at her from the table where he had been laying out wooden sticks to represent the barricades. Asoori had studied military history in Gremeshkenn Tem and she found the commander's approach alarmingly simplistic. He seemed unable to hold the details in his mind for any length of time.

'No. I am planning to send the Bakkujasi Swarm in to snatch it tonight, during the next stage of the battle.'

Before Asoori could respond, Cion himself interceded, *'What?'* He looked aghast. 'When were you planning to notify me of this? If you had consulted me, I would have already refused.' Fodukiz opened his mouth to respond, perhaps even try to pull rank on the Bakkujasi, but Cion remained coldly adamant. 'How do you think the Temple City would react if you were responsible for the loss of a Swarm in battle? Its wings could easily be damaged if it were flown so close to the conflict. I will *not* risk that.'

Fodukiz at least had the guts to glare back at Cion. 'Then what use are you to me, Bakkujasi?'

'It is not about what I can do for *you*, you—'

Asoori interrupted, her tone insistent, 'Someone has already tried to take the egg. I saw him myself during the last attack.'

The commander frowned – although he was probably glad of Asoori's distraction of Cion – and exchanged worried glances with his closest officers. 'Who would try such a thing?' he mused.

Though no one answered, each had his own thoughts. If Gremeshkenn Tem did not trust Fodukiz to do the job properly, it was possible they had sent someone else – using the commander's efforts simply as a diversion. Unexpectedly, Cion threw the man a lifeline, saving him some pride in front of his officers. 'If this was anyone from Gremeshkenn Tem, I would certainly know of it,' he assured him. 'We Bakkujasi all know one another's thoughts – so secrets are hard to keep.'

'Then perhaps it is . . . other heretics,' Fodukiz nodded in ready agreement. 'I have heard that they are gathering force across the border in Mecinia. Whoever it is, we cannot risk losing the Swarm egg to them. How soon can we be ready, Lieutenant?'

'Within the hour, sir. We are girding up against the archers. The men will now be better prep . . . protected, sir.'

Fodukiz chose to ignore the man's unfortunate slip of the tongue. 'Very well, we will renew our attack at dusk.'

❧

'RIGHT, THIS IS the plan.' Viv sat upright with difficulty, a sheen of sweat covering his skin. He was in pain – but pain which he had no time to suffer.

'Viv, I think we should just g-go. Maybe we can try for the egg l-later, when they're transporting it b-back to Gremeshkenn Tem maybe.'

'They'll fly it back there, Stief,' Viv replied. 'There's a Bakkujasi Swarm waiting over the river, and you can bet they sent it to take possession of the egg.' Viv had no idea that the Swarm's flights were being curtailed – in the normal course of events his assessment would be correct. 'They'll take it back to the Temple City straight away,' he said. 'We can't let them do that.'

Kalia had returned with a long strip of cloth. She had done a good job of binding up Vivreki's ribs; at least one was cracked and the bruising was already turning purple. He was lucky Uriel had not killed him. The self-appointed guardian of the Swarm egg had halted his second blow in mid-swing. No one was really quite sure why he had done this, except that someone had called him from the front where the archers were grouped. The moment he moved away, Sevim and Stief had raced out and recovered Viv's unconscious body.

'I've got an idea,' said Viv, 'but we'll only get one chance at it – and we need to be ready by sunset. First of all, I need you two,' he nodded towards Sevim and Kalia, 'to go back to Masu's house and fetch all of his Quirzel. He's probably got nets and bags in the aviary. Stief, I need you to find me some large pieces of steel – burnished, so that they reflect the sunlight. I imagine you might get them in the old temple. We need to keep all the combatants down by the barricades, away from the egg platform – the hardest part will be blocking off the main street leading into the square from behind. Sevim, I need you beside me when we're ready to act. I'm afraid we'll need Spall to come

– you can use my blood. We need that flash he creates when he . . . arrives.'

In the gloom of the boathouse Viv's blue-grey eyes looked tired and sullen, fighting against the aches which assailed him. But, on glancing around at the complete bafflement on the faces of his friends, he managed a wry chuckle. 'We're going to make the egg vanish.'

'Vanish?' Sevim repeated. 'But what good will that do us?'

'Well, then we can steal it.'

CION WAS READY. Fodukiz intended to throw his energies into another frontal attack on the palisades and, although the commander's reasoning capacity seemed almost laughably thin, he was perhaps unwittingly correct. For repeating the same action as before would surely lure the fighters of Releeza into reciprocating in the same manner. Cion had persuaded him to send a detachment of Brengarmah to cross further upriver and attack the town from the west – the barricades there would not hold for any length of time. He had even managed to convince Fodukiz it was the commander's own idea; Cion understood much about pride and, while the man was a fool, he had no desire to leave him nameless. At least, not while he needed his co-operation.

Cion had meditated for an hour whilst struggling to quell his impatience. He had not eaten all day, and had drunk only water – his mind must be clear, his purpose set. He would fly the Swarm into that godless town once its resistance was quelled somewhat – then he would show them the futility of their heathen belief in dragons and their supposed goddess. Asoori's assertion that she had seen someone attempt to remove the egg worried him though. Whilst it would be possible to make contact, and seek advice from, the new Hani by sending a message via the Bakkujasi, he was reluctant to do so until the egg was safely in his possession.

He had been standing staring fixedly across the river for some time, a stiff breeze from the east snapping at his robes and tousling his silver-white hair. The clarity of the light and the rugged elemental beauty of the landscape was not lost on Cion – he possessed the heightened sensibilities of a Bakkujasi after all – but, unlike other men, the brightness of the day simply made him yearn to fly. The air was his element, where he belonged.

His fingers were becoming numb as they clutched at the cold edges of his mask. He stared down at the inanimate lacquer thing and a faint expression of disgust or horror crawled across his placid features as he considered it. The masks enslaved the Bakkujasi despite their vocation being a thing to which most could only aspire. There was no retirement from such bondage; a Bakkujasi was what Cion would be, forever. When he died, his mask would be hung up in the darkened shadows beneath the Abax, and a new one cast for the next Bakkujasi chosen from amongst the Shemari to fly his Swarm. His existence was both an honour and a curse.

When first he joined the Gremeshkenn Tem flight, Cion's youthful arrogance had known no bounds. Secretly he had pledged that he alone would not allow himself to become defined by his mask, that he would still retain some part of himself that was separate and individual. Most of the other Bakkujasi did not even entertain such a thought but sometimes, when Cion looked at his counterparts, they appeared as empty, ghost-like wraiths who only truly came alive when they were masked and flying. Cion could not make such total commitment and he knew this was a failing, a weakness which burned in his gut when he considered it.

'Cion.' Asoori saluted him lightly as she walked past. He noticed she was dressed in her uniform beneath a black cloak, and that she wore both of her swords at her waist, while a long dagger hung lower on her hips.

'Asoori, I thought you had orders to exclude yourself from the combat?' he frowned angrily. 'Where exactly are you going?'

'Just to watch our men crossing,' she replied, deliberately vague. 'I only have my weapons to defend myself with.'

Cion stared at her coldly. He didn't believe her. But then, if the stubborn, glory-driven bitch wanted to get herself killed, he could hardly be held responsible – even by the Hani. It would be clear that he was otherwise engaged when the facts of the battle were later recorded. And no one would know of this brief exchange. 'Very well,' he nodded.

She bowed her head briefly and turned to go, walking purposefully across the frosted mud of the riverbank. After a few paces, she stopped and turned back towards him. 'Cion,' she said, 'I wish you good fortune. Oshi protect you.'

Cion remained exactly where he was, as activity in the encampment increased around him. He would still be standing in the same place when the unthinkable happened . . .

'STIEF, I DON'T understand what we're planning.' Kalia struggled with the knots on the net bag she carried, her fingers nerveless with cold. She had to get the bag untied ready, but not pull it open until she saw the signal. 'What Viv's doing anyway? Is he magic, like Sevim?'

Stief ground his teeth in irritation, wishing the girl would just shut up. His gaze was currently fixed on the grey-clad figure of Uriel, who was standing only twenty paces or so in front of the plinth he guarded. He was still not far enough away from the egg.

Further down the slope, towards the palisades, the Releeza archers were stoking the fires for burning pitch. They were expanding the swathe of archers, building on the success of their strategy from the last encounter. From his higher vantage point, Uriel was watching the river for signs of activity. Occasionally, he would move towards the riverbank to speak to someone or keep the archers informed; at some point he would have to walk further away . . .

'Come on . . .' Stief whispered, as if to encourage the man forward.

'What?' Kalia shifted nervously from foot to foot. 'What did you say?'

'Nothing.'

They had managed to keep the space immediately behind the plinth cleared by shutting off the alleyway which accessed that side of the square. It was audaciously simple, as the warriors' attentions were fixed elsewhere, while the women and children were mostly closeted back in the town hall again. The blocking of the alley had managed to deter people from using it as they assumed the barrier had been put there for some military reason. By now, all activity was focussed on the river. So far, after almost an hour of waiting in their positions, their luck was holding, but if Uriel did not move soon . . . if someone approached the plinth from behind . . .

'It's not going to work,' Stief groaned.

Kalia wittered on. 'So is Vivreki going to do some magic? Is he?'

'Not exactly. Kalia, j-just concentrate. Remember exactly what you have to do.'

Even as he spoke, Stief noted Uriel beginning to walk even further from the plinth, pointing at something excitedly and calling out to the warriors ranged below him. At that very moment, Stief spotted the red cloth being waved from behind the plinth. It was their signal.

'Now! Do it *now*!'

THE SWARM EGG vanished; literally, in the blink of an eye. Cion was about to don his mask when he heard a shout of excitement. At the same instant he saw a flash of bright colour as a flock of Quirzel – green, red, blue and yellow – flashed across his vision from left to right. Simultaneously, a dazzling flare rippled outwards from the plinth itself. He blinked, just once, but by then the egg was gone.

The soldiers began a mindless chorus of exclamation, their curses tinged with fear.

'Icanti's tits!' Fodukiz and Kilmer came running towards him, like everyone else unable to believe their prize had simply disappeared.

'It has to be a trick,' Cion breathed.

'I don't think so – just look at them,' Kilmer said thoughtfully. The Releeza warriors visible on the bank seemed as stunned as the Brengarmah were. Some had even fallen to their knees, presumably to beg forgiveness of the gods they had abandoned. The grey-robed figure of Uriel could now be seen running back upslope towards the plinth.

'They might have hidden it away. Perhaps the soldiers were told how to act. Perhaps they will seek to convince us the egg has hatched into their accursed dragon.'

'We must get over there quickly,' Fodukiz growled. 'We must find out what is going on. I'll lead the Brengarmah across myself.' He turned back to his bedazzled troops and began shouting orders.

Kilmer regarded his lover silently for a moment, watching the strange conflict of shadows which played across his features. 'They are certainly passionate about keeping the thing,' he remarked carefully. 'And their courage at least does them credit.'

'They have gone too far now,' Cion hissed, before slipping on his

Bakkujasi mask. When he turned towards Kilmer again, it was as if a complete stranger was looking out at him. 'The whole town is a god-less cesspit, and they seek to make fools of us all. Whether I recover the egg or no – they must all be *punished*.'

Kilmer watched him as he made his way back towards the waiting Swarm without further comment. Cion's dark zeal turned his stomach. He suddenly thought about the prospect of returning with Asoori to Cantroji and fathering children. In the thunder of encroaching battle that seemed more of a comfort than he might have previously imagined.

ASOORI SAW WHAT was happening even as Cion and the others guessed at the solution. She had travelled further along the row of buildings this time, and was almost level with the display plinth, her curiosity driving her to move closer than she knew was safe.

Her intention had been as before – to hide herself amongst the buildings and watch the progress of the Brengarmah. If they stormed the square, she would join in the melee and no one would be any the wiser. She wondered distantly if Kilmer would mourn her if she ended up getting killed tonight, but then chided herself for being mawkish and sentimental. As she reached the level at which she now stood watching, however, events had overtaken her rather immature thoughts and plans.

There were two figures, hiding behind the egg. Asoori could see them quite clearly from her vantage point. One was tall and slim, quite good-looking – he moved with a lightness in his movements. The second was much shorter and slightly hunched with long black hair hanging in lank tatters down his back, and obscuring most of his face. He clutched a dagger in his fist like an assassin preparing to strike.

In front of the plinth stood the man she had been told was Uriel. He was intently watching the preparations down along the palisades, constantly shifting from foot to foot and muttering to himself with increasing frustration. Obviously things were not being done to his satisfaction on the riverbank. Eventually he could bear it no longer, and began to stride down the slope, calling out to someone and pointing.

At the moment he reached the palisades all hell broke loose.

Hundreds of Quirzel rose into the sky, soaring above the square. Asoori glanced back at the assassins and was mystified to see the hunched man drawing his dagger across the forearm of the other. As blood spurted from the wound, he lifted the unresisting man's arm to his mouth; and in that very same second, a flare of blue-white light exploded outwards from the strange couple. It was so bright, she instinctively flung her hands up to protect her eyes and she staggered back, her senses reeling.

When she was able to look back, the hunched figure had vanished. In his place stood a young man in white robes. His accomplice did not seem perturbed by this and already they moved in some pre-arranged plan, sliding something swiftly across the base of the plinth, obscuring the egg from view. This was done in a moment and they lifted the precious egg from its stand to put it into a large sack. Asoori was completely confused over what was happening, even more so when she glanced towards the river and saw the reaction of the Releeza fighters. They seemed afraid, although the massive flash of light had passed without harming anyone.

Uriel meanwhile, began running back up the slope towards the plinth, his face a picture of abject consternation. He didn't seem aware of the two men hurriedly packing the egg away. His gaze was on the front of the plinth. *What the hell is going on?* she frowned.

As Uriel panted towards his goal, the thieves behind it were slipping away towards the cover of the nearby buildings, and they must have made some sound which the Guardian heard. Behind them rose a shout, fraught with anger and grief. 'Nooooo!'

Spall carries the egg in a bag slung over his back. Vivreki feels uneasy about this, not believing that anyone else would look after it as carefully as he would, but that would be impractical now because of his damaged ribs. As Uriel comes screaming up the slope towards them, Viv pushes Spall away. 'Go on, run! I'll catch up . . .' He pulls his blade and runs forward to confront the enraged man, fighting to ignore the pain as he has done all day. Only once he reaches the safety of Ayshena, can he give in to it.

'I don't want to hurt you,' he warns. 'Give it up. It is the egg of a Swarm. You don't know what you're dealing with.'

But Uriel is in no state of mind for persuasive argument. He has armed himself with a curved blade he has snatched up from a dead companion. He comes charging towards Viv in a hysterical onslaught. His weapon is raised for a sweeping blow, though he wastes his breath on a tirade of curses.

Viv drops to his knees and then to the ground and rolls over and over, aware of the swishing arc of the blade whispering above him. He times the dangerous spring back to his feet for when he hears Uriel – grunting with effort and frustration – pulling the steel back for another clumsy swing. He then leaps up again, catching Uriel hard across the back with the flat of his blade. The impact snaps it apart just below the wooden hilt. No matter, because Uriel is unbalanced by the force of the blow, and trips forward, his sword tumbling from his grasp. The Guardian lands face-down in the wet slush, but Vivreki sees him immediately raise his head to look for his lost weapon – he runs and snatches it up before Uriel can gather his wits . . .

There is a moment of indecision. Vivreki recognizes the Guardian's misguided passion as so genuine that his heart is moved to furious pity. He is only protecting the egg, he thinks. He hurls the sword away and it spins across the square in a bright pinwheel, its lambent energy like the star.

Vivreki only watches it for a second before he realizes Uriel is struggling to rise. 'Just stop it,' he snaps. 'Let it go.' Agitated by Uriel's intransigence he kicks out in a pushing motion with the flat of his foot, sending the man sprawling in the mud once more. Then he turns to catch up with Spall, but as he reaches the shadow of the nearest building he sees with a stab of annoyance that Spall has turned and waited for him. He is about to curse him aloud for this stupidity when Spall pushes him aside, and thrusts both hands forwards with fingers splayed wide. A noxious black spasm of sin erupts across the square, appearing somehow bright against the gathering dusk. Vivreki catches a brief glimpse of Uriel's expression before his view is obscured – it is one of utter grief, as if his sanity is slipping away, his world falling apart.

They turn and head up along the side of the town hall, towards the steeper slope of the hill. Ayshena will be waiting there, and Vivreki feels a surge of joy. We've done it, Ayshena! We've done it!

PERHAPS URIEL'S TENTATIVE grip on reality was really a blessing. He watched the cloud of sin before him and made no move to run from it. In fact, for long minutes, he sat back on his heels in the slush and observed the nightmarish vision with the kind of blankness one might reserve for staring at an empty sky. His mind was aflame with denial – *the egg could not be taken* – and resolve built within his gut, almost as a force independent of his consciousness. It now animated his limbs so that he found himself standing upright before he knew his own intention. Then he simply stood there, shoulders slumped, jaw slack, as if still waiting for coherent thought to return to him. He didn't know how long it took, but he became vaguely aware of sounds behind him as battle was rejoined in the shallows and on the banks of the Rel.

He was about to step forward, regardless of the sin cloud, when a whooshing dart of movement in the sky overhead caused him to look up.

What he saw was a Bakkujasi Swarm, and never having seen one so close before he felt his limbs begin to tremble at the sight of the massive creature in flight. The motion of its wings stirred up an unnatural wind. As it came closer to the ground, Uriel's robes were snatched and buffeted about his quaking frame. Pebbles and sand were lifted through the air in a whirling vortex. The awesome creature's front legs were trailing a container of something burning white-hot. The slipstream of its passage acted like a bellows to fan the flames and, as it passed just in front of Uriel, a large chunk of something molten was dislodged. Uriel stared at it aghast as it hissed in the mud, but it was soon clear that he was not the object of the Swarm's intent. It passed overhead leaving him rimed in debris which stuck to the sweat of his fevered skin.

A young woman in Brengarmah uniform ran out from between the buildings at the side of the square, her gaze fixed on the Swarm. 'What the hell is he doing?' she yelled, though the question could only be rhetorical. Uriel's dumbstruck mind reached the same conclusion as she did at the moment the creature stopped to hover above the town hall.

'No!' Uriel broke into a run as the Bakkujasi's righteous fury was unleashed on the innocent women and children of Releeza. 'Get out of there! Get out!' he screamed. But he was still too far away to be heard by those inside.

The occupants of the hall were totally unprepared. The wooden building caught fire in moments, its thatched roof going up like tinder and collapsing inwards. The flames were tenacious, as the blaze caught hold. The doors burst open and the wailing, choking inhabitants sought to make their escape . . .

Asoori stood motionless, unable to believe what she was witnessing. The Swarm wheeled back towards the Brengarmah encampment. Cion did not even pause to see the results of his action. She just could not believe any Bakkujasi could act so despicably, but she had to acknowledge that, to Cion, this destruction was merely a mass burning of heretics. He no longer viewed them as people, just irredeemable, spent souls. She dropped her sword and, ripping her cloak off, broke into a run trailing behind Uriel. Her intention was to help the people from the burning building. As she put her head down to run, watching her own feet flashing through the mud she realized, distantly, that the first casualty of battle was often honour.

Some people could live with that but she did not think she was one of them.

'WHERE *ARE* THEY?' Viv's voice held the first creeping edge of panic.

'They will be here soon, Vivreki.' Spall gave him a faint smile which was intended to reassure Viv but failed miserably as it looked somewhat less than sincere. Spall seemed almost impervious to human reactions like panic, but Viv's agitation was contagious. 'They promised.'

'Well I *know* that,' Viv stormed. 'Stief would never let me down on purpose. If they don't get here soon, it means something has happened to them.'

'Kalia. Something might have happened to Kalia.'

Viv gave an exasperated sigh but fought to contain his irritation. It wasn't Spall's fault he wasn't quite as emotionally developed as real people, and the Sin Eater's avatar had been more than useful to them so far. They had been waiting at the agreed meeting point on the hillside for ten or fifteen minutes, and Viv's worry only increased when a huge fire gripped the buildings down by the square, sending a lurid orange glow up to meet the encroaching night. Releeza would be easy prey to the Brengarmah now, so they needed to get their prize out of the town as quickly as possible. Ayshena wasn't helping his mental state either. After he had communicated to her the success of their mission, the Swarm was so overjoyed, she was crowding Viv's mind with colour and light which kept sparking at the edges of his vision as if some garish and entirely inappropriate party was occurring in his head. If Ayshena did not leave Releeza soon, he feared for whatever passed as her sanity. Meanwhile, his eyes had begun to glow again, burning in mute reflection of the beleaguered town.

'Maybe you should just go ahead, Spall. Take the egg to Ayshena. I'll wait behind here for the others. She can always fly back for me, when—'

'They're here,' interrupted Spall pointing back down the track, where Stief was heading slowly towards them. He was supporting Kalia, who was limping heavily and fighting to remain conscious.

'What happened?' Viv rushed towards them.

'We got caught up in the f-fighting.' Stief looked dejected but otherwise unharmed. The Brengarmah have b-broken through, and the town's ablaze . . .' Before he could continue, Spall scooped Kalia up into his arms and turned back up the hill path. After a silent glance back at the devastation of Releeza, Viv and Stief began to follow.

&CHAPTER FOURTEEN&

O NCE THEY COULD see Ayshena on the horizon, it was obvious to everyone, not just Vivreki, that the huge creature was full of excitement; her wings kept juddering and her abdomen pulsing up and down in a faintly disturbing manner.

Spall had slowed his pace as they reached the top of the rise, feeling the encroaching tautness of his muscles and hearing the whispered protests from Sevim in his mind. He put Kalia down gently and she limped along beside him.

'We did it, Ayshena,' Viv called out. 'We have the egg.' The Swarm seemed to respond silently to him because he then broke into a fragile smile, which stretched the tired lines of his face.

'What did she say, Viv? Is s-she pleased?'

'Yes, she says it was the egg of a Swarm named Sandeshi, who died in trying to keep it safe, away from the Temple City. Ayshena tells me she is both joyful and sad.'

'That is a *lie*,' the voice was a broken, rasping sound. 'The Temple City has sent her.'

Everyone turned to the speaker, who stood wavering on unsteady legs. His grey robes were now smeared with black soot, his singed hair and his face coated in grime – tears washed unchecked down his cheeks, tracking paths through the ash. The newcomer pointed an accusing finger at Viv. 'Do you know what you've just done? They're dying down there.' Viv shook his head in puzzlement but Uriel continued, jabbing his finger to emphasize his words.

'The Bakkujasi set fire to our town hall – with all our women and children inside it. It was a punishment on us, for what *you* did.'

There was stunned silence for a few moments, before Viv could speak. 'I'm sorry . . .'

Uriel reached behind his back for the sword which he had slung between his shoulders. 'Selfish bastard,' he grated. '*Give it back.*'

Stief was the first to move, with the soft hiss of his blade being drawn. Spall put down the bag and stepped forward, as Viv held his hands up in a placatory gesture. It was clear to him that, despite the wavering blade, Uriel was no true threat; he was already beaten and exhausted, and only the man's grim determination had brought him this far.

He stepped forward, just one step, keeping his voice soft and level. 'We *are* taking the egg away, despite anything you might say. Somewhere safe. Surely that's what you want too, isn't it?'

Uriel's lips moved, but no sound came out at first. It was as if the voicing of his accusation had used up all his emotional reserves. He licked his lips before trying again. 'Yes.'

'You cannot go back to Releeza. The Brengarmah will be looking for you, not just the egg. You have instigated a rebellion.' Viv paused as the implications of this crossed Uriel's stricken face. All the Guardian could expect should he return to Releeza now was certain death. 'Come with us.'

'What! Viv, we can't take—'

Viv held up his hand in an imperious silencing gesture. 'Ayshena will certainly take him. He's risked everything to protect Sandeshi's egg.'

'S-Sandeshi?' Uriel looked confused.

'It doesn't matter – it doesn't matter if we disagree on what the egg is. All that matters is that we are both sworn to its protection.'

Uriel nodded, but he continued to hold Viv's gaze – distrust and hatred were evident in every line of his face.

'We've got to go, now,' Stief urged in a low voice. 'I just hope Ayshena can carry so many.'

Finally Uriel lowered his blade and glanced about anxiously, taking note of the others for the first time. Kalia stepped forward and put an arm around his shoulders. 'Come on. Come with us,' she said soothingly as she led him towards Ayshena. 'She won't hurt you. She's not like the Bakkujasi Swarms . . .' As she spoke, she took the sword gently from Uriel's unresisting grip and held it behind her back for someone else to take from her. Spall took it with a wry smile at Kalia's surprising thoughtfulness.

Viv beckoned the others towards him. 'Just watch my back,' he said quietly.

ONCE THEY WERE all crammed onto Ayshena's back, she took ponderously to the air. As the ground fell away beneath him, Vivreki was seized by a rush of near-hysterical relief. He threw his head back and laughed his old, crazy laugh. It startled the others at first, but made Stief break into a broad grin.

In the darkness beneath them Asoori emerged from the undergrowth hedging the trail. She had followed Uriel from the town and listened to their conversation. When Viv spoke to Uriel something in his voice seemed hauntingly familiar.

It had begun to rain – too late for the townsfolk. Had the rain and snowmelt made the Rel unfordable things would have been so different. As Asoori looked up towards the dark bulk of the Swarm, the creature seemed to move away in an elemental silver vortex, the raindrops backlit by the moon and the star, Orlannoni.

The sound of Vivreki's laughter drifted back down to her as if through time . . .

'Snoot?' she whispered.

ACHIOS SAT IN his new audience chamber surrounded by the rich and powerful. Being men accustomed to using the church for power and gain, of course, their requests were all couched in such elegant language: thinly veiled bribes, promises of land for new temples, estates left in trust . . .

Though so very important it was excruciatingly dull, and Achios had just been idly wondering if the previous Hani had died of sheer boredom. Still, he considered as he gazed around the gold-encrusted room and shifted on his plump cushion, it was a different class of boredom. It had its consolations.

We need Falloden Sen. Get me Falloden Sen.

When Rann's voice slammed into his head with the force of a

hammer, Achios blinked to clear the tears from his eyes, and waved a dismissive hand to cut off the interminable imprecations of the Duke of Gonsha in mid-flow. 'Leave me,' he commanded. 'I must pray.'

The visiting dignitaries scrambled to obey, but the servants stood immobile, like part of the landscape. '*All* of you,' Achios insisted, staring directly at the nearest fan-waving attendant.

The man blanched and hurried to obey, while Achios smiled to himself. It was quite possible that the Hani had never directly addressed his servants before – so ubiquitous were they.

Within moments he was left entirely alone. Just for appearances' sake, should anyone enter unexpectedly, he crossed his legs and closed his eyes, as if in meditation.

Falloden Sen? Why?

Dare you ask the god for his reasons? Rann's reaction sounded almost puzzled. Achios realized that interacting with mortals in such a way was a new experience for this deity, just as dealing with the gilded rigours of being Hani was new to him. They were both learning in their own ways.

It might help me to help you, he suggested.

Falloden Sen is . . . significant, geographically.

Achios frowned, not quite understanding.

Did you realize that Cantroji – and specifically Falloden Sen – occupies the centre point of the world?

No. That's . . . very interesting.

When Rann sighed audibly, a faint breeze whirled around the room. *It is more than interesting, Achios. It makes Cantroji a place of great power.*

Oh? Achios thought of the last time he had visited Falloden Sen for his niece's wedding. It had seemed a pleasant enough place, with a grand old crumbling house set in grounds full of lakes and fountains. The climate there was most agreeable, milder by far than that of the twin cities. *When you say you want it, what do you mean?*

You must find a way to acquire the property for the church. I will arrange for the Duke and his wife to meet with an accident – but first it must be bequeathed to us. I will begin sending him some nightmares of significance.

Duke Detri will not comply. He has a son who is married – to my own niece as a matter of fact.

A son? Rann replied without pause. *Then he must die also, and very soon.*

THE RAIN WAS so numbingly cold, that everyone on Ayshena clung together, hunched against the chill. Only Vivreki seemed impervious to the foul weather; although soaked through, he sat perched at the very front of Ayshena's thorax, his thoughts seemingly elsewhere, as distant and unreachable as the stars. It was only when Ayshena lurched, suddenly losing height so fast that everyone shouted in alarm, that Viv realized something was wrong.

'We have to land very soon,' he called back over his shoulder. 'Ayshena cannot go on much further.'

Uriel, who was sitting behind Kalia, asked her, 'Where are we going anyway?'

'I don't know,' she replied. 'I think we just need to get as far from Releeza as possible, in case the Bakkujasi comes after us.'

'Tell Vivreki to follow the coastline, then. There's a flat peninsula not far ahead. It will be easy for her to land on, and we can find shelter there.'

'Is it a village, though?' Kalia asked. 'We have to avoid other people now. We don't want to bring the Bakkujasi's retribution down on anyone . . . anyone else.'

'No, it's not a village. But my sister lives there, and she'll help us.'

THEY LANDED IN the dark on the empty strand close by the sea. The rain was a deluge by now, sweeping across the beach in sheets, the sound of the droplets hissing into the waves like a bereft sigh, a grey sadness with no respite. There was no sign of any habitation, and pillars of black basalt ran like a jagged spine from the headland further out to sea, disappearing eventually as if some scaled creature were diving beneath the ocean. Some distance from the shore these rocks re-emerged in the conical spire of a small volcano.

They hurried under the shelter of one of the rocks although Ayshena could only remain out in the open because of the spread of her wings. 'What now, Uriel?' Viv snapped. 'Where does this sister live? There's nothing to see for bloody miles.'

Uriel's expression when Viv spoke to him left no one in any doubt that his sense of outrage against him had not subsided. He turned and pointed out towards the black silhouette of the volcano. 'Over there.'

'She lives in a volcano?' Viv frowned.

'C-couldn't Ayshena just t-take us a bit further, Viv?'

The rain was gusting heavily now, pushed by a sudden howling gale. It spattered almost deafeningly against the rocks. 'Maybe later,' Viv insisted. 'She's exhausted now. She needs the sun to warm her . . .' He gazed out mournfully at Ayshena's darkened form. Under the sporadic moonlight, her green and gold tones shone slickly like subdued gemstones, her wings jittering constantly in the wind. 'She'll be all right,' he muttered, but it wasn't obvious whom he sought to reassure.

'Well, good for her,' Kalia remarked acidly, 'because I don't think *we* will be if we have to stand around here till the morning.'

She was right: the shelter provided by the rocks was nominal. If the wind and rain changed their direction, their covering would be non-existent, and everyone was already numb with cold. Kalia had the infuriating gift of stating the obvious. They would have to move soon or they might end up perishing of cold here after all their efforts. Viv had just begun to wonder if the intense cold might affect the contents of the precious egg they had striven so hard for, when Kalia's keen gaze spotted something in the distance.

'Look, what's that?' she pointed.

Something white and ghostly slid silently through the dark sky towards them. As it drew near, they realized it was a large white owl.

'Oh no,' Kalia whispered, 'it's bad luck. Really bad luck.'

'As opposed to what exactly?' Viv commented wryly.

The creature landed on the rocks right beside them, gripping onto a small extrusion of the wet surface with hooked talons the size of Viv's hands. It then affixed them with an acid yellow gaze which seemed to gleam in the darkness and was surprisingly expressive. It took a few moments for Viv to realize that everyone was staring, transfixed by the huge bird and, for some reason, holding their breath. So rapt was their attention that no one noticed a small boat rounding the rocks and pulling ashore behind them . . .

And she walked though the storm, like a dream, a vision of purity and elegance. Vivreki felt so sure that only he could see her – that no one else could hold the same vision – that therefore the sensation of simply *knowing* her could only be his. His breath caught in his throat as she moved towards him, and he knew – even as his lips moved, frozen and mute – that he wanted to say: *Oh, there you are . . .*

She wore only white, as if in concert with her owl: a white gown, a white cloak with a soft cowl hood. Her long black hair was unbound but swept back from her fine features with a broad white headband. The only hint of colour was one pear-shaped emerald resting on her brow, between her dark eyes. The lower part of her face was concealed by a white scarf, bound tight against the cold and wet. This gave the impression that she stared at him from some vast icy distance.

She was looking directly at him. For the first few moments, at him alone . . .

'Losha.' Uriel stepped forward. 'Losha, we need your help.'

THERE WAS A single gash in the leathern walls, which served as a window of sorts. Vivreki stood there, looking out over the city of ghosts towards the lake. The lake, pooled in the caldera of the extinct volcano, was starkly beautiful in the daytime. A morning mist drifted across the placid water now touched by the dawn. All around the shoreline, twisted tree trunks littered the black soil like the bleached and denuded bones of huge animals, the bulk of their roots exposed. Here and there, rude shelters had been built amongst the gnarled roots of the trees, and canvas or scavenged wood wrapped around to form surprisingly large and robust tent-like structures. The occasional flowering weed had sprouted from the midst of these repairs, in a stubborn miracle of nature. Gentle woodsmoke drifted as morning fires were rekindled, exerting a softening influence on the harshness of the scene.

When they had arrived last night, huddled against the last waves of the storm, this place had seemed lurid and inhospitable, and the sulphurous smell emitted by the lake stung their eyes and throats but now, only hours later, Viv was becoming accustomed to it. Vast flocks of black birds roosted on the sharp angles of the trees, their hunched silhouettes and occasional cracked-sounding calls being unnerving in the extreme. It was difficult to see how anyone could make any home here and yet a few people did.

Vivreki himself felt surprisingly rested this morning, and yet there was some new feeling of unease in the pit of his stomach for which he could not find a reason. It seemed worse at this very moment, because he was watching Losha; and she was dancing.

He had spotted her earlier walking along the shoreline, apparently in deep contemplation. Vivreki had peered out simply by chance, and was surprised by the thrill which ran through him on seeing her. She moved with the same elegance that she had shown when first he saw her. This morning she wore no cloak or hood, and the light morning breeze wafted the sheen of her long hair behind her. She gazed out over the lake as if perpetually waiting for someone or something.

Her reverie was interrupted when from one of the crude shelters a small group of children came tumbling forth, two smaller ones and one taller. It was difficult to tell if they were boys or girls at this distance, but the taller one walked awkwardly, a roughly made wooden crutch under one arm. They spoke to Losha for a few moments, and she appeared to enjoy their company, nodding and once throwing her head back in laughter. After a few minutes' conversation, one of the children lifted its arms and made a few exaggerated dance steps. Losha watched carefully before adjusting the position of the child's arm. She then took hold of the taller child around the waist, handing the crutch over to one of the others. It was now clear the taller one was a boy, and Viv instinctively recognized the cringing embarrassment of teenage boys everywhere when confronted by the prospect of dancing with a woman.

They both raised their hands to place their palms together then began to move slowly in unison, the boy staggering clumsily. Losha stopped, to instruct him patiently before continuing. Vivreki was entranced by the sight, and saddened in the same moment. Uriel had explained to him earlier that Losha wore the white robes and the mask to symbolize the purity of her soul, because that was the only part of her which her disease could not touch. Losha, he said, had once been an exceptional beauty, but beneath the fine cotton veil her face was now ravaged and ulcerated. Thinking back to this as he watched her dance, for the first time in his life Vivreki questioned his idea of what was beautiful.

Before his mind had time to catch up with his feet, he too was standing by the lakeshore. She didn't notice him at first, so he revelled in those few moments when he could listen, enthralled by the clarity of her voice. One of the children suddenly noticed him, and pointed over to where he stood. As Losha turned towards him, Vivreki noted that the boy she had been dancing with was seriously disfigured. Not only did he have a cleft lip but one side of his face sagged as if all the muscles there had collapsed.

'Good morning, Vivreki,' Losha said. Like Uriel, she spoke with the slightly halting accent of those hailing from the far Donraj region. It seemed that parents brought their disabled children here, and some husbands brought their wives from many leagues away just to abandon them.

Viv suddenly found himself tongue-tied and nervous, aware that he had not even combed his hair, which had the unfortunate habit of frizzing up against the pillow at the back overnight. He patted at his head distractedly, then realized what he was doing and snapped his hand away. 'I . . . erm. I know the steps to that dance,' he said. One of the smaller children giggled at his discomfort until it was elbowed in the ribs. 'I mean, I could show you how it goes.'

He could tell that she smiled at this, despite the mask. 'That is very kind, Vivreki, but I do already know the dance. I was just showing Ten here. He is learning so he can show his mother his progress.'

'It might be helpful if I could watch you two do it properly,' Ten suggested.

'Good idea.' Without pause, Vivreki stepped towards Losha and held up both hands for the initial movements.

He longed to be able to make some witty remark, but the instant their palms touched, all levity eluded him, and he realized that never before had he understood the inherent intimacy of dance. Losha gazed into his eyes; and where he might have expected the coy embarrassment or even brazen suggestiveness found in the women he had danced with back home, there was none. What there was instead was simply mute understanding, a shared sense of freedom as Losha's marvellous soul was fearlessly laid bare.

His feet moved as if receiving instruction from some outside source, because his brain was proving incapable of coherent command. Fortunately, Vivreki was a practised dancer, for Calla had taught him and Stief when they were younger – the memory of stepping and wheeling around their tiny front room with Calla made him unexpectedly emotional, and he stared at Losha with morose intensity.

'Are you all right, Vivreki?' she suddenly whispered so that the children would not hear.

Just as he was about to reply, surprised that he could feel ready to divulge the truth, that he was thinking of his mother, Kalia came running down the slope, her feet slipping in the loose black sand.

'Viv, come and look at Ayshena. She's acting a bit strange.' Kalia stopped just in front of them. 'Oh, sorry,' she remarked, confusion evident in her expression. 'You were dancing?'

Vivreki pulled away from Losha with some reluctance, 'What's wrong, Kalia?'

Kalia led him back up the slope, and Losha followed them. Ayshena had sought cover in a small cave – almost too small, confining her wings uncomfortably. She looked clearly agitated, rocking back and forth on her legs and seeming on the point of collapse. Stief and Sevim were already standing at the cave entrance looking perplexed.

'Ayshena!' Viv rushed forward. 'What's the matter with you?'

Don't know. This cannot be real. I think . . . I . . .

Suddenly, something in Ayshena's movements sparked a long-suppressed memory in Vivreki's mind. Receiving an image of Ansanzi, he frowned. 'Ayshena, I think you might be going to produce . . . an egg.' He reached up and touched the cold chitin between her eyes, wishing he could discern more expression there.

'Perhaps we should let her be,' Losha remarked. 'We're crowding her, making her agitated.' She looked up at the Swarm and spoke as if she had heard Ayshena's thoughts to Vivreki first-hand. 'It's all right, Ayshena,' she said simply, 'we are here for you.' Then, turning solemnly to Viv, she added, 'She is very frightened.'

'How do you know that? Can you hear her thoughts too?'

'No, but I *can* sense fear. It is very familiar to me.'

Viv dropped his voice, as he turned away from the stricken Swarm. 'I'll sit here close to her but I think she'll otherwise be better left alone. When her mother gave birth to the egg that became Ayshena, she died the same night.'

'Do you think she'll be all right, Vivreki?' Sevim whispered.

'There's no way of knowing . . .' Then Viv seemed to confront the idea of the Swarm dying. 'We won't need a Sin Eater, though. I think her soul is probably unique.'

❧

KILMER WAS CLEARLY furious. Asoori had never seen him so angry before, and she was amazed by the sheer physicality of his emotion. They were now occupying one of the Releeza houses which had been commandeered from the defeated townsfolk for the use of the more important Brengarmah. Kilmer had started punching the only stone wall he could find. 'The man is a zealous, dangerous, manipulative bastard,' he yelled. 'You were right, Asoori. You were right all along! How could I have been so blind? I've been forced to pay over almost my whole inheritance to the bloody church in order to save these stupid people . . .'

Asoori said nothing, merely poured him another large goblet of red wine. Souls had a price, or so it seemed, at least according to Cion Gezezi. Once the fires had been put out and the townsfolk rounded up, he had been all set to undertake wholesale slaughter on the spot – until Kilmer had stepped in. He had made a handsome offer to 'buy' the townsfolk into indentured service for the local silver mines. That would constitute severe punishment enough, he argued, because Releeza would effectively become a slave settlement. Falloden Sen already owned a share of the silver mine, so this was a way of extending the ducal estates' interests. The people of Releeza had, after all, been victims of psychological possession of a kind; but now the truly dangerous heretic, Uriel, was missing. As was the Swarm egg.

In fact, Kilmer had no intention of enforcing anything so harsh upon the townsfolk – something which Cion may have suspected but didn't actually know for sure. Kilmer had simply been thinking on his feet during the earlier discussions with Fodukiz and his officers, and had been so outraged by Cion's suggestions of mass executions that this 'proposal' had simply formed in his mind in an instant.

'If there are no workers left here – or no families to support the remaining workers – the mine will have to close and the Cantroji estates will lose a *lot* of revenue.' This was a bit of an exaggeration of course, since his father's interests in the mine were not that substantial.

And Cion had haggled for every last woman and child – of which there were precious few after his act of retribution with the Swarm – because he was seeking to redeem himself slightly, when he eventually reported back to Achios. He knew the Hani would still be livid with rage, but then the church could always use the additional silver.

'It's disgusting,' Kilmer railed. 'Do you know how little a woman's life is worth to your precious church? Twenty dralchi. For a child, twelve dralchi . . .' He gulped the wine as if it were water, desperate to get drunk and erase the last few hours from his mind.

'It's not *my* church, Kilmer,' Asoori protested quietly.

He glared at her. 'Your uncle is the Hani. That means you're closer to the church than almost anyone.'

She snorted derisively. 'Don't be ridiculous, that hardly makes me in any way responsible, and you know it. Anyway, Achios is not that close to me: he is my *great*-uncle, my grandfather's brother . . .' She re-filled his goblet again.

There was a knock on the door, and Cion strode in as Asoori was still halfway across the room to open it. She had given Merric the night off, since everyone was physically and emotionally shattered by the day's terrible events.

'Cion,' she said coldly. 'What do you want?'

'I need to talk to Kilmer alone.' He stared at her pointedly, but Asoori stood her ground.

'I am not some housemaid, to be dismissed, Cion Gezezi. Anything you have to say to Lord Kilmer, you can say in my presence.'

It was normally quite difficult to tell when Cion was angry, so self-contained was he, but there was now no mistaking his ire. He just stood there for a few moments, as if fighting to keep a grip of himself, then said, 'Very well, Asoori. Kilmer, I'm sorry. My duties are of the utmost importance to me, and sometimes . . .' He could not bring himself to admit his complete and utter wrongness. 'Well, it becomes difficult. You don't know the pressure I am under from the Temple City. It seems quite likely that I will face personal disgrace upon my return – as will Fodukiz if I have anything to do with it.'

'Disgrace?' Kilmer's expression was unfathomable. 'I would have thought that the gods would be just thrilled by your own personal scourge. I would have thought that Herrukal would—'

'Kilmer!' Asoori gave her husband a warning look, sensing that the wine was having an effect on him already.

'Oh, worried about my soul, darling wife? Well, here' – he flicked a twenty dralchi piece into the air – 'you can always buy it back from him for me.' He swigged more wine. 'That's my last dralchi, by the way.' Asoori knew this wasn't true, but she wondered at the scale of the bargain Kilmer had negotiated with Cion.

Cion looked almost stricken for a moment. 'The egg was the crucial thing,' he muttered, 'and we lost it. It . . . it's vanished.'

Asoori almost gasped aloud. In all the chaotic aftermath of the battle, she had forgotten to tell anyone what she had seen. Although Cion had reacted in anger, believing that the townsfolk had simply hidden their treasured item, it was now increasingly believed on both sides that it had actually vanished – as had its self-styled Guardian. She started to give a brief, nervous laugh, a relieved reaction which had little to do with humour.

'I can see how my dishonour pleases you, Asoori. It's strange but I imagined you to have more integrity,' Cion snarled, and turned to leave.

'No, wait . . . Wait, I have something to tell you. But, in return, I want you to write off Kilmer's debt. Cantroji will help rebuild this town, but not by means of an enslaved population.'

'And what do I get in return?'

'I can tell you who took the egg, and which way they were heading when they left Releeza.'

Cion snorted in disdain at her suggestion, but then remembered the disgrace which awaited him. Anything he could use to placate the Hani's wrath might prove useful . . .

IT WAS DUSK and Ayshena's condition had still not changed. Vivreki had remained by the cave entrance all day long, a continuous stream of silent communication exchanging between him and the Swarm. During this time Ayshena revealed to him visions of his youth which had long been submerged in his consciousness; the face of his mother, Veda, his best friend, Pik, and the bright colours of the Temple City where he had spent such a privileged childhood. It saddened him and fascinated him at the same time, but eventually he ran out of questions and they both fell silent. After a while, the privations of the last few days caught up with him and he dozed off, despite the hard surface he rested on.

He woke with a start to find Uriel sitting in front of him, staring into his face intently. The Guardian seemed somehow different today, less fragile, less edgy. Vivreki hoped that once the balance of Uriel's mind was fully restored, the man might realize that he was not to blame for the punitive actions of the Bakkujasi. He smiled slightly and nodded in a small show of courtesy. 'Thank you, Uriel, for bringing us to this place of safety.'

'I saw you dancing with her,' Uriel replied, his gaze hardening with suspicion.

'Losha?'

'Yes, my sister.' He glanced around as if expecting some censure of his next remark. 'She is not what you think.'

'You told me this last night, remember?' Viv frowned. 'I understand about her . . . "deformity".' He hated using that word in connection with Losha, it didn't seem right, but it was the word Uriel himself had used before. The man seemed to be having some sort of trouble with his conscience; his face was awash with conflicting emotion. It occurred to Viv that he was trying to warn him off his sister but, since he had apparently not seen her himself for six years, that seemed to be something of a liberty.

Finally, Uriel blurted it out, 'She's a witch.'

'A witch?' Viv couldn't help but laugh at this. It seemed the people of Releeza were even more superstitious than those in his home village of Rinjisti. But his laughter died in his throat when Uriel's face remained deadly serious. 'Even if Losha is a witch,' he said, sobering rapidly, 'it would make no difference to me. I'd like to be her friend, that's all. Anyway, she is *ill*.'

Uriel was adamant. 'I know what I saw and—'

Vivreki! Ayshena's mind voice interrupted their conversation. She sounded worried.

'Just wait a minute.' Viv scrambled to his feet and entered the mouth of the cave. As far as he could tell, Ayshena looked fine. She had stopped the strange weaving and juddering movements, but he grew aware of a bright panic of her thoughts.

What's wrong?

I think something has happened.

Viv peered around the cave but there was no indication of a Swarm egg.

No, not me. It was another Swarm – Yros.

Wait. Do you mean you were simply reacting somehow to another Swarm's birthing?

I – I think so.

He felt a huge surge of relief. *Ayshena, that means you'll be all right now.*

You don't understand . . . Yros is dying. Her egg is taken already. The Shemari have it.

I'm sorry. But you should still be happy, Ayshena. You alone of all the Swarms are doing something to save the eggs from them.

Vivreki, it has happened before, just a few months ago. But then I did not realize what it meant and now I cannot sense that egg.

Vivreki reached up and touched her face. *One at a time, Ayshena. We must find them one at a time,* he soothed. *Where is this new egg?*

It is in a Shemari temple many leagues from here. Yotu Tem, I believe it is named. But poor Yros is dead . . .

Viv sighed in sympathy. *Rest now, Ayshena.*

Promise me we will find it, Vivreki.

I promise.

AFTER AYSHENA WAS calmed down sufficiently, Vivreki went off in search of food. Uriel had disappeared from outside the cave and their discussion about Losha was momentarily forgotten. He eventually found Stief and the others all crammed inside Losha's shelter looking pretty morose as they ate. Losha was not there herself, though she had helped Kalia to cook a meal of trout and vegetables which was delicious. However, even the food seemed to do little to improve the atmosphere.

'What's going on?' Viv asked eventually.

'K-Kalia doesn't want to stay here,' Stief remarked. 'The local people are not pretty enough for her.'

Kalia glared at him in answer to his sarcasm. 'I never said that,' she fumed. 'It's not their fault they're – they're diseased.' To everyone's amazement she began to cry, her face twisting into a tight little ball.

True to form, both Sevim and Stief began fussing around her but Vivreki stared at her coldly, amazed that she still had not learned the lessons of her own past. Her attitudes and prejudices remained, just like those of her father, just like the whole town where she and Sevim had come from. On the other hand, he had to concede that, at the least, Kalia was no hypocrite, and she was honest about her feelings.

'Well, that's all right then, because we're not staying here anyway. We're leaving for Yotu Tem as soon as possible.'

Uriel sat forward. 'Yotu Tem is a long way – probably a week's journey on horseback.'

'And we don't have any horses,' Kalia pouted, drying her eyes.

'But Ayshena can take us.'

'We don't think we want to fly the Swarm again, Vivreki,' Sevim said.

'We?' Viv glanced around the group, who all fidgeted uncomfortably. It was clear that they had been discussing this in his absence, and he felt stung by this small glimmer of disloyalty.

'Why do you want to go to Yotu Tem anyway?'

'There's another egg there.' Vivreki kept his eyes on Uriel as he said this, well aware that the existence of another egg should logically lead the man to question his stubborn belief that the egg contained a dragon. But Uriel's single-mindedness was unassailable by logic or anything else.

'Then perhaps you have been mistaken, and that is the egg you are really seeking – not *my* egg.'

Vivreki was too tired and irritable to point out that the egg they now had – safely tucked amongst his things – did not belong to Uriel.

'You should listen to Vivreki,' Kalia said, slightly patronizingly to Uriel – as if she were soothing a child, 'he is magical, you know. A great mage.'

'What?' Viv could not suppress a smile, and when he looked at Stief and Sevim they had equally bemused expressions on their faces. It had not occurred to any of them that Viv's audacious trick had never been fully explained to Kalia, only her own task of finding and releasing the Quirzel – so Kalia actually thought that . . .

'He made that egg *invisible*,' Kalia said triumphantly.

Vivreki burst out laughing, all rancour forgotten for the moment; Stief and Sevim joined him, laughing till their eyes watered. It had to be the most absurd, funniest thing he'd ever heard. Kalia looked confused but had the grace to smile at their hilarity. 'What? What did I say?'

'Gods bless you, Kalia,' Viv grinned. 'You do our hearts good.'

SOMETIME LATER LOSHA came in and asked Vivreki to join her as she took a walk. He wasn't quite sure where she had been in the meantime. Sevim mentioned that she helped with the children – apparently some of them lived alone with no parents or older siblings to help them. It was a strange, fragmented community but it seemed to function in its own unpredictable manner and the children survived.

As they left the shelter, Viv caught Uriel watching him darkly. He gave a scowl towards the Guardian as he left with Losha.

THE NIGHT SEEMED eldritch, almost fragile, under the glory of Orlannoni and her lesser sisters. Their reflection on the stillness of the lake gave the impression of an infinite abyss in the centre of the caldera. Losha and Vivreki walked along the shore in silence for a while, enjoying the chill clarity of the night air. After a while Losha slipped her hand into his. Her long fingers felt cold and warm at the same time, sending a pleasing thrill through Vivreki. He must have betrayed this reaction somehow, because she stopped and pulled her hand away.

'I'm sorry, Vivreki. I was being too familiar too quickly. It's just that . . . well, this morning, I experienced such a feeling of connection with you.' She stared down at the sand, 'I realize there can never be anything between us and, in truth, that is not what I want. I only want to be your friend.'

'Losha,' he said, 'I feel a bond between us also. Whatever you are comfortable with is fine by me. Let's just enjoy our walk, shall we, because' – he glanced up at Orlannoni – 'who knows how many nights we may have left before the star brings her fire down upon us . . .'

'But there is something else you should know about me . . .' she began. They continued to walk; the silence of the lake and the stars complete, except for the screech of an owl in the distance.

'That you are a witch? Uriel already told me,' he said airily.

'He told you that? Damn him. He ignores me totally for six years and then invades my refuge to cause me further heartache.'

'Losha, think about it this way, your brother was in trouble. Really bad trouble – his sanity, his life threatened, his family gone – he thought of you.' He touched his fingers to his chest, 'You were still there, in his heart.'

She laughed, but the sound had a tinge of bitterness. 'They did not tell me you were an incurable romantic.'

They were suddenly interrupted by the owl as it swooped low across the shimmer of the lake, its reflection as pristine and silent as itself. As it approached, Losha reached out her arm and the bird settled there, its talons completely circling her lower arm.

'It's really majestic,' Viv breathed, in awe.

'Shhh. He's telling me something.' After a few moments of listening intently, Losha sat down on a skeletal piece of driftwood. As she did so, the owl took off again, over the lake. 'There's something coming,' she frowned.

But before Viv could ask her any of the myriad of questions which sprang to mind, he noted something looming in the sky in the direction the owl had taken. Lights, unlike the stars, dancing and moving like motes of brightly coloured dust, still high on the horizon. They were coming closer.

'*Darhg*!' he breathed.

'Don't worry.' Just as Losha spoke, a flurry of white owls flooded the sky, with their whirling reflections turning the waters of the lake white as if the moon itself had fallen down. It only took a minute before the coloured orbs of the approaching *Darhg* were nowhere to be seen. Vivreki stood speechless with wonder and, before he could find anything to say, one of the owls flew back towards Losha. The dead tree trunk on which they were sitting still had the remains of broken branches and the bird alighted just to the side of Losha; it may have been the same bird as before but Vivreki could not tell. Within its precise yellow beak it held a soft, squirming shape. This was the insect which was at the heart of the *Darhg*-seeking spell. The clumsy moth-like thing writhed uselessly in the firm grip of the owl's beak. Losha reached out and took hold of the creature – it was still glowing slightly, with a yellow light which pulsed in wordless distress. She stared at the jittering of the insect's legs for a few moments, the light of it reflecting in the depth of her beautiful eyes. With no warning, she lifted her mask and popped the thing into her mouth, and began chewing vigorously.

Vivreki just sat there slack-jawed and speechless with grim surprise and revulsion. There were no words to express his shock. Apparently unabashed, Losha turned to him and said: 'The bad news is, they were not tracking Ayshena, but they were looking for you.'

He could feel his stomach churning, saliva building in his mouth. Worse than that physical reaction, was the fact that he felt so unsure of his reasons. The world seemed to spin, till the immensity of the stars and the lake, previously so pure and beautiful, seemed somehow to mock his naivety. Because as Losha had lifted the corner of her mask, Vivreki had seen beneath it the polished white gleam of exposed bone.

❧CHAPTER FIFTEEN❧

A CHIOS WAS IN trouble. He was a naturally stubborn man, especially when bullied into something against his will. And at stake in his present quarrel with Rann there were two lives he was most reluctant to give up – Pava's and Kilmer's.

Pava had been his friend ever since Achios could remember. It seemed like a thousand years ago since they first met at the seminary, both ablaze with passion and zeal for their calling, both determined to dedicate their lives to the church. Pava had appeared less intellectual than Achios, but showed a more natural instinct and empathy for people's souls. In truth they had ever been a mismatched pair, but had both succeeded in their calling and now become the most powerful men in Gremeshkenn Tem. When Achios was appointed Hani, Pava had been determined to be the first of the Shemari to pledge his oath to him. Even Achios was moved to see his lifelong friend make his sincere obeisance before him.

Rann wanted him dead, but Achios refused absolutely. Pava's life was non-negotiable. When Rann threatened him with dire consequences, he simply shrugged. 'Waste your time if you will,' he pointed out, 'but you will have to find a new agent to carry out your wishes. If you kill Pava, my cooperation ends.'

Rann had raged furiously about this, sending Achios such a headpain, of flashing, stabbing lights that he thought he would die anyway and his gambit had failed. Rann was a master of suffering, however, and knew exactly where the limits of human tolerance lay. When his voice next invaded Achios's mind after a night of searing agony, he did not even attempt to comfort him, but instead, moved on to his next demand: Kilmer.

❧

ACHIOS WAS ASTUTE enough to realize that Rann might be ready to concede Pava, but he would never let things go with regard to Kilmer. He stood in the way of Cantroji, and Cantroji was germane to the god's still inexplicable plan. As Achios sat, slumped and pale, in his gilded throne while listening to the morning prayers, the battle of wills continued raging in his already blasted mind.

By midday he could retire to his rooms, and there sank into deep black oblivion which was more unconsciousness than sleep, shutting his mind down, as years of Shemari training had taught him, and refusing to answer the voice of the god at all.

When he woke, hours later, two *tengu* stood in his room, one on either side of his bed. Achios sat up with a cry of fear and revulsion – it was one thing to see these vile creatures in his dreams, but their physical reality was awesome. Their wings were wrapped around the ornate headboard of his bed, shutting out most of the light, so that mottled rays of the evening light fell in weak golden stripes across his terrified face.

'What do you want?' he whispered. The *tengu* said nothing, merely glared balefully at him with their jet-black eyes. *Rann? Rann? What do you think you're doing? You cannot send them here.*

They are there to watch over you, my friend, my agent.

'But other people—' Just as Achios spoke, one of his servants entered the room, carrying a steaming bowl of hot water. Normally, he ignored the servants which was the accepted behaviour – many of them in the Hani's inner sanctum were mute, but Achios had not yet learned which ones, and so remained cautious around them.

As the young man walked over to the side table to set down the bowl, it seemed he was about to bump into one of the impassive *tengu*. But where the man's elbow should have connected with the thing's back, a bright fizz of blue light flickered, neither the *tengu* nor the servant visibly reacting. Achios was unable to keep a look of horrified amazement from his face.

The servant leaned forward, his face emerging through the *tengu's* right shoulder – 'Is everything well with you, my Hani?' he inquired solicitously.

'Yes,' Achios replied tersely, unable to force his gaze away from the bizarre sight. 'You may leave now. Send Pava to attend me.'

The man bowed out backwards, his hands clasped deferentially beneath his chin.

'He just cannot see them . . .' Achios muttered.

Why have you called Pava?

'I just had the desire to see him – to remind myself why . . .'

You surprise me sometimes, Achios, and I am not given to surprise.

'Take them away,' gasped Achios. He realized he was shaking, and he fought to quell his tremors but failed so he bundled his blankets around him for comfort. He stared up into the face of the *tengu* standing on his right. The bird-goblin-warrior creature blinked back at him and tipped its head to one side; a look which only served to remind Achios of the utter strangeness of the thing.

No, I believe I will leave them here with you, since they are slayers of vanity. And in defying me you have shown vanity truly vast for one so weak.

'Do you mean they will follow me, everywhere? Please, Lord Rann, people are bound to notice something. Those Shemari who are adept at sensing auras and arcane happenings . . . Your plan will fail if the council deposes me as Hani.' As Achios struggled to prevent any solicitude entering his voice, he also had to fight against inhaling the fetid odour the creatures exuded. His chest was tight.

No, I will take my chances on that.

Achios sighed heavily – blankets pulled over the lower part of his face. 'I will give you Kilmer Torroshi. I can arrange his death easily.'

Make it soon.

Achios felt encouraged, but the *tengu* did not vanish.

AFTER COWERING IN his room for a couple of hours, Achios decided he had to be seen out and about. Pava had still not arrived, but Achios presumed that was because he was busy over at the Sky Temple, and it took time to come back over to the main Gremeshkenn Tem complex. He found himself reluctant to walk towards the *tengu* who still stood like some malodorous statues by the side of the bed platform, so he slid to the bottom end and lowered his feet to the floor. The *tengu* did not move, and he congratulated himself as if for some obscure victory. He padded over to the basin of cooling water, looping cautiously around behind the massive black wings of the nearest *tengu*. After splashing his face with the scented water he did feel slightly calmer, and he found that if he did not look at the beings directly he could stop his stomach from churning. Pretending they were not there was self-deception on a massive scale but Achios attempted to treat it as a challenge to be faced.

It was not until he left his rooms to return to the inner-sanctum throne room where he had decided to receive Pava that the *tengu* made any move.

They did not walk or run, or even fly, but they *translocated* by magical means, vanishing from beside Achios's bed and reappearing just outside the screen door of his chambers. At the first instance Achios almost cried out in fright, as a sinister sound accompanied their movements; a mixture of feathers folding and an implosion of air. As he walked the length of the corridor, the *tengu* vanished and reappeared three times in all. Achios, his peripheral vision clouded by the movement of black feathers, kept his gaze fixed ahead of him on the doors. He would keep his bargain with Rann in this matter, he decided, because otherwise, the stench of their feathers would always be with him, till he would surely go insane.

IN HIS NEW position, it didn't take long for Achios to discover Kilmer's affair with Cion Gezezi – in fact, he had suspected it since attending the wedding in Falloden Sen. He had vaguely wondered then about the details of Asoori's sudden marriage. It seemed certain she would have married for her commission – she was an ambitious girl after all – but at the time he had wondered what was in the arrangement for Kilmer Torroshi. Everything fell into place after a meeting later that evening with the Shemari's spies.

It was the first time he had called the Neruk'eel to his presence, and he realized they would be assessing him as much as he would them – the power of their sect was indisputable, traces of it infiltrating like bloodied ribbons throughout the very fabric of society.

Disappointingly only three of them appeared at the meeting. He could not recall if these were the same Neruk'keel he had encountered when last summoned by the old Hani. He had only learned how to contact them now because of special instructions and a token he had found contained in a lacquer despatch box presented to him on his investiture. He had placed the gold and jade token prominently on the arm of his throne then left the chamber as instructed. When he returned, after an hour, it was to find a message arranging the meeting. He was unsure how he felt about all this secrecy, arrogant enough still to resent such manipulation, however oblique.

When he first entered the room he sensed a certain tension which he imagined was due to their silent appraisal of him. None of them spoke, but merely waited for the new Hani to address them. Once they were seated, however, and he asked about Kilmer Torroshi, he could sense their attitude changing, becoming faintly condescending – despite the fact that they could not see him and their expressions were almost totally obscured by deep, purple hoods. As the three heads turned towards one another – making Achios wonder if they were telepathic – he tried to attune his 'listening' to pick up any stray thoughts from them, but he knew they would sense him so did not probe too hard.

Finally, the middle one extended his hand and drew a symbol on the table, which meant nothing to Achios. 'What do you require to know of Torroshi?'

'Why did he wish to marry my niece? What is in it for him?'

'It was an attempt to disguise his true proclivities.'

'Pardon.'

'He is committed to another man. One of the Bakkujasi.'

Achios's mind raced to the correct conclusion – he remembered Cion Gezezi's enthusiasm for the mission to Cantroji. 'Cion Gezezi,' he murmured.

The middle Neruk'eel could hardly contain his air of smugness. Achios was sure he drew the quickest possible symbol. 'We are greatly surprised you did not know. Any Bakkujasi could have answered this question.'

Another fast symbol. 'It is irrelevant now, is it not? He will have offspring with your niece, to disguise his true nature, and the succession of Cantroji will be secure.'

'Gezezi must be punished. The honour of the Bakkujasi is at stake.'

A different hand stretched forth, with long, claw-like fingers. When this Neruk'eel spoke Achios was surprised to realize it was a woman – her voice was aged as leather, but still sharp and clear. 'Cion's honour is already tainted but do not delude yourself, Hani, that such cases are a rarity. How you deal with a disgraced Bakkujasi is of course your own decision, but Gezezi is a useful and ambitious young man . . .'

The third spy put a hand forward and drew a surprisingly complex symbol in the sand. 'We respect your power, Hani. Do you intend to send your *tengu* to accomplish your act of justice?'

ACHIOS CAME AWAY from his meeting in a state of shock. He was confident that he had managed to disguise his surprise at their being able to 'see' or sense the *tengu* somehow, but if they had been probing his mind at that point, it was more than likely the panic invading his thoughts had leaked out.

As soon as he was back in his private chambers, disregarding the *tengu* completely as he stalked back along the passageways, he voiced his thoughts aloud. 'Well, that went well did it not, my Lord Rann? I *knew* it would be impossible for them to remain undetected. You must get rid of these creatures at once.'

I think not. It will do your reputation little harm if rumours arise about the tengu. *They are not intrinsically evil – it depends what use you put them to – they are merely tools if you like. So, what now of our friend Torroshi?*

Achios sighed. 'He will have to be dispensed with.'

Murdered you mean. Tsk. At least have the fortitude to say the word, my friend. Denial is costly.

'As you say then; murdered.'

YOU MUST KILL Earl Kilmer Torroshi.

What? Cion woke with a start and sat bolt upright on his mattress. In the gloom he could just discern the figure of Achios, sitting cross-legged on the floor. The image was powerful, projected all the way from Gremeshkenn Tem – to the new Hani, it was merely a way of reminding Cion that he could not evade the consequences of his failure at Releeza.

I know, Cion, that you are lovers, but killing him will purge your soul and prove to us that you are still worthy of the mask you wear. Despite your ineptitude.

'No, we are no longer lovers – it is finished.' Cion spoke aloud, unsure whether Achios would be picking up his thoughts as he did in the Bakkujasi dreamstate.

I still need him dispensed with as soon as possible. Then – I don't care how you do it – I want the heretic Snoot, and I want the Swarm egg recovered.

Cion stared aghast at the indistinct figure of the Hani. How could he know about Snoot? 'I have sent trackers after them,' he said by way of justification.

Achios sighed. *He and his compatriots will reach Yotu Tem within the next fourteen days. There is a new egg there and he will try to take it. Cion, you have disgraced yourself beyond measure. If you had captured or killed the heretic at the first opportunity, as instructed, none of this would be necessary – redemption or second chances are as rare as any miracle amongst the Bakkujasi.*

'I will not fail you, Hani. My life, my soul and my sword are at your service.'

The shadowy form seemed unimpressed by this declaration. The Hani vanished as he had arrived, with no salutation or warning.

Once Achios's presence was gone, Cion examined his feelings about the task he had just been set. It did not dismay him to realize he had few qualms about the murder of his lover. For his career meant everything and, once Kilmer was gone, Cion's commitment to his calling would be renewed, and strengthened.

He fell back to sleep with no great difficulty.

IN THE END, six of them travelled to Yotu Tem, for Losha insisted on accompanying them. She had loaned them supplies and mounts for the journey. Six horses was a big undertaking for the community and the only horses they had been able to provide were the scruffy old nags which they used to fetch and carry around the village. In return for this favour Losha had demanded that she come along. There was a famed dispensary at the Yotu Tem temple complex, where she could acquire salves and medicines for the orphan children of the village. At least, that was her explanation, but Vivreki was sure it was more to do with remaining near him – which would be fine except that he could hardly bring himself to look at her since their traumatic moonlight walk.

He felt stupid. Losha had never made any pretence at normality after all and he had only known her for a day when he had witnessed her eating the *Darhg*. Perhaps he had vaguely started to convince himself that he and Losha might establish some kind of relationship. It was true, after all, that he had never felt so . . . so smitten. He had confided in his brother that same night, his voice shaking slightly as he talked about it. Stief had had the good grace not to laugh as Viv feared that he might; in fact Stief looked mildly shocked as well. 'She seems so f-feminine,' he remarked.

Vivreki glanced wistfully at Losha riding ahead of him; she *was* feminine. She was beautiful, above the mask. She was also fairly annoyed with him right now as his method of dealing with the matter had been simply to avoid being on his own with her.

They had left Ayshena behind for the moment. She would rejoin them as they approached Yotu Tem if she could. Vivreki sorely missed the feeling of knowing she was nearby, having become used to her presence, both physically and mentally. For some reason, he found himself thinking of Calla as they rode, remembering her laughter the day he had finally perfected the trick he had done for Kalia with the flowers.

He found himself smiling at this memory, and was still smiling faintly when Losha turned to look at him. Thinking he was smiling towards her, she smiled in return – or at least, that was his impression despite her veil. He sighed, knowing he would have to talk to her sometime, although he had no idea what to say.

THE CITY WHICH surrounded the sanctuary of Yotu Tem was a low, sprawling conglomeration which they approached from the north. As they drew nearer, the desert gave way to scrubland again, the patches of grey-green sagebrush giving way to thicker grass. Eventually this became meadow, which at this late time of the year was patchy green and faded brown. Although devoid of forest, small copses of trees, spindly silver birch or cedars, punctuated the view like little islands in a sea. The grass flowing around the edges was constantly channelled by the wind.

They camped in the midst of such a copse still five leagues from the city. They needed to approach carefully in the guise of temple pilgrims, as they did not want to attract any undue attention. The plan was for Losha, Uriel and Sevim to go in search of the dispensary and find the various medicines Losha needed. It was possible that she might be able to beg much of the stuff as a charitable donation, but they would have to see how the land lay once they got inside. Only Uriel had ever been to Yotu Tem before, and that had been years earlier. It was clear when he mentioned this earlier occasion that he had come to seek healing for Losha, as she had flinched uncomfortably at the mention. The tension between the estranged brother and sister remained, although they had spent some time talking whilst on the journey.

They would then make their way back to the current location where Kalia was to remain guarding the horses and Sandeshi's egg. Viv and Stief, meanwhile, would go in search of the other egg somewhere inside the temple itself. However, if they did not return within a set time or if there was any sign of trouble from the temple, Kalia and the others were under strict instruction to leave without them and begin the journey back to the city of ghosts.

If Viv and Stief had any niggling worry about this loose plan, it was Kalia. She was the least able to defend herself so remaining in as much cover as she could find with the horses was essential. Also, Vivreki did not entirely trust Uriel not to try and take the egg if he returned first – Sevim would certainly try to prevent this, but it was a concern.

THE TEMPLE WAS much less ostentatious than Kamyaaz Tem: a squat construction of black marble which was covered in decades of grime and vine-like creepers. It boasted no minarets or spires, no bells or even prayer-wheels, either inside the temple yard or anywhere else to be seen. The sombre building seemed to suck in the light of the sun and transmute it into a melancholy which matched Viv's current mood perfectly.

There were plenty of pilgrims visiting the temple though – more than might be expected considering there was no religious festival. Perhaps the approaching star had people worried and they had turned to their gods for solace. The crowd was remarkably quiet, speaking its prayers and entreaties in a whisper and ringing tiny hand bells which made only a subdued, sweet sound. The overall effect of the place was almost soporific, as if the faithful were merely sleepwalking. But as he watched, Viv realized that they were moving in a predetermined pattern, weaving arcane shapes in the dust with their shuffling footsteps. This worked well for the group, who joined in anonymously with the other worshippers, muttering prayers and stopping occasionally to light a candle at the small shrines.

After a while of dusty, dry-throated walking Sevim signalled to the others that he had spotted the side entrance to the temple. They drifted slowly towards it, keeping the same shuffling rhythm to their movements so as not to attract any attention.

'I didn't see any monks or priests,' Uriel commented. 'That's got to be good.' He seemed surprisingly animated and enlivened by their mission, and his eyes had more sparkle about them than they had seen before.

'Not really. That means they're all inside,' Stief scowled.

'We should go,' Losha urged. She nodded through the gateway where the path split – one side leading into the building and the other to the temple complex at the rear.

'Yes,' Vivreki caught her gaze. 'Losha . . . good luck.'

She nodded. 'And to you, Vivreki.'

IT WAS COLD – really cold – inside the temple. The black marble surface of the walls looked cleaner and far more impressive that the temple's exterior; it glinted in the low light of the sconces.

As they reached the core of the building, Viv let out a low whistle, and Stief stared around in astonishment.

Kamyaaz Tem, where they had rescued Kalia, had been what they had expected from their limited experience of temples, like some giant gold and curlicued behemoth. Yotu Tem, however, was quite the opposite; it was as if some wondrous phoenix had been entombed inside this slick black shell; rich yellow gold glinted everywhere, striking a note of shining opulence against the funereal background. Veins of the gold even ran through the rock of the walls in chaotic patterns that echoed the weeds on the outside like some precious, vibrant honeysuckle. Gemstones glittered from the lanterns, appearing to drip in liquid cascades, their multiple facets diffusing the reflections of the flames into delicate rainbows. At the farthest end loomed the massive golden statue of a sleeping Oshi, dominating the elaborate altar before it.

Viv and Stief moved slowly through the press of worshippers drinking in the lavish scenery with greedy amazement. There were perhaps a hundred people in the cavernous hall, mainly pilgrims but also a few monks whispering their prayers as they had outside. Here inside though, as their words of devotion ricocheted off the marble walls, the effect was amazing. It combined to sound like a moving, living thing: a sea of whispers, a lesser Swarm.

Viv gave Stief a nudge and motioned his head towards one side wall where a painting of a Swarm had been picked out in liquid gold. Each different segment of its body was adorned with an emerald, ten of them in all, from the largest at its abdomen tapering to the smallest at the tip of its tail.

Stief replied in a breathy whisper, 'It's a-amazing.'

Reaching the back of the great hall without incident, they made for a small doorway over to one side. Ducking through it, they wandered through various passageways beyond, for what felt like a long time. Eventually, Stief noticed a heavy gold-embossed door which lay open ahead of them.

Beyond the threshold of the door, the ground dropped away into a deep pit, filling the entire chamber. A long, narrow suspended walkway ran right down the middle of the yawning space for about three hundred yards. The void was lit by a succession of lanterns which were suspended out over the edges of this walkway, and at the other end two bored-looking guards stood with their longspears crossed before another, much less ornate, doorway.

Viv ducked back out into the corridor. 'What are we going to do, Stief?' he hissed. 'The egg's kept in there, I can feel it, but . . .' He motioned to the walkway and the lanterns and Stief grimaced his gloomy understanding. There was no way they could approach the other end undetected.

'Maybe we can lure the guards over,' Stief mused.

'What about the lights? If we somehow put out the lanterns as we go?'

'Might work. Scare the hell out of them I imagine. By the time we get to the other end we'd be in pitch blackness though, then we'd have to cross back over the walkway in the dark.' Stief poked his head around the door and peered over into the pit, but there was no indication of how deep it might go, or what was down there.

'If we work our way along the outside of the walkway holding onto the ropes, we could still reach up inside the lanterns to put them out, I reckon,' Viv said. 'The only danger might be if they notice our hands, so we'll have to move fast.'

'Are you m-mad?' Stief groaned. 'What if we f-fall?'

'Well, we just make sure we *don't* fall, but we have to chance it.' Viv's eyes had that old familiar glint in them, and Stief was torn between being glad to see his brother's old spark back and frustrated because he knew he would get swept along as always by Viv's enthusiasm.

'I – I'm not sure . . .' Just as he spoke, there was a soft splashing sound from down in the pit, followed by a deep-throated growl. They stared at each other, eyes wide in alarm.

Then Viv smiled. 'Let's do it.'

THE OTHERS WERE having surprisingly few problems, since no one had challenged them as they made their way round to the rear of the temple complex. But it seemed obvious now that they were unlikely to be donated the medicines as Losha had hoped. The dispensary building was guarded by two stout men carrying longspears and armed with swords. Uriel assumed these spears were to keep the 'afflicted' at a distance, for many of the pilgrims to this quieter area were lepers. He also wondered how the sight of such harsh treatment was affecting his sister.

'Why would you guard medicines?' he muttered.

'They are difficult and expensive to make, Uriel,' Losha replied quietly. Her gaze remained stony as she observed the crowds of suffering people – most of whom had been abandoned by society as she had.

'Sir, sir?' Someone was trying to attract Uriel's attention. It was a young woman who wore a strange garment comprising a leather bodice and a deep red skirt, her hair obscured by a twisted red turban, the end of which concealed the lower part of her face in a way that was familiar.

'Brother and sister,' she said softly, 'where are your bells?'

Sevim was quicker to realize the implication of her question, and he bowed his head. 'I'm sorry, *kerzi*, but I have lost it.' *Kerzi* being the correct form of address for a nun. She had assumed that Sevim and Losha were lepers. It was an easy assumption to make with Losha, and Uriel – glancing at the Sin Eater's dishevelled appearance, frizzed sandy hair and pale skin – could see why Sevim might also be considered afflicted.

'You may request another from the dispensary,' she nodded. 'Tell them Denna sent you.'

'Thank you, *kerzi*.'

She peered more closely at Uriel. 'Are you visiting?' she asked, a faint trace of suspicion in her voice. His eyes were drawn to the curved silver dagger at her waist. What kind of nuns wore weapons, he wondered.

'I'm his cousin,' he replied, cursing himself inwardly for the feebleness of his lie. 'We're from Cantroji.'

Her gaze became milder as a hidden smile transformed the hardness of her face completely. 'It's very good of you to come with him. The corrupted ones seldom receive such courtesy from their kin.'

'It's the least I can do,' he mumbled, avoiding Losha's gaze as he spoke. 'Come, Sevim, let's go and find you another bell.' They wandered off, with Uriel ahead, trying hard not to break into a run. 'Is she still watching us?' he hissed.

'Sir . . .' she called after them. 'Sir, the dispensary is over there,' she pointed over to their right, and Uriel gave her a small wave of thanks.

'Why do the good sisters wear knives?' he whispered to Losha.

'So they can amputate fingers and toes at the first sign of infection. Limbs as well – not with the little daggers obviously – their "mercy" is swift and painful.'

THEY EDGED SLOWLY out onto the walkway – one clinging to either side. Stief could hardly bring himself to breathe. He looked through the ropes to watch for Viv's hands so that they could reach up in unison to kill the guttering candle flames inside the lanterns. Stief licked his fingers and snuffed out the light, as did Viv.

There was the hiss of the flame and then Viv cursed. 'Shit, that bloody hurt!'

'For godssake, Viv, just concentrate,' Stief muttered. He glanced over at the guards who, so far, had not reacted. They had almost reached the halfway point before the guards noted the gradually decreasing light levels.

'Look,' one of them nodded over, 'must have been a draught . . .'

The other squinted ahead and so was looking directly at the lanterns as Viv and Stief extinguished the next ones. 'That's odd.'

Another light went out. The ropes of the walkway creaked slightly as the brothers reached the fulcrum of its balance.

'What's going on?' The first guard licked his lips nervously. 'Maybe we should tell one of the priests.'

Stief motioned between the ropes for Viv to stop for a moment, hoping the guards would revert to the inertia of boredom.

'And tell them what, exactly? That the lanterns are goin' out?'

Another pair of lights was extinguished, as Viv and Stief came within thirty feet of where the guards were standing. It was getting seriously dark now, the remaining four lanterns only managing to shed two weak pools of yellow light. From underneath the walkway, the sound of something thrashing through unseen water could be heard. Stief screwed his eyes tight shut and uttered a silent, fervent prayer to Oshi.

'I don't like this at all,' the younger guard frowned. Without warning, he jabbed out with his longspear. 'Who's there?' he demanded.

'No one's there,' the other guard remonstrated, faintly amused by his jittery companion. 'Looks like they didn't trim the wicks or something.' When the next pair was extinguished, only the two lanterns nearest to them were left.

Viv and Stief glanced at one another, unsure of what to do next; neither of them wanted to resort to killing the men. Even if they could send them toppling over the railing, there was obviously something lethal somewhere down there in the dark. 'We can't,' Stief mouthed.

Viv wondered if the guards might find it bizarre to know that, just in front of them, under their very noses, their fate was being silently debated. The moment of this deliberation seemed to last a long time;

Stief stared at the younger guard facing him, whilst feeling the muscles in his arm tighten with fatigue.

'I'm going to try and relight them,' the other guard said. 'No point standing round here in the dark.' As he started forward without any further discussion, Stief lurched to one side so his face wasn't visible between the ropes.

'Be careful,' his companion called out, sounding somewhat bereft. 'It's treacherous in the dark.'

'I'll keep in the middle . . .'

Viv and Stief hung on grimly, with heads tucked out of sight and their postures frozen, hardly daring to breathe.

As soon as the guard had passed them, Viv snuffed out the final lantern on his side. As Stief glanced over, he was dismayed to see the glint of a grin on his brother's face; it put everything that followed in a different light.

It all happened so fast, as the younger guard, completely agitated now, lurched forward in irrational panic. 'No!' he yelped, as if he could command the vanished flame back into life. It was almost completely dark now in the huge space as he reached out for the lantern. Stief's hand was already outstretched to snuff the final flickering glow on his own side, but as he looked over at the startled sound of the yell, he saw Viv had vaulted the ropes and was grabbing for the guard's arm. It seemed clear that he had decided to act without consultation.

'No!' Stief hauled himself onto the bridge, all stealth momentarily forgotten. There was a terrible creaking of the suspension ropes as Viv was grappling with the terrified guard who was screaming for his companion to come back. Just as Viv managed to heft the guard over the side of the hand-rope, Stief reached out in time to catch hold of the flailing man's tunic sleeve.

'What are you doing?' Viv stormed. 'Let him *go*!' Without apparent premeditation he grabbed the discarded longspear and rapped it hard across Stief's wrist.

Stief held his grip. 'For godssake, you stubborn maniac . . .'

The man was sobbing in terror now, as Stief was losing his grip, the nerves of his hands deadened by Viv's vicious blow. And beneath them, something roiled in the black water. 'Hold on, just hold on,' Stief gabbled uselessly. Behind him, Viv had raced off into the now unguarded room beyond leaving him to deal with the situation. The guard kept knocking his hands away, which didn't help. It was obvious his mind was too panic-stricken to realize Stief was trying to help him.

There was a ripping sound as the thin fabric of his tunic gave way. Stief caught one last glimpse of a face paralysed by fear as the guard plummeted away into the darkness below, his arms jerking and scrabbling as if by some miracle he might get back onto the bridge. As soon as he hit the water, there was an exultant roar from the mysterious creature below. The screaming and thrashing were mercifully brief, but Stief knew he would be hearing the horror of it in his mind for weeks after. A smell of displaced fetid water wafted up to him, followed by a wet, smacking sound which made him want to gag. His dismay at the young man's unnecessary fate was quickly replaced by fury, and he turned and ran towards the door through which Viv had disappeared.

The room was quite small and hexagonal, more reminiscent of a gazebo than part of such an impressive temple, despite the ornate filigree and gold drapes which lined its interior. But it overflowed with treasure: brooches, necklaces, gold dralchi, uncut stones, all piled high in willow baskets. Clearly these were the offerings from the more affluent pilgrims to Oshi's shrine. Viv did not even stop to glance at such bright temptations but lunged straight towards a nondescript hessian sack tied with a single rope. He loosened the neck of the bag and pulled it apart eagerly. There it lay, what could only be the egg of a Swarm. It glinted with a kind of dull silver obstinance in the glow of the only overhead lantern. This one was slightly smaller than the egg from Releeza, which Stief now thought of as 'Uriel's egg', and it may have been a different metallic colour, but it was hard to tell in the muted light. There was something unnerving about the way it seemed to suck in the sparse light which made Stief fight to remain calm.

Viv could not hide his rather avaricious pleasure on seeing it. '*Yes*,' he breathed. 'Yes, we've got you.' Tugging the drawstring tight again he swung the sack onto his back, lacing his arm through the rope for extra security. Once he jogged the load into a comfortable position he glanced at his brother, and the look of triumph faded from his face.

'What?' he frowned back at the look on Stief's face as if his actions of only a minute before were completely forgotten. 'Come on.'

'You bastard,' Stief groaned. 'You didn't have to do that. D'you know what just happened to him? He got eaten alive down there . . . eaten alive.'

Although Viv's expression twitched slightly he was resolute. 'It was necessary,' he snapped, 'and if we don't get out of here quick, may be necessary again.' He turned away abruptly and began to walk back along the bridge. As he passed Stief, his brother had an irrational urge to haul him over the side and watch his precious egg go with him. Instead he simply turned and followed, his fury and dismay unabated. It wouldn't be the first time Viv had overstepped the line, by a long way, but he had never been responsible for a death before now. There would have to be a reckoning for this, but for the moment it would have to wait . . .

THE BROTHERS RAN back over the bridge in almost total darkness; the weight of the bag did not seem to slow Viv overmuch. They concentrated on staying firmly in the middle in order not to make the bridge sway too violently. As they reached the far end the older guard reappeared in the doorway carrying a lantern in one hand and a long taper in the other. 'Taj' he called. 'Taj, I got a taper. I'll start lightin' from this end.'

Stief felt further sickened on hearing the youth's name. It made it seem so much worse – although for Taj, of course, it could not possibly get any worse. He moaned inwardly as hot saliva coursed into his mouth, wondering if he was going to vomit – the sound of the young guard being devoured was still fresh in his mind.

Viv simply carried on running, his shape looming out of the darkness so suddenly that the other guard had literally no idea what hit him. A punch, which Viv landed squarely on his face, broke his nose and sent him toppling to the floor with an abrupt scream of pain. Stief grabbed at the back of Vivreki's jerkin, unsure whether his brother intended any further injury.

'Leave him alone, Vivreki,' he snarled, 'j-just leave him.'

Viv glanced back at him as if offended. 'Gods, Stief, what d'you take me for?' he frowned.

They raced on along the narrow dark passageways, ducking into doorways whenever people approached. A woman worshipper who looked lost managed to jog Viv's arms, which were now cradled around the egg, as she hurried past. He scowled at her ferociously.

'Going to k-kill her as well?' Stief spat. They continued in grim silence.

❧

'PLEASE, SIR. PLEASE, I know you can help. I sense it.'

Sevim stared in dismay at the recently deceased, who must have only been about seventeen years old. Although this was a place where families regularly abandoned those unfortunate enough to have contracted leprosy, it seemed to him that she had probably died of some other disorder of the blood.

'You *are* a Sin Eater, are you not, sir?' The voice of the old woman who had accosted him acquired a wheedling quality, a certain edge borne of desperation which could lead to trouble if denied. With Uriel and Losha he had finally managed to coax from a sympathetic monk a supply of precious salves that might last the city of ghosts for a couple of years. The mention of Denna's name and the vague inference that she had given permission for such generosity had helped persuade the monk to their cause, but it would be better if they left the sanctuary before any questions were asked.

Uriel glanced a warning at Sevim. They had been under specific instruction about not attracting attention with Spall, but Sevim merely shrugged in response. He knew Uriel would not understand that he was bound by his calling to respond to her plea.

'She's so young,' he said trying to deflect the old woman. 'It is likely she had no sin. The nuns will take care of her.'

She snorted in bitter derision. 'The nuns, why would they care? My granddaughter worked on the streets to support us both. She was a whore, you understand, Sin Eater?'

'Yes. You were her grandmother?'

'Yes.'

'Sevim,' Uriel muttered urgently, 'we've got to go.'

'It will only take me a minute,' Sevim replied.

Uriel grabbed hold of Sevim's arm and made to pull him aside. When Sevim did not budge, he leaned in closer towards him. 'If you release Spall now, we're bound to attract attention.'

'Then we will prove a diversion.' Sevim wrenched his arm back, an expression of anger building in his grey eyes. All the inherent queerness, the *otherness* of the Sin Eater, was suddenly apparent in his gaze, making Uriel flinch back from him. 'Help me move her corpse out of sight,' Sevim hissed.

And Uriel obeyed, compelled by whatever force it was that enabled a Sin Eater to keep the balance of souls; unknowing that the very act – an act of mercy to the soul of a nameless whore – was balancing an act of thoughtless violence perpetrated at the same moment by their friend. As the grandmother reached out a palsied hand to help them, Sevim snarled at her. 'Do not touch her again.'

As they carried the pitifully light bundle between them into the shadows of the nearest building, Uriel remarked, 'That was unkind, Sevim. She has lost her granddaughter.'

Losha laughed cynically at this comment. 'Do you think being sick makes you a good person, Uriel?'

'I hadn't really thought about it that way.'

Sevim's cold glare flickered back to the grandmother still standing by the corner where they had left her. 'What choices do you think she had? Her grandmother used her up.'

'How do you know that?' Uriel frowned.

'I just know.'

IT WAS THE fastest he had ever worked. In truth, since being in the company of Ayshena, Spall was harder to contain, and seemed more energized somehow. Now, Sevim could hear his young wise voice inside himself, so full of glee it bordered on malicious; *I'm coming out, Sevim. Spall is coming to do it. See Uriel. See Losha* . . . He seemed particularly fascinated with Losha, who he had not physically met yet.

When Sevim had first became aware of Spall, he used to wonder why the voice inside his head sounded so like a child and yet, once Spall manifested himself, he spoke perfectly normally. It gave Sevim comfort to realize that Spall was dependent on using the basic frame of his body and his thought processes and it was *he* who gave Spall the veneer of calm and assurance other people saw.

He cut her arm with his knife, and touched the blood to his lips, knowing it was diseased but he had no choice. There was instantly the bright, hot taste of copper in his mouth, and then the blinding flare which was always the last thing Sevim was fully aware of . . .

THE MIDDAY PRAYERS were now at their height, and the temple was crowded. In an effort not to arouse any suspicion with their burden, Viv and Stief made their way across the central sanctum by passing behind the statue of Oshi, where the faithful were not permitted to go. They picked a path gingerly through stray votive candles and highly scented wreaths that had been thrown onto the statue of the sleeping goddess. Stief suspected the flowers – sold in the temple grounds – were chosen for their soporific effects; he could feel his heart rate slowing and his mind calming down from the cold fury he had felt towards his brother.

But Viv was allergic to the flowers and eventually began to sneeze. Unable to see where he was putting his feet over the bulk of the bag he was carrying, he kept standing on the offerings, crushing the delicate blooms and releasing further pollen. On the third sneeze he managed to knock over a stand of flowers which crashed outwards causing a cascade of offerings to fall from the goddess's carved leg.

The young woman whose family had just given the display was still praying and so she was looking at the blossoms as she chanted her prayer. She let out a shrill wail of surprise and horror that carried high above the sibilant whispering sounds of Yotu Tem. The goddess Oshi had rejected her obeisance! People began to crowd around her as she pointed excitedly at her scattered tribute.

Viv began to panic slightly – even though he was obscured from view by Oshi's legs – and reeled back, cursing and staggering along behind the length of the goddess's statue in an effort to flee the unwanted attentions of the crowd. In his clumsy haste he managed to knock a few of the candles over, sending them rolling into a narrow channel behind the altar, which was full of withered offerings.

'Viv.' Stief, apparently unruffled by the chaos which Viv always attracted, strode between the wreckage of crushed blooms. 'Calm down.' He touched his younger brother's arm and made eye contact as if reassuring a child. Viv frowned at him. 'Are you all right, Stief?'

Stief had to admit there was something odd about the scent of the flowers. Before he had the chance to examine the state of his sobriety, however, a blaze of light flashed through the temple like a tsunami. The worshippers threw themselves to the ground.

'Spall,' Viv growled.

❧CHAPTER SIXTEEN❧

S PALL STRETCHED LAZILY, enjoying the feeling of being in possession of the body again. Maybe this time he would not relinquish
it. 'Hello, Losha,' he said. He pushed a stray lock of hair back from
his face – Spall was not afraid to look at the world, he had seen the
worst of it.

Or so he thought. The corpse of the young woman drew his
attention immediately. He could see vividly the unclean colours of her
wounded soul, and her sins enrobing her like a malignant caul. Near
her heart, the one tiny uncorrupted area of pink revealed how she had
clung on to hope once.

Reaching out his hand, he took hold of the drifting caul. Only to
a Sin Eater would this manifest itself physically – it was at once both
insubstantial and turgid, its vile colours nausea inducing. He ripped
the dreadful apparition apart, dim daylight surging through the
new-made rents like a sweet reclamation. He scrunched it into a ball,
tossing it up into the air, where it floated like some dirty, unnatural
bubble. Spall grinned nastily, with sparkling-white canines which were
unusually feral.

Then he proceeded to eat the dead woman's sins.

THEY WERE TRAPPED by the mass response of the worshippers;
before them the floor of the temple was a patchwork of multicoloured
robes as the faithful had prostrated themselves in reverential obeisance, believing the flash of power had come from Oshi. As the Sin
Eater was situated behind the temple building at the moment of

transformation, it appeared that the light flared outwards from the statue.

'This way!' Viv pointed to an ornate side door which looked as though it led somewhere important. Stief scrambled behind him. From behind them, a babble of noise was coming from the worshippers as people frantically compared what they had just seen – with the moving offerings and then the lights, people were sure they had witnessed a miracle of Oshi.

Viv and Stief lapsed back into silence until they reached the end of the corridor, which opened into a large chamber lit only by candles. There the two brothers came to an abrupt halt, for in the corner of the space was a Bakkujasi, *the* Bakkujasi. The man was not looking at them, but was in deep meditation; his legs were crossed and his hands in the classic position and, fortunately for them, his eyes were closed. He was levitating fairly high above the table platform from which he must have started.

'It's him,' Stief breathed. 'The one who killed our mother.'

The Bakkujasi remained so motionless it would have been easy to mistake him for another temple statue. Viv had the impression that there was no one else in the room, contrary to the evidence of his eyes, and this unnerved him. Behind the golden mask, the distinctive silver-white hair was tied in numerous plaits, and at his hips he wore his swords, the longer one of which had murdered Calla.

With a snarl of rage Viv lunged forward, only to be jerked back instantly by his brother. He glared furiously in response, pretty sure that Stief would resort to reason as he always did: the Bakkujasi would kill him, Stief would argue, he was more skilled than Viv, more highly trained. All of these things Stief might say, because he wanted to protect him as he always had. Vivreki shrugged off his older brother's grasp, scowling furiously.

Stief licked his lips nervously. 'A-at least give me the egg. I'll – I'll keep it safe for you.'

Without hesitation Viv slipped off the rope strap and, pulling his blade, advanced murderously towards Cion. Suddenly a young woman appeared in the opposite doorway; she wore the *yurik* and mail of a Brengarmah officer. She gazed directly at Vivreki, as if unsurprised by his presence, almost as if she had been expecting him.

'Drop your weapons,' she ordered. 'Now.'

❧

Viv froze. For a long moment nothing seemed to move in the silent chamber, just the slight stir of the woman's hair in the few currents of tenacious wind which somehow managed to seep into the building. Shifting on the balls of her feet, she ostentatiously drew both a long, thin blade and then, a vicious-looking dagger. The hiss of steel leaving its scabbard was a high clear sound which rang loud amongst the highest reaches of the vaulted ceiling.

Viv blinked stupidly. 'This is a trap?'

'Of sorts.' Her stance did not change, and Viv knew she would not allow herself to get distracted. Still, it didn't hurt to try.

'How did you know we were coming?' he ventured. No answer. Viv stepped back a pace, his stance unguarded. He gave a wide, relaxed smile to the woman, whose ready posture was almost rigid. 'I only came in to pay my respects to Oshi and . . .' he moved forward slightly as he spoke, just a couple of steps but he was just outside her reach.

'Drop it,' she commanded again.

'*No, I don't think so.*' She was only a woman, after all – how difficult could it be? That surge of confidence evaporated when the Brengarmah officer suddenly attacked. Viv had never imagined there could be others as good as he. She came in close and tried to disarm him of his blade with a quick twist of her own. But it was a move he knew – even stupidly thought he had invented – and he countered by changing the balance of his grip and managed to hit a glancing blow to her forehead with the heavy pommel of his sword, before having to fling himself backwards as she slashed across with the dagger. He allowed himself a couple of steps backwards, knowing there was plenty of space behind him, but the woman gave him no respite as she ran towards him to press her attack again.

'Stief, go!' he gasped. 'Just get the egg out of here!'

Viv took an almighty gamble and, side-stepping, kicked out at her right hand, sending the dagger flying from her grasp. She cursed, but did not hesitate as a less experienced swordsman might have done. He grinned ferociously at the knowledge that he had evened his chances. Even better, he noted that she seemed to have some problem with her right leg. A previous injury perhaps. Swiftly he decided to make her bring the fight to him, and so tire her out. It wasn't going all his way, however, because his long coat was impeding his speed.

His opponent frowned at him as he sped over to the far side of the hall, near where the Bakkujasi still meditated, immobile, in the corner. She was clearly puzzled by his flight, having imagined he would simply stand and duel. As she ran towards him again, the limp in her right leg was more pronounced over a larger distance.

Just as she reached him, Viv laughed his crazy laugh for the first time in ages, a wild energy coursing through him. She stopped short at the sound of it, just outside his reach, as if he had slapped her.

'Come on then,' he taunted, twitching his sword.

This mockery only served to break through her hesitation, and she lunged forward bringing her blade up to meet his. Viv had no time to speak again, she was so fast; her light-looking weapon was impressively strong as they locked together, pushing forward, each seeking to unbalance the other. With supreme effort Viv managed to shove her back a step but as he took a pace forward, intending to stay under her guard, she kicked his legs from under him. He scrambled to his feet again, running fast from a crouched position. His sudden laughter rang to the rafters, not quite as spontaneous this time, but deliberately goading her.

So sharp and fast was her blade, he was not aware at first that he had been cut. It took moments before realization sunk in, that she had sliced him across the back as he had recovered his balance. As he stood up fully, out of her reach, he felt the jagged fire of severed nerve endings, and his laughter gave way to a curse. He hoped her first blood was not too deep a gash.

Despite this advantage, she had paused and was staring at him curiously. Still, she did not drop her guard and neither did he. He felt nauseous for some reason, and was totally unprepared for her next words.

'Snoot?'

'Huh?'

'It *is*. It's Snoot, isn't it?'

Viv's mind reeled; he had avoided thinking of that name even after Ayshena reminded him of it. 'N-No,' his denial was more to stop the woman voicing it once more. 'I don't know what you mean.' He stepped back, flustered, and skidded slightly in something on the smooth flagstones of the temple floor. It was blood, his own blood – he was bleeding heavily.

'Drop your blade, Snoot,' she urged. Viv felt sick and his head was beginning to feel muzzy. But if he dropped his weapon, the Bakkujasi would arrest him – and bad things happened to those the Bakkujasi arrested . . .

He bluffed, swishing his sword again with more vigour than he was presently feeling, his thoughts racing, trying to find a way forward from this. The Bakkujasi would most likely take him to Gremeshkenn Tem, and he'd be burned there, just as they had been going to burn Kalia . . .

She stepped forward, sure that he was going to surrender his weapon. 'You don't remember me, do you?'

As realization dawned on him, Viv bared his teeth in an instinctively feral snarl. 'Asoori Pikresh? Pik. I should kill you now. Do you know what you did to me?'

She did have the grace to blanch slightly at this, then she said, 'But you're hardly in a position to threaten me, are you, *Snoot*?'

Vivreki made a sudden unpredictable move, so fast that Asoori was momentarily fazed. He lurched to one side, grabbing the discarded dagger from the floor, and threw it, not at Asoori but at the Bakkujasi, Cion. As the silver streak arced across the space between them, Viv offered up a silent prayer that his aim was true. The dagger thudded into the top of the man's breastbone, just below his clavicle. Cion dropped like a stone, an exclamation of surprise and pain breaking through his trance. As soon as he recovered, however, the Bakkujasi was swift to assess the situation. Without any hesitation he pulled the dagger from his chest and flung it aside, a sneer crawling across his face. Stief groaned in terror from the other side of the room, as Viv was now trapped between Cion and Asoori.

'Stief, get out of here,' Viv repeated. He was about to drop his blade and surrender, just to buy Stief time, when high-pitched screams erupted from the main temple beyond. The Bakkujasi did not react, keeping his gaze fixed on Viv, but Asoori glanced away towards the source of the sound.

'Icanti's teeth, what's happening?' she muttered.

Suddenly there was the thunderous sound of running feet coming down the passageway, then a hysterical crowd of worshippers burst into the chamber. A gout of black, noxious smoke followed them.

Vivreki only just had the presence of mind to leap backwards, so that there were now at least ten people between him and the Bakkujasi. There was bedlam in the room as the mindless crush of the crowd tried to squeeze through the small door opposite. Viv joined in the crush, hoping that Stief would do likewise.

THE SCREAMS AND cries as terrified people erupted from the main temple doors carried across the whole temple compound of Yotu Tem. Black smoke now wafted from tiny vents at the rear of the building, as if the squat edifice had become a sleeping dragon. Uriel broke into a run, with Losha following.

'I do believe Vivreki has set the place on fire,' Spall remarked, catching up with them.

'You don't know it was Vivreki. It could just be a coincidence.'

Spall did not respond. As they reached the front doors some unfortunate monk ran past them screaming, with his robes ablaze. The smell of burning flesh already permeated the air. Everywhere, people were moaning, crying and gasping, reeling with shock.

'Oh gods, where are they?' Losha's voice was tight with panic. Just then, Viv came staggering out of a side doorway, fighting for breath. He was smoke blackened, his hair badly singed, and also bleeding heavily from a gash to his back.

Uriel hauled him to one side and began to pat out the remaining embers in his hair. Viv turned a furious scowl on Spall. 'What happened?' he was gripped by another spasm of coughing.

'Where is Stief?' Spall replied calmly, choosing to ignore Vivreki's question.

'He's still in there, with the egg.'

They all turned to look at the inferno engulfing Yotu Tem.

STIEF HAD JUST secured the sack behind his back and had no choice but to head back up the corridor when the small door became blocked. He couldn't make out what had happened to Asoori or the Bakkujasi, but knew they would take any opportunity to grab the egg from him. He ran on through the main temple – now mercifully half-empty – to join the press of people pushing through the bottleneck created by the main doors. It was a hellish melee with some people already crushed and unconscious on the floor, or staggering around in a shocked daze.

A little girl was sitting on the ground screaming in fright. Her face had been injured and blood spattered on her white temple robe. She seemed to have plenty of air in her lungs which she was expelling in high-pitched screams like some little banshee. Her mother, or any other adult, was nowhere to be seen – probably caught up in the crush by the doors. Stief scooped her up, hardly breaking his stride, and she stopped her noise abruptly, her eyes widening in silent surprise.

But before he could reach the body of the crowd, something snagged at the back of his robe, yanking him backwards so that he almost lost his footing. He glared back angrily, and realized it was the Bakkujasi. Even seen from arm's length, the man was half obscured by a cloud of thickening black smoke.

'Give it to me,' Cion demanded. In that moment Stief understood that the man valued his own life little against the egg of a Swarm.

'Let me go,' he coughed futilely. Time was short, he knew. Glancing back to the escape route, he noted the crowd there was thinning. People *were* still getting out over the bodies of those unlucky enough to have fallen. He tried to pull himself away but the Bakkujasi's grip was tenacious. Panic seized him and he slapped uselessly at the priest's hands.

'Let me go . . .' he coughed. His legs buckled and he slumped to his knees, despite the pulling of the Bakkujasi from behind him. He set the little girl down on her feet and pushed her towards the exit – she ran off but he could not see her after a couple of paces.

There was a loud crash from the rear of the temple hall. The huge statue of the sleeping goddess had begun to collapse. Beneath the gilt and the diamonds its framework was merely wood.

As Stief sagged further under the resultant blast of heat, the Bakkujasi pulled his unresisting body back towards him. 'The egg,' the man repeated insistently, and he began to pull at the strings of the sack with frenzied fingers. Stief stared numbly at the golden mask which was increasingly filling his field of vision. He would have laughed had he any air left – what good could the egg now be to him? The priest was surely going to die, just as he was – the thought gave him some vague satisfaction. Behind the looming Bakkujasi an orange wall of flame billowed out towards them.

THERE WERE A few monks outside the hall holding wetted cloths to their faces. They were sensibly – and quite forcefully – stopping frantic people from going back into the inferno in search of relatives. They didn't even challenge Spall – it was as if something about the young man was so unnatural that no one would consciously choose to confront it. Uriel stayed close behind and scuttled through before any of them could react. His heart was breaking at the sights of the disaster, a sick certainty growing in his stomach that they were probably too late to help Stief.

They had left Viv in Losha's care, wrapped in Uriel's cloak and propped up against an outside wall. As realization set in, he had begun to shake uncontrollably, his grey eyes growing huge and round with fear for his brother's safety. All he kept repeating was that Stief had been right behind him.

Now the doors were almost cleared, thick black smoke was being blown back, amassing like a giant thunderhead towards the rear of the room. Uriel bit back a gasp of dismay at the sight which suddenly greeted them. In the centre of the ravaged open space stood a golden-masked Bakkujasi wielding a dagger. He appeared about to plunge it into the unresisting frame of the man he held before him; it was Stief.

'After I take the Bakkujasi, grab Stief and get him out of here,' Spall said. His voice was calm, unemotional. Uriel nodded silently, although unsure precisely what Spall meant by 'taking' the priest. He had little time to wonder.

'You there,' Spall's voice rang out with crystal purity amid the chaos, so unlike the sound from Sevim's damaged vocal chords. Cion looked up, startled, but Spall had no intention of engaging him in dialogue. Flinging his hands outwards, the Sin Eater threw a mass of the black, deadening anti-light which Uriel had seen him use once before. The Bakkujasi was unprepared, and staggered back before the onslaught, dropping Stief into a crumpled heap. Loath as he was to draw any nearer to the dark cloud of sin, Uriel ran forward at a crouch to shake Stief roughly by his shoulder. 'Stief . . . Stief, can you walk?' Stief's eyes were still open, and he frowned at him in muggy confusion, till Uriel briefly took the cloth away from his face.

'Uriel?' Stief breathed.

'Yes.' It was obvious that Stief was in no state to get out of danger on his own, so with some difficulty Uriel managed to manoeuvre him upright, and then hoist him over his shoulder. He ran a few staggering steps towards the doorway, then stopped, with horrified fascination, to look back towards Spall and his prey.

URIEL DID NOT know that previously, Spall's repulsive projection of sin was mostly for effect, to frighten those pursuing them. He could not know that Spall was now struggling to control a whole new surge of power – engendered by Ayshena – which had taken him totally unawares. And Spall was, for the first time in his strange, symbiotic life, *frightened* by what he was doing. All Uriel could see was a seething mass that was somehow sentient, the sheer energy of it pushing the flames and smoke back, stealing the oxygen from the fire, sucking the life force from everything close to it.

THE CLOUD STOPPED directly above the head of the Bakkujasi, who stared up at it in disbelief and horror, his blue eyes stark behind the holes of the mask. Spall moved his hands slowly downwards, and the mass of sin responded, beginning to move to engulf Cion.

With a shriek of rage, Cion dropped to his knees in order to avoid its attentions. He held his hands palms upwards, long fingers curling inwards like talons, and his lips began to move silently as he desperately babbled an incantation so powerful it could not be given true voice. Blinding white light blasted upwards from his palms as Cion became transformed into a conduit for the power of the Abax – the power of the god Herrukal on Myr.

Spall's power was strong but not that strong; the sin fought hard to shroud the Bakkujasi in its malignant caul. Light and dark roiled around Cion's kneeling figure as each energy sought to eclipse its rival. There arose a sound of animalistic screaming, but it was difficult to know if it was ripped from Cion's throat or whatever hell the sin had been summoned from.

'Spall, come on!' Uriel coughed. 'We have to go.' As he turned to stagger out from the temple in disgust, he didn't stop to look back –

if he never set eyes on Spall or sin again, it would only serve to gladden his heart.

Spall stared transfixed at the coruscating battle for long seconds – barely able to discern the form of the Bakkujasi shimmering indistinctly in the midst of the fury. He wondered how the man could hope to keep his sanity. 'Go away.' He whispered this command to the sin as if not wanting anyone to hear and know he was responsible for the whirling darkness, despite the evidence to the contrary.

Suddenly the flames, the destruction of Yotu Tem, seemed like a clean thing. Spall turned and ran to join the others.

ASOORI FOUND CION lying amidst the flame-scoured shell of the great temple. There were numerous corpses, piled by the doors, and it was difficult to steel her heart against the pitiful things she saw, especially the dead children, but Asoori went about her business with as much calm as she could muster.

Few had been as lucky as Cion, who at least had survived, though he was in a terrible state. She dragged his unconscious body outside and yelled for help, as he rasped and spluttered to draw clean air into his lungs. Despite the Bakkujasi's status, no one came to their aid, for these first few hours after the fire were the province of the grieving. The sound of wailing filled the air, mingling with smoke and the smells which no one would care to name.

It became clear to Asoori that Cion's injuries were not only burns. Something strange had happened to him – frizzled bits of some bizarre resin were scorched onto his chest and arms. The wound he had suffered from Vivreki's dagger had closed as if it had been cauterized, but perhaps the most worrying thing was that his Bakkujasi mask seemed to have become burned tightly to his face. She first tried to remove it while he was still semi-conscious, but it would not budge. A minute later, when he was awake but still stunned, she tried again, but Cion's hand shot up and grabbed her wrist.

'Leave it,' he rasped.

'Cion, I think it's—'

'Just leave it.' A fit of coughing followed, and Asoori surprised herself with a surge of sympathy for the man, even though she despised him. 'Did we get him?' he croaked. 'The heretic boy?'

She shook her head. 'I'm still checking the bodies . . . but we did get what we came for. Look at this.' Asoori dragged a sack across the floor towards him, and pulled down one side of the sacking. The upper surface of the egg gleamed, a rich dullness in the still dissipating haze of the fire.

His eyes fixed on the wondrous object, Cion's expression became one of sheer awe; he whispered a prayer in some arcane language Asoori did not recognize. She couldn't help but smile, wanly triumphant, forgetting that her legs were cramping and shaking from her exertions. She sat down on the ground next to him.

'What d'you think?' she crowed.

'By Herrukal, it's a miracle,' he breathed. Then, with him leaning against her for support, they staggered back into the empty temple to find one of the monks to tend Cion's wounds. As they passed the pillars flanking the temple entrance, Asoori was unaware that her footsteps trailed through the blood of her injured prey; Vivreki Monvedrian the Swarmthief.

VIVREKI IS DREAMING – at least he's sure it can only be a dream. He's flying again on the back of Ayshena but this time they have soared so high – higher than ever before – that he cannot even see the land far beneath him, just the gilded topside of the clouds. Under the dazzling sun, they look surprisingly solid; fiery landscapes made from spun sugar or yellow-white clay.

He loves to fly. He totally loves it. Since the first time Ayshena took him up, and he whooped and cheered, the exultation of it has remained with him. There's no fear for Viv, and he cannot understand Stief's reluctance *every* time. The worst that could happen, plunging to his death from the back of a Swarm . . . what a glory that would be!

Still in the dream, he gazes down and imagines that, even should he fall, the clouds would somehow hold him up so that he could run through their softness – the skies are so still, so free. And just as he thinks this, the awful thing happens and Ayshena vanishes. But not by dispersing into a million moving, flying creatures – no, Ayshena just becomes a green and purple light, whose colours somehow glow unnaturally in the crystalline serenity of the sky.

Viv is suddenly falling – it's as if he made it happen with his thoughts. He can hear the wind rushing past him, whipping at his clothes. He stretches his arms out, as if he too can fly, but this is not flight; there can be no denying he is falling.

Just as he reaches the cloud layer, which displays its treachery by being only mist, Viv begins to lose his calm. Now he glimpses the land beneath him: forest, rivers and mountains. Mere seconds of falling have elapsed but it feels like a lifetime.

'Vivreki.' He hears a voice beside him, and when he turns to look, he finds it is Ayshena. Well, he just *knows* it is her. Except now she looks like a woman rather than a Swarm. Her voice is just the same. She flies effortlessly, as if she still has the use of her wings; her long black hair seems to be defying the gravity of their descent. Wreathed in diamond-bright lights of purple and green, she is quite the most beautiful thing he has ever seen.

'Take my hand,' she says.

He does reach out for it but somehow he misses and, as his plummet continues, Ayshena is left behind. He braces himself – praying he will wake up before he crashes to the ground. But then someone catches him, and halts his headlong descent.

He turns around, as he is floating again now, the air becoming still around him, with calm coldness. There are five other women, goddesses surely, they look so sublime. They are like Ayshena in appearance, but clothed in other bright jewel-like colours. They have caught gentle hold of his cloak, his sleeves, his ankles, making him drift above the clouds in the same way as they do. With quiet laughter they propel him between them, as if amusing themselves with the seed head of a flower which has blown into their sky.

There is some vague purpose to their game however – Vivreki senses it but he cannot fathom the reason. Each of the goddesses takes hold of him by turn, clasping his shoulders and staring deeply into his eyes, as if they mean to imprint their images onto Viv's consciousness. In that, they succeed, although they are so much alike in their appearance it seems almost an irrelevance. Not that Viv objects to this playful interaction . . .

'Viv? Vivreki . . .?'

'No, don't wake me . . .' He knows it is Ayshena's voice again, but not in the dream. Not part of the delicious dream. 'Leave me, Ayshena,' he mutters.

'Viv!'

Stief? It's Stief's voice now. What's he doing here? In the dream? With a reluctant and miserable groan, Vivreki wakes up.

※

COOKING SMELLS AND humid sweat replaced the brilliant primal colours of Vivreki's dream. Stief was sitting beside him, watching intently for any sign of wakefulness. They had camped in a large cave, and outside it was raining. Lashing torrents of water fell like a bead curtain across the entrance; the sound of it was fresh, and not unpleasant to listen to from the warmth of the fire.

'Stief, you bastard. Why did you wake me up?' Vivreki moaned. 'I was just having the best dream . . .' Then memory hit home, and his half-serious admonishment trailed away. 'Oh gods – the temple. Stief, is everyone safe?'

Stief nodded, but there was a dark disquiet about his expression which Viv's befuddled mind could not fathom for the moment. Losha came over to them with a steaming tisane which smelt distinctly unpleasant. 'Here, Viv, I brewed this especially from linden bark. It will help to strengthen you again. You lost a lot of blood.'

'Thank you, Losha,' he whispered, fragments of memory beginning to drift into his consciousness. Then he frowned, 'Did I see Asoori?' he asked Stief suddenly. Stief nodded in reply.

'Who is Asoori?' Kalia asked.

'Asoori Pikresh. Pik, I used to call her. She was a childhood friend before she stabbed me in the back.' As he said this he gave a small, bitter grimace. 'And now she's done it again.'

Kalia frowned, not quite understanding, but just as she was about to ask for clarification Viv pushed himself upright in his bedroll with a further moan of dismay. 'The egg. Stief, we've lost the egg, haven't we? Asoori will take it back with her to be destroyed.'

※

ACHIOS FOUND HIMSELF alone, and solitude had been something of a rarity over the last few weeks. He stood amongst the ashes and debris of Falloden Sen, gazing east towards the ocean. It was snowing again and the chill wind whipped a flurry towards him, the flakes

DEBORAH J. MILLER

quickly dissipating against the warmth of his skin. He was beginning
to feel cold but he welcomed the feeling. So stifling and cosseted had
his life at Gremeshkenn Tem become, the freshness of the sensation
was like freedom.

He had arrived at Falloden Sen on a Swarm almost a week earlier,
after the Duke, Detri Torroshi, and his Lady, had died in a freak
accident when the central dome of Falloden Sen mansion house had
collapsed on them. Three servants had also been killed in the tragic
event – somewhat messy considering the god Rann had personally
engineered it, Achios thought. By chance, Achios had already been
travelling that way in order to notify them personally of the death of
their son and heir. As a result of this tragic coincidence, since Detri
had no surviving heir to succeed him, Falloden Sen fell into possession
of the church.

Achios had feigned surprise and sympathy so well that he was
shocked by his own deviousness. He even managed to shed a tear or
two for the demise of the Torroshi dynasty – then he had dismissed
most of the servants and retainers, since his own people would be
arriving within a few days. If anyone thought it strange that the Hani
had ordered his full retinue to begin the journey before he could have
known that Falloden Sen was about to become church property, no
one had the nerve to speak up. Strange things were afoot. The sounds
of destruction echoed from within the encircling walls of the great
estate and the villagers living on the periphery began to lock their
doors at night and keep their children safely inside.

Rann had sent *tengu*, a small army of them, and it was they who
were now demolishing the old house, so as to leave standing only one
small residential section and the massive atrium by the side of the lake.
It was the atrium which the god seemed fascinated by, and Achios
understood this to be the place Rann had referred to as the centre-
point of the world. The *tengu* spent most of their time there when not
destroying the main building and, consequently, Achios did not go in
very often.

Achios had since sent a letter to Pava, explaining that he intended
Falloden Sen to become a place of retreat for the Hani and his suc-
cessors, so he would stay there for a while to oversee the structural
adjustments to the buildings. He kept his words sparse, not wanting
Pava to sense any problem. Indeed, it was a relief to escape from
the Temple City for a while, especially since becoming aware that

members of the Neruk'eel could somehow sense the *tengu* who shad-
owed him. He had tried to explain away their constant presence by
claiming that after he had prayed to Herrukal to curb any lapse into
vanity and hubris, the great god had sent the *tengu* as a constant
reminder of the Hani's mortality, and so provide a walking, pestilent
lesson in humility.

The Neruk'eel seemed satisfied and impressed with this explanation for now. In fact, Achios was sure the direct intervention of
Herrukal made him appear both appropriately humble and the right
choice for Hani.

Not everything was going to plan however – not that he was any
nearer to finding out what the ultimate plan actually was. He had lost
touch with Cion Gezezi after his last communication instructing the
Bakkujasi to murder Earl Kilmer Torroshi. It was a stark choice, even
for someone as coldly ambitious as Gezezi; murder your lover or be
expelled from the ranks of the Bakkujasi in disgrace. Achios never
entertained any doubt that Cion would comply, but he had sensed the
man's extreme resentment at being forced into such an action.
Resentment, but not sorrow, it had seemed. Achios realized then the
full magnitude of the younger Bakkujasi's ambition; he had been
securing the future Lord of Cantroji's patronage and wealth for the
Bakkujasi, and that had to be admired. The Neruk'eel were right:
Gezezi was proving a strong candidate for future high office in the
echelons of the priesthood. The miracle hunter was indeed a calculat-
ing, sly man – but, sadly, he was now missing. Achios had already
spent hours sending out *kelephi* incantations that would return to him
once they had located Cion's thoughts, but nothing had come back
so far. A pity, when his obvious long-term goal of acquiring control of
Falloden Sen for the church had now been so easily achieved. Perhaps
he might have rejoiced in the Bakkujasi's gain, more likely he would
have simply set his objectives anew.

The cold was now beginning to bite, and Achios was about to
return to the remaining building of the once sprawling residence,
when something caught his attention from inside the atrium. A flare
of orange light suddenly lit up the elegant glass and iron framework like a giant lantern. It lasted only a few seconds so, at first,
Achios thought he may have been mistaken. Then it happened again,
the entire atrium flaring warmth against the cold backdrop of the
encroaching storm. Achios frowned and began to walk towards the

entrance. Unable to wait for the evidence of his own eyes, he sent out a worried thought: *What is it, Lord Rann? What are the* tengu *doing in there?*

The reply came swiftly. *It is not the* tengu, *Achios. Take a look.*

Anxiety overcame him and he ran the last few steps, flinging open the double doors. An unexpected smile creased his face despite the humid, reeking air which assailed him. All around the periphery of the atrium, the *tengu* stood chittering and shivering their wings in excitement. Normally Achios would feel intimidated to see so many of them grouped together, but now his attention was gratefully diverted.

In the middle of the open space stood a Swarm, the new Swarm just hatched from the mysterious egg – a giant dragonfly of such breathtaking beauty that Achios was as entranced by it as the *tengu*. Radiant in gold, orange and black, her great wings were fragmented by a tapestry of rich black veins, and her eyes were massive orbs of rich, almost liquid, red-gold. Achios knew now that the fire had marked her birth somehow, as she had emerged, almost impossibly large, from the egg.

She is named Farzull, the god told him.

Undiminished, wrath
transmutes to flame, but then
directionless, burns only self

❧CHAPTER SEVENTEEN❧

W HEN VIVREKI NEXT awoke he lay silently for a long time, lost in thought, his eyes sullen and listless. The others were all by the campfire, talking in low voices which drifted into the cave on snatches of warm woodsmoke. He could hear Kalia's constant chatter and her high, clear laughter, the deeper, almost booming tone of Stief, and the quieter more level tones of Uriel. He felt separated from their camaraderie by more than simply a few paces; they were distant somehow, different from himself. The details of the failed raid on Yotu Tem came back to him in glimpses and sense memories, the smoke of the campfire acting as a conduit for his tired consciousness. He groaned softly as he remembered why Stief was angry with him.

'Vivreki? Are you well?' It was Losha, who he had not realized was sitting nearby in the shadows of the cave. She leaned forward to peer at him, her whiteness emerging from the shadow like one of her beloved owls.

'Yes, I . . . I suppose so.'

'What ails you, my friend?' she said softly.

'Losha, am I still your friend? I've behaved stupidly, haven't I?'

'No, not stupidly, just . . . well, perhaps you were a bit thought-less.'

He groaned again and put an arm across his face, feeling the pull of the scar on his back. 'That's just it. That's what I do: act thought-lessly when I get carried away. It's like an insane rush of blood to my brain sometimes.' She did not reply to his self-pitying comments so he looked towards the rear of the cave, but was unable to see her face so as to discern any emotion there. 'Look at them,' he said softly. 'Stief's mad with me, because he thinks I'm a murderous berserker that has to be contained. All I've ever done is get him into trouble. It's my fault our mother, Calla, was killed . . . As for Uriel, huh,' he laughed weakly, 'he just hates me. Thinks I'm responsible for the death of all those people in Releeza. And Sevim and Kalia, they're only here because they've got nowhere else to go . . .'

'Not true,' Losha said. 'Kalia thinks you are a great mage.' There was quiet laughter in her tone. 'Stief told me.'

He almost smiled at the memory of Kalia's remark but there was little mirth in him.

'Losha, I'm really sorry about . . .'

'Perhaps I should have warned you about my divination methods. It was partly my fault.'

Vivreki took a deep breath, and did Losha the courtesy of being truthful. 'It wasn't just that, Losha. I – I saw beneath your mask. Gods, I feel like such a shallow, insensitive bastard now, but I care about you and I want you to know that . . .' he struggled to find further words.

'My deformity repulses you?' she supplied. Her tone was strangely without rancour.

'I'm sorry.' He was amazed to hear a quiet chuckle in response from the back of the cave. 'That's not funny,' he frowned.

'No, but Vivreki you possess more integrity than any man I've met – you found that truth as painful as I do – and perhaps that's why your friends are still here, because they see that too.' Losha moved over and knelt beside him. She smelt good – despite the rigours of their travel – perhaps it was part of her enchantment. Her eyes were now deadly serious. 'Perhaps I was unfair to you. I already knew the truth, that no man could love me once they saw my face,' she took his hand and rested it on her knees. 'If only things were different, Vivreki . . .' She sighed and paused to re-organize her thoughts. 'I never reveal my face to anyone – I feel it spares everyone by cutting out the anxiety of pretence. But you are different, even if simply as a friend. If you would like to see my face, I will show you.' She reached up to undo the lacing at the back of her mask.

'No.' He grabbed her hand, seeing the fear in her eyes, knowing how it would change things between them. 'Losha, I do not need to see. Listen to me, it doesn't matter. I will always be your friend – nothing about you could disgust me. I will always . . . care for you.'

'Then I am content.' She smiled.

SEVERAL DAYS HAD passed since the fire at Yotu Tem, when Asoori and Cion rode out to meet with Kilmer. Asoori had tried her best to persuade the Bakkujasi to remain with the monks at the temple and receive further healing, but Cion had been adamant about accompanying her. They knew Kilmer would be travelling from Releeza to Cantroji in an effort to procure supplies and resources for the damaged town from his father's coffers, so they had deliberately set their own course to intercept him on his predicted overnight stop.

Cion had seemed particularly strained since the fire. He had left behind the strange puzzle-box which contained his dissolved Swarm in the care of the monks at Yotu Tem and this was an unheard of thing for any Bakkujasi to do. Also, the monks had confided in Asoori that, on removing his mask, his face only had scars on his brow and temples where the heat had made a scorching seal with his flesh. Cion, despite this, had taken to keeping his mask in place the whole time. For some reason, this disturbed Asoori greatly but the Bakkujasi did not care to be drawn on the subject.

What she had no way of knowing was that Cion was feeling bereft. Since utilizing power channelled from the Abax to save his life, his very soul, from the sin that Spall had attacked him with, Cion was no longer able to 'hear' the mind-voices of the Bakkujasi. It was as if he had used up his lifetime's magic in one massive act of self-protection. He was truly alone now, and although he could probably still move his Swarm with some effort, there seemed little point when he was unable to communicate with its mind. His mask was now simply an impotent, hollow shell, but he wore it constantly in the hope of reviving some shred of contact.

THEY HAD BEEN planning to return to Cantroji with Kilmer after intercepting him, but now Asoori wanted to take the egg straight back to Gremeshkenn Tem, with Cion, to present to her great-uncle. She hoped that the new Hani would confide his plans to her with regard to its future. Also, if she was honest with herself, she was beginning to seriously wonder if Achios had been right about training her for the

Shemari and if she might persuade him to allow her to specialize as a healer.

They arrived very late at Kilmer's campsite but Merric had kept the fire well banked. There were no other servants travelling with him as Kilmer had wanted to travel both fast and light, and it was noticeable that he and Merric had already shared a drink together before the fire. Kilmer listened to Asoori's breathless recounting of the events in Yotu Tem with interest, tempered with mild amusement at her enthusiasm. Merric's cheeks were flushed by alcohol, as he listened to her with unconcealed admiration. Cion meanwhile said very little, and after a while wandered off into the darkness as if to meditate.

Kilmer frowned. 'Why does he keep his mask on all the time?' he wondered aloud. Asoori put a finger to her lips and gave a warning shake of her head. Like her, Kilmer now despised the Bakkujasi – especially since Releeza – but there was something about the changes in Cion which bordered on pathos. Asoori called after him before he vanished into the darkness.

'Cion, are you coming back to us tonight?'

'I am not sure, Asoori. But I will not disturb anyone.' He bowed before turning on his heel and walking beyond the light of the fire.

SHE COULD NOT say what woke her – and in all the time after that day, replaying the events in her mind, she still could not say why she woke just when she did. Two minutes, one minute earlier, things could have been so different.

As she opened her eyes, first of all, a bright, clear blue sky, promising a beautiful morning, filled her vision. She remembered how they had finally just curled up where they were by the fire – all three of them drifting into reluctant sleep because the company and drink-fuelled banter was such fun, or at least, so it had seemed. Though wary at first of the lack of formality, Merric had gradually relaxed and joined in with a will.

She turned over towards Kilmer's bedroll – and froze.

Cion Gezezi was standing astride the prostrate body of her husband with a dagger dripping blood.

❧

SHE ALMOST CRIED out. She did not – those one or two seconds of restraint probably saved her. She was unarmed and equally vulnerable, so instead, she snapped her eyes shut again, desperately fighting her body's reaction to the dreadful image which would remain burned on her memory forever. Fortunately, Cion had not turned to look in her direction *yet*. While fighting to keep her face impassive as if she were still sleeping, Asoori edged her hand behind her, under the blanket, praying that her sword was still easily within her reach. She was in luck. Her training was so ingrained into her, that even drunk as she had been, she had laid the weapon near her as she fell asleep. Her heart thumped wildly even as her fingers closed around the hilt. She heard Cion drop something back onto the ground; it made a faint *whump* kind of noise and Asoori fought to quell a whimper in her throat as she realized it was Kilmer's body.

She knew she could not surprise the Bakkujasi – standing up would take precious seconds she did not possess. Fighting every natural instinct Asoori remained motionless as she heard his footsteps move towards her, the crunch of his boots in the shingle soil unnaturally loud to her strained hearing.

Cion stopped beside her, was apparently looking down at her, perhaps weighing up in his mind the consequences of murdering the niece of the Hani. Asoori's instinct was to hold her breath, but she forced herself to continue breathing evenly. She prayed he was not quick-sighted enough to notice she had her blade concealed just under the edge of her blanket. It was happening within seconds – heartbeats and seconds. Deep within herself she realized she could not defeat the Bakkujasi in a fair fight, or controlled, disciplined duel, so, just before she surged into action, she resolved to make this as devious a contest as she had ever fought.

Moments dropped away into gut-wrenching infinity as, slowly, Cion squatted down beside her apparently sleeping form. All the while, Asoori chanted incoherently in her head: *not-yet, not-yet, not-yet . . . now!*

She sat up fast, slamming the flat of her palm hard into Cion's face, her fingers hooked to catch his eyes if she was lucky with her aim. The Bakkujasi was caught completely off-guard, toppling backwards as soon as her hand made contact – unfortunately lessening the impact of her blow. He had removed his mask now, and his face was unprotected.

Both were even now, however, both scrambled to their feet – Asoori having bought herself the precious seconds she needed. At last able to vent her fury, she screamed at Cion as she brought her blade into view. He did not react to the tirade, which was a rather stupid expenditure of energy, merely nodded as if in mute acknowledgment that her anger was justified.

Although she sorely wanted to, she did not rush to the attack, but instead waited for Cion to make his move, knowing he would be at a disadvantage if she forced him to rush forward. Pausing where she stood, she twitched her blade restlessly.

She knew Cion was good but she had never seen him fight seriously before, and she wasn't prepared for the sheer speed of his onslaught. The same movements that looked so graceful and aesthetic were designed to sever or dismember when pressed into real service. Asoori knew that, better than most, but had hoped never to face such a skilled opponent. He was currently attacking so fast, that she literally had no time to think.

Inevitably, she found herself stepping back, although she was successfully deflecting the blows he kept aiming at the tops of her arms. She recognized the strategy – *suru*, many cuts – which eventually would cause the biceps to struggle, the sword arm to spasm and fail. Perversely, Asoori knew this was a compliment to her – Cion was deliberately playing a 'long game', which meant he did not underestimate her as an opponent. As if the gods meant to punish her for this fleeting vanity, she suddenly tripped, as her foot became entangled with the discarded blanket. As soon as she hit the ground she rolled, four times, over and over, keeping her sword arm extended at shoulder height, forcing Cion to run a few steps in order to prepare for a strike once his target stopped moving. Asoori cursed involuntarily as she rolled across a sharp stone, but enough adrenaline was coursing through her to allow her to ignore the pain.

Her manoeuvre would not be enough, however: Cion was going to be ready as she scrambled to her feet. Without reaching a conscious decision, she lunged forward without getting up and with her free hand tugged hard on Cion's legs sending him crashing backwards to the ground with an exclamation of surprise and probably disgust. *To hell with it*, Asoori was thinking. *To hell with your cursed rules, Bakkujasi.*

With another scream of rage, Asoori launched herself onto his fallen body, grabbing him by the hair and banging his head back into the gritty soil. She knelt across his chest, her knee pushing hard between his ribs, and Cion, thrashing his arms, dropped his blade. Asoori moved her hands and began to shove his face sideways into the dirt. For the first time, he tried to speak to her. 'He's not dead,' he gasped. 'Asoori, he's not dead.'

'Liar!' she screeched, pressing down harder. Cion was bleeding now, rivulets of blood streaming down his face; somewhere Asoori's nails had dug deeply into his flesh, the red in bright contrast to his white skin.

'It was a leech . . . I was only cutting a leech out.'

She instinctively *knew* this wasn't true, she *knew* he was dead, but Cion's ruse was enough for her to pause in her ill considered mangling to glance quickly towards her husband's body. A tiny cessation of pressure – it was all Cion needed. A second later she was face-down in the dirt herself with Cion astride her back and her arms pinned beneath her.

'Do you think you are the only one who can fight dirty?' he grated.

Asoori realized she was sobbing with rage and frustration, but there was no time for such indulgence now. As Cion pressed her face down in mute revenge for her own recent action, she struggled to hang onto some degree of coherent thought. She watched with bizarre detachment as a black ant scurried past her eye, hauling a tiny section of leaf on its shiny back. Her body went limp.

'Oh very good,' Cion snarled in her ear. 'I'm not that stupid.'

She saw his left hand come into view, the dagger aiming for her throat as he pulled her head back by the hair. As his hand came down across her face, she craned her head forward and sunk her teeth into it, biting down so hard she broke through the flesh. Cion yelled out involuntarily and dropped the dagger, but had enough presence of mind to keep his knee pressed into the small of her back. In fact, he was pushing her so hard that Asoori had made an indentation in the loose earth, which gave her precious room to move. With a grunt of effort she twisted over, lashing out as her arm came free of Cion's pressure, catching the priest a blow beneath the armpit. It was a clumsy, undignified blow, but enough to unbalance him, and she scrambled out from beneath him as he toppled to the side.

It seemed the shock of having his flesh bitten through to the bone had somehow stunned the Bakkujasi – maybe he had never suffered the indignity of such a wound in combat before – but he did not recover as fast this time and Asoori leapt up, grabbing the dagger.

There could be no dignified touching of the blade to Cion's throat and claiming victory, no quarter given, even if he had asked for it, which she knew he would never do – so without giving herself time to consider, Asoori swung round and stabbed him in the back. He was already pushing himself upwards on his hands when she dealt the blow. He fell forward again with such suddenness that she could have almost believed he died instantly. But she could not take the chance – with another scream of rage, she stabbed him twice more, her mind reeling away in a red fug of denial at her own violence.

As Cion's blood blossomed across his clothes like some lurid flower, Asoori threw the dagger aside. For a moment she stood simply heaving for breath, and dully watching the Bakkujasi's death. Eventually, she approached and flipped him over with her foot: there was no sign of life in his wide-open eyes. Asoori felt no remorse, for he had denied her her husband in every sense.

HER LEGS BEGINNING to shake, she staggered over to Kilmer's bedroll and collapsed to her knees beside him. Blood had pooled around his torso in a huge stain, already soaking into the earth. His throat had been ripped open, a ragged gash hastily inflicted, violent splashes covered his face, already congealing strands gravitating into his ears and neck. Kilmer was still warm, his death so recent it seemed as if his breath had only just left him. Asoori wanted to weep but her body was still reacting to the fight, a massive knot of grief and fury gathering in her chest. Her limbs twitching and trembling, she hugged her arms around her knees and rocked backwards and forwards. On opening her mouth as if to either scream or vomit, only a strangled wail escaped her.

Time passed – she didn't know how long – and the breeze picked up, sending the lighter grains of shale hissing and drifting across the melancholy scene. Asoori's unbound black hair whipped unchecked across her face. A desert lizard skittered past the corpse of Kilmer Torroshi without stopping to investigate. A large, ominous-looking bird stalked cautiously towards them. When Asoori threw a stone at it, it merely flapped its wings lazily and retreated a few feet.

Eventually, as her heartbeat slowed and Asoori began to feel as if she were back inside her own skin once more, coherent thought returned, and with it the realization that she had not yet seen Merric. She stood up numbly, and staggered a few steps in search of him. Merric was also dead. Cion had killed him first by suffocating him. As he had been sleeping quite some distance from Kilmer and Asoori, it would have been an easy matter for Cion to murder him with some stealth without anyone being alerted. The young squire looked for all the world as if he were sleeping peacefully, except that his lips were blue and the flush of his cheeks now more akin to bruising. Beside him lay the bedroll which Cion had shoved down onto his face. Asoori felt mutely responsible for his fate: he had been so young, both in outlook and years, so proud and excited to be chosen as her squire. She dreaded the thought of informing his parents. She glanced back at Kilmer again, realizing she would have to tell his family also. She just hoped the truth of Kilmer and Cion's intense relationship would not be revealed in the process of any subsequent investigation.

After a while, she wearily managed to rekindle the fire. She seemed to be unnaturally cold, so she wrapped a blanket around herself as she prodded and poked the embers back into life. Next she threw a blanket over each of the corpses, even Cion's. Her mind was still a confused whirl of dark thoughts and raw emotion, so that after a while it was as if everything fazed into a blur. A comfort blanket of numbness seemed to cosset her senses. Sitting upright, rocking back and forth, she was not sure if she slept at all.

Sometime after dusk, Asoori Torroshi Pikresh stood up and wandered into the desert. The only thing she took with her was the canvas bag containing the Swarm egg, which she dragged along behind her. She could not even have said *why* she took it; belief in miracles was far beyond her now . . .

'I'M TELLING YOU –' Uriel scowled – 'the one goddess created the city, and dropped it onto Myr in a bead of water.'

Over a week had passed since the raid on Yotu Tem, and initially the friends had planned to ride east, straight back to the village of ghosts. The only benefit of their long journey they could claim was their haul of medicines for Losha's community of orphans and lepers. But they soon discovered that Brengarmah troops were now moving between Releeza and Yotu Tem, and in their efforts to avoid them the small party was pushed ever further north skirting the fringes of the Gurz'taal desert once more.

During their journey little had occurred to mend the silent rift between Viv and Stief. The physical scar on Viv's back was now healing but the distance between the two brothers remained. They talked to each other civilly enough, but Losha in particular noted the sad coolness between them. Only the brothers knew the heart of what had occurred at Yotu Tem and neither would discuss it openly.

Two nights earlier Uriel had announced that, once they delivered the medicines to the village of ghosts, he intended to head off for a place Stief had never heard of, called Nia. Much heated discussion followed this, because to the others, Nia was known as a stronghold for fleeing heretics and wielders of magics, yet it was far from confirmed that Nia was even a real place. Whether legend or rumour, belief in Nia implied a belief in the one goddess, Mauru, and that was where Kalia and the brothers had difficulty.

Uriel had neglected to mention whether he secretly planned to take the Swarm's egg to Nia with him, and the others exchanged uneasy glances over the fire on realizing that the dispute between Uriel and Vivreki would not be settled any time soon. In fact the only solution would be if the egg hatched and settled their argument, and no one – not even Ayshena herself – knew when that might happen.

Now, as they camped on the northern edge of the Gurz'taal desert, the subject of the mysterious Nia was raised again. Stief sighed, staring fixedly into the flames. It was the beginning of winter now and the weather had turned for the worse. Sleet and snow had lashed down unrelentingly for the past couple of days as the travellers plodded on slowly, wrapped in every piece of clothing or blanket they owned. It would get even worse now as they moved into the desert wastes, with no trees to provide shelter. Perhaps snow would not actually fall in the middle of the desert – Stief hoped not, but he had noticed that since the event of Orlannoni the weather had become far from predictable.

❧

URIEL'S VOICE SOUNDED weary and richly old as he narrated the tale of Nia. 'The goddess is named Mauru,' he began, 'meaning love in the old language of Myr. For aeons she existed alone in the emptiness of the sky. Then, one day a strange feeling she could not explain crept over her. It was the ache of loneliness, but she had no word for the feeling. She began to weep and her tears made first the stars, and then Myr itself. Mauru looked at the world and saw that the light of the stars, shining through the tears, had made many colours on the world. She played a while and made tiny creatures to run and live amongst the colours: animals and birds, men and women.

'But Mauru could not stop crying, and soon the world was covered in oceans, and its people shouted and prayed for the goddess to stop. In their fear and anger they made other, false gods.' Uriel shifted slightly uncomfortably as he said this, but no one challenged him as they were too caught up in the story.

'These new gods said to Mauru: To punish you for weeping, we will erase your memory from the hearts of men, and you will fade. This is what they did, but before she vanished, Mauru wept one final tear and hid it in the wilderness for men to find eventually, so that they might remember her again. This last tear is called Nia, and it was discovered by a mystic almost a hundred years ago . . .'

❧

THERE WAS A short pause as the others considered this story, then launched a whole gamut of sceptical remarks and questions towards Uriel.

'Oh, come on, that's so simplistic . . .'

'How come, if we can hear about this in a story, the church itself doesn't know about it?'

'How do you know they *don't* know about it?' Uriel retorted. 'Naturally, they would keep it a secret, lest everyone should get to know about the one goddess. That would be why all the heretics take refuge there and . . .' Uriel began poking a stick towards Sevim to emphasize his point, then suddenly trailed off, his eyes fixing on the other side of the encampment. Everyone else turned to follow his gaze.

There was a man standing there, indistinct, just outside the nimbus of light from the fire. Even in the semi-darkness it was easy to see he was in some state: he stood hunched forward, wavering slightly, a startling shock of white hair falling over his face. Just as Viv and Stief, who were nearest him, started up, the figure pitched forward and fell face-down in the dirt.

As the firelight caught his collapse, two things were immediately obvious: firstly that he was covered in dried blood, and secondly, from the tattered remains of his distinctive clothing, he was, or had been, a Bakkujasi.

⚜CHAPTER EIGHTEEN⚜

A s they flipped the body over, both Viv and Stief cursed in surprise.

'I recognize him,' Vivreki frowned. 'He's the same Bakkujasi from Yotu Tem. He killed our mother and he's a friend of Asoori Pikresh.'

Kalia looked up from where she was kneeling beside the prostrate body of the Bakkujasi. 'Well, you won't be too upset to know that he's dying, then.'

Sevim was also kneeling beside the stricken man and Stief couldn't help but wonder if his attentiveness was more to do with ghoulish expectancy than concern. Perhaps Spall was jostling to the forefront in the Sin Eater's mind, all salacious anticipation at this imminent demise.

'Yes, I remember him,' the Sin Eater said. 'Uriel, he was the one Spall attacked in the temple using sin, was he not?' Uriel did not reply; he had tried not to think about it too much in the days since. 'Well, he's not dead yet . . . Kalia, perhaps we can move him closer towards the fire and find him some blankets.'

'I'm not touching him,' Viv snarled. 'As far as I'm concerned, the sooner he dies the better.' Stief did not join in his brother's condemnation, but he did not move to help either. It was as much restraint as either of them could manage in the circumstances. Between them, Sevim and Kalia manhandled the wounded man over to the fire, and managed to prop him upright.

Losha crouched in front of Cion. 'Can you hear me?' she asked, as Sevim wrapped a blanket around him. 'What is your name, priest?'

'It is very strange,' Sevim frowned. 'By rights he *should* be dead. And Spall agrees with me.'

'Maybe he's using some Bakkujasi magic to keep himself alive,' Kalia suggested.

'Yes. I think you are right, Kalia.'

Cion opened his eyes which were crusted with dried pus. Judging from the smell of sour decay emanating from his body, the battle for Cion's immune system was already lost. 'Ah' – he raised his upper lip in some kind of rictus which was probably supposed to be a smile, revealing a mouth and gums that were shockingly bloodless – 'the Swarmthief.'

Viv glanced towards Stief when the Bakkujasi said this. 'Do you think he knows about Ayshena?' he hissed.

Stief shrugged, his face impassive. 'Does it m-matter now?'

Cion sat up quite suddenly, his eyes snapping open wide. 'Swarmthief, I know where the Yotu Tem egg is. I know where Asoori will go.' Then he slumped back onto his blankets.

'What's he telling me that for?' Viv was confused.

'It is a gamble. Perhaps he thinks we will try harder to save him.' Sevim said. 'He knows his magics are failing and that soon, he will die.' He gazed contemptuously back at Cion. 'It is the way these people think: that *anything* is tradable, even souls.'

'You mean he's just trying to save his own skin?'

'It is much more than just his skin, Vivreki. He holds almost the most sin I have ever known anyone to possess.'

'Sevim,' Losha touched the Sin Eater lightly on the shoulder, 'we must still show him compassion. However much he's sinned, some-one else has now sinned against him.' She shifted the apparently unconscious form of Cion forward so that he slumped forward in a sitting position. On his exposed back three deep and clearly infected gashes oozed gore, and a crust of blood had formed around each one so that they resembled minute volcanoes. In shifting him, they had managed to knock the scab off the biggest wound, so it was beginning to bleed afresh.

'She stabbed him in the back,' Viv sneered. 'Not just a bitch but a coward – and probably stole the egg from him as well . . .'

'We d-don't know what happened, Viv,' Stief cautioned.

'Nor will we,' Sevim sighed. 'I think he is finally gone.'

'What's to know? She betrayed me when we were young, and it looks like she's continued in the same vein her whole life. If I ever see Asoori Pikresh again, I swear I'll kill her.'

❧

AN ARGUMENT BROKE out amongst them almost straight away.

Viv had gone off to try and commune with Ayshena. He was unsure if she would detect his mind-voice at such a distance, but the appearance of Cion had made him uneasy and he wanted to check that she was safe and well. Fortunately for him, Ayshena was already on her way to find them, so was now within twenty leagues of their camp. He returned there at about the moment the mood turned ugly. Sevim had suggested that he take the Bakkujasi's sins but Uriel and Stief – who had both been on the receiving end of Cion's brutality – were against it. The man deserved to die with his sins intact, they argued. Eternal torment was probably what he had earned.

'But you cannot *know* that,' Sevim was protesting, despite his earlier assessment of Cion's soul. Perhaps Sevim considered himself bound to his duty even if his personal feelings dictated otherwise. He now stood in front of the corpse, barring access; and there *was* something inherently menacing about Sevim when he reverted to his Sin Eater persona. In any case the others held back warily.

'That's enough,' Viv said loudly, and there was something authoritative in his tone which made everyone turn towards him. 'Ayshena thinks he's lower than scum – well, she didn't put it quite like that – but she wants me to bring him back to life.'

'What?'

Viv stared directly at Stief. 'Like Jest,' he added. 'Look, I know this doesn't mean much to you all, but he does know where the other egg is, assuming it survived the fire. The Shemari will be determined to destroy it if they can.'

'We don't kn-know that,' Stief scowled.

'Ayshena seems sure. Anyway, I think we can all benefit from the resurrection of this dammed priest.'

'How?'

'Well, he must be pretty important, even amongst the ranks of the Bakkujasi.'

'Yes,' Uriel frowned. 'But I don't see where you're going with this, Vivreki.'

Viv grinned brightly – that same old grin which Stief used to love, but which now filled him with tinges of dread. 'How much d'you think the Bakkujasi will pay to get him back?'

ASOORI SPOKE TO Kilmer every night. Perhaps she spoke to him now more than she had ever done while he was alive – but then, losing one's mind was always going to change things somewhat.

She had no idea how long she had been wandering aimlessly through the desert. Initially she headed south, though not for any specific reason, until she was almost back within sight of Yotu Tem. But then she had swerved away and looped back towards the mountains lying to the west. She survived by eating bugs and snakes, and carrion, at first not even bothering whether they were cooked or raw. Her body became ever more taut and weather-blasted by the elements. If she saw people in the distance, she would quickly deviate to avoid them.

One day she just stopped dead. By chance it was the evening of the same day Cion wandered into the outlaw encampment – but she had no way of knowing this. She simply stopped her endless walking and stood for a while staring at the sunset. After a few minutes she sat down; she had the blanket wrapped around her which she had been wearing since her departure from . . . that place, and beneath that, she still wore the white cotton shift of her nightdress.

'My love, I'm tired.' He didn't answer her, but Asoori was not deterred by this. She stared placidly around her. Perhaps she would even sleep; her body felt strained beyond the point of exhaustion. Even as she thought this, she began to black out, not drifting into sleep exactly, for her vision, burned by the glare of the constant sun, began to fill with black, floating masses so that it was like having a chequered pattern in her head. She blinked a few times to clear them, but she did relent and eventually closed her eyes.

WHEN SHE FINALLY awoke early the next morning, Asoori lay blankly staring into the middle distance, watching a lone bird wheeling through the dawn skies. 'Hello,' Asoori said eventually, though she knew there was no one there. She wasn't even talking to Kilmer this time, merely testing out her voice. The silence of the desert had become a distant humming in her ears.

'I expect you need to get a drink or something . . .' she said to herself. Then she sat up, coughing. 'Awww . . . yuk,' she said, spitting grass seeds from her mouth. 'You need a bath, Asoori.' Then, after a moment she repeated more slowly, 'I need a bath. Asoori Pikresh.' They were the first coherent words she had spoken for a week.

THE SWARM HAD arrived within the hour and Viv sat with her for a while, finalizing his plans for the re-awakening of Cion. Then he drew everyone else near to him after making sure they were armed.

'Stay close,' he warned, 'because I'm not used to controlling this. It's possible this won't just bring him back to life gently; he may feel pretty energetic. And we know how dangerous a Bakkujasi swordsman can be.'

The group shifted uncomfortably, Uriel throwing his sword from hand to hand in order to wipe his palms on his trousers. They had taken the precaution of binding Cion's wrists but that had been done pretty loosely, since no one felt quite right about trussing up a corpse.

It was very late now, way past midnight, and their fire had been banked up to a roaring blaze. Orange light flickered across the anxious faces of the group. Viv sat himself on a saddle, which he'd placed on the ground beside the corpse. He had a pensive expression on his face, but nothing appeared to be happening. Uriel rocked back and forth on the balls of his feet in anticipation, till Viv's eyes suddenly flared with blue-white light as if some giant firefly were burning inside his skull.

Reaching forward, Viv touched Cion lightly on the forehead – which was quite possibly the worst decision he had ever made. A juddering spasm seemed to ripple through the length of Cion's body, and Viv straightened up suddenly, wrenching his arm back. He blinked rapidly as if some of the strange light had bounced back to him in an aftershock.

Everyone else craned forward. 'Be ready,' Stief muttered.

Even by the flickering light of the fire they could see that Cion's wounds had healed – even the deep gouges on his brow vanished instantly, as a charge of the blue fire pulsed up and down for a few seconds, then vanished.

But nothing else happened.

'Viv?' Stief tensed further, remembering the way Jest had recovered, as if awakening from a deep sleep. Before he could say anything more, however, the Bakkujasi suddenly sat up. For just a second an expression of confusion flitted across Cion's face . . . then he tilted his head and grinned dangerously towards Viv.

'You again,' he said, then, before anyone could move, he whipped his arms up and looped the bindings around his wrists across the back of Viv's neck, pulling him off the saddle seat and bringing his face nose to nose with his own.

'Hey!' Stief was the quickest to react as he jabbed a blade to Cion's throat. 'Just gimme a reason, Bakkujasi,' he growled.

At that, Cion pushed Vivreki away, but kept his gaze fixed on his prey – ignoring the drawn weapons which currently surrounded him. 'What did you do to me, Swarmthief? I should be dead now, and we both know it. How long do you think you can deny the gods their due souls?'

Viv stared back angrily, fighting to regain his aplomb while sprawled across the ground. 'I don't think they'll miss your company for a while, Bakkujasi. But meanwhile, you're worth more to us alive.'

Cion turned a cold, un-intimidated gaze on the outlaws – only Uriel remained impassive in the face of his glacial stare; the others flinched from it, in tiny ticks or twitches. The Bakkujasi nodded slowly, and there was something about his complete relaxedness which made Viv glance nervously at Stief.

'Am I a hostage then?'

'Yes. And we are considering hacking off your ears to send to Gremeshkenn Tem, as evidence,' Kalia smiled nastily.

Cion nodded again, glancing up at the ever-present brightness of Orlannoni. He realized that, on the day the gods chose to send Orlannoni to her ultimate rest, men and women would still be waking to make breakfast, maintaining the fabric of their world with quiet desperation . . .

'And how do you propose to contact Gremeshkenn Tem?' he frowned in apparently earnest enquiry. 'Surely you realize we're at least a hundred leagues away?'

'Yes, but we've got a Swarm and—'

'*Shut up*, Kalia,' Viv fumed. Kalia looked slightly crushed so he added more kindly. 'Maybe you could heat up some wine for us all.'

'Oh good,' Cion said with dripping sarcasm, 'let's all have a drink together. Mine's a large one. Being dead's a bitch.'

ABOUT AN HOUR later, Cion lapsed back into sleep. He had been unable to reach out to the other Bakkujasi, which meant that his power was still missing, but he had managed to convince himself that once he had finally fulfilled his orders from the Hani he would 'hear' the joyous sounds of the Swarm in his mind once more. Now, he felt completely alone and he had murdered the only person who might have ever cared how he felt.

ASOORI WAS FEELING stronger now. That same evening she set up a minimal camp for herself – the first time since her erratic wanderings began. Finding some twigs of sagebrush, she piled them into the makings of a fire, but she knew they would not burn for long, they were too thin and twiggy. After a short reconnaissance, she found a dried-out tree stump, bleached silver by the weather. Rather stupidly she tried to pull it up at first but its roots ran deep under the surface, so in the end, she brought her meagre pile of sagebrush to the stump instead and managed to light a fire within its dried-out bole, by rubbing a couple of sticks amongst the twiggy leaves. It took an age, but she managed it eventually and the fire began to burn with a satisfying smell – the only light visible for miles around, apart from the star, Orlannoni.

That star would eventually fall to Myr, she thought sadly, and Kilmer had not even lived to see the ending of his world. It seemed an ironic injustice to die just as the world came to an end (and she was silently sure now that it would) and sitting beside the flaring tree-stump, her hands reaching out to the warmth, she decided that she must go and inform Kilmer's parents that he was dead, and Merric's also. The news would bring them no comfort, but she knew that the death of both sons had to be known for she could not mourn them alone. She gazed towards the north where the last faint tinges of daylight stained the horizon a faint purple-pink – that way was Cantroji and Falloden Sen. If she kept moving, she could be there in three days.

She wondered if anyone would mourn for Cion Gezezi. She hoped not.

KELEPHI INCANTATIONS CAME back fast, and normally Achios would be awaiting their return, ready to snatch the little orbs out of the air like so many troublesome wasps. This time, however, he had to accept that the pair he had sent out were gone for good; which meant that the minds the incantations had been questing for – both Cion's and Asoori's – were dead. So it came as some surprise to be woken by one of the *kelephi* returns smashing against his arm with stubborn persistence. Reacting with instinctive irritation, Achios almost made the mistake of slapping it out of existence before taking the time to examine it.

Kelephi were similar to *Darhg*, but far more sophisticated and far-reaching; the little orb pulsed and flashed between his fingers, first green and then blue in frantic sequence, the brightness of it spilling forth to illuminate Achios's face with an uncharacteristic glow of innocence. He grinned, 'Cion, where have you been?' before he pressed the light to his forehead, where it dissipated, instantly firing his brain with the knowledge it had brought.

Just as he was about to try contact with Cion he realized the second *kelephi* had also returned. He quickly overturned a drinking bowl, trapping the *kelephi* beneath it. He was keen to contact Cion first. The Bakkujasi should be in possession of another Swarm egg, but he had been missing for a week, so Cion Gezezi had a lot of explaining to do.

❧CHAPTER NINETEEN❧

Asoori was within a day's journey of Falloden Sen when it happened. She was feeling a lot calmer now, although it seemed strange to her that she was still furious – with Kilmer himself – about Kilmer's death. Considering she had since avenged him by killing his murderer, she would have expected to have a sense that the matter was dealt with, but then, grief was still new to her. Perhaps this was normal – perhaps she was angry and blaming Kilmer for the whole situation. She had only just begun to genuinely hope about their future, and now there was none. Even though she had regained coherent thought, sometimes her mind would still reel away from the whole issue: the readjustment to the fact that, so recently a bride, she was now a widow.

She rested again in the mid-afternoon; she had reached the eastern edges of the Gurz'taal desert again. Far in the distance she could see shapes that may have been buildings against the horizon, but it was difficult to tell. There had been little snow here, and that, as much as anything, told her she must be within striking distance of Cantroji, as the place enjoyed its own micro-climate, warm winds coming from the south-east, along with the currents of the southern ocean. She remembered suddenly her first impressions of Falloden Sen, when she had travelled there with Kilmer, and the amazing arboretum that Kilmer's grandfather had built. She smiled sadly.

As she continued staring into the middle distance, her fingers playing thoughtlessly with the Cantroji crest necklace, a movement on the sand nearby caught her attention. She glanced over, and then did a swift double-take: it was a scorpion – a large, *golden* scorpion?

Asoori liked insects and arachnids from Swarms to bugs and she knelt down to look at the thing more closely. But as it scuttled towards her, she realized that the creature was not simply a gold *coloured* scorpion, but that it was actually fashioned from gold like a brooch or charm might be; it shone, brightly metallic in the harsh direct light of the afternoon. As it clipped its pincers together, Asoori could even hear a tiny noise.

She was too slow to react; at the same second the realization came that the creature was *unnaturally* alive, the scorpion leapt forward, springing from surprisingly powerful back legs. It landed on Asoori's cheek, its legs biting sharply into the soft flesh of her face and, even as she reacted, it arched its tail over and drove its venom straight into her temple.

Asoori screamed in panic and instinctively tried to knock the thing off. When it didn't unlatch at the first attempt, she grabbed onto its abdomen and tore it free, despite the pain. Flinging it away from her, she rolled across the floor and ended up on her back before sitting up, her hand already feeling her cheek for the damage.

She looked at her fingertips coated in blood, and her vision begin to swim. A choked sob came unbidden from the back of her throat; the shock of the encounter had shaken her badly. She was certain the scorpion had poisoned her, and the toxin was going straight to her brain.

Touching the side of her face again, she closed her eyes as a wave of nausea and fear washed over her. *So soon* . . . she thought, *Kilmer, so soon* . . . She began crying at the futility of everything. Then she remembered nothing else for a very long time.

THE COMPLEXITIES OF the human mind were a mystery to Sevim, for he had experienced the darker side of humanity first-hand and this made him by nature a pessimist. But he knew that the Bakkujasi was up to something, and he could only marvel that the others were so quick to trust their hostage.

Cion Gezezi was a charming and erudite man. It had been two days now, but he bore his captivity with little complaint, joking affably with the outlaws who constantly guarded him and being quietly solicitous towards the women in the group. Kalia and, to a lesser extent, Losha, were obviously flattered by his attentions, although Losha was far more difficult to engage with.

Sevim watched him keenly from behind his veil of hair and Cion knew he was watching. By the time Cion asked to speak to Viv again, the level of outright hostility towards the prisoner had lessened, which could only go in his favour. Like Viv, Sevim had the distinct feeling that Cion could easily escape if he really tried, even though he was trussed up like a felled stag. It was difficult to quantify this instinct, but when Viv came over to talk with him there was a real sense that these two were equals rather than captor and hostage, and Sevim had to silently admire such innate dignity on the part of the priest.

'What do you want with me, Bakkujasi?' Viv demanded. He always looked discomfited when speaking to Cion directly.

Cion did not smile this time, rather he approached the discussion with some gravitas. 'I have been thinking, Vivreki, that we are still a long way from Gremeshkenn Tem. It will take us a long time to get back there.'

'You don't need to worry about that,' Viv said quietly. The Bakkujasi knew about Ayshena now. It would have proved impossible to keep knowledge of her existence from him in fact. 'I will go ahead and take notice of our intentions straight to the Sky Temple.' Still Cion did not react, even though Sevim sensed that the Bakkujasi thought this idea was risible.

'I have a better suggestion, which would make this easier all round. Deliver me to Cantroji – to Falloden Sen, not the temple. The Hani is currently in residence there. He was going there when Asoori and I went to Yotu Tem. We were ordered to deliver the egg back to him personally. That was before Asoori Pikresh lost her mind and murdered her husband . . . and myself.'

'But how could we contact them? The Sky Temple would be much easier – they land Swarms there all the time, don't they?'

'Yes, that's true, but there are also temple guards on duty constantly.'

'Huh,' Viv smirked. 'They've never given me any trouble.'

'Well . . .' Cion paused as if considering something seriously. Sevim, watching them from the entrance to the tent, was staggered by how easily the brothers played into his hands.

'Well, what?'

'No, no . . . that probably wouldn't work.'

Viv tutted: 'Just tell us priest or stop wasting our time.'

'I could contact them first. Remember I have the mind-talent as is the way of the Bakkujasi.' To their credit, Viv and Stief both now looked suspicious – though it was more suspicion of the unknown than of the inherent deviousness of Cion.

'What's in it for you?' Uriel asked, as he wandered over to listen to their exchange.

'Well, nothing really – only that I achieve my freedom sooner. Then I can return home to Gremeshkenn Tem more quickly.' Cion shrugged, 'Doesn't matter anyway, it was just an idea. I guess we'll reach the Gremeshkenn mountains in about two weeks, eh?' He shuffled back towards the tent, moving with as much decorum as he could muster in his restraints. Viv and Stief turned away from him, their heads together conspiratorially, their voices lowered.

'He could have a point,' Viv admitted. 'We could all do with getting this over with quickly.'

'There's got to be something else in it for him,' Uriel fretted. 'Why would he propose such a thing?'

'Does that matter if the end result is the same for us? From Cantroji we could make our escape by sea, then drop Losha off by ship and carry on up the coast.'

'If we're going to change our p-plans we should talk to everyone together, make sure we all agree.'

'Yes,' Viv screwed his face up in apparent concentration. 'What I want to know is, will they have enough money at Falloden Sen to pay us a ransom for him?'

'Course they will – the Torroshi family are really rich.'

'But we're not asking them, are we? We're asking it from the church.'

Sevim came forward. 'I could not help but overhear, Vivreki, Uriel. I do not trust him.'

'Neither do we . . .' Viv began.

Sevim held up his hand. 'What I mean is, I feel that he – well, he'll escape if given any chance.'

'He's well tied up,' Uriel insisted.

'I know what Sevim means – I've had that feeling as well,' Viv said. 'And if he has got the mind-talent, how do we know he has not been in touch with them already? How do we know a band of Brengarmah or Bakkujasi is not on their way here to rescue him?'

'Icanti's tits,' Uriel breathed, 'I hadn't considered that. What should we do?'

'Nothing we can do about it. We can't stop the man *thinking*.'

'Maybe if we knocked him out, kept him unconscious?' All three of them turned in unison to look at where Cion was sitting, tied up, amongst his nest of blankets.

'We do not know even that would work,' Sevim said.

Viv sighed. 'Maybe we should ask him to contact them. I'm all for getting rid of him soon. If it all goes wrong, we can just kill him and go our separate ways.' He was deadly serious.

THE DEBATE RAGED for another half an hour. Cion sat calmly watching this shabby band of travellers discuss his fate as if he were a piece of carrion. He could not blame them, he supposed; he even vaguely admired their criminal mentality. As far as he could tell though, the only real intelligence belonged to the Sin Eater . . . possibly the Swarmthief as well, but he was so impetuous and suggestible he was hardly likely to present any problems.

Achios had at last communicated with Cion earlier that morning. It had been both a massive relief and a shock. The Hani demanded to know where he had been, and how he had lost the precious egg to Asoori. Cion sought to redeem himself by the news that he was travelling with a band of heretics in possession of a Swarm that had allegedly hatched from an egg. There had been a brief pause in Achios's thought trace and then he had come back to him.

Lure them towards Falloden Sen, Gezezi. I will contact you this evening. There were no empty threats or promises this time about this being Cion's last chance. Neither of them was under any illusion that redemption of Cion's career was still within his grasp.

Yes, Hani.

So, although Cion watched the outlaws' debating with feigned equanimity, his stomach was churning. He was considering, if his plan failed, how best to kill himself when his honour was broken, his name taken away – because they had removed his swords when he staggered into their campsite. And only a Bakkujasi's own blade could be used for committing suicide. He realized now, after the weeks of silent isolation from the Swarm mind, that if he was not a Bakkujasi, he was as nothing at all.

It had begun to snow again, only lightly, but it was enough to draw their debate to a close. Finally, the two brothers came over to Cion's shelter. They had tied him up to the main support so that, should he attempt to escape, the whole thing would collapse, giving them early warning – much good it would do them if he got loose, Cion thought sourly.

'We've decided to divert for Cantroji estates,' Viv announced, his gaze flickering across Cion's face, watching for any give-away reaction. 'But we'll be watching you, Bakkujasi, so if we get any sign that you're leading us into trouble, we *will* kill you. Do you understand?' He was perfectly sincere about this, which surprised Cion. It was interesting though, that as he made the threat, his older brother looked discomfited by the idea.

'Yes.' Cion nodded gravely. 'I will try to contact the Hani and make arrangements for the exchange. It is just money you want, isn't it?'

'Just money will be sufficient.'

'Very good. Well, it shouldn't take long. We are within two days' journey of Falloden Sen once we cross the canal.'

Viv nodded dumbly. He hadn't actually known this, never having been to the place before. He felt his mouth go dry at the thought of effecting the exchange and now wondered how he'd ended up in such a stupid situation. He'd argued in favour of the exchange being made at Falloden Sen purely to get things over with sooner. Actually, he wished Cion Gezezi had never walked into their campsite.

Everyone else was obviously feeling the same way. It was as if some noxious cloud of doubt was emanating from their prisoner's tent. The mood in the campsite was sombre, but once the decision had been reached no one seemed willing to express any further doubts. There seemed to be no going back now: the alternatives were either to murder the priest in cold blood or just leave him trussed up in the middle of the desert. Although the latter option had its attraction, there was no doubt the church would hunt them down remorselessly once they found him.

Viv was about to turn in for the night; he would be woken at three to take his turn at guarding the prisoner. But for now he needed to sleep, though his mind was still ablaze with the whole situation. Just as he entered the tent he shared with Stief, he heard Cion call out to him. Mystified, he stepped back out into the snow.

'Vivreki, I thought you might like to know. The exchange will be made by Asoori Pikresh. And, as far as I know, she still has the egg in her possession.'

THEY AGREED TO meet at dawn. They pitched camp the night before among the last dunes of the Gurz'taal. The mood of the group had not lifted; only Cion seemed in anything approaching good spirits. With each light-hearted remark their hostage made, the group became further resentful, the balance of power between them bizarrely at odds with any physical evidence to the contrary. Cion's constant chatter became a stick with which to bludgeon them.

However, as the rendezvous hour grew nearer, and the atmosphere tense, even Cion fell silent. He had to accept there was every chance that the exchange might not happen and that Achios had deceived him. In that case, it was likely he might not see the sunset on this day – he was the whole focus of the bargain after all.

He even offered to say a prayer, and no one objected. Losha stood on top of the ridge keeping look-out, but the others stopped their nervy, useless weapons practice for a minute and stood around with their heads bowed. This apparent devotion surprised him somewhat, and a comment Asoori had made to him about the church creating heretics by its very condemnation came back to him unexpectedly. He was about to encounter her again, and he felt a perverse respect for Achios's great-niece, even though she had almost killed him. She had assessed the situation correctly as they fought, knew she would be unable to win against him in a fair fight, and had amended her attack accordingly. Despite his exclusively masculine training and prejudices, Cion knew Achios had been right – she should have been a Shemari.

Just as Cion's prayer ended, Losha came running back down the steep slope of the dune; her feet ploughing deep into the gritty sand, the only thing stopping her from toppling over in her haste and excitement. 'Come and look!' she gasped. 'Good grief, come and look at this!'

Everyone grabbed their weapons more securely and started forward.

Wordlessly, Vivreki cut the bonds around Cion's legs, although leaving his hands tied. But there was nothing to be gained by trying to escape now. Cion was as drawn into the inevitability of the confrontation as they all were.

CION CRESTED THE dune just behind Stief and Uriel, who were already cursing and making warding signs before they saw the object of their apparent terror. When finally he too saw it, his lips moved in silent exclamation – as shocked as everyone else.

It was Asoori Pikresh. She was walking slowly across the stretch of gritty sand towards the base of the dune. She was wearing a white robe – which appeared to be just a nightgown. Both her arms were outstretched from her sides, one hand dragging a sack along the ground. There was something strange about her progress towards them: some stilted, unnatural movement . . .

This was not the cause of so much dismay, however, for behind her rose a huge wall of swirling, gritty sand. It filled the horizon for what seemed like a league across, forming a barrier from the sky to the ground – a vortex of roiling stinging energy. From the cloud of sand issued a high-pitched wailing and shrieking of wind, like the mourning keen of a thousand voices. As Asoori walked forwards, the sand cloud followed her, but mercifully she was moving so slowly that it would be some time before she covered the ground between them.

Not unreasonably, most of them turned away and scrambled or slid back down the dune towards the camp, but the two brothers and Cion remained, transfixed by the sight of her. The sand did not overtake or consume her, but rather followed behind as if she were in control of it. Only the priest guessed that this was not the case.

'There's v-voices – voices in the sandstorm,' Stief whispered, his voice dry and cracking.

'She has no weapons.' Viv frowned. He felt cheated somehow.

Sevim – who had come back for another look – commented, 'She's already dead, I am sure of it.'

'No.' Cion tried not to react too keenly. If Vivreki thought she was dead – and Cion was not entirely sure of that himself – the Swarmthief might change his mind about the deal as his comrades apparently had. 'No, the Hani would never allow any harm to come to his niece. She is probably protected somehow – see how the sands do not even touch her.'

Vivreki nodded, uncertainly.

'She's stopped m-moving,' Stief said. 'What now? What are we going to do?'

For the first time since ascending the dune, both Viv and Cion turned back to view the campsite. Already, under Uriel's instruction, the two women were packing their belongings onto the horses.

'Looks like you first have to rally your troops,' Cion remarked wryly.

※

THE NOISE DIDN'T help. They could hear it from the camp now: it was the kind of visceral, disturbing sound which infiltrated on a purely instinctive level, moving directly to the brain by way of the stomach, insidiously creeping through their pores – or so it felt.

Viv was not about to berate his friends as cowards – he had lived with them long enough to know that was not so. But their courage was fast failing them in the face of something apparently 'supernatural' – not in a beneficial way like Ayshena, nor induced by the gods, but rather by the malevolent powers of the Bakkujasi and the Hani. Though simple and pragmatic people, they were astute enough to know that the Hani was personally capable of pressing such powers into use for his own ends.

'We've come this far,' Viv pleaded, 'and she's carrying enough gold to allow us to live in comfort for the rest of our lives.'

'The rest of our lives?' Uriel snorted with a sarcasm borne of raw fear. 'The rest of our lives will be bloody short if we go down there. What use would money be then, Vivreki?'

The others muttered in agreement. Then Cion stepped into the argument, which made Sevim pay close attention. The weird sound was working on all of them, and the Sin Eater as much as anyone was loathe to go back down. 'The sandstorm is probably only intended to protect Asoori Torroshi Pikresh. After all, she is the niece of the Hani, and he will not want any harm to befall her. If we make the exchange as agreed, she will then walk with me back through the barrier. I detect there is powerful magic at work there . . .'

'Oh, you think?' Uriel jibed.

'I mean, I believe she has a barrier of force around her to stop the storm from touching her. If you were to be caught in the sand, it would flay you alive, would it not?'

'Viv, could you not just f-fly in on Ayshena?' Stief suggested.

'I wish I could, but I doubt she'll be able to move in very close because of the storm. Also, I think . . .' he looked down, shuffling his feet slightly. 'I think she's afraid. She won't talk to me – she hasn't been speaking to me all morning.'

There was a discomfited, silent pause after this admission. Viv sighed, 'Look. I'll go ahead with Cion. You can all follow at a distance, and watch my back.'

'I'll come with you, V-Viv.'

'Thanks.' Somehow the word did not convey enough, for to know Stief would be there beside him was like receiving a gift.

'I will come also,' Sevim offered.

'Are you sure?'

'Yes.'

Even Uriel relented. 'Look, we won't be far behind you. We'll stay and watch from the base of the dune. If you're in trouble we'll . . . we'll do something to help.' He sighed heavily.

'Then that's all I can ask,' Viv nodded unhappily, and began to hug or shake hands with his companions as if he were taking his leave.

'I'm sorry, but if I were going to share a fortune in gold with people I'd want more of a guarantee,' Cion scowled.

'Yes, but then you probably haven't got any friends, Bakkujasi,' Viv grinned mirthlessly. 'If Uriel says they've got my back covered that's good enough for me.'

Viv had already taken Cion's swords from the cache and began brandishing them in experimental circles, trying to decide whether he could truly fight two-handed. He knew Asoori was a very dangerous swordswoman, and it was possible she had weapons concealed. The continued wailing of the sandstorm was making him feel as jumpy as everyone else, and if they didn't make a positive move soon he was likely to lose his nerve.

'We've got to go,' he said. Then, they were ready.

AS THEY WALKED across the space of the sand, Vivreki had never been so glad to have Stief there for him, though Stief, in his turn, had not considered for a moment staying by the dune with the horses. Cion was positioned between Stief and Sevim, both ready with daggers drawn and pointing towards his body. The Bakkujasi now seemed as nervous as any of them, his cold blue eyes flickering back and forth, a slight frown of puzzlement on his face. If Cion was acting, he was very convincing, Vivreki decided.

In fact Cion had little idea what was going on – but his silent instructions had been clear: when the heretics were 'distracted' take the Swarm. He could not guess the nature of the distraction, but Ayshena had made things easier for him at least: she had followed Vivreki. She was not flying, she walked a short distance behind them, her spindly legs quick and light across the surface of the sand. It seemed she was determined to be near Viv; perhaps she would attempt to fly him out of trouble as she had done in the past.

❧

ASOORI HAD STOPPED moving; she simply stood in the midst of the wailing chaos, waiting and still as if she were the calm at the centre of the storm. They walked on, dry-mouthed and terrified at the immensity of the sand-wall.

'Look, there!' Stief yelled. 'I thought I saw something.' He had to shout to be heard over the surrounding howl. 'Something's there, i-inside the sand.'

Sevim shook his head in disbelief. 'Nothing could survive in there.'

'Something's wrong with Asoori Pikresh.' Viv frowned. Everyone stared directly at the young emissary, now they were close enough to make out the details of her face.

Perhaps Sevim had been right in his assessment – she looked as if she were dead even though she was standing upright. Her face was contorted in an expressionless slack-jawed rictus; it was as if someone or something had *twisted her around inside*. There was no animation in her eyes at all; a thin sliver of drool escaped her mouth and was plastered to her cheeks by the storm. Although the flaying sands did not touch her, the vortex was close enough to buffet her clothes and her hair – her black tresses whipped and moved around her, perhaps the biggest indicator that Asoori was not actually *there*. Cion remembered how vain the young woman had been about her hair and, although he had little reason to like her, he felt a small stab of regret that she should come to this.

To Vivreki the revenge he had sworn seemed pathetic and useless now. Although he still held Cion's swords ready before him there could be no duel or any action at all with his recently avowed nemesis – she was destroyed.

'What now?' Viv yelled.

'Go and take the money from her. And the egg,' Cion replied. When Viv hesitated, he repeated, 'Go and take it!'

There was something in Cion's overeager expression as he said this which made both Sevim and Stief shout out instinctively at the same time. 'No!'

But Viv had already stepped forward. Despite the howling immensity of the sand-wall behind her, the most identifiable threat seemed to be Asoori. He kept his blade pointed towards her as if she could still understand the implied threat, and reached slowly for the bag.

Within an instant, Vivreki's world was chaos and fear. Something lunged out at him from the sand-wall, hitting him squarely in the chest, and knocking him flat on his back. It saved his life, despite the fact it was trying to take it. As he wrestled with his unknown assailant, Viv was aware of the cessation of sound. The sand-wall dissolved so instantaneously that its ending was like a blow to the head. Immediately after, he heard shouts and yells of fear behind him, but he had no time to look.

For long seconds, Stief stood transfixed, hardly able to believe the evidence of his own eyes. He had never seen anything like it – no one had. As the sand-wall dropped it was clear that he had been right, there were dreadful things inside it: *tengu*.

They were foul creatures, their evil intent writ large in the glittering beads of their eyes. There were perhaps thirty of them, and in a line and behind them loomed a Swarm, the same size as Ayshena but orange and gold. On its back it carried a Shemari priest that Stief guessed must be the new Hani.

'By the gods,' Cion shrieked. 'What has he done?' He fell to his knees in the sand before the array of unnatural might, while both Stief and Sevim ignored their hostage, their minds too overwhelmed by the awesome sight to keep to their simplistic plan.

Stief was nearest to Vivreki, and he managed to tear his gaze away for just a second, intending to kick out at the first of the *tengu* which had a struggling Viv pinned to the ground. When he looked back, a *tengu* was standing right in front of him, a sword and a stabbing-spear in its vicious-looking claws.

Even as he reacted, another appeared to his right. The creatures simply blinked in and out of existence, so they did not need to walk, and there was no time to react – no time at all. Their scabrous wings soon blotted out sight of Cion, and nearby he could hear Sevim yelp in fright also. Stief slashed out with his dagger, hitting the creature in the powerful muscle of its wing. Its beaked mouth opening, it emitted a shrill, harsh cry of complaint, noxious breath washing across Stief's face. He reeled back in disgust even as a second *tengu* pressed its attack and, unable to retrieve his dagger, he stumbled and fell, crashing his arm into a protruding rock. The first *tengu*, with Stief's knife still lodged in its wing, vanished from sight with a faint snapping sound, but the other lunged forward to where Stief lay, dazed in the sand. Far behind him he thought he heard the thunder of approaching horses. *Please don't come here*, he thought wildly, knowing it was the others. *Flee* . . .

He scrambled backwards at speed, now bleeding heavily from his arm. His questing fingers found Vivreki's shortsword, which had been knocked from his grasp by the first attacker. As the *tengu* moved closer to deal him a fatal blow, he lashed out with his foot and unbalanced the creature. It toppled forward, blotting out the light, and he plunged Viv's sword through its belly. Hot bile sprayed across his face even as the *tengu* vanished. Stief had only seconds to glance back before the next demon appeared. He noticed Losha, Uriel and Kalia bearing down on horseback at a full charge. Considering what lay before them, their courage was remarkable.

Viv finally defeated the first *tengu* by bashing a large stone across its skull. It was either dead or just unconscious but he had no inclination to care. The creature had cut into his chest and torn his ear, and he was bleeding fast. Too furious and energized to stop, Viv staggered over and grabbed the other fallen sword, before stabbing the nearest *tengu* in the back, square between its wings. As the riders drew nearer, each second became a race for survival, moments blurring into one another, as the world became a flickering confusion of sunlight and the black shadows of *tengu* wings.

Sevim was down. The Sin Eater had never been quick on his feet and the first *tengu* to reach him had stabbed its spear into his shoulder. The demons fought chaotically, with seemingly no premeditation – Sevim followed his instinct to turn away, to run blindly. But there was nowhere to go; he was surrounded by masses of the creatures. Something else jabbed into his side and he fell, but continued crawling across the sand. Grit and blood filled his mouth and he was gasping and moaning for air. Before him, a sea of stinking, scaly talons – another stab, to his leg this time.

No Sevim, noooo. Spall was frightened and angry.

Sevim choked back a sob and touched his own bloodied hand to his lips. *I'm sorry, Spall,* he thought. *I cannot do it alone. Help me . . .*

There was a sudden blaze of light, and the *tengu* leapt back from their fallen prey, yammering in fear.

WHY ISN'T AYSHENA *helping me? What is she doing?* Viv's thoughts were interspersed by grunts and yells as he managed to hold back three *tengu*. He was under no illusion that their sheer numbers were destined to bring him, and the others, down. This would be a massacre, not a battle. The bastard Bakkujasi had led them into a trap, just as Sevim had warned earlier.

Still, for *this* moment he was alive. He stole a glance back towards Ayshena – just as the flare of light heralding Spall's arrival caused the massed *tengu* to reel back, earning him precious seconds of respite. Ayshena still stood immobile, though the sand-wall had dropped away so she could have easily escaped to safety. 'Ayshena!' he yelled out to her, even as the *tengu* turned their attentions back towards him again. 'Ayshena!' When she did not respond, he knew there must be something terribly wrong with her.

Something else caught his attention. Cion. He was easily noticeable amid the press of *tengu*, his white hair shining out like a beacon. But the Bakkujasi was not engaged in any combat – in fact the *tengu* were ignoring him. It was as if Cion was not even there, slipping amongst them like a breeze. And he was now pushing his way through, towards Ayshena.

A spear gouged into the side of Viv's arm, deep and painful enough to register even through his battle-charged fury. He screeched in agony, his vision beginning to swim. Just as his fingers went numb and he dropped his blade, the red-brown flanks of a horse intervened between him and his attackers. Slashing out with both a sword and an axe, Uriel was steering the terrified beast with his knees.

'Viv! Viv, get up!' Uriel yelled. He laid the sword across his pommel for a second and held out his hand.

Viv backed away – there was a small gap in the crowd and he could see Cion had almost reached the Swarm – *his* Swarm. 'Get Stief. Please, get Stief.' he yelled. He didn't look to Uriel for any response but pressed ahead into the crowd. Off to his left was Kalia on a black horse – he had a fleeting impression of her red hair – and she was flailing around her with a staff. Almost witless with fear, as she had been the day they rescued her from the heretic's pyre, she screamed and squealed as she slashed around her, and her obvious terror made her the bravest woman Viv had ever seen.

He had almost reached the Bakkujasi before he realized he had no weapon. For a giddying moment Viv paused, motionless, as the world fell apart around him. A weird sound began from somewhere – it was the sound of the *tengu* making their fear noise – and the source of their fear was Spall. The Sin Eater's avatar strode amongst the minions of Rann with seeming impunity, casting out cloud after cloud of sin which reduced any *tengu* unlucky enough to be in its path into a disgusting heap of gore. Not the brightest of creatures, the *tengu* were running mindlessly in their panic – a few even took to the air, but they seemed reluctant to share the sky with the foul emissions of Spall's sin.

Viv felt a wild surge of hope. He grabbed a discarded spear and ran after Cion, willing his swiftly numbing legs to carry him further. '*Bastard! You did this – you did this* . . .' he shouted.

Cion had been just about to climb onto the Swarm's back. Viv did not know how he expected Ayshena to obey him, but he had a sick feeling she would be given no choice. Hearing his cry, the priest turned back towards Vivreki with a snarl. He had somehow shrugged of his bonds – they had been right about his ability to escape – and he grasped one of the *tengu*'s spears in his hand.

'She belongs to the church, heretic, and I'm taking her back.' He turned again to the Swarm, and with a scream of rage and indignation, Vivreki hurled himself forward . . . so he was touching Ayshena, unknowingly in her protection, when the fire came.

THERE WAS A second of confusion as all of the *tengu* vanished as one. Relative quiet fell upon the battlefield, except for the soft metallic clink of the horses' bridles and the solid stomping of their hooves.

Someone began to speak. Kalia, possibly. 'What is . . .?'

It was the last thing any of them said.

FARZULL. THE SWARM born of fire, could create her own world of searing heat and flame. She reared up, her spiky forelegs clawing at the air before her. When she touched the earth again, lines of fire erupted from her feet, turning the sand molten before her. A jagged whiplash of flaming light hissed out from her mouthparts; and she could direct its blast. First Uriel, then Kalia, then Losha . . . they died screaming, those last few seconds of terror dropping away into infinity as their bodies turned to blackened charcoal.

Viv turned, instinctively looking for Stief. Those few still able had begun to flee, lashing their horses into a panicked gallop. Stief was nowhere to be seen at first and then Viv noticed his cloak, a blue tatter, beneath the still smoking remains of Uriel's horse.

It all unfolded so fast – too fast to offer any hope of survival. The only one left standing was Spall and he seemed too stunned to move, torn between gathering up the souls of his friends and his own self-preservation. As Farzull's flame arced out again, Spall was only just quick enough to respond by casting a thick cloud of sin towards the Swarm. It held her off for mere seconds as the fire consumed the negative energy, burning brighter and brighter. Then Spall was forced back, his young-boy face contorted in an agony of effort. As his shield of sin collapsed, Spall was flung backwards with the sudden force of the flaming onslaught, his body crumpling to the ground, limbs twisted like a broken doll's.

'STIEF? STIEF!' VIV began to choke from the acrid smoke drifting towards him from the burning bodies. His eyes were streaming, as he took one last glance at Cion, who was now firmly astride Ayshena's back. The Bakkujasi's face registered shock but little fear – he knew he had possessed immunity. Viv gave his actions no thought at all. He let go of Ayshena and began to race across the field of destruction, his gaze fixed on the patch of blue fabric lying under Uriel's horse. As he passed the corpses of Kalia and Losha and their mounts, a raw sob escaped the back of his throat. He threw himself to the ground, to roll for cover behind Uriel's remains.

TOO SLOW. Viv screamed as a blast of fire lanced across his legs.

❧CHAPTER TWENTY❧

SILENCE . . .
   Tiny sounds begin to creep back onto the desolate finality of the battlefield. Small tongues of flame lick idly at the remnants of dead men's clothes, and crackle as they consume the denuded skeleton of any surviving scrub. In patches, the superheated blast of Farzull's deadly energy has baked the sand to glass – a tiny brittle sound can be heard to underlie the dying fires.

For a long time, Cion Gezezi sat motionless on the back of Ayshena, his face a blank, unreadable mask, should anyone have remained alive to observe it. After a while, ahead of him, Farzull began to move. The hot thrumming of her wings started to beat, indicating that she was ready to fly Achios back to Falloden Sen. As she took flight, almost vertically into the clarity of the afternoon sky, downwind of her own iniquity, Ayshena prepared to follow her, unbidden by Cion.

The two Swarms flew east, one behind the other, their exquisite beauty thrown into black silhouette against the low winter sun.

❧EPILOGUE❧

ASOORI PIKRESH WOKE up in the comfort of a warm quilted bed. She felt as though she had been asleep for a long, long time and, as her brain struggled to remember anything that happened before the drift into sleep, she realized her body was weak, her hands trembling and her legs stiff from inactivity.

The room had pleasant, ochre-coloured walls and large, almost tree-sized plants gave it an air of comfort. Outside the window the occasional shrill call of a peacock could be heard; it was this sound alone which made her sure she was back at Falloden Sen.

She sat up, feelings of inexplicable alarm flooding through her. There was a gold hand-bell on the bedside table. She reached over to pick it up but – still disorientated – managed to knock it to the ground. Nevertheless, it had the desired effect, and she heard voices from outside. Within moments the screen door slid back and Cion Gezezi stood there.

'Where is Kilmer?' she said. She spoke even as the thought formed itself in her mind. Cion walked over and sat down on the side of her bed, then he took her hand – which she felt sure was an unusual level of informality between them – but she said nothing. Deep within her, something was forming, some thought, some kernel of . . . something. Rage? No, that could not be right.

'Asoori,' Cion suddenly smiled, his blue gaze locking with her own, 'I don't think we should discuss that now. I don't—'

'Where is he?' Her voice was quavering and weak, and tears of frustration spilled down her cheeks.

'Shhh, we will talk later, I promise. Go back to sleep now.' He rearranged the pillows behind her head, and she sank back against

313

them gratefully, vaguely wondering what state her hair was in. She felt herself drifting and realized she was still studying Cion's face.

'Will you brush my hair?' she whispered.

AND SO THE days went on. Asoori would never be sure how many times she woke up and was lulled back into sleep. She was aware occasionally of someone pressing water to her lips – perhaps it was drugged to calm her. Her thoughts remained as smoke or cloud: unformed, gathering, and then dissipating . . .

Achios was there once too, and while it briefly cheered her to see him, his dark eyes haunted her dreams for what seemed many days afterwards.

THEN, QUITE UNEXPECTEDLY, Asoori Torroshi Pikresh woke up during the night. This time there was no one to hear her, no one watching . . . She could not have said what woke her, but she sat up suddenly as if frightened into wakefulness. At the end of her bed rested her bag with her few belongings inside. Something there was gleaming, a rich golden glow in the tired light of the oil lamp. Asoori slipped out from under the covers and reached out to take the object in her hand. It was cold in the room, so she sat back under the blankets to examine it.

'It's pretty,' she muttered – then she gasped aloud. For, as she gazed at the Cantroji phoenix crest, with the suddenness of a physical blow, Asoori remembered.

Asoori remembered *everything*.